LATER DAYS

LATER DAYS

CHIP JACOBS

RARE BIRD
LOS ANGELES, CALIF.

RARE BIRD

THIS IS A GENUINE RARE BIRD BOOK

Rare Bird Books
6044 North Figueroa Street
Los Angeles, California 90042
rarebirdbooks.com

FIRST HARDCOVER EDITION, SEPTEMBER 2025

Cover Artwork by Anton Rivages
Author Photograph by Maggie St.Thomas

For more information, address:
Rare Bird Books Subsidiary Rights Department
6044 North Figueroa Street
Los Angeles, California 90042

Set in Adobe Garamond
Printed in the United States

10 9 8 7 6 5 4 3 2 1

Library of Congress Cataloging-in-Publication Data available upon request

To Tom: the space cadet who saw around corners.

"Hello you. Hello me. Hello people we used to be."

—Ray Davies

NOTE TO READERS

This book is a work of fiction, and while many of the events described are based on personal experiences, this remains a novel constructed on imagination. It's also, in part, a Valentine's to a late-seventies brotherhood, our old prep school, its coed revolution, and era that I'll always treasure. Interactions with public figures are fictionalized and derived from my research into their noteworthy lives. The language, expressions, and behavior reflect that culture, not today's.

PART I

CHAPTER ONE
THE PIT

March 1976 Lance Drexx, or "D-Rex" as us lesser creatures nicknamed our feral classmate, was never one to miss an opportunity to wreck someone's day. So, when he noticed me alone in one of Stone Canyon Prep's most notorious hunting grounds, it must've whetted his appetite for something mouthwatering to devour at his toothy leisure. Despise the tuna-fish-breathed, maize-haired prick as I did, I'll cede him this: He had a promising future ahead as a bouncer or mafioso, the sort never happier than ambushing victims from behind with a one-finger jab in the scruff of the neck, then whipping them around for a rag-dolling that'd eventually come for them in their sleep.

Poke. Crash.

D-Rex had me pinned up against the lower-school's wall of lockers, where Stone Canyon bullies unmasked their true selves, wham-bam fast; think Trans-Am-driving seniors peeling out for weekends. His blindside was so effortless, so casual, that it was as if yours truly was constructed from hobby-store balsa wood, not a hundred-twenty-three pounds of rotating, adolescent insecurities.

The last punch I'd thrown? A third-grade fracas over a cafeteria sloppy joe.

D-Rex's dominant right hand, whose bony knuckles half a dozen of us knew on a first-name basis, bunched into a mocking fist brushing against my not-so-brave chin. Nothing new here, your basic terror-by-numbers, though mouth-breathing D-Rex pretty much bombed every math test where he couldn't swipe the answers.

"Say it! I want you to say, 'Luke Burnett is a flaming rump ranger.' You know it's true, um…Ranger-boy."

More from his greatest-hits collection, menacing someone to proclaim looney things about themselves. For variety, he sometimes was maniacal that I confess I was a "Snoopy Luke-Ass."

Well, not anymore. Not this boy. *Uh-uh.* Impulsive, suicidal: I'll take my chances. The days of him manhandling me so I'd be his puppet were done. I'd find the spine to defy him, that or risk hating myself more than I did him. Ol' Lance/D-Rex would have to grab someone else to make himself feel better about the shitty hand life dealt him.

"Tick, tick," he said, up in my face, so close that a leftover shred of Wonder Bread in his teeth loomed like half a slice.

"I'm not a Ranger, so I won't say I am. Sorry to disappoint you." I couldn't believe those words leaked out of my windpipe. It was exhilarating, even if it meant I was about to be reduced to pulpy heap.

My refusal to parrot his magic words turned his scowl into a drape of bewilderment, but not for long. With his right hand still pressing me against a locker, he un-balled his left fist, stroking his jaw in cartoonish deliberation.

"You back-talking me, Millie-*Can't?*" hatchet-ing the embarrassing, Caltech-inspired middle name D-Rex knew made me flinch. Luke Millikan Burnett. *Millikan*, really? My parents should've just had "*Freely Abuse Me*" tattooed on my forehead. "How 'bout I sock you in the nose?"

But I couldn't wilt. Wouldn't beg. I needed a strategy, not a white flag, and the only rung able to climb above the fear was, don't laugh, Henry David Thoreau, who we'd just learned about in English. If civil disobedience was kryptonite against the tyrannical machinery of government, why not the unjust, ass-whooping promised by a boy tyrannosaurus?

Adopting that, I braced myself for a jolt of pain, D-Rex's native language. His signature move was a between-classes "dead arm," a compact punch directly in the shoulder joint that numbed your bicep and pulsed fire down the funny bone. How could it not? At thirteen, the guy could flex muscles he probably had coming out of the womb.

"Go ahead and punch me," I said. "I don't care." Clearly I did, or my eyes wouldn't have welled up, straining to contain hot tears.

"Oh, *wah-wah,*" he said. "How about something different?"

Before I could wrap my head around what that'd be, he got busy manufacturing it, sniffing and snorting, followed by a hammy *wuhick* from the back of his throat. He worked his jaw, swished that "something" inside his mouth, presenting for my horror a tongue holding a disgusting, yellow-green loogie the size of a wad of Bazooka bubblegum. I saw the future, and it was spelled ultimatum. Either I'd relent in acknowledging my mythical ranger-ness or D-Rex would refashion my face into his spittoon.

There was no one around to stop him, notably me and the worthless Henry David Thoreau.

Jesus, I wanted to scream into his Neanderthal face. *You want to make me bleed? Oh, maybe you didn't hear: I've already been bled out.... You ever see someone who mattered to you laid out in a box, looking like a wax figure at that stupid Madame Tussaud museum? Thought so.*

As if that'd repel him from terrorizing me. No, shrieking about the worst moment of my life would only gift-wrap him material for another verbal slice-and-dice. Speaking of unfair, it's drubbings like this when a kid learns the true nature of a world prettier from space, how it owes him nothing—an explanation, a rentable Billy Jack—in the silent winds of its desertion.

Trapped, I retreated where I normally did when a planet of billions of people double-downed on cruelty or loss. I floated out of the present, into the castle between my own ears, where the monster whose superpower was sniffing out prey more flight than fight couldn't hurt me.

As an eighth grader still adjusting to this "historic," all-boys junior high/high school shoehorned into a sloping corner in La Cañada, a one-street town northeast of mega-Los Angeles (and just west of my native Pasadena), I was learning what those happy-face guides neglected to mention during our punch-and-cookies orientation. The *Lord of the Flies* wasn't merely a future reading assignment about a fictional island of juvenile, plane-crash-survivors-gone-tribal. It was an echo of what we lived. Heavy coursework delivered by committed teachers dissolved into a vat of *anything-goes* at the clang of the bell. Walking through the spiky-shadowed hallways, an algae smear on the food chain, you never knew if sinister hands would lunge for a collar-shake, ear-flick, or lip-biting titty-twister. When, on a whim, upperclassmen hijacked a random kid into the bathroom for an "atomic wedgie"—the type known to stretch boxers into turtlenecks—the adults seemed to chalk it up to boys being boys.

Like that roughhousing built character. Or school spirit.

Being a bookworm, in a lonely house of vacated rooms, I'd read William Golding's classic the summer before, haunted by the painted faces and pointy spears, the lifeless parachute man and distant mushroom cloud. But after a November field trip to the Hollywood Cinerama Dome to watch *2001: A Space Odyssey*, I revised my comparison. It'd been a circus of a bus ride there, kids popping zits at each other, practical jokers tying shoelaces to seat legs so the unsuspecting tripped standing up. Halfway through the film, before the part about the HAL 9000 mainframe turning on astronaut Dave, I got the chills, realizing there wasn't all that much daylight between us uninhibited children of late-seventies Southern California and those skull-bashing apes from millions of years ago. The first dead one must've been named Piggy McPrimate.

Back in my own ape-land, D-Rex's nostrils flapped for air while his palate struggled to maintain the foamy goo-ball on his tongue. A reflex took over, an unconscious choice not to be his target practice. I wriggled sideways, never expecting it'd briefly free me from the locker air vents carving factory designs into my vertebrae.

See, you're showing balls. He's human like you.

Um, no he wasn't. He was a hope-killer, slamming his hand into my outside shoulder, which knocked me back against the lockers with a thunderous crack. Fate of the Chicken Hawk.

I scurried back between my ears, searching this time for the self-loathing logic of why? As in *why* had D-Rex lumped me, the greenie from east Pasadena, in with the other clay-pigeons he delighted blowing out of the sky? As in why a sicko universe would permit it? I guess, considering my flaws, it was more like *why* shouldn't he?

Like most thirteen-year-olds, I was prisoner to the "awkward" phase dragging me toward hormonal pubescence from larvae, little kid. Radar-dish ears that'd gotten me teased as "Dumbo" in elementary school were taking their sweet time receding behind untamable, hickory-brown hair. A mouth full of metal, even inside Stone Canyon's kingdom of orthodonture, where every other classmate smiled silver-gray, was hardly macho, either. Nor were my scraggly physique and chicken legs, both trying to catch up with the hairy fascinations blooming under armpits and between thighs. My hitchy, top-end gait, which D-Rex lampooned as "The Spaz Pony," was bonus, comedy material.

The icing on the Luke-bullseye cake? A nervous system with a motor of its own. For the life of me, I couldn't be still, whether sitting at my desk or standing in a group. Neither could I quit ravaging fingernails down to their cuticles when anxious. Paired with a right foot that involuntarily tapped to an inaudible beat, it shaped the portrait of a vibrating boy.

What I hadn't wanted was my dad stomping into the administration building demanding action against you-know-who. Asking if *this* is what he got for his money? And he nearly did after a vicious stretch early this spring semester, when D-Rex some days stalked me from opening bell to carpool line. I moped in class, fake-smiled at lunch, and withdrew at home, so emotionally beaten down I exaggerated a chest cold to stay home from school an extra few days.

Not long afterward, the father who'd never won a playground fight in his life walked into my room with advice I hadn't sought. He egged me on to confront my nemesis directly; pop him one, he said, and you'll find he's a paper tiger that crumples at the first blow. Either he'd enroll me in karate-lessons or he'd intervene, which I begged him against. When I idiotically confided my father's theory to a bigmouthed, now-ex-friend, the grapevine did what grapevines do. Within hours, D-Rex socked me with such a debilitating dead arm I had to write with my opposite hand for the first twenty minutes of social studies.

However much I feared his PEZ Candy dispenser of abuse—busted nose, kidney punch, charley horse, or now loogie between the eyes—I'd take those any day over the reputational Scarlett letter we all dreaded: the Big P. None of us understood the nuances of that elusive female organ, but being stigmatized class-wide by the cowardly implication of having a dad fight one's battles? A humongous no thanks there. I'd rather be slugged than be branded a pussy.

Question was, why was he feasting on me today, when he'd actually laid off me the last three weeks? *Crack it, Luke.* It took me a sec to flash back to Thursday's math class to realize why I should've had my head on a swivel since. It was so obvious. I'd refused to let him glimpse answers off an algebra pop quiz, a decision less out of swelling pride than paranoia about getting caught. Left on his own with quadratic equations, D-Rex had zero chance to find X. Predictably, he scored an F and hungered for revenge.

"Don't make me thwait," he lisped to reorient my attention. "Thay, 'Luke Burnett is a Gay Queen' or you'll be saw-we."

If my neck wasn't in his stockade, I'd have laughed he had nothing on Gilda Radner, who performed that lisp-y impression of Barbara Walters on *Saturday Night Live*. But my neck was, so I didn't.

Deep down, we all knew why D-Rex gleefully cast himself as arch villain. We spoke it in hushed voices, never too loudly. That he had no business in a place as academically cutthroat as Stone Canyon wasn't even the root cause. It was the disfiguring, "lazy" right eye he'd been born with that had him forever lashing out. Only under duress would he wear the dorky, black, corrective glasses required to align it. Without them, that lazy eye bobbed inside its socket with haphazard direction, reminding you of a cheap, keychain compass that weeble-wobbled toward magnetic north inside its sudsy, plastic dome.

In class, I was never sure if the fickle orb was glowering at me, foreshadowing a bone bruise, or was merely taking an optical Sunday stroll around the room. When D-Rex flunked a test he took glasses-free, someone always paid for it on the blacktop. He'd stomp out of the room, throw his quarry to the ground, and grind his knees into their shoulders until they yelped, both parties probably questioning what God had against them? I could relate now as that roaming eye tried putting me in its sights, a breaching Moby-Dick overshooting its coordinates.

That I was its prisoner was all my doing. Besides D-Rex's fury at me over the quiz, I'd also strayed from a Stone Canyon sacred commandment. Rule 1: Never dare step on a blade of grass known as the Senior Lawn, unless you were a senior or comfortable being gang-tackled and tossed, in front of half the student body, into the frigid waters of the school's Olympic-size pool. Rule 2: Never slack off on homework or missed tests for more than a couple of days, because the slog of the makeup, coupled with fresh assignments piling up daily could bury you alive. Rule 3: Barring a Teflon stomach, avoid at all costs Wednesday's snack-bar bean burritos, whose aftereffects fouled the already icky bathrooms with boys' gastrointestinal strife.

Rule 4 was the one I'd just violated into hostage-status. I'd meandered unaccompanied to the junior-high lockers on the school's lower level. Stupid-cubed. What made the spot so hazardous was the wraparound deck for the science room and chemistry lab, which blocked sightlines from multiple directions, including the upper level where most of the faculty buzzed around.

Long ago, someone named the bruising alcove "The Pit," supposedly after a head-knocking Ernest Borgnine flick, and sure enough, it lived up to its billing. Daydreamer that I was ahead of weekends, I forgot Rule 4, entering this no-man's land after soccer practice, all tra-la-la, to retrieve my copy of *The Ox-Bow Incident* and sweatshirt before my carpool ride home.

"Hurry thup," D-Rex said, agitation growing. His tightening grip on my long-sleeve, "Keep on Truckin'" shirt meant it'd sag forever. "I don't hath all day for you to admit you're a big rump ranger. Thay it, or I'll thmash your nose into your, uh, whatever's bethind it?"

Again, killer timing. We'd studied the pituitary gland in science this week, and I was rather fond of mine.

Still, I wasn't buckling. Wasn't shaming myself as a wuss, gassy Snoopy, Spaz Pony, or other unsavory critters. Something weird, I guess, happens after suffering through this for the nth time, an *I-don't-care* air liberating you to rebel, to resist, regardless of the blowback. It'd first reared up a few months ago after a Christmas I'd rather not remember. Amid the school holiday decorations and good cheer, I'd taken to hiding from him in the main bathroom to throw him off my scent, and I got others in return. Trust me: Nibbling a bologna sandwich or crunching Frito's commode-side, sniffing deodorizing urine cakes and porcelain-bowl deposits with every bite, isn't as glamorous as it sounds.

Late at night, between the russet, vinyl walls of my bedroom, I'd try white-washing away my disgust for not rabbit-punching him, no matter the carnage it'd invite. *It wasn't so bad what he did. It's not like the shit-kicking Neil Katz gets.*

"What's it going to be wittle nail biter?"

I grinned, answering by non-answer. He replied with a blurry-hard slap across my cheek that rang in my ears. This wasn't one of those white-gloved, French Foreign Legion slaps from the movies. It was a stinging, real-life, bitch slap that felt like he'd forever imprinted his palm's lifelines on my soft tissue.

"You're such a jerk, you know that?" I ripped my arm up to massage the tender flesh. He yanked it away and re-stuck out his tongue. Somehow, his mucous spitball had gone neon green.

Our standoff dragged into its fourth minute. And to think: The gory portion of the show was still in the wings.

"Thimes up," he said. "You didn't thay it, so I'm spraying it."

Truer words were never lisped as he pelleted the payload at me, point blank. My hands, caught in a defensive X across my chest, had no shot deflecting it. The loogie would've soaked my eyes or jawbone had I not on instinct wrenched my head sideways at the last second. Of all D-Rex's reprehensible acts, this was the vilest, the most unforgivable. And more was building.

When I squared around, D-Rex's right arm—the arm our baseball coach dubbed the team's "beautiful flamethrower"—was recoiling for a right hook.

"C'mon, Lance." My voice cracked pathetically on his name, more out of self-preservation than puberty's follies. "This isn't going to end well for either of us. Let me go."

Our potential Major League All-Star, already the staff ace of blacktop thuggery, shook his head no, while the gunk he spat at me trickled down behind my ear like a liquid spider.

Just when I figured I was dead meat, his casualty again, I sensed motion on the perimeter. Off to my right, I noticed what my lazy-eyed captor failed to detect. Someone was racing toward us on the trampled grass bordering our monolithic, white-brick gym. I squinted at it for just a blink, because what if it were only a mirage? Only a lowly maintenance man trotting toward a spurting valve? D-Rex had gotten away with so much so many times before as our star athlete, why should he lose his protection today?

And, of course, he was onto me. "What cha looking for over there, ranger? Your vagina? *He-he-he-he.*"

He cracked himself up, head dipping in self-congratulations. I used that to re-check the object streaking our way.

And the nearer it got, the more surprised I was by its improbability. Denny Drummond was among the puniest boys in eighth grade, and to me its most mysterious. Yet here he was, all elbow nobs and churning knees, galloping in a pair of dirty, Converse high-tops and a faded green, Blue Öyster Cult T-shirt showcasing a laughing Grim Reaper. How he wasn't freezing without a jacket on this chilly afternoon I have no idea, just as I can't explain how a stoner-brainiac like him, dirty blond hair bouncing off narrow shoulders, could cover so much ground so quickly when he always loafed off in PE.

Adding to the confusion was a sound rustling from my left, a rhythmic, scuffing sound of someone's shoes descending the filthy, concrete staircase connecting the split-level campus. As our only path in between, it was a cattle chute at high traffic times, and empty others, meaning it could be anyone heading our direction. Senior? Substitute teacher? Popcorn-munching ghost here for the spectacle. Why not, time distorting itself with me in D-Rex's clutches?

Swinging my chin back to my right, the stranger on the staircase disappeared from my crisscrossing thoughts. That's because Denny was near enough now to pick out a rip in his shirt's inseam, though the blaze in his seething, pale-blue eyes stuck out more.

The runt a good fifteen pounds lighter and two inches shorter than D-Rex skidded to a stop in front of the lockers. Wordlessly, he unhitched his charcoal JanSport, corkscrewed at the waist, and swung it behind him with both hands. Then, redirecting that momentum like an amateur discus thrower at the start of his motion, he spun the opposite direction, thrusting the book bag on an upward trajectory that walloped D-Rex with a ferocious haymaker on the lazy-eye side of his face.

The whomping collision of factory nylon and human rearranged us all. It lifted D-Rex up a foot off his Adidas, a welt that would've fit nicely in a prep-school, "agony of defeat" clip for ABC's *Wide World of Sports*. I should know, observing it up too close and personal. Because D-Rex was gripping me when he got clocked, I was knocked to the ground, too, entangled with my monster. Denny, meantime, was five feet away, self-toppled by his own heave-ho.

I pushed D-Rex off me, and everything hurt: an inflamed cheek, a back gouged by locker vents, and a bruised hip that'd absorbed the brunt of two plunging bodies. Most painful was the flushing shame that *I'd* needed to be rescued. I popped up, craning my neck, relieved to discover there'd been no rubbernecking classmates around to blab everything to the campus rumor mill.

D-Rex tilted up onto his butt with the expression of someone KO-ed from outside the ring. His face—those squashed features, his crazy eye—gazed skyward. Fingertips accustomed to mauling others massaged the tender cheekbone where Denny's backpack blew him its violent kiss. I'd never seen him hurting before, never heard him mutter *"ouch."*

He lurched to his feet, more shellshocked than incensed, and just in time for Denny's second surprise. Curiously, he hadn't peeled himself up for the sake of pride like me. Uh-uh. He began rolling on the oily asphalt, hands clutching an eye. Once he stood, it was act two of a bogus performance it took me a minute to decipher.

"*Crap*, Lance," Denny said. "You're not happy just thrashing Luke. You had to attack me, too. What's wrong with you, psycho?"

D-Rex was speechless. And this time, unlike ancient history class, it wasn't because he couldn't name a single one of Zeus' offspring, despite people coughing an answer in mercy. *"Eh-he-em, Apollo."*

"You better hope you didn't blind me." Denny's outrage, voiced in a baritone octave you wouldn't expect from someone so short, was rolling. "I'm not winning the Nobel Prize, no offense, as some cyclops."

Cyclops? Did he have a death wish, too? Or, true to wispy murmurs, was our classes' "space cadet" so dippy he'd lost his mind? I worried for his life, though I barely knew the dude.

"Shut up, asshat." D-Rex said in a whiny growl, kneading the side of his head. "You hit me when I wasn't looking."

"Stop lying—you gave me a shiner. My head's killing me."

Whatever stranger had been on those stairs now strode toward us, and that's when Denny's plot broke through Good Friday's afternoon marine layer. His acting: all devised for an audience of one.

Sherman Pike, our watchful, first-year headmaster, approached us wearing a houndstooth blazer and a judgmental frown. He was a broad-shouldered, middle-aged man who'd supposedly been a lacrosse and debate team champ in his native Maine (by way of a family from Athens, Georgia). Above a broomstick mustache, joked in the hallways as camera-ready for low-budget porn, was splotchy, red skin. Reviling authority figures was practically mandatory for upperclassmen. And this late-forties figure, with jet-black hair parted like a Kennedy and a cards-to-the-vest demeanor, qualified as their automatic enemy.

Not to me. Mr. Pike ran our universe, eight-to-three daily, seer of all.

"You bunch. What do *you* think you're doing?" he snapped. "I can tell there's been a fight. I need answers. Like now!"

None of us supplied any.

"Taking the Fifth, eh? Spare the bull, gentlemen. I'm not averse to suspending the bunch of you, coming midterms or not."

Ten seconds of his stare-down was all the Boy Scout in me could handle. I cleared my throat to explain that I'd been ambushed, but Denny beat me to a backstory.

"A jumping of two classmates—that's how this started, Mr. Pike. Luke and I were going over our history exam when Lance attacked us." Denny next walked over to him, pointing his index finger at a yellow-magenta ring under one of his eyes. "See? He went after Luke, then sucker punched me"

"I, I, I did not," D-Rex stuttered. "He's ly…"

"So, you're saying a black eye is lying?" Mr. Pike interrupted.

Denny, actually, was the one twisting facts. A second before he bashed D-Rex with his JanSport, I saw his face and it already sported a shiner.

"He's a whack job," Denny continued, not a quiver in his voice. "I don't care how many batters he struck out this season." Still in character, he cupped his eye and, whimpered "*youch*."

Mr. Pike gave us the once-over as a light breeze ruffled his Brylcreemed bangs. D-Rex, finally appreciating he was being played the patsy, raised his hand, as if required to comment. Mr. Pike, who'd memorized the names of the entire student body, small as it was, ignored him.

"Is Drummond's account accurate, Burnett? Did Drexx instigate this foolishness, or whatever it was?"

I hesitated, factoring everything in: D-Rex's Clint-Eastwood-esque glare at me; hambone Denny, pretending to see if he could blink out of his swollen socket.

"Yeah, I mean, Lance, well…" My tongue flopped fish-like around my cheeks.

"Quit looking at them, Burnett," Mr. Pike said. "Tell the truth. Unless you want me phoning your parents."

Good luck reaching both of them. "OK," I said. "I hate being a narc, but, yeah, this is on Lance. Now can I go? I don't want to miss my ride home."

I fast-forwarded to the next time I ran into Lance when he was being D-Rex. Would he buy I'd confessed, and minimally at that, under stern interrogation? Yeah, that had no chance. It'd be back to lunch besides the urine cakes.

"That's not true," D-Rex protested. He rotated his sore neck, though I wasn't sure if he was attempting to out-fake Denny for injuries or only in the grips of angry disbelief. "I didn't touch him, I swear. Denny slugged me with his backpack."

Mr. Pike's stern jaw gave away nothing in the shadows of the deck whose absence would've revealed two out of three of us were liars. "Who didn't you touch, Drexx? Right now, I'm seeing two, minorly injured boys who may be eating Easter jellybeans with bags of frozen peas on their faces. Is that on account of you?"

"I'm hurt, too," he said shrilly. "And I didn't hit nobody."

"Correction, you didn't hit anybody. My God, son. Were you in a coma in English class when they taught double negatives? For the last time, did you, in any fashion whatsoever, initiate contact with both or either of them?"

The clunky wheels of D-Rex's mind spun. "Yeah," he said a moment later. "I tapped Luke on the shoulder, which the baby took the wrong way. *Uh*, what was your question again?"

"Can I split, too, Mr. Pike?" Denny asked with a croak. "I need Tylenol. Bad."

Our headmaster thrust his large hands, which had swallowed all of ours in obligatory handshakes he insisted on if he hadn't seen you in a while, into the pockets of his beige slacks. "Stop going for an Oscar, Denny. Point made."

He pivoted back to D-Rex for a final cross-examination. "Drexx," he said, asking what he'd already deduced, "if you're innocent, how do you explain this situation? Are you suggesting your classmates struck themselves in a conspiracy to frame you?"

Game over. D-Rex had no defense, ensnared in a web of his own making, which Denny had just tightened into a Venus flytrap. Unless he confessed, which he wasn't going to do, he needed another cover story. And he had one, rolling out the same, get-out-of-jail-free card he'd used after torquing a kid's arm in a chippy game of "Smear the Queer."

"We were just horsing around, sir, on a Friday afternoon."

Mr. Pike, tamping down a smirk, had heard enough. He fished a pack of Marlboro Reds from his coat pocket, tapping the open end against his palm. Out came a cigarette, then a silver Zippo lighter, then a little nicotine cloud that made me queasy. "Burnett and Drummond: you're free to leave, though permit me to express how disappointed I am by your conduct, however it began. This isn't some public school where students maul each other carte blanche. This is an institution that aspires to live its motto, not just print it in a pamphlet. That's why I accepted this job. Obviously, we have some rough edges to saw off."

We nodded our heads, all solemn-like, to win our release.

"One last thing," Mr. Pike said. "While I step back to finish this cancer stick, I want you three to shake hands. And to promise me there'll be no reprisals. Understood?"

We bobbed heads again for the peace accords, D-Rex clasping my hand with a tungsten squeeze. *He doesn't know what reprisals mean. Only revenge.*

When D-Rex gripped Denny's hand, raised voices from inside the woodshop room thirty yards away diverted Mr. Pike's attention. I kept mine. As they made contact, I watched Denny lean in to whisper something into D-Rex's ear, and blood drained from his face.

Adjourned, Denny and I scooped up our respective backpacks, my burgundy one innocent, his gray JanSport guilty as sin. D-Rex collected his stuff, too, assuming he'd be exiting with us.

"Not so fast, Drexx," Mr. Pike said after losing interest in the woodshop. The two fingers pinching his red-tip Marlboro gestured at his upper-level office. "You and I have further business to conduct."

That was our cue. We headed west, toward the lower-school parking lot, which sat beneath a colossal Foothill Freeway overpass not only the width of an aircraft carrier but also colored the same gunmetal gray. Halfway there, we turned to watch Mr. Pike escorting D-Rex on his perp walk.

"I don't know how to thank you," I said as the line of idling cars pumping out tailpipe exhaust broke into view. "I thought I was toast."

"No thanks needed." The conversation stalled for a second while Denny seemed to debate asking me a sensitive question. "Hey," he said, "I don't suppose you got any weed on you?"

I stammered, still the drug virgin, though the weekly pot consumed by our student body could've been sold by the bale full.

"Shit. I don't. If I did, it'd be all yours."

He took it well. "No problemo. I need a dime bag for the weekend. I'll try someone else. Next year, I'm growing my own plants to earn some bread. Already picked out my secret spot."

"Really? That's cool." Cool as in how can Denny be my age but act twice it? "Can I at least treat you to a Big Mac?" The Mickey-D's a block away on Foothill Boulevard was Stone Canyon's unofficial bistro.

"Nah. I'm good."

I spotted my ride home, and it wasn't going to be pleasant. Mrs. Tomlin—retro, Susie-Q hairdo, face full of moles—was grouchy you if you were a minute late climbing into her white, Oldsmobile Cutlass. And now I'd left her there, with two hyper boys bouncing in the backseat, for eleven minutes. She threw me an ornery look.

"Before I split, I got to know: What did you whisper into D-Rex's ear? It scared the hell out of him."

Denny, staring blankly ahead, was nonchalant. "I said if I ever caught him hassling you again, I'd sneak plastic explosives where he least expected them and blow him on top of the gym. The moron lapped it up."

"Wow. Explosives? Why'd you do it, though, you know, riding to my rescue. You could've gotten your ass kicked."

He checked his Converse's and touched his shiner before responding. "Honestly, I don't know. Something came over me. I just saw red."

"I'll say so."

I wanted to hug him. Give him all three dollars in my wallet. Promise to name a son in his honor, though I'd only spoken with him a dozen times, if that, since September. "You made my year," I said. "But we both know he didn't pop you. How *did* you get that black eye?"

Denny ignored the question while he took out a black hoodie from his JanSport, wiggling it on over his Grim Reaper T. "Oh, that? A story for another time, Lukester. Later days."

He flashed me a smirk, then walked over to a folded-back gap in the fence separating our school from the electrical substation whose hissing, dark cables powered campus. From that opening, Denny dragged out a long, woodshop-lathed skateboard, under whose laminate rested Alfred E. Neuman's face from a *Mad* magazine cover. Done talking, he dropped the board on the ground and rolled past me on polyurethane wheels, his long, blond locks bopping behind.

"Hey," I yelled before he was beyond the gates, "Happy Easter!"

He replied with a flip of the back of a hand.

Getting into Mrs. Tomlin's Cutlass, my gut told me what I'd grow to learn. Denny had heavier things weighing on him than tin-foil eggs and hollow bunnies.

CHAPTER TWO
THADDEUS LOWE'S LAST RIDE

Under the wire-caged lights of our paint-flaking gym, behind aging championship banners the color of horse teeth, a tweedy Sherman Pike stood at the lectern, aiming to give us a hero we could believe in. Gathered before him was Stone Canyon's future, the entire high school, all one-hundred-seventy-four strong, for the customary, first-day-of-school assembly. He'd already delivered the welcoming remarks and passed the microphone to department heads for the standard announcements—the coming school calendar, academic tips, recycled rules of conduct, club-sign-up deadlines, etc.

The older boys greeted the drumbeat of "circle this date" and "never hesitate to reach out" with a glazed surrender. Everything they said, after all, was regurgitated on a stapled handout they'd press into our hands on the way out the door. "Our queen has arrived," I overheard an acne-necked senior murmur to a friend. "Her majesty, duplication."

Such a Stone Canyon thing to say. Then again, what did I know, me being a squirrely freshman, eyes wide, trying to shake off a case of summer-vacation brain? Hot damn, though: us larvae had made the majors, grown peach fuzz. My classmates and I wouldn't be packed into a building reeking of anticipation—let alone the vague stench of tube socks and jock straps—otherwise.

In four tight blocks of chairs partitioned by grade, those exhalations you heard were our last gasps of freedom. Everyone, except for dedicated loners and foreign-exchange students, busied themselves catching up after a three-month separation. Class schedules were compared, big fish tales embellished, corny jokes retold. If it was after Labor Day, this was where our keisters were supposed to be. But what wasn't in the open might've been the most palpable; I felt pangs of it myself. Disguised inside the perky chatter—the "What's crackin?" and "No Way!"—was a swirling cloud of invisible nerves. For seniors, pressure-cooker

SATs only months away; for juniors, make-or break GPA; for sophomores and us freshman, continuing proof we had the Wheaties to grow into *them*.

Whoever you were, whatever your notch on the campus pecking order, today was the soundless blast of the starter gun for months of bondage to inky textbooks and demanding teachers, their weighty expectations versus our zigzagging, teenage endurance. The "academic meat grinder" they called it.

Bring it on. I was so amped about this new beginning, so riveted by the atmospherics, I was about to shimmy out of my skin. Twitchy fingers, which hadn't stopped twiddling since I was eight, cycled between mouth, hair, and JanSport. They crept under my hard metal chair, tracing metallic welds, all the way to island chains of lumpy, dried gum possibly there since the moon landing. Distracted to the nines, I didn't realize I'd greeted my first day of high school with my boxers visible through my unbuttoned Levi's, until a classmate's nudge in the ribs.

The single thought I could keep intact: *No sight of him so far today. Chill out.*

I had no shortage of trivial distractions to keep me occupied, beginning with nearby objects: the backs of seniors' heads arrayed in the row directly in front. There were narrow skulls and pumpkin-shaped ones, elongated necks and missing ones. There was shoulder-length hair (though nothing Aerosmith-long-crazy) and shaggy, Chia-Pet fros, neat trims above the ears and crew cuts of boys from military families. I inspected every shade of brown and blond known to mankind, and gingers, too. Some seniors had wolfish sideburns, some greasy skin sheening in the lights, others with dandruff sprinkles their mothers forgot to brush away.

"Only good thing about these assemblies," the pimpled senior told his buddy, "is they shave an hour off school. Rest is phooey."

Mr. Pike, back at the lectern, double-tapped his hot mic not because it glitched or fed-back but because he had sixty-odd conversations to stop. Though his appearance was identical from last semester, there was a difference about him in how he spoke, how he carried himself. It was the command of someone making an alien land his. "Gentlemen," he said in an assured voice. "Situate yourselves. We have plenty to go over. Plenty, indeed."

If there was anything confirming he'd situated himself, the summer letter he mailed to every returnee's family cemented it. His rookie year of careful observation was done. As his correspondence made clear, our second-year headmaster was more like a sheriff firing his six-shooter at school traditions that'd outlived their usefulness. The first ritual he took out were those scratchy, Navy-blue blazers disliked by all, yet previously mandatory for assemblies and formal events. Just because they bore the school crest, Pike reasoned, was no reason to keep saddling us with them. That was obvious today in the regular clothes (minus rancid flip-flops, foul-mouthed T-shirts, or hole-ridden jeans) everyone wore. He attacked our long-standing calendar next, adding two extra days of review time before nerve-racking "Final's Week"—and letting us out at noon this Friday for everyone to get their feet under them.

Mr. Pike's reimagining of Stone Canyon hardly ended there. On page two of his letter, he announced—confetti please—that he was "imposing harsher penalties" for bullying, which could make a guy euphoric if it wasn't lip service. He was also, to hear adults tell it, making a daring break from prep-school convention. Beginning this semester, he announced he was phasing out Latin, which earlier classes welcomed like gamy liver, no longer requiring it to advance into honor courses. In his "considered opinion," it was illogical for Stone Canyon to continue harping on a dead language, last spoken by ancient Romans, when Spanish would be the West Coast's second language of the 1980s.

"Communi sensu supra consuetudinem," he'd wrote. (Common sense above custom.)

Showtime now built with buzzy guessing of the identity of the guest speaker handpicked to close out these festivities. Normally, they rolled out someone from our deep bench of alums and patrons to urge us to reach for the stars, something other schools reserved for pomp-and-circumstance at graduation. But Stone Canyon prided itself on being a different animal, less snooty than our rivals, more free-spirited, so why save for June what you could have in September? Hollywood. Industry. The Law. Scientific Nobel-Prize winners. We had our pick.

The gym's overhead lights half-dimmed, movie-trailer style, and except for a few catcalls, the audience perked up for another tradition-snapper. No "distinguished" person paraded across the stage, either, because Mr. Pike had anointed himself guest speaker.

"Power move," that senior commented.

"Or a little fascist," his buddy responded.

Mr. Pike unfolded his speech, smoothing it on the lectern. The icon he selected to rev our engines had been gone for sixty-three years. It was the school's original founder, a man depicted in Stone Canyon literature, as well as glossy, coffee-table books, as a hobbling, white-haired fossil from history. Our chain-smoking headmaster aimed to bring Thaddeus S.C. Lowe back to life by entertaining us with a backstory that'd been lost in hibernation.

"By the time he arrived in Southern California before century's turn, our Mr. Lowe should've been dead—or worse, irrelevant—multiple times over," Mr. Pike said. "Self-educated farmer's kid with an unquenchable drive for knowledge. Overcomes childhood illness. Hears a lecture on lighter-than-air hydrogen that ignites a lush imagination. Becomes so obsessed with hot air balloons he vows to cross the Atlantic in one, knowing he could drown or become shark pâté."

Kitty-corner across the aisle, an attention-hogging junior piped up with a *"Dun, dun, dun, dun"* in an ode to *Jaws*. A mimicked throat-slash from a frizzy-haired English teacher, a Berkeley grad sitting to the left of the lectern, shut that down.

"Thaddeus' first test flight," Mr. Pike continued, "nearly does him in when the skin of his balloon shears. No quit in those bones, though. He meets Abraham Lincoln on the Civil War's brink. Volunteers to gather combat intelligence for the Union Army from his inflatable. To confirm his technical chops, he sends the president the first telegraph from hundreds of feet up."

At the word "up," Mr. Pikes motioned to someone in the rear to kill the master lights. The building fell dark as a projector that'd been quietly wheeled out hummed and a silver screen behind Mr. Pike lit up. It stunned even cynical seniors. "Cinema verité," one said. "Who's got the licorice?" another added. I was dazzled, too, both by the story and its brisk pace.

Onscreen, there was Thaddeus, dashing and walrus-'stached, waving from his silver, teardrop-shaped balloon, then gripping hands with an Honest Abe grim-faced in his stovepipe hat. There was emotion seeing the two together like that, grainy history rendered into flesh-and-blood stakes.

"He's soon surveying the First Battle of Bull Run in Virginia. Bull Run, fellas. Keep in mind that flying a balloon over combat is a quantum leap of modern warfare, and just as perilous. Snipers shoot down Thaddeus' hydrogen-gas airship, 'The Intrepid,' forcing it to crash behind enemy lines. Lowe's wounded ankle prevents any escape. The Confederates who round him up threaten to execute their Yankee spy by firing squad. Wouldn't that rankle Lincoln? They well might've if his wife lacked as much gumption as her husband. She disguises herself as an old hag and persuades his abductors into releasing him. Unfortunately, he contracts..."

"VD?" someone from the peanut gallery yelled. "Happens to the best of us."

The rabble-rousing junior shushed before had struck again. But this time, it wasn't our English teacher who set upon him. Us students knew it was Rueben Yates, a bony, carnie-looking kid who swanned around with a classmate supposedly able to fart the first line of "The Star-Spangled Banner;" "Thing 1" and "Thing 2" was their handle. Yates' father, a grant-winning USC geneticist, probably would've disowned the son for mocking a man of science. As it were, a chorus of boos pelted him, and Mr. Pike, whose narrated slideshow had us eating out of his palm, let self-policing do its trick. There'd be no further interruptions.

"As I was saying, he contracts malaria. After Lincoln frees the slaves and is assassinated, Thaddeus returns to being a whirling dervish of innovation. He builds revolutionary machines for heating, lighting, heck, cold-storage refrigeration that we still rely on. His friend Horace Greeley's 'Go west, young man' advice resonates, and he relocates to Pasadena. Mr. Unstoppable draws up plans for the first-ever electric railroad into local mountains, defying experts warning it's too treacherous to access. Yes, for the ordinary. Lowe conjures a veritable playground up in the clouds. Time-warping yourself back, you'd see a whimsical, Victorian hotel and alpine tavern, a zoo and tennis courts, a formidable telescope and a carbon searchlight able to reach Catalina Island. Still, even great men of their generation cannot elude fate. Should I stop here?"

Cunning narrator, that Mr. Pike, leave 'em wanting more. Rising out of us was a collective *"Nooooo"* that could've bounced off the windows at the Jet Propulsion Laboratory down the hill.

More slides came from the Thaddeus time-capsule: the old-man riding a funicular to his "White City in the Sky" resort; him in a trolley cranking along a hairpin curve while his passengers turn green; him on the hotel balcony surveying the checkerboard landscape below, before subdivisions and superhighways; him posing with an imported tiger, piney forest behind. Awe-inspiring, every image. As if Mr. Pike didn't know.

"In 1912, after his railway files for bankruptcy, but before an unholy sequence of fires, floods, and lightning destroys everything he painstakingly created, Thaddeus craves one last ride, one last voyage into the blue yonder. On a shimmering afternoon in 1913, while the Colorado Street Bridge was still in arch-work, our ill, beleaguered hero totters into a small, hot-air balloon, taking off from Echo Mountain. He sails around a Pasadena more Old West than Rose City. A fierce, westerly gale, however, blows the balloon this way and that, slamming him around, and nearly into a church spire. He's forced to land, and guess where?"

In the pin-drop silence, you could hear the projector's mechanical hiss. Even resident loudmouths knew better than plucking the long-hanging fruit of his rhetorical question. There's no snickering "The dark side of Oz" or "Uranus," accent on the anus.

"Biographers long presumed Thaddeus crash-landed in a radish field in the upper Arroyo Seco. Our esteemed Mr. Burr, dean of the history department and still an avid digger, combed the Huntington Library's archives this summer to conclude history was flat wrong. His balloon came down right here, on the coordinates of this very gym or parking lot."

A ripple buzz-sawed through the crowd, slouchers sitting up, commentaries whispered. The past now felt present. I pictured a dazed geriatric crawling out of his airship's busted, wicker basket.

"Now we know why he chose, with the remnants of his depleted fortune, to purchase acreage for a future school, the type he never could attend. The eternal part of Thaddeus knew the value of a strong education and connections to the future. So, to our adventurous friend, wherever you are, I say on all our behalf, you ensured death is not the final word."

There was a stunned hush at this closing line, a breathless vacuum that momentarily put a lid on us before everyone leaped out of their chairs for a thunderous ovation. Mr. Pike hadn't anticipated the reaction, or he wouldn't have stepped away from the dais to take a modest bow with a blushing neck. For all the factions us newbie freshman were about to merge into—the pocket-protector geeks and grade-chasers, the stoners (aka "loadies") and Lacoste-favoring preppies, the theater kids, athletes, and clique-skimmers—we united in that explosive applause, embracing Thaddeus Lowe and even Mr. Pike, sheriff or not, as one of our own. When the assembly concluded, we flowed in waves out the double-glass doors, grabbing our handouts with energetic mitts and lots of opinions.

Up ahead, Denny was in a kitschy tuxedo T-shirt, pantomiming with his hands to show someone how Thaddeus' wayward balloon must've plummeted into our world. I slalomed through the masses of boys to reach him on the grass behind the southernmost, football goalpost.

"Gnarly story, huh? So, how was your summer?"

Denny rolled his eyes. "Got an hour?"

"No, but I got two minutes."

Marching toward the battered stairs and our first-period classes, the raw electricity from Mr. Pike's speech leveled off into a din on a thousand other subjects. Kids split off from the throng to ensconce themselves in friend groups. Denny and I discovered ourselves shoulder-to-shoulder on the steps, funneled upward in a noisy stream of boys moving like a hundred-legged centipede.

Right on cue came the reminder we remained scum on this food chain.

"Out of the way, maggots," said a stubbled senior in a letterman's jacket, bulling between Denny and I near the top. "I got places to go, people to charm."

—

Soon, I was fidgeting in the second row of Mrs. John's harshly lit science room, pinching myself at all we were shedding. It was goodbye juvenile homerooms, "Parents' Night," flag football, and *Willy Wonka & the Chocolate Factory*, and hello to *Farewell to Arms*, Friday-night mixers with the plaid-skirted cuties at Westridge girls' school, and tackle football (the eight-man variety). A choice apprenticeship on the picky yearbook staff, which elevated sarcasm into art form, could be in my offing. Or maybe a role in a dozen other after-school clubs like the "Stanley Kubrick Appreciation Club," where members reportedly quarreled over who got to dress up like the monocled Dr. Strangelove. No "2001" ape-club yet. Whatever I joined, I wanted it to be in pursuit of a Luke my forty-year-old self would admire.

But in the present, mental attendance-taking was my foremost concern, and it was comforting to know I wasn't alone. Among Stone Canyon's sweatiest Day-One rituals was discovering who'd been invited back here and who'd been informed to go elsewhere. Dismal grades were the primary reason people got the boot, though misbehavior and parental cash-shortages also factored in. Every fall, nine percent of the student body turned over, and all eyes stayed glued on the door to welcome or curse whoever Sherman Pike let in.

Please, God, deliver me from that eye.

Each rattle of the door handle, each whooshing sigh of the hydraulic opener was a real-time game show, just with not with polyester-clad hosts or Frigidaire giveaways. Between now and June, the thirty-eight kids making up the future class of 1980 would be living inside one another's shirts, cooped up together in poorly ventilated, barracks-like rooms. I was side-gnawing my thumb and foot-tapping by minute two.

I tried self-calming by field observation, and again there was a bundle to marvel at, starting with how dramatically we'd all changed since June. Whether genuinely glad to be back or smiling over clenched teeth, it was hard to tell, but the physical differences weren't. Like me, some had tacked on a few inches of height and spoke from Adam's apples lowering voices. Maturing fashion senses had classmates in Hang Ten and Izod shirts, autumn corduroys, and crisp, Levi 501s; so long to Sears Tough Skins, pliable as tree bark. There were laminated belt buckles inscribed with favorite bands and a constellation of new footwear—suede desert boots, Topsiders, or for me, sky-blue Puma sneakers. Fading too were the days of sleepy-headedly throwing on whatever was in arm's reach, unless sloppiness was your chic. People's hair was better brushed, with a few mussy exceptions, and hygiene improved by squirts of Right Guard. Unfortunately, along with this improved grooming were puberty's evil twin: outbreaks of acne, whiteheads, and whatnot blemishing previously clear skin.

Filing into Mrs. John's room first were friendly acquaintances that'd become reliable chums. Kyle Hartsung was the easygoing Altadenan, tanned as brown sugar from weeks surfing Newport Beach's harrowing "Wedge," a likable guy with a squinty-grin and Prince Valiant haircut. Rupert Bing had wavy, brown locks, a sweetly reserved nature, and a sharp dislike of socks. Mitch Wilkins, a pretty-boy jock and marginal student, returned to Stone Canyon with feathered, blond hair and a deep, AM-deejay voice. Skinny RG Moon (RG short for Rick Geronimo), pale-skinned and black-haired, tucked his feelings inside; only D-Rex was the better, natural athlete.

Neil Katz, the smallest kid in class and easily its most picked-on, entered next. Whatever hell I suffered last year, it was light purgatory compared with what ash-blond-haired, squeaky-voiced Neil had. In the doorway, he gave a little wave with a timid smile to test the waters; only four people acknowledged him. In his blue-checked, short-sleeve, the class mini-mouse didn't so much walk to an empty desk as sidestep along the wall against the Dormer windows. He had his reasons, namely that no wall had ever stuffed him in a closet or baited a ravenous chipmunk into his backpack with a bag of pretzels. No wall had pantsed him in a drizzle, leaving him shivering outside the gym while his jockstrap swayed on the barbed wire around the pools perimeter.

I was most tickled to see Carl Dieter, my best friend here, outfitted in a psychedelic *Alice in Wonderland* shirt, wiggle into the seat I'd reserved for him. Carl was hitting puberty's air pockets himself—zits flaming up behind his neck, greasy hair—but with an unfazed attitude that asked what's-it-to-you? We had multiple classes together this big-step year. He lived ten minutes away, on Beulah Drive, just up the block from the only La Cañada store worth shopping, Sports Chalet. He and I said hello with the silly handshake of juxtaposing thumbs and fluttering palms that we perfected in July between Slurpee's and slingshot practice at telephone poles. I just wish Denny wasn't in Mrs. John's other section.

Still, that bell was about to chirp, and the math favored me. Seventeen of the nineteen desks were already occupied. Come on down, I thought, Lars, our new, Swedish foreign-exchange student, a lanky boy who rarely spoke. Give the remaining seat to anybody: a transfer, someone repeating freshman year, a hitchhiker off Angeles Crest Highway. Just anyone not named Lance Drexx.

The door handle jiggled; my stomach knotted. Clench and *phew*: it was Roland Peters. Wiry, a tad aloof, he told us last year that he'd already mapped out his life. From Stone Canyon, he was going straight to West Point for a career in Army camo, just as his Vietnam War hero father had. He rushed in as if tardy for a battalion parade.

Things were looking up. The name's Luke. I'd mind-trick my preferred reality.

"Don't have a cow," Carl said while classmates sorted Pee-Chee folders and notepads or goofed around while they could. "D-Rex wasn't there when I passed the other room. You're probably in the clear. Not sure I am." With a demoralized look, he directed his chin behind me to show why.

It was Mack VanDoren, a freckle-faced, red-haired boy with a tetherball-wide head and a decided jealous streak. Mack, better known as "Raggedy Angry," was smart and intense, a decent athlete, too, but never willing to accept that Carl was a better student than him. Known for cackling punches to the belly, he'd dropped Carl to his knees in the lunch line last May upon learning Carl scored a ninety-eight on his math final, three points higher than him.

"Fucking-A," Carl said. "He couldn't have moved to Guam? Or one of Saturn's rings?"

Sudden movement at the door stopped our conversation cold. Another *phew*: it was Mrs. John walking in, arms clutching reams of paper. *Yes.* Lars must be on her heels.

A split-second later, I learned life owed me nothing.

There, in unmistakable silhouette, wasn't the Swede but a bigger, more muscled Lance in black, corrective glasses thicker than last year's. My gut reaction: Buddy Holly reborn as a barbarian.

"Lance-a-Roni, what's up man?" Mack said. "I wasn't sure you were coming."

Join the club. Lance/D-Rex swaggered down the row toward him for an exuberant high five. He scooched into a desk against the back wall, where class ruffians usually hunkered down, kitty-corner to Neil and rows behind me.

I squeezed my eyes hard, though there'd be no wishing this away. I'd been run over. Screwed over. Fucked over. Forsaken. You can't escape into the tower of your own head when you're falling through the floor.

I'd been guardedly optimistic when he was a no-show during JV football practice that kicked off three weeks ago. During stretching last Wednesday, after our coach hollered at us to roll onto our backs—"Brown eyes to the sky, sissies"—he prowled the columns of us mostly shrimpy kids in shoulder pads, measuring our talent this season. At day's end, all of us bushed and dehydrated, our bellowing coach said unprompted: "All's not lost. There's still a puncher's chance Lance will be back. Let's hope Arcadia High doesn't nab him. Kid's worth a couple wins by himself."

Arcadia High: how could you? Stone Canyon: how dare you? To borrow something I once heard on the radio about an ancient comet, this for me was an extinction-level event.

I swept my pencil off my desk for a quick peek at the rear wall. Lance was already reverting to old form, snickering a mean comment one of his crew directed at Neil. Rather than ignore it, Neil demonstrated he hadn't matured emotionally either, plugging his ears with his index fingers.

Most of us felt crummy he tiptoed the grounds with a misery index off the charts. And yet, few of us, especially me, stuck up for him. Half of this abuse Neil brought on himself by posing asinine questions that any semblance of a filter would've blocked. As to the unprovoked hounding, many of us bought into self-interest, knowing the beasts pummeling Neil would have less malicious energy to devote to us a shameful bargain never openly discussed.

Neil's fingers were out of his ears when I looked over and mouthed the feeblest of consolations. "It's OK." But it wasn't OK—not for him, not for me, not for anyone, really—and Neil plopped his head into his little hands, squashed before the semester even began.

"Boys, settle down. Fun time's over," said Mrs. John, standing behind a wide, Formica counter that served as her desk and moonlighted as lab-experiment platform. The sophomores who'd had her last year, in her first teaching stint out of grad school, had this to say: She was even foxier in person than in yearbook photos, and totally out of her league maintaining classroom order. For this girl-crazed boy, labeling her foxy was like labeling the Grand Canyon a gorge.

After fifteen seconds gaping at her, I was smitten, her only displeasing feature that chunk of ice on her ring finger.

Our back-row classmates disregarded her request for order, launching a rubber band that bounced off the back of Neil's left earlobe. "*Oww*," he said shrilly.

Mrs. John frowned at D-Rex and Mack, knowing their reputations. "Listen up," she said. "If you want to be treated like you're in high school, act like it. I appreciate today's a milestone, a rite of passage. But you better get over the novelty fast and cut the juvenile antics. As the older teachers who's covered this subject always remind me, this course is an acid test that…"

"You mean like yellow sunshine?" It was Jim Perrini, the youngest of four brothers to attend here, who said it with a toadying wink at the back row.

"Thank you for illustrating my point," Mrs. John said. "And stop tilting back in your desk, Jim. Now!"

Jim, who'd tell you he was your friend one day, then gossip about you the next, did as she asked, still smug.

"Anyone else need to get things out of their system?" she asked. "I was at the assembly. Those interruptions reflected poorly on you."

The creamy skin around her gorgeous cheekbones tightened with her irritation. Much as I enjoyed messing around, I was glad she was seizing control. For a second, only the buzzing fluorescents made a noise in the staid air. The September heat that'd taken it easy on us in the gym was setting itself to broil, with no functioning air conditioning to neutralize it.

"Good. As I was saying, if you fail to take this class seriously, you're going to be in deep yogurt. Your brains need to be hungry little sponges, people. I promise the math won't be grueling. But science can be a challenge, and there's no substitute for the hard work it requires."

She breezed around the two-tone platform, distributing a stapled syllabus hot off the school Xerox machine, making the scent of camphor our air freshener. When she got to me, I saw the faint outlines of her bra through her light-green blouse, and my eyes enlarged. I worried she caught me leering at her breasts, but she strode past to commandeer an origami, paper football Kyle was constructing. She slammed the paper triangle into the trash can with an angry windup. The resounding message was obvious: She'd blow her stack if this continued.

"I guarantee, you're going to feel overwhelmed at some point in the semester," she said, doing her rounds. "I'll also guarantee that you'll be grateful you kept at it years from now, taking your SATs besides kids sorry they weren't pushed as hard."

Between D-Rex's arrival and Mrs. John's warning, it was as if Thaddeus Lowe's pulse-pounding adventures were fabricated to dupe me into false hope. I was the youngest son of a Caltech grad and mathematical savant, the kid who'd excelled in algebra but scraped by in geometry with a C+, flustered by triangular equations that read like hieroglyphics. Not that my father accepted hieroglyphics as an excuse for squandering an A.

"We'll take it step by step, though," she said back at her desk. "We'll delve into names you only heard in passing before: Aristotle, Copernicus, Galileo, Newton, Darwin, Edison, Curie, Einstein. Their work are building blocks you'll need later for chemistry, physics, and calculus. Give it a chance. It can be thrilling."

Thrilling? I got the jitters just contemplating that murderer's row of subjects.

"Hey, what's with your foot?" Carl whispered. It was unconsciously tapping the linoleum. "SOS signal?"

"Not funny," I said back.

Before we met the Aristotles, Mrs. John said we'd need to speak their code, be it the periodic table, laws of thermodynamics, or the paradox of Schrödinger's cat, whatever a vanishing cat had to do with anything. Master these, and by spring we'd transition to "the cool stuff," experiments utilizing Bunsen burners, test tubes, and petri dishes.

That last part didn't sound too excruciating, and from her red-tartan thermos, she filled a plastic cup of coffee. "If you're the least confused, visit me. It's the ignorant ones who believe they have all the answers. They'll probably end up working the deli at Fedco."

By the time the bell rang, I wondered about the odds of a piece of sky junk taking out her husband.

CHAPTER THREE
STONE CANYON'S FLIES

Lunch on the quad, under metal umbrellas shading a dozen tables, was already less rambunctious than junior high, free of widespread taunting and grab-ass at someone's expense. It was by the railing overlooking the Pit where I realized old habits would die hard. There, I watched Lars get the "Nadia Coma-Flipsky," a whiplashing prank inspired by Romania's champion gymnast, Nadia Comaneci. We'd all fallen victim, one second standing there, minding your own beeswax, the next cartwheeling backward from a shove in the front and a cohort sneakily down on all fours behind. Head over heels you toppled, usually onto concrete.

So far today, D-Rex had ignored me, except for flipping me the bird when we'd made direct eye contact. Neil should've kept his own distance, but in trying to buy himself peace for the year, did the opposite with a butt-kissing comment that D-Rex's clunky, new glasses were "tubular." Evidently disagreeing, he snatched Neil's sandwich out of his hands and chucked it down the embankment.

After eating, Carl and I wandered around our H-shaped upper campus with divided brains, on the lookout for known hazards while chitchatting about everything: football game after-parties, Thaddeus's balloon ride, first impressions of teachers, even "Bohemian Rhapsody" by Queen, Carl's favorite band. When he veered off to take a whiz with a "Galileo Figaro," I drifted over toward the Senior Lawn for a look-see at Stone Canyon's squash-court-sized DMZ. My Pumas never got within a foot of grass.

"Hey, punk, keep the hell away," barked Arnie Hosarian, lounging there in a beach chair, shirt unbuttoned, wrist-deep in a sleeve of Pringles potato chips.

Arnie, even us freshman bottom-feeders knew, was the closest thing to an untouchable here, a golden boy with a gorilla's hairy chest and a meatpacker's beefy limbs. He was student-body president, the ex-chair of the student-conduct, judicial board known to reduce even confident kids to tears, and a two-hundred-pound, All-CIF nose guard last year. No one questioned whether the oldest son of a famed, Armenian-American defense attorney would soar in life, only into what tax bracket? Fearsome Arnie had a supposedly, unblockable forearm shiver and a high chance to graduate summa cum laude.

"I am keeping away," I said. "I don't want to get thrown in the pool on my first day."

"Yeah," he said, mouth full of chips, "but you're still here, existing. That's annoying."

"OK, OK. Got it."

"Now shoo. Save yourself from dying a bad death. Probably."

"I'll take probably," I said, reversing course toward the bathroom.

From his low-riding chair, Arnie lobbed his now-emptied Pringles can at me. It sailed end over end, landing at my ankles. "*Probably*," he said in a Myna-bird squawk, leaning back into the sun with a bottle of Coppertone on his furry belly. "Do they ever learn?"

—

The final class of a memorable day found us jostling for desks inside Harvey Burr's classroom, which Stone Canyon's longest-serving teacher decorated like a mini-museum of Americana. No other teacher here besides the legend himself could've gotten away with blanketing the walls, nearly up to the water-stained ceiling tiles, with their personal affinities of national greatness and gullibility.

I was giddy in Mr. Burr's presence, and even giddier because of who wasn't in this section.

Tacked along the wall by me was one of his pastiches. Top to bottom was a framed copy of the Bill of Rights, a sallow photo of Teddy Roosevelt in the White House kneeling by his pet bear, Elvis's *New York Times'* obituary, and a *National Enquirer* cover declaring the Apollo moon landing a government hoax. Every year, depending on his opinion about whether the USA was on the rise or in decline, he'd shuffle his montages.

History was my second-best subject behind English, both breathtakingly math-free and gateways to mesmerizing new worlds. Besides that, this was *Harvey Frickin' Burr!*

You entered his room one by one to receive a personal hello. In previous years, there was griping he played favorites, that he was a stuffed-shirt drunk on his own voice, that he tried indoctrinating kids to be Libertarians like him. Before class, Carl and I rushed into the library to browse yearbooks to see what our successors said about him. Last year's described him "as a natty intellectual who made his sparkling contributions with keen knowledge, a pipe that never stopped, and a munchkin stature similar to Napoleon's."

Whatever, I thought. He might've been all of five foot seven in a three-piece suit the color of tortillas and black platform shoes, but you don't tug on capes like his.

Before he welcomed us, we were greeted by the elephant in the room—a big, sweating elephant braying in a sauna. Because his classroom faced south, the afternoon sun beat down on us with a vengeance. It was in the high-eighties, and thunderheads over the San Gabriel Mountains compounded it with muggy, dense air. Dormer windows cranked to their max offered no relief. Melting classmates dribbled in, fanning themselves with spiral notebooks and tugging at soppy collars.

Quentin Wicks, a soft-spoken boy with curly, walnut hair and the waistline of someone much older, plopped into his desk, sweat moons under his arms. "We got through eighth grade for this?" he said ragged breathed. He hit off his Primatene Mist inhaler and dabbed his neck with a wet paper towel. "They're planning to drill civilization into us while we're in heatstroke?"

Carl looked worse for wear himself while taking his seat. He'd had to jog to his locker to get his textbook and returned a perspiring salt lick. He mopped a beaded forehead with a sheet of lined notepaper. My trouble was lower. The elastic band on my boxers was a last line of defense keeping briny rivulets from making it look like I peed my pants.

At the precise rattle of the bell, Mr. Burr clapped his hands to jar us sweaty boys to attention. He strode to the front, leaning against his broad desk. "*Aww,* my next crop of victims, all assembled in place. And punctually. As I repeat to every freshman class, it's my fervent desire that what you'll learn here will resonate long after you leave."

Broiling as we were, Carl and I traded *can-you-believe-we're-really-here?* glances.

I took a few seconds to look over Stone Canyon's longest-tenured teacher. Gray hair with sharp widow's peak; small, rosy lips; prominent nose. Mid-fifties, I'd say, and a definite clotheshorse judging by his lavender silk tie, immaculate pocket square, and gold Rolex. There was scuttlebutt that after *he'd* left Dartmouth, where Stone Canyon itself had sent dozens of graduates, the CIA had recruited him for overseas missions, but he never confirmed it one way or the other, teasing the intrigue with a "wouldn't you like to know."

"Not incidentally," he addressed us now, "I know the sun feels like it's ten-million miles closer. If you need to refresh yourselves at the drinking fountain, just do so discreetly."

A line of parched classmates straggled out, while the rest of us tried sitting erect, stewing in our juices.

"You'd think an old-timer like me would've checked the forecast to ensure we at least had a portable fan in here. Sorry. I was too busy plotting how to steal every second of your free time. Let's pray our Mr. Pike can deliver on his promise of getting us central air conditioning as well as he delivered today's speech." He tamped his own forehead with a pocket square. "Holy Helios is it cooking in here."

Once people returned better hydrated, Mr. Burr began distributing syllabi that weighed in at twenty pages. By next week, today would be our honeymoon. His classes were infamously reading-heavy, "university level." Over the years, parents had complained the workload was excessive even by prep-school standards, visiting their sons with chronic headaches, eye strain, sleep deprivation, and more ridiculous medical conditions. The administration allowed them to vent, and that's as far it went because of his track record of molding first-rate students.

Just then, I remembered Denny was behind us probably sweating buckets, too. When I peered back at him in the corner, he wasn't panting. He was hunched over his desk asleep, hands propped under chin, with the sleeves of his tuxedo T-shirt extended down to his wrists. I liked him for a lot of reasons—his swinging JanSport and brash IQ just two of them—yet after a year of him on my margins, I barely knew him. Our veteran teacher let him doze in the heat swamp.

"Pardon me, Mr. Burr, I have a question," Neil said, poking up a hand not much bigger than a child mannequin's. "If your homework is going to take up all our time, can you write notes to our other teachers to give us a break? I want to try out for the golf team."

The squall of derision that normally trailed Neil-isms like this reannounced itself in muffled insults and clucked tongues. Unlike the more untested Mrs. John, though, Mr. Burr let the mocking burn itself out, and with a knowing grin strolled toward the side of the chalkboard where he titled his Ben Hogan-brand putter. He twirled the club around, taking it by its chrome-plated head. Not only was he golf team coach, but he'd also threaten and occasionally use "Ben" to lightly whack unruly kids with its rubber handgrip, both in class and during campus patrols.

"Neil, why don't you stay a few minutes after class so I can explain to you how hyperbole works. And I won't be writing any notes, kiddo."

He returned to his desk, tapping Ben in his hands like a riding crop, and we all quieted. "Boys, you may think you know American history, from its Pilgrims and powdered wigs to Watergate, but we're going to drill deeper than facts and dates. We're going to mine the American psyche, focusing on one question: apart from the outer edges of the Milky Way, have we run out of new frontiers to conquer? By year's end, you may be sick of debates about that and sicker still of listening to me pontificate about the theories of historian Frederick Jackson Turner. If you listen well, you may, repeat may, just understand why America, as a bright light in a sea of darkness, seems to have lost its way. Any questions?"

No one lifted a hand; we were too heat-zapped, too sensory-overloaded, glassy-eyed, and stifling yawns. Well aware of that, Mr. Burr sketched out the semester—major themes, tests' schedule, paper-writing no-no's—in a fast cadence. Ten minutes prior to the closing bell, he said: "Before I take pity and let you all out early, here's your first assignment: flip through the textbook to engage in time-travel fantasy. Specifically, I want you to imagine yourselves present at the flint-lock of history when a genius, after years of slavish dedication, of costly sacrifice to family and health, discovers that which makes him immortal."

He let that hang while he returned Ben to its resting place and lit his pre-packed, cherry-wood pipe, a musky plume soon coiling overhead. "Put another way, picture a lightning bolt that'll change the future. Not an actual one, Neil, a symbolic one."

"With all respect, Mr. Burr, I'm confused," said Kyle, whose Mammoth Ski Team T-shirt clung to his ribs as if he'd already been dunked in the pool. "What's this got to do with American history?"

"Listen and thou shall learn," he said, breaking for a puff. "It's individuals who advance the world as much as nations do. That's the headline to remember."

He highlighted that by ticking off examples—examples of what it must've been like being a spectator when someone's brilliance came out of the oven. The pope's shock laying eyes on Michelangelo's *Pieta*; Thomas Jefferson dancing the minuet after reading James Madison's draft of the Constitution; Marie Curie's husband spinning her around by the lab coat after she discovered cancer-fighting-radium; bystanders waving caps as the Wright brothers took flight at Kitty Hawk, North Carolina; the arch of Paul McCartney's crescent eyebrows hearing John Lennon sing a scratch version of "In My Life."

"I get it now," Kyle said. "I think."

"You will with certainty later," Mr. Burr said with a gleam. "You all know George Carlin, I'm assuming; the comedian famous for listing the seven dirty words unfit for TV. I, however, celebrate him for his observation about misunderstood brilliance: 'Those who danced were thought mad by those who couldn't hear the music.' That's what I sincerely want for everyone here: for you to go to your grave, decades from now, having created music only *you* could compose, genius or not. Failing that, I'd like you have a ringside seat to watch someone altering the course of history."

The end-of-school bell warbled, and half the class raced out the door, forgetting both George Carlin and Harvey Burr, toward the water fountain or their air-conditioned rides home. Carl, Kyle, Rupert, and I clustered under the eave, deciding to hit the water faucet in the locker room. Three cheers: We still had JV football practice to survive.

Denny. I had to ask him what he made of our first day of high school, this barrage of the mind. I gazed in through a dormer, watching him rouse himself from his siesta and wipe sleep dust from his eyes. I also noticed that the left sleeve of his tuxedo T-shirt had bunched up above an elbow, and that's when I noticed marks on his forearm in a line of three, pink-rimmed, black-encrusted circles. Was that why he wore that absurdly long shirt on a sweltering day? To hide burn marks, as in cigarette burn marks, if that's what those were?

"Luke," Carl said with a wick of impatience. "Let's boogie or we're ditching you."

"It's cool. You guys go on."

I kneeled down, pretending to tie my shoes so I could at least walk to the lower level with Denny. While I did, a couple of devoted grade-chasers brownnosed Mr. Burr, who let them gab away as he smoked his pipe. By the time I lifted my head up from my Pumas, Denny was nowhere around, having slipped out the rear door.

That night in bed, spooned up to Bilbo the Wonder Beagle, struggling to sleep in a room beside my plastic, modular shelves and lumpy beanbag, I couldn't stop dwelling on Mr. Burr's wish for us to bear witness to genius. Maybe *I'd* already checked that box last Easter. Denny's supple mind, it seemed, had gobbled up info blips like a Bell Labs supercomputer, formulating the perfect counterstrike to incriminate D-Rex while exonerating us. Everything else about him, including why someone would want to turn his arm into an ashtray, was a riddle that kept me up till 1:00 a.m.

CHAPTER FOUR
ERASER FUZZ

We'd never heard our football coach, Jerry Hoover, so lathered up at practice before, blasting us with salty language, his beet-red checks about ready to burst. "Unless you want those snobs embarrassing your candy-asses in front of your parents and friends, you better start executing! Keep lollygagging it, and I'll run you in full-pad contact up to game time."

It was the week before Thanksgiving break, when autumn foliage and cable-knit sweaters teased poinsettias and Santa caps ahead. For Coach Hoover and us, the date that mattered most was noon Saturday for our homecoming rivalry game against "that team across town," Pasadena's Polytechnic Panthers. We'd gone 5-2 so far, more than respectable compared with seasons past, but none of those victories were notched against the school that'd given us Stone Canyon Mountaineers a little-brother inferiority complex.

No matter how you cut it—picky admission rates, trophy-case, rich alums, campus—Poly bested us, stereotyping us as "that *other* prep school" of the western San Gabriel Valley. They were the wholesome kids, Donny Osmond in orange-and-white, milk-and cookie consumers who organized blood drives and smiled with their perfect teeth. We, in contrast, co-opted our black and gray colors from the renegade Oakland Raiders, thought Marie Osmond a drag, and preferred our music heavy metal, punk, or new wave.

Coach Hoover was this booming personality with a redundant wardrobe: white, mesh shirts that stretched across his beer belly, all-weather, black Spandex shorts that left nothing to the imagination. He drove a sky-blue Impala and puffed Winston-Salem cigarettes, sometimes covertly during games when things were going south. For all his energetic screaming at us between the hash marks, he'd been a model of professionalism under the classroom lights as our eighth-grade history teacher. Everybody working for Mr. Pike, it seemed, did double duty (teacher, van driver, ski-trip chaperone) to make ends meet in a "stagnation" economy.

As our teacher, Coach's job had been readying us for Harvey Burr. The Clemson University grad, a balding, forty-something bachelor with standard-issue, black mustache, made no secret of his zeal for the Peloponnesian War, or his desire to write a screenplay about it. Classmates who ran their yaps last year while he waxed on about Pericles or King Archidamus were sentenced to a very 400-B.C. punishment. In the "Hoover Position," the guilty maintained a push-up stance atop a pair of desks for three, long minutes. "Sparta forever," he'd say.

Expert in "the skullduggery of great city-states," he expected controlled fury from us three days from now on the home-field gridiron. As the sun began to fall from the dark sky, dipping behind that view-blotting freeway overpass, three sharp toots from his whistle was Morse code for we-weren't-anywhere-ready-for-Poly. "Run the reverse handoff again," he hollered red-faced toward our helmets' earholes. "Use your technique—both sides. Those Poly, goody-two-shoes will eat your lunch if you don't."

Why he choose me, our second-best wide receiver—mediocre speed, indifferent hitter, good hands—to carry the load on this play made no sense, not when RG was twice the athlete I was. The element of surprise, all war-like, perhaps? That he had D-Rex playing both ways as halfback and slobber-knocking linebacker was a no-brainer.

Kyle, our ski-bum quarterback, flipped me the ball. The play, intended as razzle-dazzle misdirection, fooled no one since Coach already called it out. Somehow, I successfully head-faked our defensive end, Will, a tall, handsome kid with an absentee mother and a 4X4 truck waiting in his driveway for him to get his learner's permit. Racing up to do what Will couldn't was the spiteful one in sports goggles inside his facemask. D-Rex tossed aside a blocking RG with ease, homing in on me with an evil sneer. I tried dipsy-doing him with my hips, make him commit the wrong way, but there'd be no getting him off balance.

Everything afterwards was a crunching blur preceding the pain—the dropping of his shoulder pads, the lunge of his body, the launch of his Riddell helmet at my exposed knee.

Laid out, I wanted morphine, an amputation, anything to stop the throbbing, and I wanted D-Rex to throw himself against a high-voltage wire at the power substation behind us. The destroyer of my knee, who believed Nebraska was in "Central America," was smart enough to exact revenge from spring when Denny wasn't around and I was a legal target holding the ball.

Coach squatted by me while I clutched a leg simultaneously deadened and on fire. "No fun getting speared, is it?" he said in an avuncular tone. "Good news, though. No bones popping out. The trainer's gonna help you into the locker room. You'll live, Burnett."

From my back, I looked up to see him waving the entire team over ten yards away, instructing them, ironically enough, "to take a quick knee." He grabbed D-Rex, our standout jock, by his practice jersey and pushed him off. "Everybody, you see what Lance did, cheap-shotting like that. If you think we're anywhere good enough to overcome a roughing penalty, think again. For Chrissakes, when a ballcarrier's coming at you with a head of steam, square your shoulders, plant your feet, and explode into their midsection, not their legs. Got it?"

Our trainer, Barry, a part-time chiropractic student with a Fonzie pompadour and celery breath, told me we'd "take it slowly" when I wasn't sure I could take it all. Lightheaded, I threw my arm around his neck and limped off the field with a knee on fire. Behind me, practice resumed with all its smacking, grunting, and signal-calling. When Barry held the door for me at the mouth of the gym, I glimpsed back at the field. Off to the side, Coach wagged a finger at D-Rex—before a butt slap that sent him not back to the huddle but toward me.

"Coach told me I had to apologize. So there. Bye."

In jogging off, Nike cleats clicking on asphalt, electrocution seemed too kind a fate for him.

Mild sprain of the medial collateral ligament was the season-ending diagnosis. My MCL injury would cost me our showdown against Poly and our regular-season finale against the less detested Chadwick School Bottleneck Dolphins of the Palos Verdes Peninsula.

An hour later, I was still lying flat on the training-room table, with an icepack cellophaned around my grapefruit-sized knee and a pair of moldy-padded crutches waiting for me on a hook. Barry said an X-ray was optional though probably not needed. On top of everything, I'd missed my ride home and had to phone our live-in housekeeper, Charlotte, roly-poly like coach but never a yeller, to pick me up. No teenager in the history of teenagers would've wanted to be caught dead in her ride, a horrifying AMC Gremlin, but I tried bucking myself up that at least none of my pals would be around to see me gimp into her pea-soup green hatchback.

Waiting for her, knowing she'd bring her treasured "Gretel," a miniature dachshund part and parcel of her employment with us, marooned me alone with a pulsating leg I shouldn't have. Tylenol and two slabs of nostril-curling Tiger Balm gel hadn't numbed much. I decided against rinsing off; I had to preserve my energy for the acrobatics of getting into my Levi's one-legged.

An unfamiliar sound crashed my *why-me* pity party and crashed it with perfect pitch. From the steamy, tiled cavern of our group showers drifted the voice of someone singing an AM radio hit. It was Seals & Croft's "Summer Breeze," an airy, toe-tapper from years ago when I was deep in my Elton John phase. Whoever was replicating it a cappella had some pipes. Maybe it was the circumstance, or a subconscious need for distraction, knowing my season was kaput, yet something in me just had to know who was belting it out. On one crutch, I hitched over to the edge of the showers, guessing it might be Coach Hoover with the hidden, vocal talent.

Wrong as wrong could be—it was my ligament-crusher shampooing his hair, eyes closed, hitting those high notes on, *"blowin through the jasmine of my mind."* It was him humming the interlude with the same, tribute-band quality. Why, I wondered, was he still here? Had Coach made him run laps for spearing me, and he never saw his disposable-victim in the training room?

The water shut off with a screech, and there was no confusing the voice anymore. He'd shapeshifted from crooning Lance to D-Rex. "There better not be a Peeping Tom out there, or I'll knock your lights out," he said in my general direction. A minute later, I heard the shower nozzle gush back on.

Out in the parking lot later, gimping towards her on my crutch, Charlotte stopped drumming her sausage fingers on the Gremlin's steering wheel when she saw what my monster had made of me.

—

We'd been at it for an hour, my cluttered brain unable to solve a perplexing equation, his mathematical one aggravated I couldn't crack what came so lightning fast to it. The fall-semester science final was two days away—gulp—and I'd requested my father's help boning up for it on a practice test. I should've gone, after a spoonful of salt peter, to Mrs. John for tutoring. All I wanted was for him to pinpoint where my calculations took a wrong turn; he was resolved I derive the equation *myself*.

The stumper involved the second law of thermodynamics. Specifically, entropy, or how disorder in a "system" snowballed once unloosed.

"I still don't get it," I said, sitting at my desk, him beside me in a chair he lugged in from the kitchen. The atmosphere was already charged, and having to keep my knee, which had mostly recovered from the sprain, extended straight made hunching forward awkward. (Speaking of that knee, we'd lost a hard-fought game to Poly, 27-20, in which D-Rex accounted for two touchdowns and an interception, and Coach Hoover praised everyone's "grit" afterward.)

"I understand it in theory, except what does temperature have to do with the reaction?"

"See—you don't understand the theory. That's the crux of the problem. If it wasn't, you'd know temperature affects the heat in the system. This is basic stuff."

"Yeah, to you."

"I'll ignore that comment while you redo the calculations. Make it legible this time on your scratch paper."

I did. "OK, I think I got it. It's W equals QH plus Q minus QC."

Consternation, disappointment, disbelief: the three seasons of his face. "No, Luke. You don't got it a bit. You're not concentrating hard enough."

I resisted snapping my teeth-marked Ticonderoga No. 2 pencil in two. "I'm trying."

"Trying isn't doing. Erase what you have and buckle down."

I obliged, erasing my close-but-no-cigar answer in impatient strokes, leaving behind a dark smudge and little patch of pink microdots on the yellow, lined paper. I brushed the detritus off, eager to get the problem solved and him out of my room.

"There's still eraser fuzz all over the page," he said. "You know that drives me bananas."

"Us working together," I said under my breath, "does that for me."

"All right," he said icily, "that crossed the line." He jammed his mechanical pencil into his shirt pocket and carried the borrowed kitchen chair toward my door, signaling our contentious tutoring session was over seventeen minutes in. "You asked for my assistance, but I refuse doing the heavy thinking for you. Come get me when you're done acting like a child."

When he walked out, past Charlotte's room, two realities dawned on me. We were *nothing* alike, and entropy wasn't limited to abstract machines. Families themselves can fissure and degrade when subjected to the excessive heat of incompatible humans trapped under the same roof.

My mom's death, in this way, was our frying solar flare. Before it, I was her light, her baby boy, the recipient of tickle-fests and crispy mac-and-cheese, of playful swimming lessons and tight hugs after I'd memorized the Lord's prayer she'd taught me on the sly. I also took the brunt of her short fuse when I spilled Elmer's glue on the carpeting or spoken sassily or tried hiding slimy asparagus in my napkin. When she'd go nuclear or, conversely, give me the cold shoulder for hours, it could make a boy wonder why he was here.

My analytical father, superfan of charts and mathematical tables, never blew his stack like her. Where mom was melodramatic and spontaneous, he was Mr. Spock in his logic and predictable as the calendar. I was the "whoops baby" they had in their early-forties, putting me ten years behind my middle brother, Simon, and fifteen behind my oldest, Matthew. The romance that conceived us, first sparked during the air-raid blackouts and gas-rationing of World War II, was a real-life Beauty & the Brain. Mom was an ex-pageant queen and later social butterfly, dad the rangy, Caltech civil engineering student once adorably klutzy around the fairer sex. Decades of choppy marriage later, that feverish love of opposites was curdled milk. I never saw them hold hands.

Muddled as I was about her death, I recall one shouting match just before that frightened me they'd split up like so many friends' parents now divorced. She'd thrown down on his counter a *Time* magazine article about how archaeologists had carbon-dated the Shroud of Turin, its age matching the precise timeline of Jesus' death. "There's your proof, Mr. Scientist," she'd said. He yelled back, atypical for him: "What you know about science could pass through the eye of a needle that *your* make-believe savior talked about."

Their religious differences, her devout, him a staunch atheist, was the blaze that'd periodically ignite, but her Mastercard bills and daily pack of Virginia Slims was the kindling for their more everyday strife. After he'd harp on them, she'd snarl at him for being a workaholic at his industrial, air-conditioning firm in downtown Los Angeles, and having a wandering eye, especially toward visiting, Nordic lady-scientists at Caltech events.

Dad and I, best I can piece together, walked the house like zombies in the immediate weeks after the funeral. Charlotte—hired to tend to me, the cooking, and cleaning—filled some of the gaping emptiness with her bubbly spirit and easygoing nature, and a routine set in. Monday through Friday, dad belonged to his company, and I belonged to her. Come Saturdays, I was dad's tagalong, literally his errand boy on trips to Berg Hardware on Altadena Drive and the Pep Boys on Colorado Boulevard. I was the pipsqueak beside him at the Coliseum for USC football games, back when tailback Anthony Davis was tearing it up, or the Forum for a deserted King's hockey game. (After I'd once quizzed him *why* it was OK to move from our seats to abandoned ones he hadn't paid for up against the boards, it was sayonara Forum.)

What I prized most didn't require a ticket, or a trip to Macabob's toy store across from Fedco when I'd cry out of nowhere, when I'd drag around as if I'd lost a limb even though I retained all four. During the next few summers, falling asleep listening to Vin Scully broadcast Dodgers' games on my transistor radio, he'd slink into my room with a note informing me whether the Dodgers had won. Now, that was a father of a small kindnesses I needed.

By my thirteenth birthday, the gray, crewcut-topped man I'd admired and depended on was grayer and, confusingly, both more controlling and distant. My "wellbeing in this critical time" was his recurring theme. So was his pronouncements that I could get straight-A's if I applied myself (for a future business career). Rarely did he open up on his own childhood in a broken, hardscrabble family, but there was no hiding an undercurrent of resentment toward me. Here, he'd bootlegged himself from penniless college student at the tail end of the Great Depression to American success story, all to reward *me* with the trappings of a cushy-soft life in the sex-drugs-and rock-and-roll seventies. They were light years from the near-starvation and secondhand shoes he'd weathered at my age, and nobody gave him an instructional manual for empathy or, as I was finding out, even permission to be happy.

Being a moody teenager, I felt myself pushing him away. Felt myself denying him entry to my private world, willfully giving myself over to doubt him, question him, chaff at his unsolicited advice, mouthing "fine" to nearly every dinner-table question. Gun to my head, I'd admit I loved him and was proud of his accomplishments, and still couldn't bring myself to freely vocalize that. Every week now, he receded more as wise guardian, my "Shell Answer Man" on any subject, instead towering over me as a presiding judge in a sham trial where I was presumed guilty.

CHAPTER FIVE
THE MILK BOMB

Three days after Christmas, when Denny called asking if I wanted to hang out, I pumped my fist in relief by the hallway phone. "Oh, donka," I said. "Double donka actually."

I needed to be with one of my own and Carl, that screwball, was away in upstate New York visiting relatives. Being stuck in a house—a house whose minimal holiday decorations were nothing compared with my mom's candle-lighting, tinsel-everywhere excess—was suffocating, so Denny's invite injected oxygen back into me. My dad was copacetic with it after learning that Denny's father was one of *his* own: a Caltech grad and professor.

More and more, too, Caltech was becoming my teenage open sesame. Day after tomorrow, dad was jetting off on a ten-day trip to Europe with the Caltech Associates, an alumni group, to tour astrophysics sites, climaxing with a trek to some university-connected, particle-accelerator project in Geneva. Cutting-edge science was the one subject where he wasn't anti-social; he'd once said he wished he'd pursued cosmology, his dream-job, rather than his more lucrative, intellectually ungratifying career cooling peoples' offices. With him overseas, I'd be free, well, "free" defined by a louder stereo and absent sermons.

I hopped into Charlotte's Gremlin, keen to get to Denny's door, but she crossed her arms, saying we couldn't leave unless I said goodbye "like a proper son." He was in his walk-in closet, squishing mismatched clothes into a Samsonite, packing last minute as always. "Have a good time," he said holding a pair of checked slacks and boxers. "Just behave like someone's watching you. I'll pick you up before dinner."

Pulling up to the curb outside the Drummond's ranch-style home on La Cañada's southern flank, I was nearly out of the car impersonating a tin boot before it stopped rolling. On the drive here, I ducked-down in the backseat, praying no saw me in such a reputation-bruising abomination. Charlotte's wiener-dog, Gretel, who spent the majority of her time napping in her room, rode shotgun, snout out the window.

My host stood on his stoop, in a yellow, "Zog's Sex Wax" tee under his trusty, black hoodie. He was glad to see me and gladder still to get out of his own house. His first word to me? "Finally." Behind his front door was the reason: a heated argument that you could tell upset him. I didn't know who was arguing, and didn't need to, staying true to Stone Canyon's unspoken boy-code. No matter how inquisitive you were, never stick your nose into someone's complicated home life, because their dirty laundry wasn't anyone's right to know and, besides, you probably had some yourself.

"Turns out my mom's got a work appointment in the Valley," Denny said, kicking at his doormat. "Some Republican Committee or whatever. My asshole big brother is going to drive us. Buckle up."

"No problemo." That first year-Spanish was already paying off, though I bet my dad, if he spoke the language, would be grumbling *"mucho problemo"* at the notion that a classmate's unknown brother would have my life in his hands.

Daniel Drummond, a Stone Canyon senior who treated Denny like any other maggot freshman on campus, was a slightly taller, shorter-haired duplicate of little bro, uncannily similar in their upturned eyes, crooked smiles, and rail-thin frames. His irritation at being forced into chauffeuring us leaped off his tongue. "Get in," he ordered us. "We're making this quick." Denny and I slid into the backseat of the used Mercury Capri he kept neat as a whistle.

"I do this for you, you're handling the pool," he said as we whipped left on curvy Berkshire Avenue. "Scooping leaves, checking the pH. And you better not track mud into my car or..." Daniel cut off the sentence there, remembering I was listening.

"Or what?" Denny said, goading him. "You'll drop me down the chimney? *Ho. Ho. Ho.*"

Daniel sneered at him in the rear-view mirror, pirate-like, and shoved in a cassette so Eric Clapton joined us, first with "Let it Grow," then "I Shot the Sheriff." Denny bumped me, putting his finger down his throat at his brother's musical selection, but Slowhand's voice was the only one in the car until Daniel stopped the eggshell-white Capri in the turnout parking lot beneath Suicide Bridge.

"Be back here in an hour or you're hoofing it home," Daniel said.

"Gosh," said Denny, slamming the door once we were out, "forget what I said before. You truly are a prince—of darkness."

"Eat me," said Daniel, gunning the motor in idle to usher us out faster.

No objection here. Outside, that fraternal hate-fest was replaced by my hunger for adventure. I tailed Denny down a steep path beneath Pasadena's infamous bridge while cars whooshed overhead. Once we reached the bottom in dust-caked sneakers, Denny parted a thicket of vegetation that opened into a clearing that I didn't know was possible: a teenage Shangri La camouflaged by hillsides and honking bridge columns. It put to shame the dirt lots and horse acreage that my neighborhood pals convinced ourselves were California wildlands.

A couple of dozen, seemingly fancy-free teenagers were here. My mouth fell open.

"You oughta see it in the summer," Denny said, hiking his JanSport over his shoulder. "It's rockin' with people. Almost too rockin.' The secret got out. There's lines now for the Stinky Felix. It's worse than Disneyland."

"The Stinky Felix?"

"Forgot. Your first time. It's a flood-control dealio beginning right there," he said, pointing to the bridge's central arch. "Algae slimes over the concrete so you ride it on your ass a few blocks. Gets you moving pretty fast."

"I'm coming back for that. The one we have in Eaton Canyon lasts like ten seconds. Plus, it doesn't have a killer name like the Stinky Felix. What does?"

Kids on this jacket-wearing day were zipping Trac-Balls and plinking Pepsi cans set on rocks with BB guns Santa must've brought them. Three older boys squatted a ways up an embankment, passing around a pungent doobie while Pink Floyd's "Time" reverberated from their ghetto-blaster. A young couple to their right pulled a blanket over themselves and squealed, hands evidently getting busy.

Denny started up with his Hacky Sack footbag, racking up ten kicks in a row. Given a turn, I got four on my first try, soccer being my natural sport, much as I wished it were football. With so much to explore—the branch-secured rope swing, the mini-skateboard track, the graffiti-sprayed boulders, an unmarked cross (probably planted by the loved ones of a jumper)—our hour in the unpoliced shadows of that rounded bridge sped by in dog-year minutes.

Daniel reprised his snippy ways on the quick ride to the second, new place Denny picked for our hang out, but not before he made us dust off our sneakers before we re-entered his Capri. Along Linda Vista Avenue, he propped his elbow out the window, tapping his fingers to Clapton and dragging off a smoke. He let us out at the entrance of Oak Grove Park across from gargantuan La Cañada High School and gunned it out of there.

Seconds later, though, he pumped the brakes and reversed towards our shins, gears whirring, him with a quick message. "Almost forgot," he said out the window. "You're on your own getting home. Late change of plans. I'm taking Sheila to see *Rocky* at the Academy."

"Negatory," Denny said, knitting his brow. "That wasn't part of our bargain."

"It is now. Oh yeah, mom said she won't be home for dinner. SpaghettiOs for you. Outta here."

After he tore from the parking lot, Denny laughed. "He's got a rude surprise coming if he thinks I'm cleaning the pool while he's feeling up his girlfriend in a theatre." He gave a *whachagonnado* shrug, and we found a trail (for me into the unknown). Soon, we were under a virtual Astrodome roof of interlacing tree branches that cooled the air and made the sky go missing.

Oak Grove Park was perched on the western bank of the upper Arroyo Seco, in partial view of the mini-city of cosmic exploration known as JPL. Stone Canyon, our turf, resided just up the hill, but it felt distant. A plaque explained this grassy, wooded area, once occupied by Indian tribes, marked a fabled spot as the planet's first Frisbee "golf" course. My tour-guide suggested we give it a stab, removing a pair of neon-green, Wham-O "World Class" discs from that versatile backpack of his; Daniel's name was written in Sharpie on one.

We played a faced-paced six holes. There wasn't all that much to get a hang of, either. You navigated tree lines in the sprawling terrain, aiming for "Disc Pole Holes"—funky contraptions that used dangling chains to snare Frisbees and a basket below to catch them. Starved from the exercise afterward, I suggested we walk to McDonald's, since we had to go that way on what Denny groused would be a two-mile hump back to his house.

"Already ahead of you. Let's eat at a picnic table."

Now his JanSport became a clown car, able to transport more objects than physically possible. Out of it he pulled a pair of turkey-Swiss-mayo-sandwiches on pillowy focaccia bread, Lay's potato chips, Dr Peppers, even napkins to prove we weren't animals.

"Your mom get us this?" I asked as I unwrapped and attacked my sandwich.

"Nah. I drove her car to Bergee's sandwich shop last night while she was taking a long bath with a glass of wine."

"Wait. You drove? You're fourteen."

"Man, you are a choir boy. Tasty sandwich, huh?"

After inhaling lunch, Denny reached into the backpack's front pocket, removing a pack of Marlboros and his Bic. I'd never seen him smoke before, only smelling tobacco on his breath after school. He savored this post-meal ciggy like a pro, with long drags, smoke rings, ashes carefully tipped into a Lay's bag. He noticed me noticing him, without knowing why I reviled cigarettes like I did.

"Don't get the wrong impression," he said. "It's only about five a day."

"It's cool," I said. "It just brings back some bad memories." I left it there.

"Maybe you'll like dessert better."

I was expecting Moon Pies or apricot Fruit Roll-ups, two blocks of Denny's food pyramid. He snuffed out his Marlboro and back his hand went into the JanSport, this time its front pocket. Materializing now was a Ziploc with a narrow doobie in it. "Ready to bust your cherry, *err* murder some brain cells?" he said. "No peer pressure at all. Personal choice."

I was torn, late to the pot game. It wasn't a question of me being tempted because I was tempted, majorly. It was a question of confirming my father's doubts about my judgment by getting busted. "I don't know. It feels too out in the open. How about next time in a garage or something?"

"Sure," Denny said, carefully returning the baggie to the pocket. "But this pinner will be dust soon."

"Do kids really party down here?"

"Luke, Luke, Luke: I seriously need to corrupt you. Of course they do. It's not 1950. You think many high schoolers give a shit about Frisbee golf? That's why the townies call this place Smoke Grove Park. That and the boneyard. Look in the trash can; nothing but beer bottles and Trojan wrappers."

My left thumbnail whispered me to chomp it, me now squishy about whether to hit off that joint. "Yeah, but what about Brian and what's-his-face, Duncan? Mr. Pike expelled them in October for getting high."

"Actually," Denny said, flicking his Bic for amusement, "those putzes were smoking and selling hash in the parking lot—with teachers around. What'd they expect? Extra credit. But there aren't any prying eyes here."

"Yeah, but I've got a prying father."

"So I'm gathering."

I changed the subject as I wavered. "So what's the story with your mom?"

"She's a busy woman these days, trying to get Reagan elected president. Personally, I think she's in love with him....Now my turn. It must be rough not having one, a mother I mean. I heard she died in a car accident when you were, what, eight?"

"Yep," I lied, not about her but the cause.

"So, just you and your old man? That must suck donkey balls."

"We do have a housekeeper who looks after me. And you haven't met my beagle. You'll love Bilbo. He's a hoot. I couldn't have gotten through everything without him."

He dumped our trash while I stuffed the Frisbee into his JanSport, now considerably lighter without food. Something at the bottom jingled as I pressed them in, and my curiosity couldn't resist. I wiggled out another Ziploc, this one bristling with a miniature circuit board, wires, and small, plastic parts.

"What gives?" I asked, shaking the baggy.

"Oh that? My dad's old, Texas Instruments calculator. He wagered me ten bucks I couldn't put it back together after he dropped it at work. Easiest cash I'll ever make. At least he gets me."

"Your dad?"

"Who else?"

The clock was ticking on the two hours before *my* dad would be picking me up, so we got a movin'. I was dying to ask Denny about what I'd spied the first day of freshman classes: those raised, scabby, holes in his forearm no longer so visible. Were they cigarettes burns, and if so why? Torture? Payback? A dare? After today, I assumed the source of the black eye he manipulated to rescue me from D-Rex was Daniel's doing. Something told me to hold off getting too personal because I wasn't anywhere near ready to spill any secrets myself.

From shady Smoke Grove Park, we trudged up the short, steep-ass road affectionately known as "Heart Attack Hill," which took us past the other, nearby high school, this one all-boys like us. At Saint Francis, brown-robed monks herded students in mandatory buzz cuts into red, tile-roof buildings. "Jarheads," we tabbed them. Lord knows what they called us Prepsters.

Passing Stone Canyon, I tried cracking Denny up. While no toker, I still could be a joker, apologies Steve Miller. "You think," I said in the crosswalk, "the chain-link fence around campus is to keep us safe? Or prevent our escape?"

Denny laughed with a smoker's crackle. "Two birds, one chain."

We continued trudging up Foothill Boulevard, only halfway, Denny sighed, to his place below Descanso Gardens. Nearing the tallest object in La Cañada's low-slung skyline—the triangular, yellow-black sign advertising Winchell's Donuts, Denny did his chin-point thing and patted the belly of his surf-wax shirt. "Let's go in," he said. "Hope you got some money."

The advice around Stone Canyon was that if you were scheming anything illegal, check Winchell's first, because a cop with a donut and a cup of coffee was one less cop blood-hounding teenage mischief. Roving California Highway Patrolmen and county sheriff officers— "Omar's" in our lexicon, as in Omar Sharif from *Lawrence of Arabia*—were always dipping in and out of there for sugar-caffeine fixes.

Winchell's, I knew from my only time in here with Carl, beckoned you inside with its unfair advantage: the aromatic smell of fatty, deep-fried dough tempting passerby from the sidewalk. The store needed it, too, because the décor—bolted tables, industrial, crumb-stopping linoleum—had all the hominess of a janitorial closet. Softening things up this December were frosted windows with images of Saint Nick and his reindeer chasing crullers.

Only three people were there when we walked in. A pair of younger, high school kids, equally bored as us and flicking sprinkles at each other, sat in one corner, while a grizzled-looking trucker in a John Deere hat nursed a piping-hot cup of coffee in the other.

"You just don't give up, do you? The answer's still no." A long-limbed man in a slimy apron shook his head at Denny before I could even examine Winchell's offerings. A nametag said he was "Fred, Manager." "Why don't you try Sports Chalet, unless they've kicked you out, too."

I had no clue what their history was. Denny did, proceeding up to the streaked, glass counter that'd sold out most of its inventory. He screwed his face into a mask of innocence before speaking. "Fred," he said, "is that any way to talk to a couple of hungry customers?"

"Nope. It's the way I talk to someone who keeps badgering me about something he knows I don't want."

Fred, the doughnut-world's anti-Willy Wonka with his beady eyes and five o'clock shadow, glared at Denny. I pretended not hearing him to avoid getting sucked into the crossfire, faking interest in a lonely apple fritter and an éclair leaking custard. Fred wasn't buying it.

"Kid," he said, locking onto me. "You know what your obnoxious friend did?"

"No. But, um…"

"Rhetorical question, dummy. A night before Halloween, no one's here. I'm in the kitchen, working the fryer when I hear change rattling. I race out, thinking it was a robbery. But it was him. He'd jumped the counter, without asking, and had taken apart the side of the cash register with a screwdriver he had on him. He was attaching wires and gizmos between the register and a piggy bank, one of those you drop a quarter or dime into it, and they roll into the right slot."

Memory flash: I used my plastic coin-sorter to save up for a *Rolling Stone* subscription. Far ahead of me, Denny must've been trying to win a patent.

"He may look like the obnoxious, little cousin of that blond guitar player in Styx. I forgot his name."

"Tommy Shaw," I said all proud, before Denny scowled *not appreciated*.

"Yeah, that's it. I told the pest three times I wasn't interested and that he should get a job at Radio Shack."

Having seen the busted calculator Denny bragged he could rebuild blindfolded and now learning this, maybe he should.

"Let's not resort to name-calling, Fred," Denny said.

"It's Mr. Tyree to you, Lance."

Oh, my God. Denny was using Lance as his alias. Shine on, you crazy diamond.

"OK, Mr. Tyree. I was trying to automate how you make change. Handling all those coins wastes your time, and you get that gross, coin-shit on your fingers, which spreads to the food. I'll circle back tomorrow for a full demo if you give me ten minutes. It works."

"*No!*" he said in a raised voice that had those other teenagers looking over. "Someone," he continued in a lower voice, "with like five pubic hairs and zero retail experience ain't telling me how to manage my business. Keep it up and you're not welcome back. Now," he said in a syrupy tone for all to hear, "how may I serve you today?"

"*Well, excuseeeee me.*" Denny's Steve Martin impression needed work. "We'll take two glazed. And that apple fritter?"

"That it, Tommy Shaw-ette?"

"Yes, Mr. Tyree. Pay the good gentleman, will you, LB? And throw in a couple milks. Negotiating made me thirsty."

"Don't push your luck, Lance."

Outside, just in case it wasn't abundantly obvious before, I realized I lived a black-and-white existence within the lines. Denny's world was spectacularly Technicolor and boundary-free.

"Don't worry about that scene," he said. "Fred's under a lot of pressure. Probably has a coyote-ugly wife. I say we scarf our doughnuts with a view. You game?"

I should've hesitated, but why dull Technicolor? "Sure, Lance."

"I thought you'd get a rise out of that."

He took me to the rear of a one-story, stucco building besides Winchell's, set back from the boulevard disappearing west into a polluted horizon the color of rotted apricots. Doughnut-bag clamped in teeth, commando-like, Denny shimmied onto a lidded trashcan along the wall and hoisted himself onto the roof in a technique I copied.

"We got to go on our knees from here. Someone from the street could see us. Roger that?"

"Yeah, but where are we?"

"See that church to the left? We're on the rectory for it. But don't worry. No one's there now."

I retract what I said about that Winchell's sign. La Cañada Presbyterian's Church qualified as the highest object around, an aircraft-hangar-sized building promoting God on a glass sign.

"How can you be sure?"

"Pastor Bill's car isn't in the lot, so he's probably traveling. He's a good guy. Always driving around helping Vietnam vets get used to being back home."

"Let's do it," I said.

We knee-crawled over bumpy, tar shingles toward the crown of the roof. Denny released the doughnut bag back in his teeth, removed his JanSport from his shoulder, and laid down on his stomach. Given the so-so street panorama, we had no reason being here except in theory we shouldn't be.

He opened the crinkly, white Winchell's bag and passed me a doughnut. "And even if Pastor Bill was inside, he'd be cool. He and my dad are tight, or used to be."

I gashed my doughnut. "How'd they meet?"

"Our whole family used to be his parishioners. Every Sunday, every holiday, for years."

"Used to? Did something happen?" A guy can't hold off a fishing expedition indefinitely.

"Yeah. It's hard to sing a hymn as a family when it's World War III inside the house. You met Daniel."

Say something. "Mine's more like a graveyard. I hate the quiet. It's why I'm always playing my stereo. I got *The White Album* and Jimmy Page posters above my bed."

"Zep's OK," he said. "Blur Öyster Cult's my jam. Them and Black Sabbath."

"So, you want to be an inventor? An engineer? The auto-coin sorter just your start?"

"Oh, fuck no. Computer programming. That's where my future is. As you probably noticed in class, I could give a crap about any subject that doesn't involve numbers."

"Reverse for me." I licked glaze off my fingers.

Just then, an earsplitting machine rumbled into the Winchell's parking lot in front of us, and Denny scooted down the roof a foot, waving me to do the same. Us two inquiring minds peeked over to the edge just in time to watch a CHP motorcycle cop switch off his Kawasaki, remove his aviator sunglasses and helmet, and swing a black-booted leg over a spotless chopper. Off his bike, he windmilled his arms and jiggled his hips as if to get loose. From our crows-nest vantage, we saw a fit man in his mid-thirties with a handlebar mustache, curlicued at the tips, barbershop-quartet caliber. If this Omar didn't sing harmonies in his off hours, he could've been a waiter at Farrell's Ice Cream Parlour on Rosemead Boulevard, a birthday-party-hotbed from our elementary-school days. He strutted into Winchell's liked he owned the joint.

"Wouldn't you know it?" Denny said, mouth half full of apple fritter. "That goon Officer Stroud." He dipped into the Winchell's bag and extracted his milk carton, which he immediately opened.

"What do you mean, goon?" I asked, cocooned in my own sugar rush, preferring that fatty sweetness—along with the vented scent of its origins in Frank's grease fryer—to the grotesque waves of gasoline vapors billowing up at us from the traffic whipping by.

"He gets his rocks off roughing up teenagers; D-Rex would cream his pants to be him. After he popped my friend Stewey for jaywalking by Bergee's, he searched him for drugs—with no cause! Before he lets him go, he whacks him in the back of the leg with his baton. Stewey limped for two weeks. Textbook police brutality."

Minutes passed while we polished off our Winchell's. I checked my Timex and glugged my milk, though Denny hadn't even sipped his yet. "Shouldn't we hit the road?" I asked. "It's getting late."

"Good thinking."

I was stuffing wax paper and napkins into our bag as Denny wiggled up onto his knees. Gullible me: I figured he was turning around to go. He wasn't. He was getting into position to lob his milk cartoon, using a parabolic arc we suffered through in eighth-grade geometry, at the CHP-man's chopper, and doing so without alerting (never mind asking) me first.

Not only was Denny's throw a perfect bull's-eye. It was a white-liquid explosive that drenched the black leather seat and splattered the gasoline tank with the stars painted on the side. Drip, drip. "*Yee-haw.* Take that," Denny said all gleamy. "Stormtrooper's is going to have a soggy ride home."

He immediately ducked down to savor the fruits of his provocation, while I dropped my head with visions of cold handcuffs, hard batons, and a dank jail cell bashing around. *Divided we fall.*

"Are you out of your freakin' mind?" I whispered to him, struggling to articulate words, no longer conscious of anything we'd done heretofore and barely able to feel arms tingling from my chum's aerial bombardment. "Let's split before he notices and goes berserk!"

"Don't be such a namby-pamby. I need to watch him blow a gasket first. He'll probably assume us tricksters are long gone."

Denny soon received what he must've craved all along: the gratifying spectacle of an intimidating authority figure served their just dessert. Our ninth-grade eyes peeking above the crown of the low roof, we saw Officer Stroud dash out of Winchell's toward the crime scene, a fistful of cheap napkins in his gloved hand, that lame barbershop mustache twisted up in fury. Whether it was the sound of liquid detonation soaking his pristine machine or the unidentified flying carton he glimpsed on impact, he knew he'd been targeted and came running for a hasty cleanup before busting some heads—heads as impulsive as dent-able.

And, just in case those same heads were so foolish to still be in proximity, our Omar hollered skyward while mopping up the seat with those thin napkins: "Whatever you do, your ass is grass, and I'm one sonofabitch of a lawnmower."

"Lawnmower? That's the best he's got?" Denny whispered with a tsk-tsk. "Now we better boogie, though."

The instigator reverse-crawled down the roof like he did this weekly, making it onto the ground with uncanny quiet. I was so livid at him that by the time I was in place to hop down, my whole being was consumed by one urgent question. "Why did you have to go blow up our afternoon, Denny?"

"Blow it up?" he said with a jack-o-lantern smirk. "I've just made it entertaining. What's Christmas break without some danger?"

How about relaxing. Shirt smeared by crumbly, roof tar, blood Slurpee-cold, my whole being *now* ached to shove him once I was off my belly. But retaliation would have to take a number. I misjudged how close the garbage can we'd used as a stepstool for roof access was, causing my left sneaker to crash into the aluminum lid with all the nuance of a drum cymbal. Within seconds, my clumsy repelling announced our exact position behind the rectory, destroying any illusion—or delusion—we'd already beat it.

"Holy Cow, you're making it easy," the cop shouted again. "Hope you have a high pain tolerance, cheesedick."

"Now you happy?" I said to Denny in a soft bellow.

"Uh, yeah! Don't you feel alive? It's rad. Follow me. I know every shortcut home. Omar will be chasing ghosts."

Ghosts? "We can't outrun a motorcycle. He'll swoop around and have us nabbed before we can get a block."

"Hey, give me some credit, will ya? Look at the dumpsters parked in the alley. It's garbage day. He'd eat shit trying to weave around them."

"Wait, you've been plotting this?"

Denny's second chuckle of his suicide mission was followed by the terrifying sound of a four-stroke, Kawasaki engine doing its best dragster impression. The two of us lit out, running towards the sun in that alleyway paralleling Foothill Boulevard, past the backs of little stores whose names I didn't catch. While attempting not to pee myself, I kept wondering what would make a kid upend a fun-filled, Christmas vacation day for a foot flight from the law. Vandalizing state property wasn't like passing an illicit note in class.

Why Denny, why? I couldn't have been the first to ask this.

We'd gotten only about forty yards before hearing the Omar's high-torque accelerator on the other side of the shops. Just like that, we were amateurs "on the lam" in a bad *CHIPs* episode, pursued by a furious man who wouldn't let this go as juvenile brainlessness. Stroud would probably cut us off at some pass, whatever that meant when you're not on a saddle, and demonstrate what real corporal punishment, punishment worse than any teacher doled out with the grip of a putter or hole-drilled, iron paddle, looked like.

"You sure you know where we're going?" I asked between breaths, perspiring into my sweatshirt and feeling my bum knee, which I wasn't supposed to run on for six weeks, begin to throb.

"Yeah, 'course."

Four blocks later, Denny gestured at the horse trail off Georgian Road, veering us away from the alley and into a neighborhood I'd never been in.

With that Kawasaki out of earshot, we slowed to a fast walk. Denny hawked a smoker's loogie. I favored my bad leg.

"I think the coast's clear," he said. "That was nuts."

Was? The spine-tingling bleat of a siren in the distance got us running again. Denny blew by me, pointing at a gap between a pair of houses. "Hurry up," he said. "Found our shortcut."

It wasn't like I had multiple choices. Nothing mischievous I'd done, be it fart-cushions, disembodied piggy noises in class, ding-dong ditches, or prank phone calls, flirted with a rap sheet. A terrier yipped at us trotting by a window in the narrow space between the properties. Afterward, we stood panting, hands on hips, on the small block known as Commonwealth Avenue.

Denny, however, didn't smile in triumph. He stopped blinking. "Damn it," he said, seeing we'd landed in a dead-end. "I forgot they turned this into a cul-de-sac cuz of all the horse apples." He three-six-tied on his Vans, grasping at straws for his next improvisation. "I vote we reverse course and hide under some bushes."

I could hear that lurking Kawasaki a block over, and a bloom of fatalism budded inside. Our pursuer knew La Cañada's streets and coves better than my shaggy rabblerouser. *"Mr. Burnett, we've charged your son with destruction of..."*

"What's it going be?" Denny asked. "Electra Glide in Blue isn't giving up."

A movie reference? How helpful when you're in a cold sweat on a sixty-five-degree day with a re-swelling knee. Again, *why, Denny, why?* I threw my dejected head back, seeing a puffy cloud skimming over old Mount Lowe without a care in the world. Our best move, our only move had to be to quit running and surrender. If we said how ashamed our parents would be and offered to wash his bike for the year, we could beg for mercy.

I was ready to plead my case, until a sharp light at the end of the street made me squint at it. I squinted harder and in a few seconds recognized this wasn't direct light but a reflection. The afternoon sun was bouncing off a hand mirror propped up in the window of a backyard tree house not far from us. Denny had overlooked the spiky reflection because he wasn't standing where I was. My mom would've called it our Bethlehem star.

"I got an idea. Let's go."

I didn't wait to see if he was following after hearing the roar of the Kawasaki spinning around the corner onto Commonwealth. In a jiff, we were down the driveway, over a side gate, and monkey-climbing up the wood ladder. I barged into the tree house first and heard Denny slam the half door behind. Next, I plucked the mirror from the window; the kid(s) who played up here probably angled the mirror to signal friends. Keeping us company were two packs of cards (Go Fish and Old Maid), a depleted can of Silly String, and a mildewing pack of graham crackers. Everything reeked of dampness, and my sweaty self didn't help.

We threw our backpacks into the corner and laid flat, listening as Stroud dismounted his motorcycle and, walkie-talkie chattering, crunched boots our way. My pulse beat in my ears, and barfing wasn't out of the question. While I tossed back saliva, I looked toward Denny. He had his hand over his mouth, not trying to stifle ralph but a laugh.

Then *clack*—the sound of the side gate we'd clambered over, slamming against the post of a house on whose property we'd just trespassed. This was slow death, knowing an indignant Omar was about to smoke us out to face the consequences of Denny's spontaneous gamble.

The CHP dispatcher joined the party on the walkie-talkie. Best voice of the afternoon. "All available units, 11-79, accident involving a truck and passenger car. Angeles Crest Highway, at Gould Mesa."

"You lucky bastards," the CHP man said for our benefit, not twenty yards from the tree house. When he spoke again, it wasn't to us. "Patrolmen Stroud on the way. ETA, ten minutes."

We didn't twitch a muscle, even after we heard the chopper thunder off, because what if it was a ruse to bait us? When we did scooch up onto our butts to lean against the sides of the tree house, I had bile in my teeth. "I think I might blow cookies," I said.

"Nah," Denny said. "That's the adrenaline. I know just the tranquilizer."

It'd been waiting for us since lunch. He lit the doobie and took three drags off it, clouding up the tree house with a sharp, piney scent. His eyes twinkled *ain't-this-fun* at me.

"Gimme some of that," I said before I knew what I was getting. I couldn't let him bogart the whole thing for my rookie impairment. *Inhale-exhale-cough, inhale-exhale-hack*. I'd heard first-timers bitch they didn't get high. I was flying after two hits, throat-scalded and anxiety-grasped.

Before too long, we were in Denny's bathroom, snickering about our great escape. I doused my bloodshot eyes with Visine and dabbed toothpaste on a finger to sanitize sinsemilla breath. The apricot fruit roll-up we split in his kitchen completed the cover-up.

"Sorry about that," Denny said in the kitchen. "A little more hairball than I expected. Lesson learned. But Lukester, I'm proud of you. That tree house, it saved our asses. You know, you're braver than you think."

Sunk into the leathery passenger seat of my father's olive Jaguar XJ half an hour later, I replayed the scene on a loop, including Denny's confidence-booster. I yearned to get home, shower, and listen to *Physical Graffiti* before the euphoria wore off. The last of Charlotte's oatmeal-raisin cookies tantalized, as well.

My nearly-grandfather-aged father, who'd attended high school with the clean-cut Tom Bradley, LA's current mayor, and didn't drink until he'd graduated from Caltech, asked me how we spent the day? I gave him a G-rated account that didn't pass his smell test.

"Why are you looking out the window when you're talking to me?" he said with probing suspicion. "You're not hiding anything from me, are you?"

Who me? Had my big brothers gotten this third degree when they were teens in the pre-Flower-Power time, or were they spared the Spanish Inquisition because dad was a younger, less cynical parental entity than the one to whom I was sentenced? "No," I said, hopefully convincingly, as he crossed the bridge by Devil's Gate Dam. "Why would you say that?"

"Because you're reaching the age when the trouble that boys get into involve higher stakes."

I faced him, devious teenager I'd become. "Understood," I said, banking on the pacify-to-deceive tactic.

"Anything more about today? Anything interesting?"

My response had to be sharp. "Yeah, Denny said next time I came over, he'd teach me how to rebuild a calculator. He's the smartest kid in class, probably the whole school."

Dad smiled. "Now that's using the old noggin'. I want to meet this Denny sometime."

CHAPTER SIX
BOY INFLATED

They tried stroking our egos, candy-coating the titanic workload they heaped on us weekly. They reminded us we were tackling material advanced for our years. They noted that the books we were reading as freshman were junior-level curriculum at other schools. Those teachers wanted us to know that when we burned the midnight oil, it was in the pursuit of superior knowledge. That we, in effect, should feel privileged to be smothered.

Such big talk could make your chest swell when you scored an A, just as it could exhaust you into dozing off at your desk, slobber on your arm, cramming for a test likely booby-trapped with trick questions. I was getting the hang of this philosophy by the spring semester. To survive at a college-prep school was to embrace being conditioned, not by Pavlovian bells but focused essays in Blue Books and mathematical reasoning to plot Mars' orbit. So yeah, we were moldable, even with a faculty slowly cooking us to a boil.

No one cracked the whip harder than Harvey Burr, ardent that we understood history wasn't captions, wasn't sloganeering, wasn't even timelines. When, for instance, he assigned us papers on the roots of America's pre-World War I isolationism, he slapped a warning label on it. Anyone trying to BS their way to a high grade by "regurgitating" what was in our textbook and seasoning it with nuggets from *Encyclopedia Britannica* would fail. Harsher than a C was his red-pen denunciation: *"This isn't close to being good enough."*

He expected us to get into the heads of those who made history. Consider, he'd say, Woodrow Wilson after a German U-boat torpedoed the cruise ship Lusitania, killing almost two thousand people off Ireland's coast. Think of him agonizing whether to send America's Doughboys into the teeth of Kaiser Wilhelm's war machine—the chemical weapons, the machine-gun nests—while also grieving the death of his wife? Crawling into his brain required hours picking through the library stacks and microfiche. Over-cite *Time* magazine, a Mr. Burr bugaboo, and no whining if he holds up your *"meh"* paper as an example of lackluster effort.

Like Old Glory after the Battle of Fort Henry, our class appeared to have made it through the early onslaught, stray cannonballs notwithstanding. And, when we didn't have our noses in our books, we tended like flagpoles to stand around a lot. We stood in the snack-bar line for waxy Danish pastries, and stood waiting to enter the gym, last by pecking order, for assemblies. We stood outside our Spanish classroom before the bell, listening to Kyle impersonate teacher Felix Rodrigo condemning us as "a bunch of meathead burros" for acting up—or mis-conjugating.

Frequently, I stood alone on the soccer field, a left-footed wing on a JV team with a near-total inability to pass the ball to one another. (On a more humorous note, we did set a league record for scoring two times for the *opposing* team with errant halfback passes our goalie couldn't block from the net.) One game, I tipped in a corner kick in a victory over Buckley, the next, a 7-1 trouncing by Rio Hondo where I hardly touched the ball. On the bus ride home, we speculated whether any of Rio Hondo's players, all bigger than us, a few needing shaves, were ringers.

The freshman friend circle, while hardly invincible, was a deflection shield we all needed for more internal threats. Kyle was the even-keeled, B-student who'd sling his arm around you if you were down; "mondo cool" was his catchphrase. Rupert, who like Denny smiled over whatever was tormenting him, was our quiet Beatle; his defusing laugh always made you feel better. RG was usually the first at school—anything, he admitted, to escape one parent who drank morning gin and another dodging flying plates. "What's the haps, playa?" he'd say, McDonald's OJ in hand. Denny had a dozen personalities: antiauthoritarian, probable genius, clammed-up soul, endlessly entertaining.

But of all of them, Carl was my No. 1 accomplice. Our sensibilities overlapped and senses of humor clicked. We pressed each other's buttons, confident they'd snap back. I'd drool over Queen's *News of the World* album, aware Carl now loathed Freddie Mercury, his former-idol, as a buck-toothed, commercial sellout. He'd needle me for sporting *Wings Over America* in my record collection. After our tit-for-tats, we'd reach a musical armistice, lampooning fans of disco and anyone listening to the vomitous "Muskrat Love."

The Yearbook Club's decision to select us two freshman plebs for its staff solidified my conviction we were a dynamic duo, unbreakable at that. This spring, months shy of sophomore respectability, we collaborated on the two lines the senior leadership allowed us, and we were over the moon, despite the measly space allotted us. You think the grown-ups running Poly or the Harvard School for Boys would let their students conjure the lineup for a mythical convention?

A demented Dr. Seuss reads from his new, children's book. "You Only See a Mushroom Cloud Once."

Sherman Pike's defense of chain smoking, sponsored by America's Black Lung Association.

Cockiness, all the same, could be risky, for while the days of the Nadia Coma-Flipsky's and atomic wedgies may have waned, fresh dangers lurked. The cretins straitjacketed by Mr. Pike's crackdown on physical abuse hadn't changed their stripes. They'd evolved new methods for inflicting pain.

Such was Carl's lesson one day in the library stacks, where he'd gone to research a paper coming due for Mr. Burr. As he thumbed through books on Reconstruction, his nemesis helped himself into Carl's azure-blue knapsack, which he'd left behind on the reading couch. Mack's nickname really should've been "Raggedy Jealous," forever bitter at Carl's scholastic chops, and his fingers combed through Carl's stuff, fishing out pens, highlighters, house keys, a goopy tube of Clearasil. I eyeballed Mack do it from a round study table on the other side of the room and hustled off to alert my pal.

Carl was at the sofa ten seconds later, sitting down next to Mack to quietly ask what he was doing riffling through his things? The confrontation quickly shifted to begging. "That's mine," Carl said. "Put it back."

Mack, doing his best Snidely Whiplash, wouldn't. He sprang up on his feet, saying to our librarian, but for all to hear: *Mrs. Pippen, Mrs. Pippen!* Carl has pot on him." In his hand was Exhibit A—a "dime bag" of green shake— and Carl reacted by turning sheet-white. A third of us freshman had already conducted our first, minor drug deals, myself included. Everyone in our small library witnessed what happened next. Mack waved the baggie around, beaming like he'd bagged a lion, until Carl wrenched it away, bailing out of the room as some had with volcanic diarrhea after a snack-bar burrito.

I walked outside, seeing no sign of him in the shadowy hallway close to the Senior Lawn, and knew where he had to be. When I opened the door to a bathroom stall, there Carl was, frantically dumping and flushing the fine, earthy-smelling shake down the toilet, and shredding and flushing the Ziploc it was in after that.

"I hate that traitor. You don't think Mr. Pike will find out, do you? I don't want to end up like Brian and Duncan. I actually care about school."

I tried pulling him off the ledge. "Nah, where's the evidence?"

"Before he pulled out the weed and showed anyone, you mean?"

"That's true, he did." *Come up with something.* "Can't you say it was your brother's? Actually, don't do that."

Carl was too distraught to return to the library, so I retrieved his backpack for him and later reported what I saw. Mrs. Pippen, lazily described around campus as a bun-wearing spinster driven to near-insanity by past classes, was anything but. She was a helpful, thoughtful, married woman who took pride steering us to the books, periodicals, and citations to make us better students. Best for Carl, she was doing exactly what she had been before he'd been narced on: re-organizing index cards for an improved Dewey decimal system. Raggedy Jealous was gone.

We had a good laugh in the carpool lane, Carl and I, and Denny came over, with a skateboard under an arm and business on his mind. "I heard about Mack being his usual snake in the grass. You do realize, though, you couldn't have gotten in trouble? Not any big kind, anyway."

"Get real," Carl said. "Yes, I could've."

"How? He tried busting you for having oregano. Because that's what you had. Eric Timmons sold it to you, didn't he? Out of his Chevy Vega?"

"Between us, yeah."

"Let me guess: in the McDonald's parking lot? Those juniors are making a killing selling underclassmen spices from their moms' kitchens. Come to me if you want the real McCoy."

Our English teacher, Darlene Whitcomb, was the daughter of an Oregon pilot who crop-dusted in the spring and flew the wealthy around Big Sky Country when he wasn't. During childhood summers, she played his navigator, longing, she told us, to become either the next Amelia Earhart or Florence "Pancho" Barnes, the 1930's movie test pilot, and daredevil. Barnes' grandfather was our Thaddeus Lowe.

Mrs. Whitcomb, in our first week of classes, had summarized her objectives: It was getting us freshmen as motivated about writing as Barnes, her girlhood hero, was about aviation. None of us could believe she had the nerve to recite the quote she did. "Flying," Barnes supposedly said, "makes me feel like a sex maniac in a whorehouse with a stack of $20 bills." Repeating language like that bought Mrs. Whitcomb a boatload of credibility with us. Only she and Mr. Burr had the standing to get away with it.

She was a manly woman in her late-fifties, with a pixie cut, bags under her eyes, and a stumpy body, comfortable in her own skin. She told us she cared little what her bosses thought of her teaching style and probably couldn't hear their misgivings anyways. She'd gone deaf in one ear from thousands of hours in small, poorly soundproofed Cessnas.

On this day, classmate Rick Landau, resident horndog, was teed up to exploit that.

Rick was witty and jet-black-haired, with Eddie Munster eye teeth and a restless manner; actor Martin Landau, he boasted, was a distant cousin. Like Denny, he relished poking the bear, hopping onto the Senior Lawn at lunch one day to swirl a Hula-Hoop for ten seconds. Seniors had chased Rick down for his punishment, but he was equipped to be shot-put into the pool. Beneath his clothes that Monday in February, he'd donned a pair of swim trunks and sleeveless wetsuit top. The glutton for punishment had much more coming, because once Arnie Hosarian declared it "Landau Week," it was open season on him with throwback swirlies, sawdust down the shirt, a rubber cobra in his locker, and other torments.

The blowback from Rick's Hula-Hoop dance grew so intense that by Friday of Landau Week, its namesake suffered a panic attack on the field, wigging out about what the seniors were hatching next. Quentin had to let Rick drag off his Primatene Mist to calm his breathing, and Arnie, our hairy-bodied, Big Man on Campus, called off the dogs. Since then, Rick knew some of us were still cheesed off at him for drawing the senior's ire, since that could ricochet later off any freshman, and tried re-ingratiating himself. Titillation was how. Passing around during class a novel missing from Mrs. Whitcomb's syllabi was the what.

We'd all seen the blockbuster *Jaws,* and heard its *dun-dun-dun-dun* soundtrack over-imitated here. But, after pulling the book that inspired the movie down from his elderly parent's bookshelves, Rick stayed up until 2:00 a.m. reading it. Author Peter Benchley, he discovered, hadn't merely written about a bloodthirsty, twenty-four-foot great white shark off New York's Amity Island. He'd drizzled in steamy sex scenes from an affair between shark expert Hooper and Sheriff Brody's wife that never made the Steven Spielberg flick.

When our hearing-challenged teacher flipped around to scrawl the themes of *A Farewell to Arms* on the chalkboard, Rick threw me the book so I could spend time in the porno sections of Benchley's horror story. Using time-honored subterfuge, I had *Jaws* opened behind my Hemingway. For the remainder of class, much as I worshipped that novel, I got my allotment of the erotic surprises that put dirty smiles and smutty comments on my classmates' lips. Because I usually participated so much in class, Mrs. W. didn't call on me.

I gave *Jaws* back to Rick out in the hallway after the bell rang. "Much better than Penthouse, right?" he said.

Unfortunately for me, geometrically too much, because those arousing visions—the moist panties, the hairy thrusts—carried over into my next class with, of all people, Mrs. John. We were supposed to be concentrating on Newton's universal laws of gravitation. All this gutter-brain could do was envision himself as Hooper and our teacher with her skirt hitched up.

Carl, ten minutes in from the desk over, *psssst*-ed to ask if I'd done the homework? In my sexual dream-world, I didn't hear him, and two minutes later, I barely heard this.

"Earth to Luke," Mrs. John said. "Again, can you please go to the board and write out today's equation? I don't know where your head is today. It's certainly not here."

My eyes soaked up the huge blackboard. They also canvassed the respectable, pastel dress she was wearing, replacing them with frilly lingerie. "Sure," I said, unclear how long it'd taken me to reply. "I was spacing out."

"Yes, you were," she said.

Below the desk line, where she couldn't see, I recognized I had a much bigger problem than raging testosterone. I had blood-flow crisis. *Play dumb. Think of something gross, like a run-over possum.* But rodent intestines did nothing to deflate this situation.

Busted, with no orifice to crawl into, I slid my hefty, science textbook across the desk getting up, pressing it over Levi's tented by a calamitously mistimed woody. I waddled up the platform in front of the class, slightly bent at the hips, that textbook covering my crotch. A classmate named Terri had, minus any book, avoided a slap in the face using this same, hip-bowing technique slow-dancing to "Desperado" with a girl from Mayfield School off Orange Grove Boulevard. Still, that was on a strobe-lit dance floor, and this was under harsh fluorescents that spotlighted everything.

I knew I'd deceived no one with my charade from the sniggering trailing me. "Look! Luke's got a boner for teach," someone said with awe.

I spun. It was Rupert, sensitive Rupert saying what was flagrantly obvious. I continued my penguin walk, mortified and hoping for a campus-evacuating earthquake. You try being fourteen, bolted to a johnson with its own agenda. I knuckled down, grinding the chalk so hard into the board that fine, white dust sprinkled the flooring.

$$F = G\frac{m_1 m_2}{r^2}$$

"F equals force. G equals gravitational, m are the masses of the objects and…" Brief vapor lock, those panties again. "Oh yeah, r is the distance between masses. I think that's correct."

"You think or you know?" Mrs. John inquired.

"I know, I guess."

"Well done, Luke, shaky start and all. You may return to your desk."

I did in the same manner I approached, face red as bubblegum with a glossy textbook over my 501s.

Mrs. John tilted her head down, trying to mask a smile, occupational hazard, I suppose, for a knockout too young to be anyone's "Mrs. Robinson" and too old to be anyone's smokin' sister. She must've known she was getting us just as the things we'd be studying the following year in sophomore biology were sprouting now in our real-time bodies. I couldn't tell you the difference between libido and vibrato, only that slushing hormones had it in for me. I say that, too, as someone girl-crazy since I was ten, falling for one pretty face after another, none my age.

Charlotte was with me at the Pasadena Hastings Theater close to our Eaton Canyon house for my first, puppy-love crush. She'd taken me to see *Oliver!* thinking I'd like the story, never suspecting I'd leave infatuated with Shani Wallis, the Cockney actress who played Nancy, the tenderhearted, cleavage-baring thief murdered by that diabolical Fagin. Once the credits rolled, it was *Oom Pah Pah* for this kid's heartstrings.

The blonde waitress serving Charlotte and me at Bob's Big Boy became my next Nancy. Charlotte told her I'd paid the tip out of my allowance, and the waitress twenty years my senior petted my clammy, little hand. I wanted to both hide under the counter and see if the honey in the apron would meet me, for Lord knows what, after her shift. There were others, including Kyle's college-bound sister, whose long lashes and shapely bell bottoms made me hanker for a dragon for this braces-wearing Sir Galahad to slay to protect her.

Lindsay Wagner, from TV's *The Six Million Dollar Man* and its spin-off *The Bionic Woman*, followed. Mrs. John resembled her, except with Carol Brady hair and a far better comprehension of the periodic table. I didn't know why this continued happening when I had a cute, ponytailed girlfriend. Was I a two-timer at heart? A sex maniac in the making? A normal boy shouldn't have a thirty-year-old's panties on the brain.

I'd won over Kimmy Hinson at a Westridge Valentine's mixer, beating RG out for her. Humor was my Cupid's arrow. I joked about the gross fruit punch even spiking wouldn't improve; I skewered the word "foxtrot." I got her giggling, telling her about what happened making posters for this dance with buddies at my house. How Denny scarfed *my* bowl of Froot Loops, our sugary, refueling snack, while I retrieved fresh markers, and how he tried framing innocent Bilbo for lapping it up when he'd done all the lapping.

Be happy Kimmy didn't see your chubby. She'd drop you for RG like that. Telling myself this paused the self-crucifying. It was capped, too, just in time for Mrs. John to redirect the heat.

"Lance and Mack, since you two appear ready to engage from all your talking out of turn, one of you needs to write out Newton's second law of gravitation on the board. Let's go, Lance."

I kept my head forward, done with being cackled about, nervous even turning around.

"*Um*, I messed up, Mrs. John," he said. "I thought that was for next week."

"You did, did you?"

"Yes," he said, hurriedly putting on his corrective glasses. "Sorry."

"'Sorry' is completely unacceptable this late in the year. You come see me after school today for a conversation about how you're handling this class."

"I can't," he said. "We have a baseball game starting at four. I'm pitching."

"Oh, I see. Well, we wouldn't want pitching taking priority over your education." No teacher had ever confronted him this bluntly.

"How about tomorrow?" he said.

"Or how about," she countered, "you find me at lunch in the administration building. I'm losing my patience with you. Mack, you do your work in spite of your behavior. Get up here."

Before the bell, after more Sir Isaac Newton, Mrs. John announced that two weeks from now we'd conduct our final, in-class experiment. Though she said it with gusto, it elicited an apathetic response. "Why isn't everybody excited?" she asked. "We'll get to roll up our sleeves and see the fruits of our labors." She seemed disappointed we didn't clap. Freshman burnout can do that.

Outside in the hallway, a sheepish Rupert zipped up to me. "I apologize for that, dude, mentioning your, you know. I hope you're not mad."

Emotionally hungover, that's what I was. "No, but it hasn't been a great day."

"If it cheers you up, you're like the tenth guy to have that happen. You're just the first one she's called up to the board."

"Really?"

"And don't tell anybody, but my mom has been grilling me about why I'm using up so much Kleenex without ever sneezing."

We set out for our second-period class, passing D-Rex, no longer Lance, speaking to Raggedy Angry, no longer Mack, in the hallway. "That bitch has it out for me," D-Rex said, lip curled. "She must hate jocks."

—

I took her down from the shelf late, after I'd wrapped up my homework and dad and Charlotte went to bed. She was tucked into a shoebox in a closet cubbyhole, sandwiched between my Topps baseball cards and the Major Matt Mason lunar station I couldn't bring myself to junk. I brought her out only when I needed her, and did I ever tonight. A yawning Bilbo, from the foot of my bed, observed me gently remove the box's lid from the crunchy plush of my beanbag. Cooping mom up like this wasn't an ideal way to keep her ghost present, but life, as my father always said, "comes down to how well you cope."

For his own psychic reshoring, he'd had the Salvation Army donation truck here two weeks after a funeral I attended in a black-fizzed trance. The truck chugged out of our driveway hours later with all of her wardrobe and the majority of her worldly possessions. I was too dazed to block it, too young to lodge any righteous objection, satisfied clutching what she'd earmarked for me inside this crinkly, paper-lined box. Her lacquered hairbrush and Bible. A Saint Christopher medal and chrome letter opener. That butterfly paperweight and first edition of *The Great Gatsby*. My black-light alarm clock read 12:47 a.m. when I finally returned the box containing the first girl I loved to its place.

CHAPTER SEVEN
THE POISONED THERMOS

Mrs. John's big experiment day was here—*"big, big, big"* in her promotions of it—and it couldn't have come fast enough for someone who equated science-y math as quicksand to learning. Leave the coefficients and square roots, the *divide-this, parentheses-that* rigamarole to those destined for medicine or engineering, I say. Make it their gateway drugs. For the rest of us, forty-plus minutes without scribbling pencils and calculator readouts was almost holy relief.

Denny, maddeningly, sat in Mrs. John's other section, but there was no doubt from his grades that he was probably her top student. It came "stupidly easy," he said un-braggy one day. "I just stare at the page and my brain knows what to do." I'd seen it; homework that took us a grinding hour took him a simple ten minutes. Heck, he could probably knock off the work bombing down Foothill Boulevard on his skateboard, if he avoided shoppers coming out of Ralphs with grocery bags or Fred, the Winchell's guy who wanted no part of Denny's industriousness.

The two of us had forged a mutual-aid pact, where he helped me unknot hard-core math and I handheld him to decent grades in the humanities. At an after-school hangout at my house, with an empty Flaky-Flix cookie box beside us and Deep Purple low on the stereo, I pushed him for his secret to breezing through freshman chemistry? Was it all, I had to know, IQ, his natural smarts?

"Doesn't hurt, but I had a head start," he said. "For Christmas when I was nine, dad gave me a Chemcraft junior chemistry set. You ever have one?"

"I was playing with Stretch Armstrong at that age."

"Juvenile. Any-who, me and Daniel, back when he was human, had the best time with that set in our garage. But you know us, always pushing things too far. We tinkered with one ingredient we shouldn't have and blew out the side windows. I couldn't hear for a week. My dad couldn't get mad over it, not like my mom. Whatever you do, careful around ammonium nitrate."

"Ammonium what?" I asked.

"See?"

At least Carl and company were there for the day Mrs. John had hyped up as our educational jubilee. Even those of us grateful for a math-free class didn't catch her bug, soap-making nobody's idea of *Star Trek*-y technology. In fact, we'd been lethargic since we'd put things in motion weeks ago. You know, mixing the components, monitoring the cultures, listening to her excited voice on the stealthy life of catalysts.

Soap? Denny would've had us enriching uranium.

On a narrow table along the far wall were the "prizes" from our earlier scintillations. A pea-plant, grown in homage to Gregor Mendel and his inherited-traits theory, sprouted leaves toward crusty water beakers, which we'd previously depth-charged with Alka Seltzer to chart reaction rates. Wooden slots cradled test tubes stained with rainbow-y residue mined from a bottle of Pepto Bismol. By them were a pair of weathered Dixie Cups, underneath which a wheezing Quentin and a jittery Rupert had held Bunsen burners to slowly boil water without anything, themselves included, catching fire.

There was a small whiff of danger today, as well, thanks to the caustic material center stage for our efforts. "But if we follow protocol," Mrs. John assured us last week, "it should be clear sailing." She'd settled on "Cold Process Saponification," an old-fashioned, soap-making technique that she liked for its simplicity and eco-friendly style, because that was her. Sometimes during class, when she wasn't sipping coffee from her thermos, she nibbled on granola out of a Trader Joe's bag. She also tracked ozone-layer depletion in technical journals, saying everyone hoping to avoid skin cancer later in their lifetimes should.

"We almost have our soap," she told us from her raised platform. "After we add lye to the mixes, we'll give them a couple weeks for the vanilla-color preservative and proper pH to set. Understand? It's like Charlie Brown's Great Pumpkin you used to watch—it can't be hurried. As a bonus, you'll have miniature soap bars as belated Mother's Day gifts."

Carl sagged his eyebrows at me, a reminder he knew even innocent comments still broke skin.

Mrs. John was in a gray, pinstripe pantsuit. Yesterday it was an equally non-revealing dress with high, ruffled collar. She'd worn more conservative clothing since my luckless woody made me a laughingstock for the day, an incident that also reignited debates whether she or a brunette, eighth-grade teacher named Christie was campus beauty queen. People knew my vote.

Now, she double-clapped her hands to interrupt our chitter-chatter, which still came off as *Romper Room*. "No time like the present," she said. "Let's get ourselves organized."

Organized, though, meant *us* observing *her* lining up plastic soap molds and popsicle sticks to stir them, and more of the same as she positioned the measuring cup and vanilla-extract. Where the tedious turned amusing was observing Roland and Neil, Mrs. John's pre-selected "lead lab assistants," snapping on the safety equipment she'd laid out: yellow, dishwashing-type gloves too long for their arms and goggles that wrapped around most of their faces. The effect: that of kids dressing up in adult haz-mat gear for reactor time at the San Onofre nuclear power plant. Unsure what to do until the experiment began, the two stood stiffly on either side of the counter, arms dangling, eyes staring at us through chicken-scratched lenses.

At last, it was time for the star of the show to make its premiere, and Mrs. John went to the padlocked supply closet for a container with the skull-and-crossbones on it. She gripped it in both hands, carefully placing a sealed, plastic cylinder on the countertop, away from the gooseneck faucet and natural-gas valve reserved for her. (Us students wouldn't get our own until junior-year chemistry, so my flop sweat for them was still two years away.) We'd read up on the bone-white pellets to appreciate sodium hydroxide's alter egos. Handled right, lye was a dependable stabilizing agent, industry tested. Misused, it was toxic or a hydrogen-gas explosion.

Slowly, she poured out half a cup of the pellets from that container into the measuring cup.

"Oh, I can't forget this, can I?" she said, moving her familiar thermos from the countertop to the padded stool she sat on while lecturing.

Listen hard and you could hear class comedians josh those pellets were from a kilo of coke, as if any of them knew, in mouthiness not lost on her.

"A day with sodium hydroxide is no day for you to yuck it up," she said. "It's incredibly volatile stuff." She'd reminded us before that lye was the magic ingredient enabling consumer Drano to dissolve grease and clumped hair. What you didn't want was it on your skin, in your eyes, or, God forbid, an intestinal tract. And that's not counting its potential to ignite if exposed to certain fluids. "Let's recite the poem," she said.

We repeated it in exaggerated singsong, tired of its babyishness. *"Add water to lye, you may die."*

"Good," she said, asking Rupert and Quentin, both sitting by the dormer windows, to open them "in the rare event of a spill. Now that I've properly frightened the dickens out of you, how about we start?" I'd never ever heard her so sprightly.

She was unscrewing the cap off the pellets' cylinder when a rap on the door startled us and irritated her. On the other side of the threshold was Mr. Pike in a navy blazer and Oxford button-down. "Pardon my interruption," he said. "I need a quick word with your teacher."

Mrs. John's pinched mouth said what she couldn't: This was an inopportune moment to have her ear bent, what with our experiment laid out. Still, when the boss knocked, you make arrangements. "I'll be right back," she told us from the doorway. "Needless to say, I'm expecting everyone to behave. Neil and Roland, you can remove your safety gear if it's too cumbersome. While I'm gone, extra credit for anyone skipping ahead to find other uses for lye."

Other uses? The creaky hiss of the hydraulic door declared we were on our own. Rupert was the first out of his desk, parking himself by the windowsill as our self-anointed watcher. "Mr. Pike walked her over to the lunch tables," he told everybody. "They're sitting down. *Yes.* This could be a long one."

Had this been Harvey Burr's classroom, our butts would've remained in our seats. All he had to do to quell wild-child behavior was to stop mid-sentence, peer over his bifocals, and frown at an offender. "Now," he'd say, "where was I?"

But Mrs. John wasn't Mr. Burr, and advanced curriculum aside, we were still boy apes. Quickly, it was eighth-grade study hall again when the proctor stepped out for a smoke break. Pens were tossed. Twinkies jammed into mouths. Air guitars strummed. Rick Landau tried pawning off his latest dirty book,

Portnoy's Complaint, but us monkeys had no use for a novel about masturbation, not left alone like this.

"What's she doing now?" Kyle asked.

"Nodding and listening," Rupert said, now chewing on a wedge of beef jerky. "Mr. Pike's doing all the talking. Maybe he wants to show her his ruler."

Even though my thing for her was waning, I was still possessive. Rupert's words, just the same, were music to Kyle's ears. "Contest time," he announced. "Best impersonation of a Monty Python Ministry of Silly Walks gets a, let me think…"

"A silver dollar," Carl said, digging one out of his jeans. Why he had it, only my march-to-his-own-drummer pal knew.

"What happens if *you* win?" Kyle asked.

"Gold bullion. How should I know, dude? It's your game."

Ten of us encircled Kyle by the past-experiments table for the competition he just dreamed up. Quentin and his fellow chess-club mates merged close by to talk Dungeons & Dragons; Roland, stripping off his gloves and goggles, joined them. Ralph Billum, an unassuming kid who spent his free time riding "Larry," the family horse, and Jonathon Kendrick, one of only four black kids at our high school, resumed their long-running hand-slapping battle.

Not a single classmate read up on other uses for lye, Neil included. By the looks of things, he was the only one staying put, standing sentry-like by the counter, gear on.

You be you, Neil, I thought: this silly-walk enthusiast had his competitive juices whipped up. More than devising a winning silly walk, "Monty Python's Flying Circus" represented about the only TV program, besides USC football games, that my father and I could watch together without quarreling or descending into silence. Right now, judging by his whacky moves, this was Kyle's tournament to lose, so I'd need pliable legs to out-silly him.

When, over someone's shoulder, I spotted D-Rex and Mack scoot out of their desks, air billowed out of me thinking they wanted a piece of our laugh-fest. They never turned our way, strangely enough, instead continuing straight toward Mrs. John's platform, so why argue with luck? Us silly-walkers got busy trying to beat Kyle, whose knock-kneed, leg twist was Python-worthy. Challenging him were high-legged walks bordering on karate kicks, deep-knee-bend walks that stretched hips, not to mention grandstanding Carl's floppy-leg routine his mom might've fretted was a spasm. I was loosening up for my entry when Rupert tooted his bugle.

"Heads up, numbskulls. She's coming back. T-minus ten, nine…"

We scattered, all games halted. Hurrying back to my desk, I paid scant attention to D-Rex jogging by with a mouth-breathing smirk, no glasses on, or the fact Mack wasn't behind him. He was still up front, looking apprehensive, until Rupert updated everyone again.

"Five, four…."

"Apologies. That took longer than expected," Mrs. John said, stepping back onto the platform. "Mr. Pike had an administrative issue that couldn't wait. Now onward to Saponification." But something made her pause to size us up, Kyle in particular. "Why do some of you look like the cat who swallowed the canary? C'mon everyone. It's big-experiment day."

Our ape-boy heads nodded together.

"Roland," she added, "you can gear up again."

After that, her slender, red-fingernailed hands moved as they always did about this hour, switching to autopilot for her preferred chemical. They lifted the thermos off her stool, untwisted the plastic cup off the top, and set it on the countertop. Watching us watching her doing this routine in January, she confided she was a "Mr. Coffee Girl" who brewed at home because the faculty-lounge coffee was "factory dredge, to put it nicely." A half twist at a time, those fingertips loosened the threaded cap keeping the liquid sealed.

Who could've known Stone Canyon infamy was about to be made?

Neil, without warning, took off, but not just anywhere. Decked in gloves and goggles, he spun around on the platform, took two huge strides behind Mrs. John, grabbing the plaid thermos out of her hand and heaving it with a short-armed throw into the corner of the room, seemingly to destroy the thing as if it were the Riddler's ticking time bomb. When the carafe smashed into the seam of the wall, it was a surprise physics lesson: an irresistible force meeting its unmovable object, and the thermos retched out its contents in a hail of crushed, insulating glass and the Cremora-diluted coffee it'd been keeping piping-hot prior to impact. The way the screw-top popped off and rolled under the blackboard accentuated the outlandishness of it all, and a chainsaw couldn't have cut the surreal disbelief that ensued.

From the second row, near that side of the wall, I had a ringside seat to the most bewildering behavior I'd ever seen. Nobody exhaled. No jokester sniggered. In our theater of the absurd, previously hyped as "big" experiment day, I doubt anyone even cared if the Simplex wall clock was moving or the laws of thermodynamics still applied.

A classmate had publicly murdered a teacher's thermos. The sharp, mirrored glass now twinkling under the fluorescents was as good as a chalk outline for a TV detective to probe.

"*Neil!*" Mrs. John blurted. "Have you completely lost your mind?" In her shock, she could scarcely compose the rest of the sentence, but she got it out. "Why would you do such a lunatic thing?" I'd never seen a changing face become a color test pattern, going from relaxed tan to aghast-pearl to agitated-violet. "Collect your stuff this instant. I'm sending you to Mr. Pike."

At that, someone banged the wall we shared with the adjacent classroom, a salvo to lower disruptive voices. Mrs. John turned that direction as Neil walked around her and tugged his goggles down, revealing eyes as wide as a goldfish and lips beginning to quiver.

"But, but, but...you don't understand," he stuttered. "There might've been, I don't know, something in there you, you shouldn't drink."

Mrs. John sprung up off her three-legged stool so quickly it weeble-wobbled. "What does that mean: *Something* in there? Care to explain?"

Neil, with forty eyes fixed on him, answered as only he could. He swept the back of his gloved, left hand over the counter, trying to point, I guess, at the sopping, insulated-glass-strewn mess to justify his actions. Yet he swept his hand too low, inches too low, so it collided with the measuring cup holding the lye, sending the pellets airborne and scattering them in precisely the *same* area as the demolished thermos.

Gaffe-happy. Self-sabotaging. Weirdly sympathetic. In other words, Neil epitomized.

"*Jesus,*" Mrs. John said, sharper than before. "Stop. Just stop. You're making it worse, whatever you're doing." There was a second wall-bang from that other classroom.

"Oh, my God, I'm so sorry," he replied, puberty shrill. "I didn't mean to knock that over." I could see his legs, sheathed in beige ToughSkins, tremble. "Let me get a broom to clean it up."

"You'll do no such thing."

Roland interrupted their dialogue to say, "Mrs. John, behind you. Is that smoke?"

In the whiplash of the last two minutes, this development was the scariest: Two tendrils of smoke threaded up from the corner toward the ceiling tiles. A faint, sizzling sound, like bacon in a frying plan, came with it, but it sure didn't smell like breakfast. It smelled acrid and made my eyes water. The pellets—it must be those pellets. "Big" experiment day was over.

Which isn't to say we lost a catalyst. Mrs. John transformed before us from foxy teacher with shaky, classroom control to chemical firefighter protecting a room full of other people's sons.

"OK, boys," she said. "As you can tell, there's been a minor incident. Please grab your backpacks and head outside. Nothing to panic over. Go sit in the lunch area, and I'll come get you after I have everything under control. Calmly now."

We streamed out in ragged, single file, more stunned than talkative. A dozen classmates meandered toward the metal umbrellas over the tables, looking hesitant whether to sit or stand. You couldn't have dragged me away for all the frosted cherry Pop-Tarts on the continent. Six others clustered with me outside the open dormers, where smooth, concrete walkway segued to grass. Emotionally, I was in a place I'd never been, straddling a borderland between peak curiosity (would fire engulf the whole room?) and clenching anxiety (about Mrs. John's life).

"Add water to lye, you may die." Coffee is mostly water, isn't it?

Mrs. John, a stickler for protocol, practiced it now, striding first to the supply closet to loop a light, blue mask around her ears. She held a mop and bucket next, then a spray bottle sloshing with clear liquid. White vinegar: That's what she'd told us doused chemical fires. Soon, she was at the gooseneck faucet, filling the bucket. When she turned her back on us, I tippy-toed up on my Pumas to watch her squirting vinegar at the smoky floor and swab the linoleum. Like that, she was back at the sink with the mop and bucket for round two.

Though a coppery haze from the lye spill floated near the fluorescents, there was nothing more corkscrewing up from the floor.

"Our Andromeda Strain," said Carl, who, like Denny, tore through sci-fi books for recreation.

Kyle, as good a wiseass as anyone, gave him a disapproving look that said, *"Too soon."*

"Well, this can't be good." The voice, baritone and controlled, was Mr. Pike, who must've sidled up alongside us after rounding the corner, flabbergasted to see us standing outside a classroom we normally should've been in. "Tell me what's happened?"

The three of us spoke over each other to answer. Soap-making gone awry. Neil's thermos toss. The smoldering corner. Evacuation.

He listened to our staccato explanations, posing no follow-ups. When he shed his blazer and heeled out his Marlboro, he didn't say why. He just threw an arm over his mouth and barreled in through the open door. Once he'd affixed his own mask, he worked side by side with Mrs. John in a hasty cleanup. He'd disrupted our experiment only seven minutes earlier.

—

By lunch, "Soap Gate" was *the* talk of Stone Canyon's churning rumor mill and arguably the buzz of the year. Whether present or not when it went down, classmates couldn't finish their sandwiches without being tapped on the shoulder or called over to the railing by someone who just "needed to know." Snowballing gossip caused some to hear that Mrs. John was in a hospital ICU; that her "toxic" room—currently with yellow tape crisscrossing the door—would be uninhabitable for weeks; that pieces of her demolished thermos rocketed glass into people's skin; or looniest of them all, it was timid Neil who'd masterminded a murder plot against her.

Denny practically tackled me on the staircase to get the lowdown as I returned from a locker-run. Namely, "why did I have to miss Neil trippin' like that? Sodium hydroxide—even I know to tread carefully around it. That thermos, though: What do we know about it?" *We?*

Arnie Hosarian wanted to learn the same thing, blocking me walking to fourth-period class. This was no longer the fire-hydrant-built senior you were scared-shitless to look in the eye; this was the student body prez playing loosey-goosey detective, nettled I lacked definitive answers. Arnie *tsked-tsked* me when I claimed ignorance about Neil's motives, except the line being dissected from Senior Lawn to art room. *"Something in there you shouldn't drink."*

"Sounds like Pike needs Baretta," Arnie said. "Just try not blowing the place up. Least 'til we graduate." He went on his merry way, humming "Carry on My Wayward Son."

After lunch, just before Mr. Rodrigo's Spanish class, I asked Carl if he'd seen Neil, D-Rex, or Mack since the fire? When he said he hadn't, I got a sinking feeling.

—

The next day, taking our seats for first-period history, Mr. Burr greeted us with the smile of a protective uncle whose nephews had escaped a harrowing close call. There at his desk, turning his pipe over in his hands, he looked small, not just short, and smaller still when Mr. Pike entered the room to stand directly in front. He wore a different expression than Mr. Burr's, not so much distressed as the grimace of someone trying to communicate while chewing rocks. Neil was still gone.

"Morning, gentlemen."

We said good morning back, though it didn't seem all that good.

"I'm here to provide you with an update on yesterday's deeply troubling events. I'm sure you have questions, and this is what I'm prepared to answer. While we're still investigating, we believe we know what occurred and have taken the appropriate, corrective actions. You should know, first off, that Mrs. John is fine, just fine, and should be back teaching on Monday after taking a few personal days away. Anyone in her second-period class should go to the study hall by the bio lab today and Friday. Sorry to disappoint: you're expected to keep up with the homework."

Carl and I stared at each other. It wasn't about the homework grind. It was about whether another shoe was going to drop. Or multiple pairs.

Mr. Pike pressed forward. "On a related front, Lance Drexx and Mack VanDoren aren't here and won't be, because they've been expelled, a decision not undertaken lightly."

"Wow?" "What?" "Gnarly." "Yikes." That's what I heard from the dumb-struck desks around the room. My own reflex at the news—*Holy shit, it's over!*—was too feverish to enunciate, though I considered a celebratory jig.

Weirdly, though, for me and others thrilled those two were gone, you could also feel that initial burst of delirium quickly peter out. Yesterday's chaos still afflicted us in its severity and darkness, its rumors and implications, turning us into boys with questions aplenty.

"So, it's off to the gulag for them?" Denny asked. "Porridge and beatings?"

Mr. Pike, cheeks ruddy, patience in controlled burn, stared gamma rays. "I'll let that insolent comment pass, Drummond, all things considered. Drexx and VanDoren will be attending new schools in the fall."

"But what about Neil?" I asked without planning to. "Is he all right? Will he be returning?"

Mr. Pike lifted his palms, crowd control to reassert himself as the talker and us freshmen as the listeners of this predicament. "He's shaken up. Anybody would be. Neil's family and I agreed it'd be best if he came back on Monday, too. Neil tried to do the right thing yesterday. He just did it the wrong way."

"The right thing?" It was me, again unplanned. "There's a lot of conspiracy theories going around. Can't you tell us whether Neil was trying to stop Mrs. John from being poisoned?"

From the length of his pause, I worried Mr. Pike was about to unload on me for publicly challenging him. "Luke," he said calmly, "this isn't a press conference. Be patient."

"But that's not answering his question," Carl said. "We were there, too, you know."

"I'm more than aware, Dieter. Unfortunately, state law prevents me from disclosing students' disciplinary records, or the health of faculty members. If we do conclude what happened is a criminal matter, we'll refer it to law enforcement."

"So that's it," Carl asked. "That's all you're going to say?"

Mr. Pike mulled that over, searching for middle ground that didn't muddy his black-leather shoes. "Not forever. Once all the facts are in about the incident, I'll mail your parents a letter divulging what I can, after our lawyer reviews it. Everyone's entitled to due process." Then, from back molars grinding away at his own resentments about the institution he inherited, he veered away from script, lacing into us as if *we* were the truncheon-juggling savages responsible for Neil's absence. "There is, however, one conclusion I've already reached," he said, swatting aside a disobedient bang of oily, black hair. "I underestimated how much depravity existed here at Stone Canyon and overestimated how long it would take to eradicate it. That's going to change."

Mr. Burr retook command after Mr. Pike departed, sensing we could use some TLC. "I'm just so relieved," he said, still lodged behind his desk, "that none of you were hurt, and beseech you not to lose faith in our institution. I've been at Stone Canyon since, as they say, Christ was a corporal and have seen any number of episodes where it took time for the truth to emerge. As your history guru, I suggest you wait until the facts are in. Mark Twain always said it best. *Here it comes.* 'A lie can travel halfway around the world while the truth is putting on its shoes.'"

Personally, I wondered how the author of *The Adventures of Huckleberry Finn* would react hearing adults, well-meaning as they may be, categorize this as an "incident?" An incident to me was an absentminded student losing the tip of his finger to a workshop bandsaw, or an office secretary tripping on a loose step inside the shabby, clapboard house Stone Canyon embellished as a quaint, administration building. An incident, as I'd heard from classmates here before me, were kids locked in closets, duct-taped to trees, or strapped to chairs in vacated rooms, forced to listen to Barry Manilow on repeat.

Grown-ups hiding behind privacy laws to sugarcoat their own blame in this wasn't "incident" management. It was the opposite—teenage mind control.

CHAPTER EIGHT
D-REX'S LONG WALK

The Yearbook Club's meeting ran ten minutes long on the day I was set free, making Carl and me late for JV soccer practice, even though it never started on time. Dashing? Not us. The deeper into the day it got, the less Mr. Pike's information blackout ruffled the spirit.

"It's Christmas in April," Carl tittered entering the gym.

"And Santa left ponies under the tree," I said.

Bopping into the recesses of the locker room, some of our fairy dust dried up, seeing Kyle on a bench consoling Roland, who'd burrowed his face into a gym towel. Noticing us approach, Kyle got up and looked around to ensure we were alone. Only a handful of people were in here, with no sign of our soccer coach so far, and he sat back down.

"Tell 'em what you just told me," he said to Roland. "Including the burrito."

"A burrito?" I asked.

Roland could speak car-salesman fast, and even raw, this was no exception. How could he know what'd been embargoed from us? Cinchy: a hollow door had let him eavesdrop on *the* conversation—a heated one between Mr. Pike and D-Rex's father, who'd phoned from Belgium, where he was on business, after learning his son was in hot water again. This was five-ish yesterday, and Roland said he and his nagging conscience had been in the adjoining waiting. He was there to describe what he'd seen when Mrs. John exited the room yesterday: Neil pointing at D-Rex and Mack, "like he was trying to get them to stop whatever they were doing crouched behind the counter."

Crouched? So that's where they went.

"I heard Mr. Pike tell Lance's dad that Mack had already confessed while bawling his eyes out. He said Lance could deny all he wanted, but this was the last straw for both of them."

And that last straw truly could've been Mrs. John's final breath. According to Roland's unwitting espionage, it was D-Rex who advised Mack they should toy with Mrs. John's thermos. It was D-Rex who snatched it off her stool while the rest of us were goofing around, and D-Rex who removed the cup of lye pellets off the counter. He was the one who suggested, in a Pete-Puma-cartoon voice, they should drop "three or four" pellets into her coffee so she'd be too sick to teach, until Mack objected that dose could kill her. And it was D-Rex who called Mack a "pussy," and upon hearing that Mrs. John was returning, snorted and spat into her thermos before putting everything back and skedaddling to his desk.

"What a dirtbag." It was Denny, joining us after the Stanley Kubrick Appreciation Club meeting was over. "Luke, sounds like what he did to you."

"Let me finish," Roland said, blotting a teary face. "It gets worse."

That hollow door, a replacement for a solid-core one too uneven to plane anymore, sure wasn't constructed for confidentiality because Roland heard every syllable through it. That included Mr. Pike notifying Mr. Drexx what his son had done yesterday, *after* he released him from the administration building, where he'd been cooped up since the chemical spill. "Mr. Pike called it the most egregious act of bullying he'd seen in twenty years in education."

Guess who, Roland asked, D-Rex ran into on the lower level? It was Neil coming out of golf practice. Despite being warned not to say anything to him until the school's inquiry was done, D-Rex stayed true to himself. He demanded Neil immediately go tell Mr. Pike that whatever he'd said to him about Soap Gate was wrong, and that he actually hadn't seen him or Mack do anything unsafe. Neil's reply, evidently, wasn't what D-Rex wanted to hear, and he hiked the pressure to intimidate him.

How? He pried open the drainage grate in front of the lower lockers and stuffed Neil inside. Yeah, inside. After dropping the grille back over him, he unwrapped the cold burrito he hadn't eaten while in Mr. Pike's custody, and as his hostage moaned and begged from below, D-Rex gave him something else. He unzipped his pants, grunted, and told Neil that what was splattering the top of his hair was the runny diarrhea he'd deserved as a narc.

"That's the God honest truth," Roland said.

It was a janitor who heard wailing fifteen minutes later and dragged him out of the hole, Neil able to stammer out what'd happened before he shook so hard he turned noncommunicative. "Mr. Pike said any longer down there, Neil might've needed to go to a mental institution. He asked Mr. Drexx, 'So, think Lance is innocent now?' But I could've stopped the whole thing. *Me*. If I wasn't talking Dungeons & Dragons while Mrs. John was out, I could have kept them from tampering with her thermos. I abandoned my post. What would my father say?"

"That it wasn't anyone's fault but those assholes," Kyle said.

The same stupefying, tongue-tying blanket of silence cast over us in the seconds after Neil's actions yesterday crested again. The silence didn't last, broken by an unexpected messenger.

We heard the normally imperturbable Quentin before we saw him—the wheezing, the bowlegged footfalls. At the bench with us, panting in tight gym shorts, he managed a smile you'd get if an ice cream truck pulled up with free, summer Fudgsicles. "A special someone is cleaning out his locker in the Pit," he said raggedly. "Want to come see?"

The pack of us trotted out of the windowless gym, across trampled grass browning in the spring heat. At the outdoor locker bank beneath the deck, D-Rex was looking Lance-like, glasses on and glum. There'd been no agreement among us to surround him in The Pit. We just did it as any respectable, revenge-psyched victims would.

At D-Rex's uncommonly large feet was his unzipped gym bag, which he'd crammed with a decorated letterman's jacket, ankle weights, baseball cleats, and pitcher's mitt. Squished in there, on top and out of place, was a crimson Harvard University sweatshirt.

Quentin, the nicest, pear-shaped asthmatic you'd ever meet, claimed that in the fall, someone had filched his. "I'll take that," he said now, yanking it by the sleeve out of bag. "That was a gift from my grandad."

Ordinarily, D-Rex would've snatched it back and dead-armed him. But today wasn't ordinary. "I found it on the ground."

"You're a real…" Quentin, who never swore, did his best potty-mouth. "A real turd-bird."

And this turd-bird couldn't fly the coup fast enough.

D-Rex removed his black glasses to get his villainy back. It was me, Carl, Kyle, Denny, Quentin, a red-rimmed Roland, plus latecomers Rupert and a few others. We had him cornered in a turnabout-is-fair-play spot. Jacque Bliese, a gangly boy just growing out of a lisp that D-Rex never let him forget, high-fived Quentin for his "turd-bird" comment; I'd never seen Quentin lift his arms that high, even during a PE free throw.

"We all know what you did to Neil," Roland said, sniffling. "You tried to dump lye into Mrs. John's coffee, and when you couldn't, you spit in it. Then you stuffed Neil in a grate, fake-shitting on him with a burrito. Maybe you need to be put into your place."

This was all the news that Mr. Pike, in answering to lawyers and fairness, hadn't deemed fit print (or pass on).

"*He what?*" Rupert asked. "He did that?"

"Yep," Roland said. "And Lance, you are aware there's no cure for stupid."

"Say it again. Dare you," D-Rex said, clenching his right fist.

"S-T-U-P-I-D.," Roland replied. "Sounding it out with phonics might help."

"Ouch," somebody behind me said. "Burn."

D-Rex three-sixty-ied on his heels, searching for an ally. Four of us were his JV football teammates, *were* being the operative word.

"Hart-man," he said toadying to Kyle, using Kyle's pet last name, Hartsung becoming that. "You going to let these wusses talk shit to me like that?"

"No, I'm not," Kyle said. "I'm hoping they'll punk you worse."

"Why don't," Carl added, "you take a flying powder? You can spell powder, right?"

People were done being his prey. Quentin (bent glasses, stomped-on new shoes, stolen sweatshirt); Jacque (mockery, crumpled sandwich, four Nadia Coma-Flipsky's); Roland (pencil-stabbed, kiped homework, gay rumors); Ralph (called "Jew boy," told beloved horse was dead, elbowed in face in "light" basketball practice; Neil (all inclusive); me.

"Seriously," Carl said, Happy Face T-shirt juxtaposed with the tucked chin of a bull about to charge, "how do you sleep at night?"

"Sleep? Huh?" he said. "I sleep fine."

"You hear that, everyone?" I chimed in. "*It* doesn't even know what a sick puppy *it* is." D-Rex stomped up to me, inside the circle pressing in. "Better be careful," I said. "Neil might want revenge on you someday."

"Shut your piehole, Luke."

"Mrs. John could've died. And why, just to get out of a test?"

"You know what, ranger? I call bullshit on your mom dying in some car accident. She probably killed herself... So she didn't have to raise *you*."

He slammed his locker closed, picked up his bag, and tried cutting through us. *Killed herself. Didn't have to raise you.*

Inside, my blood roared plasma-hot, and my left arm drew back to do what it should've long ago. If I couldn't sock him right in his lazy eye, which caused all of us pain from the pain it blackened through him, I'd roundhouse him in the back of his skull.

It sounded like reasonable violence, and still my punch didn't land as designed, for I hadn't accounted for Carl shoving him from behind in my defense. Instead of the back of his head, my fist grazed him at the junction of neck and spine. D-Rex stumbled forward, but he regained his balance with that athletic footwork of his. His safety was something else.

"*Fuck you!*" I said, so dizzy with rage I didn't know whether to lunge at his throat or run screaming into La Cañada's hills. He'd made the dead speak, stooping like that.

He tried walking away from his hectoring mob, but we followed him toward the parking lot, trolling him ten feet back. Once-stifled names flew. "*Cyclops.*" "*Dickwad.*" "*Knuckle-dragger.*" "*Thugopoles.*"

Denny, fittingly, reached inside his JanSport for our coup de grace: an uneaten, dodgy-looking egg-salad sandwich. He underhanded it to Roland, who jogged up and smooshed it on the side of D-Rex's face, a la shaving-cream pie. The recipient spun for retaliation, until he saw us foaming at the mouth, picking up his pace.

We continued hissing and jeering his every other step, though our ridiculing voices canceled each other out, which didn't seem right, and I was thankful for sudden inspiration. When our varsity basketball team had its game in hand, the bleachers chanted a pointed farewell. I tweaked it for this occasion, and it became a chorus of brotherhood.

"*Na-Na-Na, Na-Na-Na. Bye, bye Mr. Lye.*"

I never loved Stone Canyon more.

CHAPTER NINE
THE NOTABLE IN-BETWEEN

Sophomore year, they loosened the shackles, wallets becoming passports once a magical driver's license snugged inside of it. And, provided we didn't smash up the family's cars, neither of which my two fender-benders qualified, and made curfew that magic was everything we'd hoped. Going to the midnight showing of *The Rocky Horror Picture Show* at South Pasadena's historic Rialto theater, packing rice to toss at the wedding scene, knowing when to yell, *"Don't mess with the monster"* was watershed entertainment. When you're watching a BDSM, transvestite vampire onscreen at 2:00 a.m., adulthood couldn't be all that far off, right?

Our mischief evolved in kind now that the class troglodytes were gone. So, when the occasional packaged rubber or unlit cigarette slid under somebody's desk during a tedious lecture, it wasn't only for amusement. It reflected a collective headspace, a group prerogative that tobacco and sex were no longer aspirational. Besides, the school trusted us more, and we had to trust it, since our futures rested in its picky hands.

That's what brought Rupert and I one rainy Saturday to Stone Canyon's creepy biology lab, tasked with identifying gender by eye-color of a hundred common fruit flies (ol' *Drosophila melanogaster*). Every sophomore had a weekend assignment like us. We followed everything to a T, chloroforming the tiny insects, determining their sexes under a microscope in painstaking monotony, tallying the stats on graph paper.

In that smelly room by ourselves, tracked by live mice in cages, frogs in tanks, and a famously aborted kitten in orange-y formaldehyde, the freedom now afforded us was too enticing to lock up when done, good boys we were (generally). Hence, Rupert only deposited ninety sleepy-headed flies back in their aerated bottle, purposely leaving ten out in his caper to see what'd happen.

Everybody visiting the bio room for the next month couldn't help but know, because the liberated *Drosophila* mated faster than the instigator calculated, and a thousand-strong swarm of baby insects dive-bombed heads and ears in Rupert's boomeranging joke.

Rather than pest husbandry, I'd scrawled my contribution, with my opposite hand, on the blackboard behind the projector screen, where we'd been shown slides on gene-propagation. The Darwin-ian limerick: some of my finest work.

"Natural Selection Gave Me An Erection."

Questioned by our benevolent, sixty-something bio teacher about this, Ottawa-born Mr. Newell, Rupert and I blamed sassy freshmen. "Sure they did it," he said drolly, wiping crud from his glasses with the back of his tie.

Junior year, sanctified as upperclassmen, Stone Canyon gave us more wiggle room (electives, off-campus privileges) while cranking the pressure (practice SATs, extra-scrutinized GPAs, red-eye workloads). At lunches that spring, we posed the grandest question of them all: What would *our* legacy be? The class ahead of us would be setting the gold standard here with double-whammy-ing Senior Pranks. It'd planned a silent, photographed re-enactment of the iconic, Iwo-Jima-flag image when Mr. Burr left to tap out his pipe, and the hiring of a Mr. Pike doppelganger during Final's Week to make the student body wonder if he'd been cloned.

On the girl front, the goalposts moved as well. Slow dances and doorstep necking no longer constituted "getting some." We reserved that for secluded bluffs and closed-curtain rooms in which things got unbuttoned and, if fortunate, unzipped. Weekend parties were no different. The pot smoke grew more copious, the pony kegs more prevalent, the stereo louder, unless neighbors phoned Omar. Certainly, nothing said freewheeling like an all-nighter camped out on the Rose Parade route on Pasadena's Orange Grove Boulevard, along with thousands of other youngsters itching to party, flirt, and catapult marshmallows, pushing the envelope up to misdemeanors' edge. Not that any of us stayed for the floats to roll, bagging out grungy and tired around 5:00 a.m.

That summer, between part-time jobs and family commitments, was a concert lollapalooza, one ear-ringer after another at the Fabulous Forum, Greek Theater, or Universal Amphitheater, no grown-ups frisking us before we left. Up on these stages sashayed Van Halen, locals who'd performed at backyard parties and neighborhood gigs on their elevator to superstardom, giving us the right to insider-winks. There was Bad Company, Cheap Trick, Foghat, the Clash, with a side of Tom Petty and Oingo Bongo. When I had car keys and that Ticketmaster paper, anything seemed possible, a wooly rush I felt in my veins. I was soon taking guitar lessons at Hasting Ranch's Dr. Music, where Eddie Van Halen himself, long, black hair past his hips, would park his jeep sideways on the sidewalk to pick up his strings and pedals, always swiping at his nose.

It took a night swim with my pals to remind me of a disconcerting reality. My independence was still not all of my own making.

Between Denny's purple-haired homegrown and the fifth of Bacardi that Carl picked up at the Altadena mini-mart that'd probably sell hooch to a toddler with a fake ID, it was chlorine-soaked revelry with no one saying "don't." Raft wars, diving-board cannonball contests, vertebrae-risking Frisbee catches off the slide: you were only this age and reckless once.

Then the slap of the screen door announced killjoy was here. Home unexpectedly early from another first date where there wouldn't be a second, the father who'd usually snoop on us from the living room window descended the steps, sure we were up to no good. He sniffed one of the mugs we'd unwisely left out, smelling more rum than Coke, and on the warpath he went.

"I'm not happy about this, Luke," my master sergeant gruffed. "Where's the bottle?"

I hid my shame by feigning offense, saying *I* didn't have it. Which I didn't, because RG did—inside the mesh of his Hawaiian swim trunks. He'd been the first to detect my dad's presence, stuffing the half-empty bottle we'd been passing around down by his willie, and breast-stroked into the deep-end to disappear. When he panicked that wouldn't work, he hid the Bacardi in the skimmer, and only my dad's search for it under the pool furniture prevented him from noticing that the bottle had floated into the *middle* of the pool, out in the open, before Johnny-on-the-Spot Carl chucked it down the embankment.

After I told my friends they better split, my dad and I got into yelling match pitting my "reprehensible judgment" against his imperial parenting, and I began counting the days until I could leave home. I also decided against showing him the leeway the school granted Carl and me months earlier because some Caltech math geniuses don't speak tongue in cheek.

—

Yearbook 1979—Random Notes by Juniors Luke Burnett & Carl Dieter

Quote of the year: "I've been reading so much about the dangers of gambling, booze, drugs, and loose sex that I'm taking a moral stand against reading" —*Unknown*.

Best Male Rock Performance: William Shatner Sings "Rocket Man."

Dogs' Choice Award for Worst Female Performance: Yoko Ono screams the Sex Pistols' "God Save the Queen." Luke's beagle, Bilbo, purchases earplugs.

Jimmy Carter's Favorite Animal: Georgian Swamp Rabbit.

Best Highbrow TV Program: Tie. *The White Shadow* and *BJ and the Bear*.

Favorite TV Show Too Popular on Campus: *Saturday Night Live*. You can hear grating impressions of "*chezburgher, chezburgher*" and "Jane, you ignorant slut!" only so many times before Lorne Michaels becomes public enemy.

Proposed New Yearbook Categories for the 1980s: Most Likely to Be a Cult Leader Addicted to Tab; Most Likely to Sell Timeshares to Mobsters in Witness Protection; Most Likely to Require Surgery for Deflated Expectations; Most Likely to Encounter Serial Killer Who Doesn't Drive Van; Most Likely to Need Rehab for Atari-Brain Syndrome; Most Likely to Be Running Mate to Future US President Wally George.

Prediction for Coming School Year: Whether you consider the "change" a welcome, alien invasion or a disastrous break from tradition, Mr. Pike's credo for the expected bathroom shortage boils down to this: *You're just going to have to hold it.*

PART II

CHAPTER TEN
PILGRIM CINDY

A glowing Harvey Burr, in brown platform shoes and bold, eggnog suit he could've stolen from Colonel Sanders' closet, stood by his classroom door, clasping palms in a meet-and-greet ritualizing us as campus Gods of the Stone Canyon pantheon.

"Never doubted you'd make it, Burnett," he said, leaning in with shiny dentures and owlish eyebrows. "It wasn't like you'd had to decide between here and Honors Calculus. I read your transcript, Archimedes."

That gibe warranted a comeback. "I tanked my math placement to take your class."

His tongue lolled around a mouth gifted at getting in the last word. "Yeah, yeah. Never forget who's the lead jester. Take your seat, Shecky."

A Mork-ish *"Nanu, Nanu"* would've slashed him, but I knew in a battle of wits with someone of his rank, it'd be the flippant who died young, so I sheathed my sword.

On the day I'd been dreaming of, it was the little things—the rich, loamy scent of his recently-snuffed pipe, how his bifocals lent him a Peter Sellers flair, the way our grown bodies dominated desks that used to swallow us—that never felt so big. Senior status also meant never being sorry for sloppy chic, in my case a Kinks *Misfits* T-shirt, black Vans, and Levi's whose back-pocket artwork was an inky, Rorschach stain from a leaky pen. I could almost hear my clotheshorse mom sermonize from the afterlife: "Luke, are you trying to look slovenly on purpose? Impressions, impressions. You don't have to pick the first thing in your drawer."

Neither the stab of her absence, nor the fat wad of Juicy Fruit I'd need to ditch could dampen the zeal of this certified, high school senior. We'd been recognized at the opening assembly as "the first graduating class of a dynamic new era," and ambled to our first class beaming at our now-exclusive lawn. After Mr. Burr's glorious putdown, I floated toward an open seat, eyeballing tacked-up posters of his ever-shifting cast of history's most illustrious minds.

All in all, a time warp to our freshman days, when I knew less than nothing. And today, in September 1979? I'd made it to Honors History for "The Turbulent Twentieth Century."

One by one, the admittees got the Mr.-Burr-treatment conferring them as pyramid toppers.

"So, your big brother's now a Yalie," he said deadpan to Carl. "Big potential that kid, if a terrible dresser. My question for you, Dieter: What are *you* going to do to make me forget his takedown of William H. Buckley? You've got some big, ugly shoes to fill."

Carl walked to a desk by me not insulted but crowned, doing a chicken-neck-thrust and dishing out low-fives. He was dressed for the occasion in an olive Che Guevara T and matching beanie.

Kyle came in next in a jean shirt and blue Adidas, his skin coppery, an under-eye nicked by a surfboard tip in a Zuma Beach wipeout. "What's crackin'?" he said. "Stoked as me for this year?"

You bet we were, except perhaps for Rupert, reacquainting himself after being away for a year. He'd dared to out-dress us today in a crisp, button-down shirt and pressed pants, though he partially redeemed himself going with sockless Topsiders. Sartorial joshing aside, we all felt bad for him, knowing his near-broke parents had relocated to Bismarck, North Dakota so his engineer dad could dig them out of debt helping the Pentagon dismantle some old, mustard-gas arsenal there. Taking the new Rupert in—rustler's mustache, wide-set eyes, tousled hair—he could've been twenty-five, and plowing fields way out of our reach if he tried. In his last letter to me announcing his family was returning to Pasadena, after JPL hired his dad, he described Bismack as a "barren refrigerator" where the only temporary pleasures were no-sweat academics and beer-fueled cow-tipping. He'd hated it.

I rose to hug him in time to hear Mr. Burr torture Quentin. "Back under my thumb for a final time, my pretty?"

"I wouldn't want it any other way," said the stubble-less boy still hooked on those khakis.

The last member of the posse to arrive was the last one you'd expect to enter at all. I was stunned Mr. Burr accepted Denny, him being the lazy, sometimes-slumbering, B-student dependent on me to outline his history papers and quiz him before tests. Was it because the faculty believed he was the most brilliant kid in school, as his near-perfect math score on last year's practice SAT hinted? For me, just another Denny mystery to crack, even as his step-by-step tutoring had kept me out of C-minus land in chemistry and pre-calculus.

But there was something wrong, a listlessness about him winding back to summer, and he stayed clammed up about it. This last Fourth of July, he was supposed to have caravanned with us to see the band we mocked, KISS, at Magic Mountain for the campy, patriotic-day spectacle. When he phoned me the night before to flake out, he blamed it on an achy wisdom tooth. I didn't buy it then, nor did I buy his other flimsy excuses for dodging us the rest of the summer—the summer our drivers' licenses afforded us luminescent possibilities, him retreating into his "trouble at home" wormhole.

"In the flesh," I said, as he passed by me. "We're kings this year."

"Yay," he said without any spark. "Waving from the balconies."

I went over to him, because this wasn't the entertaining imp I knew. "What's going on? You've been like a hermit. Are you pissed off about something?"

Hard stare, minor shake of the head. "Let's not get into it here. Or ever."

"Jesus, whatever."

He flicked my shoulder when I turned back to my desk. "Sorry, Lukey," he said above a whisper. "My dad, he's a mess. As if the family wasn't already screwed up enough."

"Geez, dude. What can I…"

"Nothing."

He trickled over to his usual corner spot, and I thought about what could've become of his laidback father, who I'd met maybe a half-dozen times. His mom: she was trickier to decipher, cold smiling and superficial, making us sandwiches once while dabbing lipstick and repeating what "a perfect day" it was. A gray-aired, ninety-two is "perfect?"

At our annual welcome-back barbecue, on the Saturday before classes began, fathers worked the grills and doled out the grub while mothers could relax. Every one of my friends' parents were there except the Drummonds, who'd attended past barbecues. Thinking about that, something clobbered me that explained a lot around here: Prep schools designed to launch kids into elite colleges had a darker tinge, a-setup-for-failure tinge. In a sense, places like ours was where the "Great Men" of Los Angeles enrolled their sons, both to sharpen their brains and also as an acid test determining whether they had what it took to escape their long shadows. Their legacy, our burden: that's the game within the game, even possibly for 160-IQ Denny.

Exaggeration? Flipping burgers and hot dogs or shucking corn like average schmoes were the men who paid Mr. Pike's tuition fees. There was a Nobel Prize winner and a runner-up, a National Medal of Science awardee and JPL's flight director, an Oscar-awarded cinematographer, a doctor who'd operated on foreign dignitaries, even ex-military like Roland's dad (now a Northrop bigwig). That went right on down the line to the salad and dessert stations.

High-priced defense attorney Allen Hosarian, who'd sent two other sons here after Arnie, was always in the *LA Times*, saying noble things about the questionable politicians he represented, and today, he was crisping the buns. At his elbow were some of the scions to Pasadena's Old Guard (families of the Budweiser, Wrigley, and Proctor & Gamble corporations), as well as the chief executive of the Western US's largest sheet-metal company and a former-California treasurer.

Spatula in hand, my own dad, whose chief kitchen skill was spreading crumbs everyplace, was in hog heaven, surrounded by the type of world-class brains he wished I'd inherited. Later, eating across from each other on a rented table set up on the field, he was elated. I asked why, and he said that he'd stymied that Nobel winner with a physics question.

—

The first bell of my farewell year, on what otherwise would've been our collective victory lap, was eclipsed by history. And not one-dimensional history commemorating dead people—history celebrating a ceiling-crasher with blue eyeshade by the name of Cindy Lummis.

She was the granddaughter of LA's proverbial jack of all trades, a man of slashes: reporter/editor/publisher/builder/curator/weirdo/party-thrower/ explorer/Indian-rights defender Charles Fletcher Lummis. The Craftsman palace it took her Great-Man grandad thirteen years to cobble from stones in the early nineteenth century was now a museum. Even if she felt little pressure to outrun his considerable shadow, there was other weight on Cindy's slim shoulders. She was poised, assuming she maintained the grades, to go down in the annals as the *first* female ever to graduate from the previously named Stone Canyon Preparatory School for Boys.

You heard that right. Mr. Pike had taken us coed my senior year, making her the only girl in a class of thirty-eight.

I'd nearly plunged through the Earth's crust when D-Rex sauntered through Mrs. John's door years back. Observing Mr. Burr speak to Cindy, as the last person inside today, I recognized that terror. She was a deer in the headlights—a deer in neat skirt and blonde, Dorothy-Hamill doo—standing by a diminutive teacher reassuring her she'd be all right. Once the bell rang, he kneaded her shoulder, shepherding her towards us in a *you-got-this* fashion. Her skittish walk to a desk, smile tight, said the opposite.

Most of us had introduced ourselves to her at the welcome barbecue, but that was no road test for school. Nobody had any hard facts why she'd submitted to being the guinea pig, even if she'd been joined by twenty-six other girls scattered through the junior, sophomore, and freshman classes below. Still, she was alone with us, expected to be *their* leader, their Billie Jean King, when she was as much an outsider as them walking the hall or using a ladies' room jackhammered from the men's john.

Mr. Pike had declared his coed revolution in a batch letter to every student's family between our sophomore and junior years. My dad let me read it, and a minute later, I was on revolving phone calls with the posse, hot with excitement, not doubt. This was "a long-overdue time to swap hallowed tradition for equality of the sexes," he'd written, before turning to the nitty-gritty reason. "Stone Canyon also had little choice but abandon a unisex student body. Since the early-seventies and the court order desegregating Pasadena-area schools, fierce competition among local prep schools for capable boys had dwindled the ranks of potential candidates. Given grim financial projections, it was either embracing a coed culture, as similar institutions have, or contemplating possible bankruptcy as soon as 1983."

Record skip there. School extinction could've hit before our five-year reunion?

Cindy sat two desks from me in my sweet-spot second row. Try as we did to act nonchalant, to avoid outright gawping at her, everybody stole glances. Everybody sniffed her fruity Ralph Lauren's perfume, or whatever she'd spritzed herself in.

"You think Mr. Burr dressed in all white as a message for us to clean up our act?" I asked Carl. "No ape behavior around the girls?"

"That," he replied, "or he's dying to sell us a bucket of fried chicken."

Mr. Burr dropped one of his cherished books, JFK's *Profiles in Courage*, on his desk, his method of gaveling us to order. Ben, his disciplinary golf putter, tilted in the corner, reserved for younger classes.

"You did it," he began. "You survived the gauntlet not everyone can." He twirled his pipe, walking center stage of his poster-plastered theater of history. "This is my third year teaching this class, and you should regard it as both reward and opportunity. If I were you, and you're worried about GPAs, I'd dwell on that second part. Before I cover the obligatory housekeeping, let's give a warm hand to our newest pupil, Cindy Lummis."

We clapped, following Mr. Burr's lead. "Would anybody care to say anything making her feel at home, in what must seem like Mars to her?"

Kyle opened his mouth to say something. Neil, who'd grown a whole inch and spoke less like Mini Mouse, seized the initiative. "On behalf of the Class of 1980," he said from his wall-side desk, "we welcome you with open arms. Neil Katz: at your service, my lady. Our castle is, you know…su casa."

A sea of eyeballs from summer-sunned faces, mine included, rotated upward toward the rebuilt ceiling bankrolled by the female surge in enrollment. If you were trying to make someone visibly awkward in the spotlight dash for the exit, listening to a new classmate talk like a smarmy Renaissance Faire guide was the ticket. And her guide wasn't done.

"Think of us as your knights, here to serve with a cape over any muddy puddle."

"On behalf?" "At your service." Oh, brother. Two years since D-Rex's expulsion, after he'd been prescribed Valium for a month, amassed goodwill afterwards, and received the kit-glove treatment from there, Neil had newfound confidence, yet, as he reminded us, the same foot-in-mouth disease. He'd brought English

class to a standstill once because he "didn't get why Shakespeare put witches in Macbeth." He forced Mr. Newell in bio class to explain what he meant when he said, "waking up with sticky pajamas is your reproductive systems activating," a quip even our foreign-exchange student understood.

"My lady didn't happen to bring a gag with her, did thy?" Kyle said in a sardonic, Old English style. "I'll search my satchel for five pence to pay for one."

His zinger at Neil's corny chivalry was the icebreaker that elicited laughs from everyone, and Mr. Burr piggybacked on it, passing around his syllabus before his lecture.

The rest of the morning, us veterans walked about with lively steps and minorly, discombobulated brains. It was one thing having bouncy cheerleaders culled from neighboring, all-girl schools present on game days, another to digest the massive influx of females strolling "our" corridors in packs. All those blouses and sleeveless numbers, the hip-hugging denim and girls' corduroys, more footwear (mini-boots, tennis shoes, clogs, espadrilles) and hairstyles than a teen fashion show. It was an invasion by another name.

At lunchtime in the upperclassmen parking lot, which Mr. Pike admonished us he'd personally police this year, we tried stabilizing ourselves.

"Whatever happens, don't let them divide us," I said. "Right, Denny?"

He laid on the hood of "his car," his brother's hand-me-down Capri, puffing a cigarette. "Sure, yeah," he said, still indifferent.

"Don't forget the jacuzzi party at my place this summer," Carl said, bolstering my *all-for-one* plea. "I don't think you made it, Denny. We'd agreed bros over hos."

"I wouldn't advertise it with that language," Kyle said. "But yeah, pretty much."

By that first afternoon, however, Mr. Pike's revolution was pretty much weakening resolve. When a clutch of junior girls flashed smiles at four of us reclined on the Senior Lawn during a free period, we smiled back unrestrained. We entered classrooms pantomiming wolves encountering scents more department-store cosmetics counter than last year's mimeograph central. Down by the woodshop, a pair of sophomores necked in what must've been lingering hormones from summer. I watched a freshman boy hold a mislaid scrunchie as if it were an archaeological relic.

Being a fly-on-the-wall, infiltrated by a species that we all knew inside was more mature than us, I should've jotted down what I overheard in the hallways.

"It's hysterical watching the boys fight over who gets to open doors for us. They must think we're amputees. Or, super easy."

"Of course, we shave our legs, dummy. You ever heard of Nair?"

"The seniors wouldn't throw a girl in the pool if she stepped on their lawn, would they? I don't want to toss out my tank tops."

"You guys are doing exactly what under the bridge? Is that even safe?"

"Tell me the three-hours-of-homework-a-night thing is just a scare tactic?"

"Mr. Pike smokes more than my mother when my dad's at a Las Vegas convention."

"Does your side of the locker room always stink like there's something decomposing in it?"

I phoned Denny that night from my own new line, outwardly to get his impressions of this momentous day, more specifically to learn about a home scene bringing him down. He was in no better mood, and no more forthcoming. "Look, my mom and dad are at each other's jugulars, and you wouldn't believe why, so don't grill me. And I know you're only trying to help."

"OK, OK," I said, probably too sharply. "See you tomorrow."

—

By Friday of that first week, the wobble in Stone Canyon's magnetic field was undeniable. Before the first bell—where you'd usually hear groups converging like gabby cicadas, or the squeal of the morning's first titty-twister, or the howl of a forgetful kid reminded it was exam day—the decibel meter dropped to normal conversational levels. Even slobs turned vanity-conscious, and at the snaking lines into the cramped bathrooms, boys with full bladders swayed, waiting for their turn at urinals reduced from eight to five, while the girls marveled at the new world into which they'd parachuted, and whether any of us had seen a Tampax machine before.

Taken together, it was anyone's guess whether the renegade personality that'd given Stone Canyon's its public imprimatur and private soul had much of a future; Neil's "my lady" hokum, while code to get into Cindy's pants, hinted the clumsy here soon would be joining other misfits who groveled for prom dates (and beat their meats with resentful grips). In the era Before Girls (BG), it was a testosterone realm powered by seniority and competition, friendships and machismo by the barrel. Often, it was camaraderie-by-necessity, too, cool kids and dorks alike gutting out the same tests, or reeling in a free-for-all climate in which the vicious could go unpunished teasing a kid with a deformed hand as "The Crab" or an effeminate boy as a "maximum faggot." Where getting away with a prank or outrage was just another Thursday. Yeah, go ahead and line up the firing squad. We were creatures of our environment, Kubrick's late-seventies apes, stomping about with *attaboy* pre-SAT scores on less hairy feet.

Now, in a reshuffled student body of the With Girls (WG) period—estrogen no longer confined to bio-class lectures, its force sure to eye our throne—the question wasn't just whether the lesser angels among us boys would be tamed in the short term. It was how long, as Mr. Burr's rhapsodized last year, Stone Canyon's "feisty esprit de corps," the bubbly rebelliousness that distinguished us from Poly and the other white-shoe, prep-schools would persevere?

I'd give it five years, *Gloria Steinem.*

Food-wise, the WG infiltration coincided with our maiden week of full, off-campus privileges, and we ate like the XY-chromosome pigs we were. On Monday, it was Hutch's, a BBQ joint with sawdust floors near the Pasadena Police headquarters. Tuesday, it was Georgee's Pizza, a thankful addition to La Cañada's food desert. Wednesday was Mickey-D's, because of tight class schedules, and Thursday was Burger Continental, which mainly served, go figure, Greek food. Neither Carl nor I liked it, but post-North Dakota Rupert did. By Friday, all of us had blown through our walking-around money, and we brown-bagged it like lowly underclassmen.

Walking out to my car that day, I was one gung-ho seventeen-year-old, upbeat about my prospects for the year ahead, if ambivalent about what Mr. Pike had unleashed. Readying to cross the street into the upper parking lot emptying out for the weekend, I heard our newest voice.

"It's Luke, isn't it?"

The school's most watched individual was by herself. While everyone had darted up to Cindy to stick out their hands, I'd kept a distance, zigging while others zagged, confident around the fairer sex (while always thinking about it).

Jenny McInerny, my post-Kimmy girlfriend, was a Sacred Heart Academy senior who lived with her divorced mother in a stuccofied condo in Sunland northwest of us. I'd met her last spring when Rupert and I, Ray-Ban's on, KROQ blasting, cruised up the hill to her all-girl campus to scope out the action. The headmistress nun, none too pleased with Stone Canyon boys on the make, charged at us by the carpool line with an impressive, cat-quick, first step. We peeled rubber, returning the next week, and that's when I met Jenny. She pinched my arm in the car window and said I was cute, and I asked the junior with carob-hair, green plaid-skirt, and dangerous smile if I could drive her home? This wasn't puppy-love. This was steamy petting on a ratty couch while her mother was gone and Supertramp's *Breakfast in America*, her sonic aphrodisiac, played on the stereo.

Back to Cindy: "Tell me: on a scale of one to ten, how would you rate your first week in the madhouse?" We scanned both ways in the crosswalk, rushing to avoid a jack-rabbiting sophomore who must've recently gotten his license.

"Maybe eleven and a half," she said, blowing cornflower bangs from her eyes. "Don't get me wrong."

"Wrong? About what?"

"Everybody's so nice. It's just nobody here knows the first thing about me. I mean, what if I were some girl Jack the Ripper?"

In the upper lot seniors considered their asphalt clubhouse, fabled in school lore for honor-code-smashing behavior, the girl unaware of its reputation dropped her head. This, I'd noticed from afar, was how Cindy reacted to the crush of attention orbiting her. Every time she tried catching her breath, there was someone else glad-handing her—a starry-eyed freshman, a teacher who'd "yet to have the pleasure."

"Then I'd want to stay on your good side," I said. First time I'd heard her laugh, or seen an unguarded smile. "I've been thinking how strange it must be being you this week."

"Strange. Suffocating. Overwhelming. Strictly between us, k?"

"K."

"Where's your car?"

"Over there," I said, "the whale with the Kinks bumper sticker on it." I pointed at a hideous Pontiac Grand Safari station wagon with faux-wood sidings and countless dings. My dad bought it from an employee, believing he needed to protect his ever-distracted son in a steel-wrapped sedan as big as a troop carrier. "I'm saving up for a Celica, four gear. What about you?"

"There," she said, going over to a yellow VW bug with a flower decal on its bumper. It stood out from the Trans-Ams, Camaros, aging Land Cruisers, beaters, and squat, economy cars monopolizing the blacktop. No Porsches or Mercedes-Benzes here. Stone Canyon wasn't that "other school"; it was more middle-class than our "rich-kids" rep.

"So," she asked, making conversation, "what's the story on the music around here? Punk rock seems like the favorite. I'd never heard of Black Flag until this week. I thought it was an insecticide."

"You're funny. I lean more mainstream myself. It puts me in the minority with the music Gestapo. You?"

"Fleetwood Mac. It used to be Heart, but Stevie Nicks and her shawls. They speak to me."

"Whatever you do, never admit you like anything Top Forty, unless you want your house tee-peed. Kidding. What else you into?"

"*Hmmm*, let me think. No one's asked that. I do love Katharine Hepburn movies. In another life, I want to be her. Her own woman, you know? Anything but plain Jane like me."

I waited until she stopped re-inspecting her shoes. "I beg to differ. Look where you are."

"You're sweet. Honestly, though, I don't know why I agreed to this, other than shooting for an Ivy and getting tired of LaSalle. I'm wondering if it was a mistake. If another boy insists on carrying my books, I might scream. I better go. Thanks for listening."

She threw her bookbag with attached rabbit's foot onto the passenger seat. Rolling by, she stopped, bunch-faced, swatting tears smudging her mascara. "Just what I promised I wouldn't do," she said out the window. "Long week. You take care, Luke."

"You, too," I said. *Weak.*

As her muffler-rattling VW eased over the hated speed bump, which Mr. Pike had installed two years ago after repeated complaints about careless driving from school neighbors, including a Catholic church, I flashed a peace sign.

Cindy made a left out of the lot, a right onto Foothill, and another quick left on the freeway. Seconds later, you could hear her Bug grinding gears to climb the steep on-ramp as if were Hemingway's Mount Kilimanjaro.

CHAPTER ELEVEN
PUKE SKYWALKER

Cindy's confession became an immediate test of the Luke Emergency Broadcasting System. I'd pledged to keep quiet about her second-guessing transferring here, and I wasn't about to stab her in the back. Still, *hello*, this was a king-size scoop that I needed to tell someone without, I guess, elaborating on it. Torn over how, I trotted back onto campus to take a much-delayed whiz before driving home, feeling, to quote urological specialists Cheech & Chong, my "back teeth floating."

And who should I see in the boy's room, dressed in his lineman's football jersey, primping in front of the mirror? It was Carl, my confidant, and someone I owed twenty bucks to after he'd spotted me for a Velcro wallet at Sports Chalet. I peed, washed up, and handed him a pair of tens. "The wallet, remember?"

"Yeah, thanks," he said, stuffing the bills in his jeans. He resumed sweeping his chestnut hair to the side, going at it hard, his mouth an "O" in concentration for the more handsome him.

All this was novelty, for as long as I'd known Carl, his appearance, whether readying for parties, mixers, or field trips, was as high a priority as his tidiness. Unlike me, he never made his bed, consigned his bedroom floor to clothes hamper, blasé even to our gripes that the open, fish food atop his aquarium left his confines stinking like a pet shop. And today, he'd packed a brush.

"What gives? You already got a date or something?"

"Sorta," he said, still molding his hair just so. "You catch that Lisa Boston-chick? Junior. Brown eyes. Built like a brickhouse. She wants me to tutor her in chemistry later tonight. An upstanding scholar like me couldn't deny her, could he? Those hams."

Bangs fixed, Carl watered down paper towels for a French shower, blotting them under his pits and across an oily forehead.

"Hams? And they say romance is dead. You better keep your windows rolled down if you're going to drive her anyplace," I said, referring to Carl's weather-beaten Dodge Dart. "It's all that junk-food trash you never get rid of."

He turned toward me, and not appreciatively. "Jeepers. What would I do without advice I never asked for? Oh, I forgot: You're God's gift to girls."

"*Yow*—that was bogus. I was only noticing you fixating over your hair like Mitch and his hair blower. Moving on, impressions of Cindy so far?"

"She's cool, a little distant," he said, still tamping. "I'm swimming in the shallow end first."

"I should say."

"You good for the post-game party tomorrow? Should be a big crowd. The 'rents are out of town, so everybody wins, Puke Skywalker." Carl flung his used paper towels into the metal bin and began re-brushing hair that said Brian Wilson of the early Beach Boys.

Puke Skywalker? He just had to keep invoking that, knowing it dug under my skin, whenever he felt jabbed.

"No," I said. "I thought I'd stay home with Bilbo and watch *Barney Miller*. 'Course I'll be there, *Car-earl*. Now, can you please eighty-six the *Puke Skywalker* stuff, once and for all?"

"Wow, touchy, touchy."

Tomorrow at one p.m., our varsity football team would be kicking off the '79 season in a home opener against Chadwick, who we normally stomped. Teen actor Mike Lookinland, the youngest of *The Brady Bunch* boys, was on their roster, and I'd juked him last year for a touchdown. But this year, I wouldn't be suiting up after I quit the team during two-a-day practices a month ago. Playful flak over it had waned, though Carl still reserved some as friend-ammo.

The stars had other plans for me besides football, or so I tried to convince myself with varying success. It began with my dad never forwarding me the team letter from our new coach in July, which recommended we get the jump on conditioning ahead of "the hardest practices" of our lives. I wasn't home to read that, having spent half the summer in the High Sierra toiling as a counselor at Gold Arrow Camp. As I'd appreciate, home two days before practices commenced, managing cabins thick with hyper, homesick third and fourth graders was no way to build stamina, the football kind.

The coaches' blueprint was to toughen us up by running us into the ground. In our second week, that constituted a two-mile, off-campus jog, in full pads, under a roasting sun and filthy skies that lopped the tops off the San Gabriels. At the end of this misery-index run, they forced us to slog up the twenty-degree hill by Saint Francis while they monitored us from the air-conditioned comfort of a Buick, frosty Cokes in hands. They craved our dirty looks, our burning calves in pursuit of a successful year, despite the fact that us mostly-average athletes, RG and Kyle notwithstanding, had no shot at a Division I scholarship. We did at beating Poly, however.

While out of shape, I hung in there, barely. The "gasser" wind sprints, the blocking sleds, the burpees, the repetitive plays: this was last year's varsity two-a-days redux. What wasn't? Four days before "Hell Week" ended, I contracted something, and that something was a case of *what-the-fuck-am-I-doing*?

In the "Oklahoma Drill," two opposing linemen opposite the other ram into each other, trying to knock the other over or out of bounds, in a mano-a-mano, pad-popping battle of wills. Depending on your point of view, it was either pro wrestling in helmets or Billy goats dueling it out for mountaintop supremacy. For me, it smacked of something worse after our classmate Adam Hosarian, Arnie's two-hundred-pound, bowling-ball "little" brother and the team's center, squared off against junior Rodney Phillips, an underweight, six-foot-two defensive end. A crunch and cry later, blood squirted from Rodney's hand. An assistant coach swiftly wrapped a gym towel around Rodney's arm, and he was gone, bustled off in that Buick to Huntington Memorial Hospital with nine-and-a-half fingers. Not making the trip was his severed knuckle, which Rodney had gotten entangled and twisted off in Adam's thrashing facemask.

We stood there afterwards, rattled and grossed out, before they ordered us to be the search-and-rescue for the half-digit souvenir. Nobody wanted to, so it was thank you Barry Tollner, a giraffe-necked classmate, who came across it by an orange cone. When Rodney later showed us the swollen, sub-gangrenous monstrosity that'd been surgically reattached, nobody, let me tell you, was hungry afterwards.

Two practices later, on a cloudless, hundred-degree-day, we were stretching, helmets off, when I sighted a stray tabby across the fence line. We'd noticed the cat around for years, nicknaming it "Mew" for its tendency to rub against your pantleg, begging for scraps. For some reason today, "Mew" had launched itself from a transmission pole by the lime-green power station to a high-voltage cable strung like industrial, black licorice. I was about point it out to Carl when everybody heard a *rrrrrrr-errrr* for the ages. We all watched as the brown-striped kitty stiffened, spasmed, and fell, dead before it bounced off the ground. For minutes afterward, black smoke steamed off Mew's crispy, electrocuted corpse.

Between that image and Rodney's knuckle, plus sneaky dehydration, it was system overload. I ran the opposite way, making it all of twenty yards before dry-heaving on the chalk line, and heard Bronx clapping behind me.

This might not have been my breaking point if our JV coach (and Peloponnesian-War zealot), Jerry Hoover, had been in charge. Shade, Gatorade, a breather: he'd let me recover. Johnny "Bucky" Mullins, Mr. Pike's new, handpicked varsity football-baseball coach, was a more *no-pain-no-gain* disciple. Foul-mouthed, twangy, and mildly sadistic, he demanded results.

"Shake it off, Number Twenty," he hollered, after allotting me time at the water fountain. "Don't even think about wriggling out of the next drill."

Who me? Coach Mullins lined us up to practice punt blocking, where you basically throw yourself at a high-velocity object, hoping to disrupt the kick with an outstretched hand or arm. Few volunteered for it, but at this practice, everyone was enlisted. Why our hesitation? Coach Mullins himself, an ex-All-Conference punter at LSU, was doing the kicking off his size-twelve Nike cleat.

Out of twenty attempts, there'd only been two blocks, and one tip, which he sneered as a "sissy ratio." At my turn, he tooted his whistle, I ran headlong at him, and he went to hammer the ball off his cleat. When I saw I'd come in too hot, that it wouldn't be an arm blocking anything but my fully exposed belly, instinct slowed me down and the consequences were painful: a football blasting off my face-mask with a force that wrenched my neck backwards.

Mullins piercing whistle could've woken up any JPL guard dogs. "You call that effort, you gutless wonder?" he shouted. "Do it again like a kamikaze or get the hell off my field."

His field? Right there, I decided three years of eight-man football were sufficient. I had too many other interests and aimed to play soccer for a fourth year. There also was this little exam on our horizon called the SATs. Our Bayou-Country coach should've read up on them.

"Excuses, excuses," he grumbled later in his office when I told him I was leaving. The thirty-something redneck raked fingers through his minx-like 'stache. "You LA boys are Charmin soft. Come down to Shreveport sometime. Now turn your stuff in."

Nobody outright called me the quitter I was. Kyle, nursing a sore shoulder, said at Georgee's Pizza that I was "a sure bet to make the cheerleading squad. Only yanking your chain, Luke."

Carl, out to score social points, swooped in with a follow-up, and it stung worse than that pigskin off my facemask. "Don't you mean Puke Skywalker?"

His *Star-Wars* humor at my expense busted the guys up in our insult-soaked brotherhood. A day later, his *Puke Skywalker*-dig was scabbing over, though in the back of my mind, I fretted Carl had injected a thimble's worth of poison into the bloodstream of a special friendship.

"You think it'd be premature to ask her to the party?" he now asked about Lisa, straightening his mesh jersey, which players wore the day before games to turbo charge teen spirit.

I missed my jersey but couldn't tell him that, not after Denny, mood suddenly normal again, came into the men's room. He must've been staying late for the Stanley Kubrick Club, while Carl still had a walk-through football practice.

"So, what are we talking about?" he asked.

"*We?* Carl's throwing a postgame shindig at his house. No parental units."

"Ooh, ooh. Am I still invited as the world's shittiest athlete?"

"Shut up," Carl said. "You know you are. So, by the way, is Rupert, and I know who he should bring."

"Cindy," I said, forgetting she might not even be a Stone Canyon student come Monday, now recommitted to keeping that hush-hush. "You catch Rupert's goo-goo eyes for her. He just needs to get over the shyness."

"Girls, girls, girls, you have a one-track mind," Carl said, shooting me a make-up wink. "No, Rupert's got this killer, Hawaiian ganja that comes in a rectangle. There's a pineapple stamped on it."

"You're talking about Compact-O," Denny said. "Better than the stems and seeds that the nimrods buy at Smoke Grove Park. But it can't hold a candle to what I'm growing up on the fire road. Tellin' you, it's Wall-of-China good: one toke and you stand still for a thousand years."

While they chuckled, I gazed into the mirror, wondering who I was. Whether I needed to drive another nail through my hand for leaving my teammates? Before I'd taken Mullins' punt to the chops, I'd concocted this flattering portrait of myself: Luke *the* best writer in class, Luke *the* lady-killer, Luke *the* ping-pong hustler, Luke *the* charmer able to hornswoggle (bonus vocab word) any adult. Was *Puke Skywalker* in there all along?

Carl gave his hair a final sweep and shouldered his backpack. "My place tomorrow night at seven. We got some Chadwick ass to whip first."

Denny's *Blazing Saddles* retort was what I needed. "Give him room, Mongo in hurry."

I left, wondering if all newly minted gods dealt with these mortal complexities.

CHAPTER TWELVE
SATURNALIAN SURPRISE

Though it was still September, the faculty was already previewing how we'd be hearing "Pomp and Circumstance" in June, oblivious to the reality that with girls everywhere, most of us boys were too preoccupied adjusting to Mr. Pike's "Suffragette City" than salivating about something months away. But Cindy was playing a different tune, an ultimatum tune, which I was privy to inside a bizarro trio of people aware how delicate prep's coed revolution remained.

An impeccable source was one of these people, my total *blam, blam*, though everyone called Jacqueline Edna Hollister "Eddy." She was many things—close friend, quirky chick, cancer survivor—just never a liar. So, when she poked her brown, curly-haired head through Mr. Burr's threshold on our second Monday back, I'd been delivered a virtual, big sister and Cindy the sister-in-arms she'd demanded.

They'd met at Girl Scouts when they were eleven, not long before Eddy got sick and dropped out. Now, whacky fate reunited them months after Eddy applied for the slot eventually awarded to Cindy. It wasn't because she was a better student than 4.0-Eddy at Blair High School. It was because her parents had the dough that Eddy's didn't. A father working for Amnesty International and a mother teaching ceramics to the handicapped weren't doing it for the money.

Yet, as Eddy gushed on a call Saturday night, Mr. Pike just offered her admission, tuition-free admission at that. "It happened lickety-split. He called my dad at noon to ask if I was still interested in coming, and I was secretly listening in on the other extension. 'You better *believe* I'm interested,' I broke in. 'I know half the guys, too.' After they hung up, I had my hand on the phone to tell Cindy the good news when the phone rang from her. So weird. She and her parents—boy, did they have your headmaster over a barrel. They said unless he added another girl to the senior class to take the pressure off, she was *outta* there, back to La Salle, and he admitted that'd raise doubts about school management. His, especially."

"That's insane," I told Eddy, appreciating Cindy wasn't being dramatic about being smothered by "nice" male attention, and how I couldn't mention I'd known that beforehand. "The good kind of insane. Welcome, new Mountaineer."

None of us knew much about Cindy before day one. Many of us, conversely, knew gobs about Eddy, none more than me. How Rupert, Carl, and I met her was the stuff of folklore. It was early our sophomore year, before we had our learner's permits, as we closed out our prank phone-call phase. On this Friday night, we'd already dialed a dozen or so victims, most answerers hanging up curtly, the rest cussing us out or deploring our manners. It was only getting to a random number in the 818-area-code where we found a live one.

"Lady, my South American parrot flew into your lemon tree," Rupert said, trying to sound forty. "You mind me coming over with my net and bottle of chloroform to get him?"

Seconds later, an endearing comeback. "No, but you better bring a truck and a bunch of nets," Eddy said, fake serious. "There's a whole flock here squawking up a storm."

We wound up staying on the phone with her from 10:00 p.m. until past 3:00 a.m. She sipped Earl Grey tea to keep her eyes open. Us three alternated talking so the others could crash and rally. Soon, dimple-chinned, Tomboy-ish Eddy became a fixture at our rowdiest parties, but she wasn't an agent of destruction like we could be, more like a den mother with a Pinto. "Don't get wasted and drive," she'd educate us. Or hold grudges over incorrect pizza orders. "And for heaven's sake, don't be stupid." On that one, she was shaming Carl and I after we'd snuck the Dieter's backyard-dwelling goat, Snickers, inside Sports Chalet for a quick loop, and Snickers shit by the Rosignol sunglasses rack.

Eddy was an old soul, protective of us, surprised by nothing. Unbeknownst to many, she was also a year older, and I was one of the precious few to know why. She'd had to repeat sixth grade after being diagnosed with and treated for childhood leukemia. During her third radiation treatment, in the basement of Huntington Hospital, she confided that her psychic powers were awoken, including a past-life memory, a supernatural tale that was totally natural to her.

"Hardly anyone believes me, so I have to pick my spots talking about it," she'd said. "Their problem, not mine."

In order, Eddy had been our prank-call girl, despite Rupert owning no parrot and the Hollister's shady home in west Pasadena's San Rafael area absent any lemon tree. She'd been my rebound girlfriend after Kimmy and I broke up; our one date, to see *Beatlemania* at Hollywood's Pantages Theatre, ended with a comically inept kiss, followed by a unique bond that'd fill the spaces of my in-betweens. She'd be my sounding board for romantic travails, that sturdy shoulder as I warred with a father trying to master-plan my future, and, yes, the eccentric who'd spew random facts about bygone Pasadena when we were alone.

Just as Charlotte played surrogate mom, taking me clothes shopping and to doctor's appointments before I could drive, and Carl's mom hugged me around the holidays, inquiring how I was doing "inside," long after other pals' mothers quit asking, Eddy was my part-time shrink. Stop worrying, she'd say, what other people thought, "and start energizing yourself by 'shining inward.'"

And what a time, as the posse said, for "that cool chick from Blair" to transfer, with next month's make-or-break SAT's hanging over our heads, and later obligations up the wazoo.

"So as heavy is the crown, so busy is the senior," Mr. Burr told our Eddy-added class, distributing a four-page, graduation checklist. "Take it one week at a time."

"Like we have any other choice," I said, sounding put-upon.

You know us teenagers, acting the oppressed when we'd never be freer. Still, we had college-counseling sessions to schedule and clubs to commit to or drop. We had "Freshman Buddies" to fraternize with, another Mr. Pike initiative where seniors mentored individual freshmen, preparing them to be, I reckon, more responsible versions of us. In the spring, when teachers traditionally took their feet off the gas, we'd "have to" lean into coronation, getting class rings sized, portraits snapped, and yearbook-page information submitted. Post-finals, there'd be a college-announcement assembly, Baccalaureate Service Night, oh, and diploma day. Once the awards were given and we said "*cheese,*" in family photos, we'd board a party bus for the "Senior Night," shorn of ties and robes. Last year's seniors didn't crawl into bed until dawn.

June was light years away because October *was* the month, a Pasadena Convention Center annex the place. Those three-hour SAT's would define our long-term futures and short-term geography. It'd inserted the word "Prep" into the Stone Canyon moniker in the fifties. It was why they'd flogged us to aim higher, study longer; why parents sacrificed for us. Those three letters, conquerable to some, a beast to others, could be the most devouring in the alphabet.

I'd scored well on last year's practice SAT except for the more complex math questions. Denny was now tutoring me on that, and I him on essays, reading comprehension, and history. Showing my skeptical dad the results of a recent, practice test in my dog-eared, SAT guide, he said it looked like I was getting it, though I'd have to live with the final result.

I'd live with it, because I was focusing like never before, stiff-arming temptations. I postponed guitar lessons and time with my new girlfriend, Beth Krieger, a together, Marlboro School girl from West LA. I put my side novels aside, and began rubbing, for the first time in years, my polished "worry-stone" if the stillness of my room made me fidget. There was only one after-school luxury I allowed myself, and this week, Denny was his name-o.

—

The first gathering of the "Stone Canyon Saturnalians" convened at my house in east Pasadena's horse country not because it was ideal, but because other sites were blacked out. Carl's usually lenient parents—the dad a marketing guru that candymakers hired to name their chocolate bars, the mom a Century 21 Real Estate agent—said the parties needed to go elsewhere for a while after their jacuzzi stopped working after an off-the-hook party. Rupert told us his folks' place, off west Pasadena's Linda Vista Avenue, was also a "no-go;" a skimpy, home-furnishing budget meant we'd have to sit on old futons. "Stagflation sucks," he said. "My mom's trying EST for peace of mind."

Temporary setbacks for a posse nine months from disbanding.

One by one, the Saturnalians—Denny, RG, Carl, Kyle, and Rupert—assembled. We invited Adam and Rick, as well, but they were chronic no-shows. The idea was for small, after-school gatherings on late-Friday afternoons, with no alcohol, just weed and snacks, since three members had football games the next day. We'd keep these hangouts on the QT to spare others' hurt feelings.

Every one of us, regardless of cliques and fluid popularity, had experienced the sting of being iced out, frequently over the pettiest of reasons. You were like a phantom in *Space Invaders*: sentient and shimmering, until someone pressed a button and you exploded, only reanimated by video-game reset (or proceeding event with your name on the list).

Our last rule: *no* girls, because as much as we chased them, as much as they bedeviled us, we were at Stone Canyon first.

My dad's business trip to Washington, DC, where the State Department was vetting his company to install high-end heating/air conditioning systems on roofs of LA consulate buildings, was our Saturnalian opportunity. The first order of business: cannonballing bowls of Compact-O in the dusty pen where Bilbo spent the day while I was at school. It was poolside lounging afterwards—joking, nerf-ball tossing, rum-bottle-in-the-pool referencing—and then fine dining on Hostess Ding Dongs and Fritos. No worry about morsels on the deck because Bilbo, who at nine still danced and whoofed in happiness when my buds were here, was our flop-eared, Hoover vacuum.

At the end, we tromped through the kitchen so I could show off my new Les Paul and everybody could Visine up before driving home. Charlotte, who'd grown up in a Minnesota family of Scandinavian descent, had Ingrid, her sixtyish, Norwegian aunt staying with us that day. She stopped us, observing our shit-eating grins and bloodshot peepers. "You boys have got," she said, "da sparkl-yee eyes." We soon were in my room, imitating her with a yodel-y twist, knowing she'd busted us without any consequences; next time, Carl said, we should wear bags over our heads like *The Gong Show*'s "Unknown Comic."

Denny was the last one to go, more intrigued than the others with my sunburst six-string. "Let's start a band," he said. "I'll learn bass. We could call ourselves 'Sparkly Eyes,' because we do make them sparkle fairly regularly."

—

The next Friday, we assembled at the Drummonds place behind Descanso Gardens, a house diagonal from where Neil's family lived. By 6:00 p.m., I was there on his porch in shorts and flip-flops, chafing at being fifteen minutes late. Or rather, *why* I was late. My dad had discovered a new power game, tasking me with chores just before I was set to go someplace he knew about in advance.

Today's *"this-can't-wait"* job—Ridding the garage of a couple of half-foot-long, alligator lizards that'd petrified Charlotte last week. I broomed them out with attitude.

Denny's mood-swings had kept yoyoing, and today he popped the door looking carefree. He'd become the only kid living at a home of splintering parents, his big brother, Daniel, at UCLA, his sister, Denise, a freshman at Vassar. Neither of them, from the little I knew, missed home much, and Denny and his hidden sides exploited a house now frequently empty.

I followed him onto the deck, glimpsing Friday-afternoon Saturnalians who'd begun without me. They'd splayed themselves on rattan, pool furniture, whose pewter tone set off the gingerbread-painted ranch home nestled in one of La Cañada's woodsiest corners. The awning and umbrella were color-coordinated, too, with striping reminiscent of a Victorian, beach-changing hut. Denny compared his *"everything-is-wonderful"* mom to one of *The Stepford Wives*, and the woman did have an immaculate knack for decorating.

Under her canopied patio, our smoke show was in progress. Several doobies made the rounds thanks to Kyle's Zig-Zag-rolling fingers and Denny's homegrown ganga, which he loved boasting was better than Compact-O, the student body's strain of choice. Neither of his parents were on the premises.

I reclined on a comfy lounger and dragged off a skunky joint, relaxing on my rattan. A floaty minute later, I sensed something was missing. And it was. For all the weed and arranged furniture, Denny had neglected two crucial elements: music and food. Nobody was complaining, owing to their buzz and, just as much, entertainment holding them spellbound.

The Drummond's dalmatian, Oscar—named not for the English playwright or golden statuette but his gluttony of Oscar Mayer products—was their performer. The large, polka-dot dog was sitting in front of our chairs in a food trance, flicking his tongue at the tablespoon of Jiffy peanut butter that Denny must've slathered on there. Just a single swipe from one of Oscar's meaty paws would've knocked the glob off, allowing him to lap it up in one bite. That was too much of an evolutionary leap, so it was *lick, lip-smack, swallow, lick, lip-smack, swallow.*

While none of my friends could stop watching his canine repetition, I could hear my stomach rumbling. "Hey, most gracious host," I called out, "aren't you forgetting something? Munchies? Jams?"

Denny slapped his forehead from his own lounger. "Damn, I knew I spaced out."

"As only a cadet could," Rick said, joint between lips.

"I'll fetch our grub. Luke, since you know your way around, go grab my ghetto blaster and some tapes from my room. None of that retro-Kinks junk, though. Or Elvis Costello."

"Yes, your majesty."

"Or the Dead Kennedy's," he added by the door. "Sorry, Kyle. This here is heavy metal territory."

—

Every time I'd been inside the Drummond's house, there was never anything out of order in the public areas. The sofa pillows were fluffed, carpet vacuum-tracks always visible, the powder room sink spotless. I was by Denny's room where there was no order, second only to Carl's as disaster area, as the guest-bathroom door cracked, and I heard a voice from days of freshman past.

"Oh my God, Luke, is that you?"

Stuart "Stewey" Freeman was a childhood friend of Denny's who'd attended Stone Canyon our first year of high school. Everyone except for Denny had lost touch with him after Mr. Pike quietly expelled Stewey seven weeks into the fall semester. His sin wasn't uncommon, cheating in Geometry I, which most of us were fortunate to eke out a B-minus in. Back then, I remember Stewey as a smallish, anxious boy in an academic crusher that could roll over anyone. This "anyone" was the only son of a pair of older, Depression-era parents who, like my dad, pegged us as late-seventies slackers continually corrupted by a druggy, decadent culture.

His name had cropped up last year on the Rose Parade route, and Denny, somewhat reluctantly, spilled his story when I pushed him.

On the night of the worst day of Stewey's life—the day he was booted from school—he'd foraged through his parents' medicine cabinet, searching for downers to kill himself. This just after his white-haired, country-club father laid into him as "a major disappointment who'd tainted the family reputation." After an alarming call from Stewey, Denny pedaled his Schwinn half a mile to the Freeman's hedged estate, climbing into Stewey's room through a window.

His first order of business: dumping those pills down the toilet. His second: sitting on Stewey's bed to give him perspective. "What happened isn't the end of the world—it only seems like it because we're pollywogs…If you wanna go auf Wiedersehen in ten years, call me and maybe we'll make it a two-for-oner. For now, forget this. You're gonna be fine."

And, *abracadabra*, fine he would be. Sent packing to an all-boys, New Mexico boarding school, Stewey reinvented himself into a poised, outdoorsy kid on the dean's list and championship, long-distance running team. I was talking to *that* Stewey now.

"I'm flying back to Albuquerque tomorrow. But when Denny invited me to your little club, like, how could I say no? See ya outside."

Outside Denny's room, thinking about Stewey's redemption, how Denny never publicized his acts of valor (just the potency of his weed), the *other* Denny was still taped up. He'd cut out mismatched letters from various periodicals, serial-killer-like, on a sign as a message to would-be trespassers.

"Enter At Your Own Risk, Clowns."

No risk for me. I was here ten days ago, practicing my SAT math.

Inside, his obsession with computers was, as Mr. Burr would say, "manifest." Spread around, on his desk, carpeting, and cinderblock workbench were soldering boards, pliers, a disassembled, Atari Model 800 microcomputer, cables, a voltage meter, and the BASIC programming textbook he'd breezed through, despite it not being assigned until spring. It was like a disorganized electronics lab for someone plotting to take IBM down.

Given my two cents, his lab could've benefited from my father's air-handling expertise to eliminate the ashtray-air quality that attacked your nose two steps in. Only Rick smoked more Marlboro's than Denny, and I wished both would quit, loathing cigarettes as much as the well-paid killers who made them. The walls of Denny's room was a separate mirror into him. A Blur Öyster Cult "Godzilla" song poster cited the line reflecting a cynical world view. *"History shows again and again, how nature points out the folly of men."* His black-and-white poster of Alan Turing, Denny's hero as father of modern computer programming, signified individuality.

Get back out there. Jams, remember?

At his black, plastic cassette holder, I ran my finger down the candidates and back up again. Selecting a crowd-pleaser wasn't as straightforward as it used be when we had crossover tastes playing on KMET, KLOS, and edgier KROQ. Our unanimity dissolved last year after some fell for full-throttle punk. Later on, they'd see the Dickies or the Germs, in seats or in elbow-swinging mosh pits, at venues like Perkins Palace or the Troubadour. *Rolling Stone*, my cultural bible, had written a piece on this phenomenon, where prep-school kids searched for identity as "disaffected youth listening to clothespin-pierced musicians scream death to the Establishment, only to return to homes with ice-cube-dispensing fridges."

Compared to them, I was a square, a British-Invasion/classic-rock kid at heart, now spreading his wings into New Wave groups—Cheap Trick, the Pretenders, the Police, Squeeze—with melodic originality. Once upon a time, we'd all hunted for bootleg albums and deals in the same rows at Poo Bah Record Shop. Today, we took separate cars to avoid sectarian music violence.

Denny's collection simplified that. There was no punk or New Wave here, just every Blur Öyster Cult and Black Sabbath album in existence, along with a respectable selection of AC/DC, Skynyrd, Zep, etc. Someday, I needed to baptize him that Ray Davies, the gap-toothed leader of the Kinks, the band he always dismissed, deserved its due. You think Sabbath ever sang about atomic war, men-in-drag (under "electric candlelight" no less), hypocritical snobs, gas crises, flailing superpowers, frisky sleepwalkers, or dead celluloid heroes? Nope, negatory.

At this point, I should've snatched up the best of the bunch and gotten back to the patio, but since I'd never been in here alone, I "let" myself get sidetracked by his walnut-grained bookshelf. Let my curiosity inspect a top shelf with disorganized stacks of *Popular Mechanics*, *Personal Computer World*, *Mad*, and *Penthouse*. Denny's lower shelf was better organized, if not more packed by sci-fi from Isaac Asimov, Philip K. Dick, C.S. Lewis, that sort. One leapt out at me because he had raved about its prophecy. What could it hurt thumbing through Dick's *Do Androids Dream of Electric Sheep?*

A quick peek wasn't a tug away, though, because the book's spine was wedged so tightly against the bookshelf's side. It took a strong rip to dislodge it, and when the *Electric Sheep* came out, the surprise that came with it rolled onto the floor. A slim, orange-and-white Chicklet's box: that's why the book was stuck, and I knew it couldn't have been accidentally squished in there.

Instead of replacing it where I found it, I pried the gum box open, and dumped the contents in my hand, the hand supposed to be handpicking heavy metal. I knew exactly what his keepsake was because I'd grown up around Diamondback rattlesnakes.

The lopped-off tail was bumblebee-colored, two-inches long, light as a feather. The rugged foothills below Mount Wilson where I was from were habitats for the camouflaged snakes and the critters they sunk their fangs into. I always feared Bilbo would end up like a neighbor's cat, killed after one slithered up out of the ivy and bit it. Once, retrieving a wayward basketball on top of a retaining wall, I would've planted my arm on top a sunning, four-footer if it hadn't rattled. The next summer, my dad signed me up for Tom Sawyer Camp, which culminated with a trip to Joshua Tree for a "Real Live Rattlesnake Hunt" that sent us grade-schoolers walking the sandy desert at pink sunset with our little pocketknives out.

I was reliving that now, a spontaneous face-your-fears moment, holding the tail up to the natural sunlight. A click of the door and a shadow on the wall was my karma coming.

"What cha got there?" Denny asked.

I stood up hastily with his snake tail in my palm, and the air pressure in the room plunged.

"What the fuck, man? Give me that back."

I dropped it in his hand, trying to explain myself. "I wasn't snooping. I wanted to check out the book you're always going on about, and this fell out. The box. Accidentally." I pointed to the top of the shelf, where I'd set *Electric Sheep* and the Chicklets container.

"Not snooping? Dude, I caught you *red-handed*."

"It's not what it looks like, but I'm sorry. I shouldn't have touched anything."

"Yeah, you are sorry—a sorry snoop. You were supposed to come in for music, something that should've taken like twenty seconds. Sonofabitch. This is personal."

Only positive: that his room was too far away from anyone to hear us wrangling. "Can we just forget it and get back out there?"

Denny snatched the Chicklets box, re-deposited the tail inside it, and walked over to slam it into a desk drawer. "No," he said, steam coming out of his ears. "I can't forget your dick move."

"I'm not apologizing twice. Rattlesnakes and I go way back. Besides, why were you keeping this?"

"Because I'm training to be a snake charmer," he said with a dagger squint. "It's none of your fucking business why I have it."

"Is this part of why you've been so up and down?"

"Conversation's over. You know, I thought you were better than this. Take whatever music you want. I need a minute."

In a daze, this snoop pulled out two tapes, put the ghetto blaster under an arm, and lumbered onto the shaded patio already eager to go. The vibe here was breezy, chill, opposite to Denny's room, with mythical bets being placed on how many licks it'd take Oscar to lap off the rest of the Jiffy.

"Took you forever," Carl said. "What were you doing in there? Spanking something?"

I didn't say anything, dropping the tapes and cassette player down onto a table by them. Kyle reviewed my choices: ZZ Top's *Fandango* and UFO's *Strangers in the Night*.

"Caveman rock?" Kyle said. "Not even X?"

"You heard the host's orders."

The sliding glass door opened, and Denny appeared with an armful of goodness—dry salami, string cheese, Moon Pies, and Dr Pepper—that sent up buzzahs from the Saturnalians and Stewey. I sat down not wanting any, declining the joint that came my way while my nervous foot tapped out my regrets, my guilt. Ten minutes later, unprompted, I stood up, saying, "I gotta take off. Girlfriend issue."

Everyone said bye except for one. I doubted I'd be visiting here soon.

CHAPTER THIRTEEN
UNDER THAT SHEET

Being a forward-looker, I always needed something circled on the calendar, and today I had my reasons to play a mean air guitar on my drive home from school. In a month's time, I'd be trading in the lane-eating whale for a burnt-orange Toyota bankrolled fifty-fifty with my dad. For the next half year, it'd be my wheels around town, and after that a highway transport ferrying me to a university with lecture halls bigger than our gym.

With just five days until the SATs, it was impossible blocking out the implications connecting that Celica and the exam. If I scored in the eighty-fifth percentile or better in the math-science section and aced the rest, my college adviser predicted it'd get me into my top three choices: Cal, Columbia, or USC.

"Think of it this way," Matt, my oldest brother, said on the phone. "You bomb the test and barber college is still an option."

This Monday was so hectic, I nearly forgot about how last Friday, Denny wanted to wring my neck and I wished I could've left by black hole. In the morning, Mr. Burr OK'd my topic for our required local history essays. After lunch, I learned which kid the faculty was pairing me up with as my "Freshman Buddy." Nick Chance, a cowlick-haired smarty-pants, would be shadowing me on certain days, including ones I'd be researching my paper. Mr. Pike believed cross-school relationships like this would, among other benefits, curtail food-chain bullying tough to stamp out. How much Nick would be my buddy as much as I'd be his after-school babysitter I didn't know.

Around 3:30, I turned the key on our redwood, back door, ready to buckle down. After a snack, I'd plant my nose in my SAT guidebook and not look up until dinner. As always, I Frisbee-d my JanSport onto my beanbag and cut a path toward the kitchen for cheddar slices and Wheat Thins. I was in the pantry for extra, Pepperidge Farms Milanos, when Charlotte walked in from the screened-in lanai connecting our pool deck and weed-strewn backyard.

"Am I ever glad to see you," she said, winded, chubby cheeks flush. "Bilbo got out the door again and won't come back." She poured herself a Dixie cup of water from the sink, swigging it a gulp. "I almost had caught him, but he heard squirrels and ran off. You know how slippery he can be when he's outside."

I held up a finger as I laid waste to a Milano. "Especially," I said, "when the moon is out and he's baying at it. How long since he took off?"

Charlotte checked her watch. "An hour, maybe hour and a half."

"*Pffft.* Long time. Did you check the balcony outside dad's bedroom? Last week he was sitting there watching the neighbor's horses. He even ignored me when I called him for dinner."

"Good idea," Charlotte said, refilling her cup. "I'll look there and do another sweep. He's got to be someplace."

He did, though the known escape artist and avid roamer never strayed far. Or he hadn't in the couple of years since we'd better guarded the back door that'd been his jailbreak when deliveries arrived or Charlotte went for the mail. If he ran out in daylight, he'd usually riffle through nearby trash cans or stalk cats until we whistled him in a house or two away.

The hallway phone obsolete now that I had my own my number rang as I passed by it with a snack plate. Probably a telemarketer or survey-taker.

"Yo-lo," I answered.

"Is this the Burnett residence?" an unfamiliar male voice asked.

Definitely a telemarketer. "Only if you're not selling anything."

"What? No, this is the Walnut Street Veterinary Hospital, and we have your dog."

Oh, thank you. But huh? The vet/kennel was at least four, citified miles away, and a scenario crystallized. Bilbo must've gone street-rover again, wiggling his white, brown, and black torso through a small hole in a chain-link fence he hadn't shown interest in for years. The Good Samaritan who found him probably called the number on his dog tag from the Arco station phone booth on Altadena Drive and unable to reach anyone, with Charlotte outside huffing and puffing for him, dropped him off in our area's best-trusted place for dogs. Seemed logical.

"That rascal," I said. "I'll leave now to come get him. When do you close?"

Charlotte reappeared with less red in her cheeks but more concern in her eyes. I cupped my hand over the receiver. "Don't worry," I said. "Someone found him and took him to Walnut Veterinary. I'll take care of it."

She scrunched her face, gave me a thumbs up, and waddled toward the kitchen.

"Sorry about that, mister," I said to the stranger on the phone. "Since he's there, do you have time to give him a quick bath and check for fleas? He's been itching like crazy."

"I don't think you understand," the caller said. "Who am I speaking with, by the way?"

A horrendous coldness sunk down into me hearing the first part of that sentence. "Luke Burnett. Bilbo's my dog. He is there, isn't he?"

I could hear the Walnut-Veterinary man sigh, and the coldness got worse. "I'm afraid I have some heartbreaking news. A car hit your dog on New York Drive this afternoon. The driver didn't stop. Someone else did and brought him here. Unfortunately, he didn't make it. Our condolences. This is merely a courtesy call to ask what you'd like to do with the body?"

Merely a courtesy call? This man was a liar.

—

It was weeks, a month, I'm not sure, because time was playing hide-and-seek with my grief processor back then. Sometime in the blur of losing my mom, my father walked out the front door and directed me into his then-Caddy. "We're going shopping."

"Do we have to?" I asked, preferring to mope around on my Macabob's skateboard.

Our last time "shopping" was his first attempt at restocking groceries after the funeral. It was a misadventure, to say the least, him throwing up his hands in frustration after forty minutes of hardly finding anything on his list. "I can't do this?" he's said in the cereal aisle. Two blessings emerged from that dispiriting excursion (where he only bought Ginger Snaps and batteries): my dad hired Charlotte, who knew her way around the supermarket from her prior nanny gig, through an employment agency. And, on the day I wanted to skateboard, we returned with merchandise for me from a squalid breeder near LAX.

The five-month-old Beagle, with the softest ears you ever stroked, and the most understanding, cow eyes a wounded kid could ever crave, would be *my* everything. From his first night with us, Bilbo slept on my bed under the crook of an arm. Whenever I was home, he was my wingman, trotting with me around the house, yard, even the air-conditioning-condenser shed, where I could wail in private and my consoling, spirit animal licked away the tears as fast as I shed them. This was four years before I went to Stone Canyon, so no one knew the lifeline supplied by the dog that smelled despair and ran in circles seeing me step off the school bus.

Bilbo got to know the posse during our freshman year, and what an impression he made. When we cranked "Lido Shuffle" on the radio, he barked along. When we'd attempt ill-advised moves off the slide or diving board, he watched us protectively. My version of Snoopy worked guests for butt-rubs and seemed to grin campaigning for leftovers. As we got older, so did his comprehension, and he'd nuzzle us while cramming for finals and roto-till his tail when we tried maintaining straight faces watching *Make Me Laugh* after school. He *hmm-hmm*-ed me when I began sneaking out of my sliding-glass door on weekend nights to meet up with Kyle, or fool around with a local girl in her father's Winnebago. Later on, Bilbo threw tantrums outside my door when I wooed various girlfriends inside, even if he knew I loved him a thousand-fold more than I could ever love them.

———

They're wrong. Mistaken identity. I'm coming, boy!

Charlotte, beside herself, ran out to the garage, flapping her arms for me to stop as I revved the whale's V-8 engine, palm on the reverse lever.

"Let me take you," she begged. "You're too distraught to drive. You'll get into an accident."

I ignored her, then Father Time meddled with me again. While my fists pounded on Walnut Veterinary's door, I couldn't precisely account for how I got here from Eaton Canyon. Traffic lights, signals, the world outside: nothing.

I could only recall the last thirty seconds making a hairpin U-turn that provoked an angry honk, then fumbling my car keys onto the street.

The sign on the fifties-era, brick building, which rested between a Shakey's Pizza and an In-N-Out Burger drive-through under construction, said it closed at 5:00 p.m. It was now 5:07 and I demanded in; my hammering on the door wasn't subtle about that. Finally, a woman with rosy lips in a light blue uniform stuck her head out, concerned perhaps I had an emergency in my arms. I gave the door a two-handed shove, shouldering past her and up to the front counter.

I recognized the manager, "Francis," a heavyset, older lady with penciled-in eyebrows. She stopped reading her paperwork listening to me describe why I was here, looking alarmed as my voice rose. "I have to see my dog *right now*, or I don't know what I'm going to do."

She told me to wait and disappeared into a hallway for a few minutes. In that unbearable void, I paced the homey waiting room with fireplace and green-leather furniture. I rubbed my eyes and listened to the distant barks from the kennel, praying one of them was the Wonder Beagle woofing: *"Back here, my human. Take me home."*

In returning, Francis' downcast expression didn't say *all's well that ends well*. It said there'd been no misunderstanding, and she ushered me into a small, exam room. Cold before, my limbs went numb, my heart thumping harder than any sweaty football practice.

The slim, snowy-haired vet, who'd taken care of Bilbo since he was a puppy, walked in through an interior door with a solemn face. Behind Dr. Max Higgenboom was a younger vet-in-training; he may have been the blackheart (in that bowl haircut) who'd phoned to say, *"We have your dog."* The three of us stood, separated by a metal exam table.

"Luke, we know you're devastated," Dr. Higgenboom began. "Everyone here is. Bilbo was a favorite. There's no words."

I wasn't ready for sympathies. I was ready to deny something irreversible had transpired. "I don't believe he's gone. Why aren't you showing me my goddamned dog?" It was my first time cursing an adult not named dad.

"That's not a good idea," Dr. Higgenboom said.

"I don't care. I want my dog."

The vet shook his head. "Take my word for it. You don't want your last memory of Bilbo to be how we received him. That'll do a number on your psyche. It'd be healthier for you to picture him in his heyday."

"Please give me *my* dog," I said less stridently, leaking tears.

"We should contact your father first."

"How about you don't. Bilbo needs me."

"I disagree, son. Your call, though."

Moments later, he wheeled in a cart with a lump under a white sheet, and my molecules began to separate. The vet settled a hand on top, looking at me from eyes that'd seen hysterical people around their deceased pets. "A dog is spirit, life…what's here is none of that," he said. "Lean on your faith, if you have it. That's my recommendation."

"If you have it." I was no heathen: My mom made certain of that.

Doc Higgenboom hovered as I went to the steel cart. I peeled back the corner of the sheet and peeked underneath. He was right: This wasn't Bilbo.

It wasn't anything, in fact, except a sickening, run-over replica. His charming, whiskered face was a flattened skull of mangled bones, snapped teeth, and blood-smeared fur. Greasy, black tire marks were streaked over his neck, and the tongue that used to lick the sorrow from my cheeks hung by a ligament. Farther down, intestines oozed out of the belly he loved getting caressed; I'd be dead, too, if I closely inspected that.

I let the sheet drop, and that was my last conscious thought before the exam room's bright lights spun and the speckled floor lunged up at me.

I woke up from after fainting an unknown time later, in the same room but now myself lying on the metal table onto which Doc Higgenboom and the trainee must've lifted me up. The cart holding *The Thing That Was Bilbo* had been rolled away.

It was now only me and the vet extending a mug of water. I propped up on my elbows, took a sip—and splashed the rest in my face. He was surprised I did it, but I had to wake my brain up to ask the question whose answer I already knew. "He is dead, isn't he?"

"Yes. Sadly, he is."

My hands brushed away the water dripping down my jaw. "I don't understand… How someone could hit a dog and keep driving?"

"Assuming they knew it, it's despicable," the vet said.

I shook thinking this not may have had to be. "Could he have, you know... lived if they'd stopped?"

"Probably not. If he'd been partially clipped, yes, just not run over. Don't play those what-if games. Your dad's on his way. Are you feeling well enough to go to the waiting room until he arrives?"

"Yeah."

I handed him the mug and exited. Not just this room, the entire building that'd shape-shifted into a morgue. I felt myself spiraling into the darkness of 1970, where there'd been no last hug, no final "I love you," no parting goodbye, no "you saved my life, don't go!" Whatever sleezeball did this to Bilbo deserved to be throttled, left to bleed out on the side of the road, and I hoped I could be there *not* to lend any aid.

—

Back in the whale, I rolled down the windows to channel air into my lungs and keep the Pontiac on the left, *err* right side of the yellow lines. Bilbo, not *The Thing That Was Bilbo*, would've told me to get arms wrapped around me before the stillness did. How I traveled from Walnut Avenue to Carl's front door on La Cañada's serene Beulah Drive was another time-space blur. I rang the doorbell, and Carl's mom, in her flaxen Century 21 blazer, answered it.

"Luke, something's wrong, isn't it? It's written all over your face."

More than there. "My dog, Mrs. Dieter. He got killed by a hit-and-run driver. Today."

She covered her mouth with a hand. "Oh, honey. I'm so very sorry," she said, hugging me before I knew it. "Why don't you come in and wait for Carl? He's still at football practice."

Of course he was. "No, I have to keep moving. Have him call me as soon as he gets in."

From my rearview mirror, I saw her trot down the driveway to do what Charlotte couldn't: keep me from compounding disaster.

Denny would've been next up in my grief-blast support circle, yet I'd snooped my way out of his good graces thanks to that rattlesnake tail, and he'd no more want to console me than receive a fresh batch of sadistic cigarette burns to his arms. Aware I was persona non grata, though only two bending turns from his wide, oak-canopied block, this muddy-brained speed-demon headed out of La Cañada toward Eddy, careening across Berkshire and Linda Vista avenues, past Suicide Bridge, cutting a sharp left onto Avenue 64 right before Stoney Point Bar & Grill. Everywhere I punched it in my post-Bilbo spiral, I left some Goodyear tire behind as offerings to no one. At Eddy's cross street, I stomped the accelerator up the steep road to a corner house two blocks up. She would know what to say. She always did.

Yes, *if* she was around, and today, instead of her chocolate-brown Pinto in the driveway, there was only the oil stain marking its place. *This is hopeless. Abandoned again.*

How could I return home without Bilbo there; how could I stare at his silver water bowl that'd never be refilled, or his rawhide bone or tug-of-war rope, without needing to break something? The whale knew where to point, and that was the reverse direction—I direction I'd rejected twenty minutes earlier.

Suddenly, almost involuntarily, I was at the lushly hedged property I slumped out of on Friday, this time not dejected but in lightheaded shock flecked with hot thoughts of revenge. Answering the door, my last resort reacted as you'd expect. He crossed his arms in a manner that communicated, *"You have some nerve coming here."* Even the houses' flagstone siding glowered.

"Bilbo," I said slack-faced, with no hello. "A car struck him. The motherfucker didn't stop. The Wonder Beagle—he's dead, Denny. I saw his body. It wasn't him anymore."

Before he responded, I heard his sometimes-there-mostly-not mother walk up, though he blocked my view of her. "Hello, Luke," she said. "Pleasant surprise. You and Denny hitting the SAT practice tests again? You're always welcome to stay for dinner, dear."

He twirled around and said, "Mom, I think I smell something burning on the stove."

"Excused again," she chortled. "You teenagers and your secrets."

A barefoot Denny, in a yellow, short-sleeve Izod with the alligator snipped off, shut the door, motioning me over to the side gate I'd schlepped out of Friday. He unlatched it, and we walked me to the corner across from the shaded patio. Oscar barked greetings from the window.

"Yo," I said. "I realize I'm the last person you wanted to see. And that's cool. I just don't know which way is up."

He leaned around to ensure his mom wasn't watching, lighting a cigarette he plucked from behind an ear. "Last person I wanted to see? *Nah.* But you almost made the list," he said with a nanosecond smile. "What the hell happened?"

I told him everything, from the "courtesy call" to passing out, allowing the tears to roll. "You don't think he suffered, do you? The idea he was whimpering for me, knowing he was dying…" I couldn't finish, the ghoulish imagery of that flop-eared corpse getting me dizzy again.

Denny crinkled his ski-jump nose and threw an arm around me. "Hey, man, it was probably over in an instant. Forget our fight—you call me night or day. And breathe. You're going to be fine, you hear me? Fine."

Even in the blackness of losing my everything dog, of the universe shanking me again, I had the clarity of a revelation. While Carl was my best friend, Denny would be my most important one. I'd gotten the "Stewey" talk.

"You want me to drive you home?"

I sniffled and exhaled. "No. Thanks. I got to find it in me to do it."

My dad's Jaguar XJS was parked in the garage as the whale rumbled in. Charlotte was in the kitchen, her face as much a drying flood plain as mine, stirring a pot of chili that looked disgusting.

"This is all on me," she said, turning from the cooktop. "Bilbo was too fast for my fat self. Can you ever, well…forgive me? I know you two were inseparable."

"There's nothing to forgive," I said, not because I'd forgiven or implicated anyone, but because I couldn't take her guilt on top of an expanding two-ton ache. "It's nobody's fault—he was a roamer," I said. Now, it was me hugging someone desperate for it.

Ours had officially become a one-dog house—her Gretel's.

Charlotte dipped her head toward the chilipot. "Your dad, he's not doing well, either."

My lanky, graying father wasn't where I usually spotted him after work: at the liquor cabinet, pouring himself two fingers of Jack Daniels, or in his closet, changing out of his suit. He was inside Bilbo's fenced-in pen, staring vacantly at the doghouse we'd built together. We saw each other only about an hour or so a day now, mainly at the dinner table. In me, he had a son from a generation he'd never penetrate; in him I had a father who wanted to restore our closeness and still couldn't compel himself to ask me how. My GPA didn't impress him a wick, not without Honors-Science classes. He recognized my skills with girls, but repeated "you better be careful you don't destroy your future in the heat of excitement."

I knew he'd grown up in a tumbledown, Oakland house after his own father abandoned his mom to start a new life with a new family in Connecticut. They were so poor that he and his sister looked malnourished in grainy photos. They could barely make rent, so a dog would've been an extravagance. Without a full-ride scholarship, my dad never would've gone to Caltech.

He appeared all of his six-plus decades, ashen and stolid when I walked up. "*Luke*, Luke." he said. "Where have you been? I've been worried sick."

We fell into the type of embrace we hadn't in forever. "Bilbo, our sweet boy," he said. "Such, a terrible, terrible shame." Waterworks burst from me again, this time in sobs. "You got to let it out. Think of Bilbo at the Pearly Gates, or whatever you call them."

"But atheists," I said mid-heave, "don't believe in that, I thought."

He pulled me tighter into his chest. "This one does today."

For the next few minutes, my tears blotted the sweater vest of the person I'd cast as the black hat of my eternal, teenage victimhood. He was six foot two, this second-string guard on Caltech's 1940 basketball team, and I was three inches shorter. When my fists pounded on his back, unable to get the *Thing That Was Bilbo* out from beneath my eyelids, they struck strong shoulder blades that didn't flinch.

The last time I lost my shit like this—wracking sobs, snot bubbles, hiccups—I was eight, and he'd just divulged, "Your mom has been in an accident."

CHAPTER FOURTEEN
GREAT MEN, BETTER WOMEN

She unbuttoned my red, flannel shirt to nuzzle my neck at the beginning of our shack-up—or "night nap" as we'd phrased it in case parental ears were in range—and all was right with the world now that my loins were the capitol.

"*Oh*," Beth said. "I'm sure you did better than you think. You're always so tough on yourself."

I kissed her on the lips and unhooked her bra strap in the flickering light of a bedroom neon for coming attractions. Our undressing of each other seemed so grown-up, so fancy in its anticipated lust, we could've been in a silk-sheet hotel, bubbly on ice. Home sofas, friends' guestrooms, the backs of cars, on itchy blankets outside: that was standard for breathy base-rounding. But this would be sex, unrestricted and private sex, under my newly tacked-up Hunter S. Thompson poster.

"You're only saying that because you feel sorry for me. Or you're hot for my bod."

Beth, daringly for a Marlboro-School girl, rubbed her palm over my crotch. "Unless those are quarters in your pocket to play Pac-Man, mister, I'm not the only who's hot for something."

And there went the top button on my Levi's, then most of the blood above my waist.

Serendipitous how all this arranged itself, and only an ungrateful heretic would question the Munificent Gods of Teenage Horndoggery, seeing those deities often took more than they gave. My father was in New York on a business trip I wholeheartedly endorsed, and I gave an appreciative Charlotte the night off. Beth deceived her folks that she was spending the evening with a girlfriend complicit in our liaison, if we later reciprocated for her.

"Whatever it is, I'm all yours," I said. "I never want to see another bubble-sheet again."

That punch-card, answer form probably never wanted to see me, either, me botching it five days after the Wonder Beagle left me with his soundless yelp.

When I'd finished the boggy portion of the SATs, the math part, at the end of last Saturday's exam, I scanned the column of answers shaded in with my tyrannically proscribed Ticonderoga No. 2. We'd been taught this double-checking technique, as well as tackling the exam's easiest parts first. In reviewing those bubbles as the clock ticked down, I froze in *we-have-a-problem* dread. On at least fifteen questions, I'd bubbled in what I believed was the right answer on the *wrong* line, as in the line for the proceeding question. A domino effect of blunders is what I'd constructed, and all my foot-tapping, harried erasing, and recalculating couldn't fix much before the proctor announced, "Time's up, pencils down."

Everything else SAT-wise I felt solid about—the history questions, the reading comprehension. I was proud of my essay about watching my big brother drafted for Vietnam, little-kid-me believing that war was heroic, good vs. evil, a *Hogan's Heroes* in Southeast Asia where no Americans returned home in body bags. Top of my list for Santa that year was a plastic M-16 rifle. As time passed, overhearing Matt on visits whisper to my parents about his list of friends "KIA," noticing all those men on stretchers on TV, I realized there might not be a guardian angel to shield Matt. That I'd glamorized killing and been a sucker for toy companies molding future soldiers. Throwing my G.I. Joe doll in the trash was my conscience's first act.

"And you're still going to wear two?" Beth asked, warm breath in my ear. "We can't take any chances."

"Abo-lutely. That's the plan."

"Plan? It's a must. I'm a Fertile Myrtle, if I'm anything like my mom."

We were down to my plaid boxers and her crepe panties, two horny teenagers, one porous heat field. I leaned away to pop my nightstand drawer, showing her a full box of condoms. "Nothing's going to break through this Trojan defense. You'll have Ronnie Lott back there to protect us."

"You and your metaphors. Who's Ronnie Lott again?"

"A USC defensive back who never got beat deep."

"Next time, maybe go with some poetry."

"OK, but don't I get credit for the room?" I said, sliding Beth's panties down to her ankles in *too-good-to-be true* arousal topping anything in *Jaws* or anything from my fitful, sexual past. When she stepped out of them, I wouldn't have cared if a comet took out the Forum. The lilac candle on my desk was the mood-setter, twinkling shadows off my ceiling and infusing the air with spring flowers. A pair of wine glasses and bottle of Chenin Blanc, which lay coaster-less on my go-to Encyclopedia Britannica, was our aperitif, courtesy of Ernest and Julio Gallo.

Lilting from my Sony hi-fi weren't my usual make-out LPs, either: *My Aim Is True* or *Frampton Comes Alive.* We'd be mining ecstasy to the Kinks' *Misfits.*

"It's no suite in Paris, though your touches are sweet," she said.

We French-kissed and Beth pushed me onto my bed. Tongues and fingers went on exploratory missions. Once her moaning crescendoed into purr and a volcano stirred in me, I reached for my double-condom, pregnancy blocker.

"SATs—what SATs?" she said into my ear as I slipped inside the heaven between her legs.

Beth had been the first to urge I postpone the SAT's five weeks, when they'd be given again, so I could better recover from losing Bilbo. The day after it happened, my English teacher requested I stay after class, noticing that her "inquisitive writer looked decidedly down in the mouth." I explained why. "Put off the test," Mrs. Whitcomb said. "You owe that to yourself."

I repeated her advice to my dad, and he hopped onto her bandwagon. "She's right. Use the extra time as an opportunity to turn your weaknesses into strengths. Geometry, chemistry."

By now my pride was slogan-proof and equally headstrong. Something about sitting out the SATs while every classmate gave it their all would've had an unpleasant aftertaste, setting a *Puke-Skywalker* pattern of ducking out where I should've soldiered through. Though taking that exam while still mourning my dog might've blown my chance at Berkeley, at least I proved I had an intact spine, and didn't that count for more?

Beth and I had the night of our lives, getting our ya-ya's out with mattress-shaking intensity that curled our toes and tangled my sheets. Our first try lasted two, feverish minutes, me climaxing before Ray Davies' final lyric of the title song. During our next shagolicious time, in a new position I hadn't known was possible, we stretched the carnal acrobatics deep into a track. Its message: tuning out the noise of a jaded world to inhale adventure.

You've gotta live life, that's all you do
Nobody gonna live your life for you
Oh, life's a mother, oh, life's a mother

By 2:00 a.m., we were spent, and I was in my bathroom cleaning up before we cuddled up to sleep. When I went to remove the double-condom. However, I noticed a puddle of me in the reservoir tip and also a few drops of milky mix spilling over the top. In my post-coital mind, it reminded me of an overexcited, root beer float that'd frothed a tad over the rim. This seepage had never happened before, just as seismic sex like this had never happened before. The soggy Trojans went down the toilet and I informed Beth.

Let's just say it harshed her mellow in the candlelight glow, ruling out any morning quickie. Whatever she was doing in the shower, it took her twenty minutes. "You better hope," she said afterward, toweling off, her square jaw jutted and hungry eyes gone, "I get my period. I'm not into close calls. And you promised to be extra careful."

—

Beth's freakout was understandable, because she was scared and so was I. Scared and feeling vertigo after the onset of a senior year that wasn't supposed to be so rocky. Still, even this so-so physics student appreciated gravity, and the biology classes I excelled in taught me male jizz wasn't equipped with spelunking gear enabling it to travel the circuitous path from near my navel to the place neither of us wanted. Or so I hoped, because what did I know about improbable conceptions, including my own?

Two Saturdays, two potentially life-changing fuckups. I chomped my nails with anxious teeth.

Mr. Burr's demanding Honor's History, given all this, was the custom-made distraction I needed. And in today's class, I'd be one of four presenting their essays. Parenthetically here, I retract my smug dismissal of Nick Chance as twerp-y nuisance. Credit him, in fact, with the left-field question that convinced me to replace my topic from something overused to something metaphorical.

Like many of Mr. Burr students before me, I'd been enthralled by the story of familial double-murder on the tranquil block where the Dieter's and Hosarian's lived. Long ago, the affluent businessman who'd founded the street named it after his dotted on, if peculiar daughter. Later, spoiled Beulah Overell thanked her parents for her gilded existence by allegedly murdering them, with the aid of a paramour, on their Newport Beach yacht; beatings with a ball-peen hammer, and thirty sticks of exploded dynamite to hide them, were more than enough to send them to watery graves. Found not-guilty in court, she relocated to Las Vegas, and in a Greek-tragedy flourish, wed a policeman who'd investigated her folks' homicides. Beulah, as if scripted, ended up an alcoholic, then dead herself.

Side by side with Nick one afternoon at the microfiche machines inside the Linda Vista branch library, which wasn't much larger than Stone Canyon's, I scribbled notes about the Overells while Nick goofed off, taken more with the machine's spools and levers than Beulah Overell and the A I was chasing. I told him to quit wasting time or I'd make him clean the whale's dusty headlights with a toothbrush. Twenty minutes of scrolling old articles later, his teenybopper voice asked, "So who's this Frank Flint dude?"

I knew the answer after reading up on him: a much better figure for Mr. Burr. I treated Nick afterward to a meatball sub at Jurgensen's neighborhood grocery nearby, forecasting an A.

Whether it was status or fortune, Frank Putnam Flint had already secured himself a place as a "Great Man" of the American West when he decided he needed his own frontier to conquer, discovering it close to La Cañada. For years, he'd be its "Lord of the Hilltops," yet as we all know, being that high meant there was only one direction to go.

Flint, Boston-born, San Francisco-bred, had no trouble making Los Angeles his own after moving south. A law degree and ambition propelled him into a succession of jobs that kept him in the news as assistant US Attorney, judge, postmaster, even adviser on William Mulholland's Owens Valley aqueduct.

At his zenith, Flint was a US Senator backed by the mighty Southern Pacific Railroad. Once the railroad's grip on power was weakened, he and his brother, Motley, networked influence elsewhere. Flint, in fact, had his fingers in so many pies—sitting on the board of a bank, serving as president of Occidental College, growing fruit, with memberships in the likes of the California Club and Knights Templar—observers might've suspected he had a third hand.

The craggy, animal-infested knolls west of Stone Canyon was the one place Flint didn't have to share any glory. Naming it after himself, "Flintridge" was to be a sparkling, bedroom town for conservative businessmen hostile to the lower classes. A silent-movie producer, who built an Italian Villa on Berkshire Avenue, and a bootlegger producing hooch on another estate put down roots. Earl M. Jorgensen, the steel tycoon who catered to shipyards, joined them. "No objectionable person," Flint explained, "will be permitted to purchase a house in this community." He constructed a Southern-governor-type mansion for himself, and next set to accessorizing his kingdom.

He hired architect Myron Hunt, who was at the dawn of an illustrious career, to design a hilltop luxury hotel, despite Hunt's warnings of inaccessibility and competition. He penciled blueprints for a country club and golf course located where Saint Francis and La Cañada high schools stand today. To entice equestrians, he established miles of trails, likening one reachable camp to "The Switzerland of America."

What intentionally wasn't there were schools, churches, post offices, or shops, for Flint expected that Pasadena to the east would pine to annex his village. He tried wooing the city's northwest citizens to support him by suggesting they change their main street's name from Linda Vista Avenue to a Big Apple-inspired "Parke Avenue." Locals spurned him, but Flint, with his powdery complexion and steely gaze, wouldn't give up.

While he regrouped, Motley, his colorful, wheeling-dealing brother, enmeshed himself into what would mushroom into a national scandal. Before it did, public stock offered for the Julian Petroleum Corporation's oil wells in Santa Fe Springs attracted investors from studio bosses like Cecil B. DeMille and Louis B. Mayer to one-hundred-seventy-five-thousand, lessor-known people. Over time, the venture soured, turning from profitable enterprise into what's known today as a "Pyramid Scheme," where privileged investors were paid with other stockholders' money.

Everything went belly up in 1927. Forty thousand Angelenos lost money, and the district attorney indicted the main players, Motley among them. Though prosecutors dropped charges against him, he was in an LA courtroom one day when vigilante justice arrived. From a back row, an Inglewood machinist who'd seen his thirty-five-thousand-dollar investment vanish stood up, removed a pistol from under his hat, and shot Motley dead before a thunderstruck audience. Police found ten cents in his pockets. Motley had sixty-three thousand dollars in his.

Frank Flint, while never implicated, fell under Motley's shadow of dishonor. Nine months before the Great Depression, he boarded a cruise ship for an around-the-world trip to recover from a nervous breakdown. It was there at sea he died at sixty-six, either from ill health or suicide. Back home, his expansive dreams perished in kind. The Flintridge Hotel typified that, sold to the Dominican Sisters of Mission Heart Academy, who'd transform it into Sacred Heart Academy school.

Historian Jackson Turner observed that "the existence of free land" was the torchlight of the American imagination. Flint's fatal flaw was equating exclusivity with greatness.

Mr. Burr outlawed applause after we read in front of the class, but I walked to my seat cocksure—before tripping over Brian Tollner's foot to laughs. Denny passed me for his dip into history on this late October day, already sulky at

9:00 a.m. He recited his essay, which I hurriedly wrote from his shallow research, in an emotionless voice. It was too bad, because his subject, with its mushroom-cloud storyline, was original.

Supposedly, there'd been a clandestine bomb-research factory for the Manhattan Project humming beneath Cheesewright Studios, a hoity-toity furniture-design store on Pasadena's Green Street, during World War II. While thin-wheeled cars rattled and pricy, living-room sets were sold overhead, subterranean scientists tinkered below with nuclear-fission and A-bomb triggers. Einstein himself "may have visited," Denny noted. Whether all true or semi-myth, I knew just where Cheesewright Studios were. Upstairs of the split-level building with a French Quarter aesthetic was where my mom once dragged me for her dental checkups and manicures.

Mr. Burr, who'd already graded us, wrote on page one of "My Man Flint" composition. "Well-crafted and researched, though immaturely pompous in tone. And there's nothing wrong with ambition." A-minus. Denny earned a B, and some scorn. "It was like Chinese food," he wrote. "Tasty going down but unsatisfying half an hour later. Next time, bring me hard facts and a supposition."

Cocooned in his hoodie, Denny had a *whatever*-expression passing Eddy as she strode up in high-waisted slacks and halter-top, which was about the most normal thing she'd worn since she'd been here. Many days, she chose her wardrobe specifically to amuse herself with our double-take reactions to what she'd harvested from her closet. There were androgynous, painter's pants over a Hawaiian shirt and flowery, sixties garb, a dainty "Little Bo-Peep" dress and her Debbie Harry fashion in a yellow "Camp Funtime" T over black slacks.

Halter top and all, she read an essay that blew both of ours out of the water. It was about a bleeding heart with a memorable name from early-1900s Pasadena. Emma C. Bangs, Eddy said, managed a boardinghouse as unconventional as it was charitable. On the ground floor were rentable rooms for wintering tourists and travelers visiting popular attractions. The upper floor was for miracles, reserved for the needy: tuberculosis patients here for the cathartic air, and a separate wing for terminally ill children. Bangs believed mindset swayed recovery, and that lively convalescence was better than melancholy window-staring. Patients in her "Busted Lung Brigade" were encouraged to view themselves as a one-for-all colony that discouraged self-pity as much as drafts.

On a lark, her ailing renters taught the house parrot to cough like a human. You couldn't see the boardinghouse anymore, because it'd been bulldozed for the picturesque Vista del Arroyo hotel.

"Emma Bangs was the bra-burner of her age, and didn't need the establishment's approval for her commerce or natural approach to health. In a city of plaques about men, where's hers?" Eddy said in conclusion

"Spellbinding, Eddy, yeoman's work!" Mr. Burr said after she was done; he'd awarded her a rare A+, and if she weren't a close friend, my green-eyed monster would've been out. "Tell us: What inspired you to resurrect her from history?"

"A unique connection."

"So unique you excluded it from your paper?"

"I avoid telling most people because they think it's crackers."

"Color me intrigued," he said, packing his pipe from his desk. "Please elaborate."

"Sure, but I warned you," she said matter-of-factly. "I was a patient there, in another life."

I knew this was Eddy's subject—just not that she'd open up on *her* secret—and a firestorm of reaction brought God into the classroom, and polemically so. Classmates, either murmuring or out loud, opined with religious conviction and personal contempt. Just me, I heard: "get serious," "that's cuckoo for Cocoa Puffs," and "got the number for 'Dial-a-psychic?'"

"Be respectful," Mr. Burr said. "She was responding to my question. Now, Eddy, so I understand, are you claiming that you died of tuberculosis in that boardinghouse?"

"No," she said, still in front, me worried someone might chuck something at her. "Some of those people who suffered from it were my friends on the other side of the wall. I died in one of her upstairs rooms in nineteen-thirteen—of child leukemia.

"Yeah, sure you did," someone said from behind.

"Progressive-Age Pasadena was magnificent to behold," she went on, ignoring the grumbling. "Even if women didn't have the right to vote yet."

"Like what?" said Mr. Burr, glancing over at Roland, who'd packed his stuff to storm out.

"Vroman's, potato-chip carts, Busch Gardens. We could hear them working on Suicide Bridge from the boarding house. There was even a man who rode a wild ostrich in shows. Its name, I think, was Mrs. Grover Cleveland."

"Grover Cleveland?" Mr. Burr said, trying to settle us down. "One of America's most tenacious politicians."

Eddy had first told me about this past life one summer night in her room, as well as the premonitions triggered by her additional radiation therapy. "If these little visions I get are right," she told everyone now, not shrinking at all, "I'll die again from cancer in this life but get to my thirties. The cycle will go on until I'm living to two-hundred or something."

Brian, from the desk in front of me, couldn't contain himself anymore. "This is incredibly blasphemous what you're saying. There's nothing about reincarnation in the Bible. Or maybe you're a Hindu who never read it?"

"*Children*," Mr. Burr scolded. "Don't make me utilize my putter."

Eddy wasn't fazed. "I'm as Christian as you, Brian. Baptized at All Saints Church."

Kamran Fazel, a standoffish, Iranian-born classmate, whose emigrating parents enrolled him at a school where he couldn't have been more of a fish out of water, scowled, unibrow in attack formation. "This is why women shouldn't read anything. They inflate. They twist." He almost never talked and, by Middle Eastern custom, showered a lot less than us.

"Good thing you are such an expert on American females," Cindy said, providing Eddy girl-power support.

While Kamran fumed, Denny, another light class participant, unholstered his disdain. "What a load of crap. You expect us to believe, with zero scientific proof, that you've had multiple lives. What's next, tea with the Tooth Fairy?"

I turned around in my desk to stink-eye him. For once, he wasn't slouching at his corner desk like the Memorex-tape guy. Or napping after being up until 2:00 a.m. programming.

"Denny," Mr. Burr interjected, "'load of crap' doesn't qualify as civil debate."

Eddy smiled and turned toward him. "Respectfully, Mr. Burr, I can defend myself." Then she pivoted back to us. "Call me crazy or a drama queen. It doesn't erase the fact that science isn't the end-all-be-all of knowledge. The universe is fourteen billion years old, and we've been studying it exactly how long?"

"Long enough to know there's no white-bearded dude in the sky as our air traffic controller," Denny snapped.

Eddy stuck her tongue into her cheek, formulating a counter. "Why is it that smart people, the kind who can solve any math problem, tend to be most close-minded?"

Classmates who'd scoffed or tuned out sat tensely, noggins ping-ponging, as the two went at it in our very own Scopes Monkey Trial of death as a no-return crossing or brainwashed mythology.

"Whatever gets you through the night—with due respect," Denny said with a tongue cluck. "You ever hear of the Big Bang?"

"Yes. You ever hear of the Tibetan Book of the Dead? Or Proust?"

"Nope. I'm a Carl-Sagan realist."

"Let's put a pin in this," Mr. Burr said, after a few more minutes of their arguing whether the hereafter or abyss awaited us at life's end. Nobody appeared evangelized, one way or the other, just emotionally ruffled, if not theatrically sucked in. "Roland, you're up before the period ends."

Why did he have to use the word "period"? Next time I have sex, I'm swaddling my entire body in Saran Wrap. This morning, before school, Beth called me to say, "I'm now two days late."

CHAPTER FIFTEEN
THE WAR WAGON

Halloween-Night hooliganism on an empty stomach was a rotten idea, which explained why we were seated at the place still employing a waiter—a huge, plastic, pompadoured waiter in red-checked overalls—as its brand spokesman. We'd been coming to the Bob's Big Boy on Pasadena's Lake Avenue for a while, more lately after some old routines grew stale. A $2.99-combo plate with pals inside those red-vinyl booths, sitting across from all manner of customers, gave the greasy spoon an enduring appeal. Nobody here knew about my crush on the waitress at the Bob's on Colorado Boulevard when I was ten, because this Bob's was all that counted, particularly when we only had so many opportunities left to commit truly imbecilic acts together.

Why Bob's management allowed us to continue trooping in was the head-scratcher because we'd provided corporate ample justification to deny us entry. At night, the restaurant was always bustling, haggard waitresses schlepping trays of deep-fried butterfly shrimp and mucky Salisbury steak, so it wasn't as though it needed us teen tightwads to turn a nifty profit.

Time and again, we pressed buttons and tested boundaries, mortifying anyone banking on us growing up sooner than later. We unscrewed the tops off the saltshakers. We left dollar tips underneath inverted glasses of water, rim sealed tightly over George Washington's face. We pretended to bend spoons with our minds. We did Gene Simmons impressions at little tots in highchairs.

Astonishingly, the badger-faced manager with clip-on tie frequently in charge during our incursions never bundled us out the double doors. It was as if he was playing the long-game, waiting us out until we graduated or took the roadshow elsewhere. Carl and Rupert sat on one side of our booth, discussing, or rather probing, whether the other thought blue-eyeshade, hair-flipping Cindy was pretty. By them was RG, scrambling to finish his computer-trig homework that saddled me with headaches. I was huddled next to Denny, asking him, in a quasi-whisper, why he'd shredded Eddy's essay instead of dozing off through it?

"Imagine the guts it took her to open up? You're a closed book about your secrets. You should've cut her some slack."

"Hey, she asked for it. Does her boyfriend even know about these *woo-woo* stories of hers?"

Boyfriend? Not random. "She doesn't have a boyfriend right now."

"She doesn't? That computes. Odd chick."

"Don't tell me you have a thing for her, and this is how you show it?"

"Maybe a subatomic thing, if that. My question is why *you* haven't been honest?"

"Me? About what?"

He spoke quietly into the ear that Beth licked last week; I hadn't alerted him or anyone what'd happened. "Don't play innocent. About your mom. What really happened to her."

I shook my head in thin pretense, on my heels for the first time somebody questioned my cover story. Thank god then the din by Bob's main entrance. I needed time to re-buttress my lie.

And this wasn't just any din, either, as we saw tilting our heads out of the booth. This was Kyle and Clip-on going at it in Bob's lobby.

"Turn around and reread the notice posted on the door," we heard Clip-on say brusquely. "It explicitly states, 'No shoes, No service.' And flip-flops aren't shoes. Leave."

Kyle might not have been wearing shoes, but he had his Mount Waterman hat on and the conviction he could still talk his way in. "Bah," he said. "Can't you make an exception? My buds are right over there. And we've given you a truckload of business."

"I'm truly touched by your concern. We'll be fine," Clip-on said. "Besides, nobody wants to look at toe jam while putting something in their mouths."

Blunted by that, Kyle hunched and exited, leaving us to deliberate whether to bag out for someplace else or order him a burger to go? Five minutes later, before we reached any consensus always thorny for our opinionated lot, he was back and not in sandals this time.

Our skier of double-black-diamond runs, our surfer of waters where great white sharks swam, had secured himself new footwear, likely from the trunk of his jeep.

"Close but no cigar," said Clip-On, who'd come around the counter to square off again. "What do you take me for, a patsy?"

"I don't know. Is that a trick question?" Kyle asked, waving at us. He had a blue swim fin snugged around one foot, an empty Kleenex box on the other.

"It's a hard answer. Scoot. I have actual customers to serve."

Now it was a standoff with Kyle standing his ground, and Clip-on unwilling to cave. Everyone at the counter near the lobby spun on their stools to watch the scene, even a crabby-looking geezer in suspenders.

"Give him a break," said a professorial-type in an argyle sweater.

"Don't be a tyrant," added a rooster-haired punk in a leather vest. "Let him in. Weren't you ever young?"

Inspired, we picked up on that, chanting, *"Let him in! Let him in!"* Half a dozen tables contributed their voices, and more joined in. Kyle had become Bob's Norma Rae.

We watched Clip-On sweep his eyes around the room, from the close-by booths to the back wall, assessing what do to, having turned himself into the foil in a silly upheaval over what constituted shoes. Easy call there: he capitulated before most of Bob's hissed at him and he'd need to hide in the kitchen, fantasizing about an early retirement. "Just this once, since I'm feeling generous," he told Kyle for public consumption. "And give the clam chowder a try, kid. It's super creamy."

It was riot watching Kyle clomp toward us, eliciting smiles and laughs, even if a few Geritol-crowd diners gumming tuna melts and cottage cheese frowned at him as he toddled past. After we made room for him to sit down, we picked out our orders, then coordinated the next foolishness for this special night. We'd request our drinks by cannibalizing the song ripping up the airwaves. The rehearsals went well, and our server cruised over.

"Can we each have a *Muh-muh-muh-muh-my-ee cola?*" we said, proudly synchronized.

Waitress Jill—bunned hair, fatigued eyes—gave us a *I-hate-my-life* expression, already over us. "E-coli?" she said, mashing her gum. "I don't get it. What are you having?"

She might not have been a fan of "My Sharona," but a Bob's customer I'd seen before sneaking peeks from a kitty-corner booth appreciated us. The French fry toss, the phony Heimlich maneuver, requesting a Coke refill from under the table: we'd sold him on our entertainment value going back months. When Kyle clown-walked toward us in that fin and tissue box, I observed him elbow his peroxide blonde girlfriend, and they fell over each other snickering.

It was former weatherman David Letterman, who was now a stand-up comedian (and one fond of sky-blue windbreakers when offstage). Carl, our pop-culture expert, claimed he'd spotted him a few weeks ago at the cheap Mexican joint we all liked, Super Antojitos, prepping for a gig at the Ice House Comedy Club. Who knows? Carl said. Our shenanigans might make his upcoming bit.

—

This Saturday, I'd be trading in the station wagon for that Celica. That meant tonight was the whale's swansong, as well as our final Halloween as a group, and we'd salute them both by piling into the Pontiac as a "War Wagon." Since I brought the ride, everybody else delivered the armaments. RG: rolls of TP; Carl: two dozen eggs; Denny: Barbasol shaving cream; Rupert: our newest weapons' platform, a water-filled fire extinguisher. In his jeep, Kyle had two, six-packs of Mickey's Big Mouth beer from Vinny's Liquor in Altadena.

From Bob's, I drove us east, toward Hastings Ranch and Sierra Madre in my neck of the woods. For the next twenty minutes, though, rolling through these lamppost-lit blocks, it wasn't much of a War Wagon. How could it be, passing hordes of adorable grade-school pirates, witches, vagrants, and others in costumes we'd long outgrown? Even us hooligans have their limits.

Our agreed-upon targets were junior-high boys—boys too old to be out trick-or-treating in waxy Michael Myers or Rocky Balboa masks, or as last-minute ghosts in their mom's secondhand sheets. We'd test them by pulling up to ask, in the sincerest of voices, directions to Disneyland (forty-plus miles away in Anaheim). Or if they knew what OPEC and the CIA stood for? They gave us any lip, they talked any smack about David Bowie (the only artist transcending our never-ending punk-versus-New Wave dispute) pumping out of the whale's speakers, and it was combat. Combat where we'd shower them in a barrage of eggs, shaving cream, high-pressure water, and smiley-face goodbyes.

The casualty count wasn't high, because we only blitzed four, back-talking groups before deciding to call it quits. This was too much of a mismatch, bullying more sadistic than playful, when our younger selves had all been on the receiving end as Stone Canyon padawans.

Battle-plans scuttled, we went to Sierra Madre's Memorial Park, where the maternal grandmother who outlived her daughter used to push me on swings, and we broke out—sorry grandma—the Mickey's and Compact-o to cook up an alternative. If there was one.

"I got an idea," RG said, walking back after tee-peeing the park's decorative cannon, having bitched about not using a single sheet of two-ply so far. "I heard a Poly jock is throwing a Halloween Party off Orange Grove. Why not go throw things there?"

"Why not" was the call, and soon we were at a darkened Shell station in Kersting Court, in Mayberry-esque Sierra Madre's town center. Everyone stayed in the whale except Rupert, who got out to refill his super-soaking fire extinguisher from a hose between the closed pumps.

Nobody saw, never mind expected, a Sheriff's patrol car, high beams on, to glide in behind us. It would've made Clip-on's year.

Before we knew it, the Omar was out of his black-and-white cruiser, ordering us to "Stay put" while he circled the Pontiac. He shone his flashlight inside, steadying it on the rear seat where we'd stockpiled the paraphernalia. All this took me back to running from the CHP officer after Denny milk-bombed his Kawasaki. This time, there was no tree house for us to cower in. We were getting arrested, simple as that.

"You guys are in major trouble," Omar said into my driver's side window. "I'm seeing alcohol, eggs, shaving cream, and your friend over there," referring to Rupert, "with an illegal fire extinguisher that says property of JPL. Anything I'm missing?" *Just Compact-O weed and probably Chinese firecrackers in somebody's jacket.*

He demanded our driver's licenses, and in my rearview mirror, I saw nothing except Saturnalians staring back at me with blank, dead eyes; I didn't know Rupert's expression, as he had his palms splayed on the whale's hood, as Omar ordered. We'd probably already be in handcuffs had we not gotten high in the park outside the car and chewed Juicy Fruit.

And to think, over three years, we'd never had a single run-in with any of the predators—your "Freeway Killer," your "Hillside Strangler," your gun-toting Vietnam burnout in a county with an astronomic murder rate—splashed across the papers. Now? We'd effectively self-arrested ourselves, and our delusions of invincibility were complicit.

By my window, the-boy-next-door-looking Omar began flipping through our licenses like a pack of cards. I expected he'd soon be radioing for backup. Instead, Kyle's ID made him smile.

"Hartsung?" he said.

"Yes, officer," Kyle said.

"Holy guacamole. It's Billy, Billy Tilbrook, you know from ski club?"

From the backseat, Kyle gazed at me in the mirror with a *here-goes-nothing*. He eased out of the car, barefoot, shorn of tissue box and swim flipper.

"I haven't since you for what, five years," Officer Tilbrook said, shaking his hand. "The family good?"

"Never better, Billy. Dang. I should've kept in better touch with you and Bill Junior. Prep's such a bear. He still at La Salle?"

"You know it. All-CIF in track. You should give him a jingle. He still can't ski the Cornice like you, but he's always off to Mammoth."

"We're definitely overdue," said Kyle, suddenly missing Billy Junior. "Same home number?"

"The same." A minute dragged by if it even dragged at all. "You guys are lucky it's me stopping you. And that I know your buddy," he said, projecting that cop voice. "My partner would've had you spread eagle. I'll make you a deal. Dump the beer and whatever illegal stuff you have on you into that trash can and get out of here, assuming your driver isn't loaded."

"He's not," Kyle said. "He's only had a cherry Coke to drink. You heard Officer Tilbrook, fellas. Get dumping!"

Robotically, heads down, we ditched the eggs, brewskis, and Barbasol; the benevolent Omar confiscated the fire extinguisher, which officially belonged to the federal government. It was salvation by identification, and I pulled out of the Shell station at sub-grandma speed.

You'd think we would've learned our lesson by the time we were back by the Arroyo Seco. You'd think we'd have been scared straight. But lessons weren't our business tonight, that Poly party was, and the Ralphs across from Huntington Hospital—where I'd been born and Eddy contended her past lives were awakened—became our convenient, egg-resupply depot.

We were up at the checkout stand with our two dozen when Carl asked where Rupert was? I offered to go find him, needing to get blood circulating into feet after the Shell Station debacle. I discovered him by himself in the dairy section, forty-fiving a can of Reddi-Wip into his mouth, sucking the nitrous-oxide out of the cream for the free buzz. This was so us, yet also just Rupert, and I knew from his little info-dumps that his family's economics remained dicey, and he was freaked at the possibility they'd have to relocate again. The Reddi-Wip can in this way was a red flag, albeit a flag to avoid until Rupert admitted the instability was gnawing at him.

From Ralph's, it was a short hop to manicured Bellefontaine Street in Pasadena's Old Money epicenter, us not far from the stuck-up Valley Hunt Club off former "Millionaire's Row." The Poly shindig that RG had talked up was happening on the lawn of a white, columned, Colonial mini-mansion, where roughly thirty kids loitered around with Solo Cups while a song from my big brother's Halloween era, "Monster Mash," played. What did they have running on TV inside: "Beaver Cleaver"?

The War Wagon passed on a five-mph recon to survey firing lines, and everything was teed up for us. Before the second pass, RG and Kyle descended into a pissing match over who had the better arm, and to make them shut up, I suggested they both throw. Neither was thrilled over the compromise, egos buffeted, but our two "arms" took up their positions anyway, winching themselves outside the car, butts resting on the bottom of the whale's rolled-down windows. They'd be opposite the party, launching their projectiles from across the Pontiac's roof.

Our battle plan, fortified by our Poly loathing, supplemented by the night's THC affections, made us modern-day Redcoats firing artillery in an unprotected field. The arms would heave the eggs, Carl and Rupert would replenish them, while Denny played lookout for an Omar (or another Omar) and any rear-guard action. I only had to idle in front, then hightail us out of there as sub-accomplice. All in agreement there, eggs streaked through the October night, Kyle and RG managing to launch twenty-four eggs in *crack-and-splat* deliveries in under a minute. Poly partygoers too flatfooted to find shelter took egg in the chest, arms, and shoes. A third of the eggs, from my vantage, missed, cracking on the lawn and a decorative pumpkin.

The message, even so: we were Stone Canyon's egg-men, enjoy the shelling?

"Fuck, Poly!" RG shrieked in victory.

I drove away, no harm, no foul, until Carl after a block nagged me to circle around to gloat on a damage assessment. I should've ignored him, on an evening of too many "should've's," so when four boys galloped toward the whale with their own eggs what did we expect but karmic retribution? Before I could punch the accelerator, a single Poly-chucked egg proved to be *that* one-in-a-million egg. The thing burst on the top of the open, passenger-side window, splattering half of its yolky payload inside while spraying the balance on the Pontiac's caramel-colored hood. I had pieces of eggshell in my hair and saw yellow smudges on the windows.

"Yo," Denny said from the rear seat. "Better go faster. There's a blue Trans-Am after us."

Of course there was. I floored it east on Bellefontaine with the Trans-Am in hot pursuit, memories of Bob's fading fast. What fun is audacity, though, without the thrill of bodily harm?

A pair of Saint Francis jocks had recently tailed two Stone Canyon juniors back to one of their homes for honking at them after they'd cut them off by Devil's Gate Dam. One of the jocks belted a junior so viciously in the jaw it lifted his feet clear over his head. Now, in my mirrors, I saw fists shaking out the windows at us and a steamed driver determined to catch us for a group pummeling.

Improvising the best I could, I blew through a yellow light, hoping to strand our pursuer behind the crosswalk, and cranked the wheel right onto St. John's Avenue. It was the worse turn I've could've made in another "of course."

Being from the other side of town, I was on a street I'd never been on before. And nobody pointed out, because there'd been no time, the city had converted it to a one-way street in anticipation of construction linking the

Foothill and Long Beach freeways. If we thought being chased by a muscle car packed with seething athletes was scary, inadvertently driving the *wrong* way—into an armada of oncoming traffic flicking their high beams and blaring horns at us—condensed into near-death experience. I had split seconds to react before a head-on collision.

Force, Mrs. John had once taught us, equals mass times acceleration. What's that formula, again, for escaping a fiery wreck?

There was no time to reverse or flip a U-ey. There was only time for me to slam the whale's brakes, then rip the steering wheel right into a stranger's driveway, coming yea-close to rear-ending the homeowner's Karmann Ghia. There wasn't a dry armpit in the Pontiac afterward.

———

Three days later, I backed it out of its carport hiding spot behind the garage to trade it in for the Toyota. The Hill Street carwash by then had scrubbed evidence of the egg splatter from the upholstery but couldn't do much to erase the asteroid-shaped stain on the whale's broad hood.

My father's detail-oriented eye narrowed in on it like the misprint on a five-million-dollar, commercial air conditioning contract. "How did this happen?" he said, rubbing his hand over the blemish. We'd been getting along better since Bilbo's death; this seemed poised to return him to gray and disappointed. "It's eaten away the paint."

I swirled facts with fiction as defense strategy. "Some Poly kids on Halloween night hurled eggs at us. They're not all goody-two-shoes. I tried tracking down who did it. No luck."

A doubting forehead called my bluff. "And you did nothing to provoke this?"

"We didn't run up with shaving cream and spears, if that's what you mean."

"I'm changing my negotiating position. Whatever the dealership deducts off the trade-in because of this, you're repaying me from a part-time job. Anything else I should know?"

That's fair. And forget me ever working for you. "Nope. That just about covers everything."

—

By that afternoon, I was breathing that new-car-smell while teaching myself to drive a stick-shift in clutch-popping practice. That night, around nine, I phoned Beth about you-know-what, praying she needed what I heard a Stone Canyon coed crudely refer to as "a cotton pony."

We'd talked by phone every other day since our night nap, each conversation more brittle than the last. I tried being her boyfriend, telling her I'd do "whatever" she wanted, and nothing I said or refrained from saying restored any lightness in her stressed-out voice.

"You can't be pregnant," I repeated. "It's a physical impossibility unless both rubbers snapped at the bottom, and they didn't. Try to relax." I should no more have mentioned "relax" than "cotton pony," which I hadn't.

"Relax?" she said loudly, cleaning out my eardrum. *"Relax?*—don't you dare tell me to relax! You're not the one about to lose everything and have to decide between being a teen mom or having an…I don't want to say. You'll still get to go to college and have a regular life. 'Relax,' he says. You say the dumbest things, Luke. I'm a week late."

Definitely dumb. "Yeesh, that long? You haven't told your folks, have you?"

She harrumphed me again. "How could I? My mom thinks I'm a virgin. What were we thinking, doing this?"

I didn't take the Toyota out for its first late-night spin, as I'd been planning, or sleep well afterward, as I expected. I was Peter Criss: *"Oh, Beth, what can I do?"* Not much after that stomach-pretzeling update.

On Sunday midday, going round and round, about to scream "why" into my pillow, still not having told anyone I could be a dad next year, I phoned Eddy. "Hey, you," she answered, as she only said to me. She promised to be over "pronto" after hearing my unspecified anguish.

She brought someone with her to help right my ship, too. "I believe you know my friend," she said outside the back door.

"I do. But what's the name of the pig flying over Mount Wilson?"

"You ought to see your face," Eddy said.

"Yeah," Denny added, "you should. Eddy, you have smelling salts in the Pinto?"

We walked out into the driveway for privacy. There, Eddy explained that Denny called to apologize for his demeaning comments about her essay a few days ago, and afterward, they got to know each other. The two-hour conversation gave her "cauliflower ear."

"I hadn't been on the phone that long since the prank call with you, Carl, and Rupert," Eddy said. "This, I must say, was way more unexpected."

"Totally," Denny said. "We discovered we have more in common than meets the eye. Food. Sense of humor. Movies. You never told me she's into heavy metal."

"I wouldn't say 'into,' but I like some of it," Eddy corrected. "I'm still a Carly Simon/Joni-Mitchell-girl."

"Ready for another mind-blower, Lukey?" Denny said. "We had our first date last night: go-carts at Malibu Grand Prix." He pecked her on the cheek and that pig over Mount Wilson executed a loop-de-loop. "So what? We disagree on the 'death stuff,'" the death-stuff in air quotes.

"On second thought," I said, "maybe smelling salts would be a good idea."

"You have a true friend here," Denny said. "She wouldn't blab why you flipped the Bat Signal. So, *um*, why did you?"

"I can't say it here," I answered, and my Celica's first passengers heard about the aftermath of my shack-up with Beth.

Passing the Pacific Hastings theater, on a drive-about with no preset coordinates, Eddy noticed the marquis for a movie she figured I'd like, *Life of Brian*, if only to take my mind off of Beth's menstrual cycle (or the lack thereof). We were in the ticket line as I started shadowboxing myself, wondering if I could muster a belly laugh, whether *I* deserved any buttery popcorn? Conclusion arrived, I suggested we bail.

"Whoa Nellie, no" Eddy said in her trademark hold-on. "Not with that face. What about there?" she said, gesturing at Bahama Lanes bowling alley alongside the theater.

Inside, the company bowling leagues and pins-crashing crowds during the workweek were gone, with only three lanes active, including a tyke's balloon-decorated birthday party. Away from them, the three of us each bowled according to our happiness. Denny and his undeveloped arms threw gutter balls and splits, laughing with his smoker's cackle no matter where his ball struck. Eddy, an inch taller than him, racked up four strikes, throwing the ball with eyes shut and a goofy smile. Unlike them, I bowled out for wanton destruction, either blowing up the pins in my lane or bouncing balls into the adjacent lanes.

Eddy herded us over to Baskin-Robbins afterward for a sugar mind-cleanse, but mainly for further discussion about what I should do. We got our ice creams, and I slumped midway down a pink, B&R booth, cushion-less of course.

"Any advice?" I asked.

"Not until I'm back from tinkling in the girl's room," she said.

How crazy that Denny kissed someone I once had. "Just what every senior wants," I said. "A college acceptance-letter shit on by dirty diapers."

"Dude, stop tripping," he said. "You were right in the car when you said she was probably being psychosomatic. If you wore two rubbers, it's the equivalent of dry humping her."

Eddy, get back here. Denny's "up" mood today was too up for me. There was also my sticky left hand, the one getting dripped on from the coffee cone that felt like a prop.

"But what if she is knocked-up, however it happened? We can't be parents. I'm not even old enough to vote."

"I think you know the answer."

I got up, walked over to the trash can, and slammed my cone into it with a vengeance. "I can't let her pay for an abortion," I said back in the booth. "I just don't have the cash. I might need to place my head on the chopping block and ask my dad for a loan. What else?"

Denny's crooked smirk formed around a glob of Praline 'N Cream on his upper lip. "I'd spot you with my weed sales, except that everybody is too in love with Compact-o nowadays. What about Jimmy saving the day? You could sell him."

"Jimmy," Denny knew, was what I nicknamed my Les Paul, in homage to guitar God Jimmy Page. "I was at Dr. Music checking out a bass, and I saw someone selling a used Stratocaster back. Betting Jimmy could net you five hundred. More than enough for Beth to get this taken care of. Which she won't need, because it's not real."

Eddy returned, yet instead of sitting back next to me, she scooched next to Denny, reaching for her Rocky Road in a cup. "You feeling any better, pardner?"

Pardner? Eddy once had a horse her family kept at a South Pasadena stable. Though her parents had to find it a new owner to help finance her cancer treatments, she clung to her old-school cowgirl parlance.

"Yeah, top of the world. If Beth doesn't get her period, I'll be building Big Wheels and trikes at Macabob's for years, then putting in night shifts in the Fedco food court."

"I'll repeat myself, *Whoa* there. You do have options."

"I know, I know. Denny thinks I should unload my guitar. As if my dad wouldn't notice it gone."

"That's not what I was going to say, Gloomy Gus. I was going to remind you have the option of settling yourself before you decide on anything. To shine inward first. Didn't you tell me when we first met that your mom had a saying for when things spun out of control?"

"Crimminy, I haven't thought of that in ages. She did. 'What ought to be, is.' Her version of let it be."

"So go with 'ought to be' for now. And you have us on your side."

"And if not," said Denny, who in no way believed in predetermination, "can I get an air rifle for Christmas, Pops?"

When he wasn't looking a second later, I snatched the cone out of his fingers and tossed it in the same trash can as mine. "Whoops," I said. "Can we go?"

—

Around dusk, well after Eddy and Denny departed googly-eyed for each other, Beth phoned to deliver breathtakingly good news with excitement in her voice and no softness in it for me. She'd gotten her period, declaring she "could've hugged my box of Tampax."

"Give it a hug for me, too," I said.

There was an awkward pause, and what felt like a prepared statement afterward. "We had some fun times together, and one scary, drawn-out moment. I still really care about you. I hope you know that. I just can't see you anymore."

"Really?"

"Really. It's nothing you did, not specifically. But those wild school parties you took me to, your friends throwing stuff off the balcony, the drinking and smoking, the long drive between us. Then this. It's all too much. I'll never forget you. How could I?"

Having sensed this might happen, and now riding my Zeppelin of relief into the stratosphere, I asked if there was anything else behind her decision to break up?

"Yes. Behind that spark of yours is a boy who fidgets too much for his own good."

CHAPTER SIXTEEN
TUNNEL RATS

Rung by rung, Denny sank down the ladder into the secret world beneath Caltech, acting like he'd been doing it his whole life when we'd only been sneaking in here for six months.

"Man, can you believe it's March?" he said, clapping grime of his hands, peering up at me inside an obscure access shed. Having a set of copied master keys, given to him by someone he wouldn't disclose, was his platinum, all-access card into here. "Three more months and no more Mr. Pike. Or anything that's a drag."

Next, it was my descent. Two steps down the ladder, I dragged the metal lid back over the manhole opening, so no one sniffed out our trespassing. Denny was midway through his usual preparations when I hopped down by him. He knotted a blue bandana around his Adam's apple in case of bad "tunnel stink," that dank aroma tinged with urine and a whiff of animal decomposition that sometimes curdled your nostrils here. Then he patted the scuffed, silver-ribbed flashlight in his Levi's pocket to keep us from stumbling over unseen objects.

"Unreal," I said. "Feels like it was last week Mr. Burr was taunting us as his freshman victims."

"Now he's brainwashed half the class about Frederick Turner," he laughed. "Even kiss-asses like you. Go forth and conquer something."

I gave his bandana a playful tug. "At least," I said, "I wasn't snoring when he was talking about the Iranian hostage crisis. Maybe you've heard about it?"

Practically everyone in the class of '80 was punch-drunk as us, popping off or engaging in unauthorized extracurriculars at a higher frequency than usual. We all had this collective, restless energy, enough of it to power Sports Chalet, and it needed someplace to go. Next week, colleges would be sending out letters whose message was self-evident in the mailbox. A plump envelope was reason for a victory dance, since there'd likely be a "congratulations" in the opening line of the *you-did-it* letter and a welcome brochure and forms tucked in. Everyone dreaded the slender envelope with only a single page, for inside would probably be the verb "regret," followed by a long night of consoling, dejection, and hope the proceeding envelope from the next, top-choice college wouldn't be so devastatingly thin.

Denny, who'd scored in the ninety-ninth percentile on the SAT math section, was a virtual shoo-in for Stanford, from what I understood. There were no guarantees for me, but I'd upped the odds getting into my Big Three, netting better test results than I expected. Either my bubble-shading mix-up wasn't the catastrophe I fretted it was or, as Eddy teased (and undoubtedly believed), Bilbo changed my answers with a swipe of a celestial paw. I went with the first scenario.

"Let us," Denny said in a mechanical voice, flashlight beaming, "go meet my sup-er-ior."

"And you're imitating the robot from *Lost in Space* like we're in fifth grade because…?"

"Because" he said, in the same syllable-halting cadence, "you're the only one I can do this with. Pro-ceed."

Tunnel explorers had multiple entrance points (unmarked doors, forgotten stairs, sheds like we'd used) to sneak in and investigate the concrete maze underneath the campus. There were miles of passageway to wander around, but it came with the understanding that unless you worked here, with the ID to prove it, it was illegal, and you could face repercussions.

As with our other excursions, we began by walking east in a shaft paralleling Pasadena's California Boulevard. Above our heads, ceiling-braced steam and cooling pipes hissed, swished, and vibrated on schedules of their own. Twenty feet below were storm drains that rumbled locomotive-like in heavy rains, a gray water churn that'd be fatal if swept into.

Visit these tunnels midweek and it could be a ghost town of scattered roamers and screechy mice. On Fridays, like tonight, there was a decent rotation. Typically, that was made up of regulars, acclimating Caltech undergrads, and high-school kids who either didn't know better or should've. We'd already passed a good, two-dozen explorers.

Within our posse, Denny was ahead of everybody, no longer requiring a map to pinpoint where he was, having memorized every subterranean-accessible building: Keck, Beckman, Noyes, Kellogg, Mudd. All of us here for the tunnels lacked his sense of direction, but we did know where to park our cars.

For us in the class of '80, leaving them in Poly's unfenced lot to the south while we traveled under Caltech was convenient and humorous. In years past, we'd lightly defaced its field before big games, once planting a rubber chicken atop a goalpost, before losing the majority of games against them. We shook it off, telling ourselves that our renegade spirit gave us the courage to break into Caltech's forbidden world, while our opposites were probably home splitting a covert beer over *The Incredible Hulk* reruns.

Denny never had to twist my arm to get me to venture under the "MIT of the West." Most of my life, I'd not been here on my volition, which made skulking in with Denny & Company something I chose on my own terms. Over the years, at lectures, dinners, and other events, I was constantly being introduced to accomplished people who'd revolutionized their fields and received standing ovations for it. In my unease here, though, I viewed them as much extraterrestrial were world changing. Whether Eastern-European-born astrophysicists with tongue-twisting names or double-PhD Americans, they formed a composite for me of a wool-wearing figure speaking an alien tongue of mathematical jabberwocky I'd never comprehend. Not even in a hundred lives.

When I'd be trooped into the ornate Athenaeum, passing walls festooned with oil portraits of Caltech's illustrious leaders, I knew I wasn't the audience for these exceptionally intelligent scientists who'd divined the inner lives of quakes, quarks, supernovas, and such. That was for peers, researchers, deans, and grant-makers. Lately, I'd occupy myself here by embracing my own bailiwicks, wondering how many poindexters inside these hallowed halls understood William Faulkner, or the subtleties of authoritarianism, or how versatile the A-7 chord was?

Small-minded, I know, but appreciate that I was born to dislike the California Institute of Technology, home of the Beavers, by the very man who worshipped it. It was my dad's fault for insisting on bestowing me with a middle name in homage to Robert Millikan, his alma mater's founding president. By grade school, playground jerks itching for something that differentiated ssomeone from the pack had their catnip in that Millikan. My mom had named her boys after three of the apostles/gospel writers in Matthew, Simon, and Luke, which my dad had accepted in begrudging concession to her Christianity. Still, where my siblings were bestowed normal middle names, my dad finally got his turn, riffing off of a physicist born three years after Booth assassinated Lincoln.

It flummoxed him why I so disliked "Millikan," which to him sounded distinguished. Likewise, I couldn't fathom, on the cusp of eighteen, how he and I could be possibly related. His Mount Rushmore—Kip Thorne, Edward Teller, Murray Gell-Mann—deciphered the material world. Mine were writers, journalists, and musicians who explained something more exhilarating: human behavior and the "why" governing it.

"Get a load of that," Denny said, jarring me out of my head, aiming his flashlight at the latest graffiti spray-painted in red on the tunnel walls. "Somebody's not renewing their membership in the Tricky-Dick fan club."

I squinted reading it, delighted Denny was having another "up" day.

> *"In the land of Nixon, where the shadows lie:*
> *One Nuke to rule them all, One Nuke to find them,*
> *One Nuke to bring them all, and in the darkness blind them."*

"I sense a pacifist," I said.

"No shit, Sherlock. Mush."

"You still keeping who we're going to meet a surprise?"

"You know it."

We picked up the pace, sidestepping Der Wienerschnitzel wrappers, cigarette butts, crumpled Coors' cans, and, if my eyes weren't deceiving me, a depleted tube of K-Y Jelly.

"We got another," Denny said after seventy more steps. "You'll appreciate this one."

I did. Someone with blue spray paint had X-ed out what was there before: "Clapton is God," which any self-respecting rock fan knew was a replication of what Clapton superfans in the late-sixties scrawled on the sides of London's Tube. But *this* was Caltech, where heaven was abstract.

> *Linus Pauling is God*

Pauling, I recalled from my many visits above-ground here, was a Nobel-Prize winning chemistry professor at Caltech, celebrated for his anti-war stances (and vitamin C advocacy). My brain was firing off in so many directions like these I nearly forgot that we had friends out there in this rabbit hutch. Carl, Kyle, and RG had driven separately, pumped up with a different vision than us. They'd eaten magic mushrooms to enhance tonight's experience, forsaking weed or beer for something psychedelic.

There was no shortage of interesting places, restricted from ground level, for them or anyone to pop into from below. You just needed moxie and the know-how. And it wasn't limited to classrooms or offices. For the more enterprising, there were accesses to cavernous rooms containing Caltech's super-machines, things such as its radio telescope and vaunted wind tunnel. During a free period at Mickey-D's last week, Denny had diagrammed routes into them for Kyle on the back of his hash brown sleeve. That was before we heard he and the others planned on shrooming.

Denny, on this point, was hellraising less than before, something I attributed to the Eddy Effect. With her as his girlfriend, he was getting regular TLC, and no small amount of tail from someone deft at leveling off his crests, softening his troughs. Unlike Denny's parents, who appeared to have little control over him, Eddy was also willing to draw red lines.

Take last month, after Denny had crowed about getting even with the "blue-haired witch" who'd ratted him out to his mom. Widower Pearl Gringle, he said, told her she could no longer abide the heavy metal booming out of Denny's car window passing her house a block from his. She railed it was "noise pollution," "a menace to delicate ears," prattling on about filing a police report. Denny bade his time, lowering the volume on his radio for a week while he got his hands on the revenge. Six feet of surgical tubing, two wooden poles, tangerines from a tree in vacant lot, and a page of trajectory calculations were the components. At three a.m. one morning, he and his long-distance slingshot replastered the side of Gringle's house in a pulpy, citrus fusillade.

"The witch never phoned again," he told Eddy and me, blowing on an imaginary pistol.

"And I won't be phoning you, either, if you repeat that," Eddy snapped. "Two wrongs— never right. Put yourself in the shoes of an old lady having her house shake in the middle of the night."

Denny never looked so humbled afterward. Even so, he wasn't the only boy whose tide shifted under the influence of coeds' moons. By Thanksgiving, for instance, Rupert and Cindy were an official couple, smooching at parties, holding hands in the parking lot. Come Presidents' Day, though they were kaput and Cindy was *now* Carl's squeeze, once he'd recovered from a minor case of mono. A simmering hostility arose between two longtime friends, which spread uncomfortably among us in unspoken pressure to pick sides in their love triangle or have an opinion. No winning here.

"Why'd he have to scam on her," Rupert grumbled to me one day when I gave him a lift home. "There's all these girls on campus, and he had to poach mine? Now I get it rubbed in my face every day having to see them together. How'd you like that?"

I replied I wouldn't and his arms remained crossed. As much as I adored Carl and liked Cindy, Rupert had gotten the brunt tip of that triangle. He wasn't alone there. Three-quarters through the school year, we had a campus contagion of romantic entanglements, reaching from us to acne-faced freshman. Between-the-bell hostilities used to pit the weakest of the herd against bullies' inner rage. Today it was two lovesick boys fighting over the same girl.

"However I slice it," Rupert said outside his place. "I still got hosed."

Scorned and smarting, he rejected joining us tonight in the tunnels. No one was shocked.

Denny and I continued walking, slaloming around mounds of trash, the last with rats making a meal of it, and a gaggle of older kids in light jackets and masks. Eventually, he splashed his flashlight on one of the endless service ladders we'd passed. This one was special, however, its bottom rung glowing from the two small, phosphorus dots my guide affixed there last time.

"That's our breadcrumb to go up," Denny said. "Ready to know who you're about to see?"

—

"Well, lookie there, the boys who came in from the tunnel," remarked Denny's instantly recognizable friend after we popped the latch into his space. "Dust yourselves off. You thirsty?"

"Only thirsty to hang out," Denny said, stretching his arms (and landing the metaphor). "Thanks again for staying late." He introduced me as his "partner in crime." He really was born forty.

The private office of one of the Milky Way's brightest humans was jumbled the way his mind wasn't, and as eccentric as his displayed hobbies. A pair of upright bongo drums, one plastered with sun-bleached Rio de Janeiro stickers, hankered for a banging by a paned window. Three safes of different sizes, all with their doors swung open, were arrayed behind his desk, seemingly as lock-picking trophies. Over his door was a relic from his Manhattan-Project days, a sign of a frowning Uncle Sam with the words: *"Loose Talk Helps Our Enemy. So let's keep our Trap Shut."*

My grammar-brain corrected "trap" to plural, but I wasn't about to scold Richard Feynman.

Up close, out of his standard suit, Stone Canyon's most coveted guest speaker appeared younger and more approachable than on stage. He had light brown, Hugh-Hefner-type hair that accentuated an expressive forehead, and a beige, Adidas tracksuit showing off a trim fit. His charismatic smile and natural energy were wraparound.

I couldn't help but notice a red nick along his neckline, proving even geniuses can cut themselves shaving.

"A pleasure to meet you, Luke," he said with a New York accent as diluted as Mr. Pike's New England one. "You thrive on science as much as our mutual acquaintance?" He smirked affectionately at Denny. "Or programming?"

"Never."

"Well, despite my incessant efforts to insert Caltech onto his college radar, he's casting his lot, so he tells me, with the wine-and-cheese crowd in Palo Alto," Dr. Feynman said. "Maybe you can talk some sense into him?"

There was my opening. "I wouldn't count on that. My dad—mechanical engineering, class of '40 here—got the math gene. I peaked at algebra two."

He *tsk-ed-tsk-ed* that, gliding over to his office mini-fridge to retrieve and hand us a pair of ice-cold Frescas. He cracked and sipped his with an *"Ahhh. Now tell me, what's in your future?"*

Steady, Luke. "Writing, journalism...still trying to sort that out."

I'd never vocalized this to any grown-up besides my college adviser. Expressing it to him, out in the open, produced something I didn't expect: a rush, the intoxicating rush of my future saying, *"Finally."*

Our host wiped Fresca foam off his mouth with the sleeve of his tracksuit, then heightened my rush with his credo. "Good for you, young man. Hoe your own road."

"Thank you." I already wanted back here another time.

"Speaking of hoeing, did Denny share with you how he tricked his honors chemistry teacher into writing out the formula for manufacturing lysergic acid diethylamide? It was enterprising, I'll give you that."

"Lysergic...Isn't that LSD? And no, he never said a word." When I looked at Denny, he pretended to be whistling an inaudible melody.

"If I'm telling his story correctly, he went in after school and said some of his classmates thought his teacher was too much of an antique to know the formula for it. Denny got his goat, so he wrote it out on the board and erased it quickly before Denny got any bright ideas. What the instructor failed to realize was in turning his back, Denny secretly copied everything he put up."

"Denny," I said smiling. "You didn't."

"No, he did," Dr. Feynman said. "He showed it to me. Now, let me say I in no way endorse consuming illegal substances, but I endorse someone that crafty to learn, for whatever reason."

"Didn't they say in the sixties, 'better living through chemistry'?"

"That they did. Your friend is quick, Denny. Now, let me see if I can stump *you* with something you can't trick you way into."

Denny rubbed his hands together in anticipation, sometimes like he would hearing the theme song to *Fernwood Tonight,* the prime-time TV satire we often watched. The professor walked to the blackboard diagonal to his desk, drumming his fingers on his lips on the way. His face turned into a time lapse of contemplation and gamesmanship, before chalking out an equation stretching from one side of his board to the other. Just thinking how to dent it gave me cottonmouth.

Done, the professor retreated a few paces to admire his challenge. I'd never seen a face light up like his, impish wonder fusing with a swashbuckler's confidence. Denny lasered in, bobbing his head, almost talking to himself, shuffling up to this Leviathan of numbers and symbols. (I later learned it involved molecular-level technology, whose potential to improve everything was only matched by its incomprehensibility to layman.)

While Denny confronted it, 1965's Nobel Prize winner timed him on his diver's watch.

"K, got it!" Denny said, ambling up to the board for his turn with the chalk. He performed some hasty calculations on the side and dashed out one hundred seventy-seven kilometers. He retraced his steps, then sidestepped toward his challenger. "You tried tripping me up with the exponent. I'm not falling for it."

Dr. Feynman pantomimed applause. "Correct. You mastered it in thirty seconds. You perused the grad-school textbook I lent you last time, didn't you, you skunk?"

"I noodled around with it, yeah."

"Not too shabby. It only took you twenty-three seconds longer than my best PhD candidate to solve this exact type of equation."

Denny wiggled his nose and raised his index finger. "Wait a sec. How long did you have the problem up on the board for him or her to think about first?"

The professor slapped his pant leg, and chuckled. "Ten minutes, give or take. See, this is why Caltech needs you. No variable slips by."

Denny, to my shock, curtsied. "Don't worry," he said. "I listed Caltech as my safety school."

"A safety school?" Dr. Feynman said sarcastically. "You're killing me. But I'm going to continue recruiting until the ink's dry on your admission papers. I've told Denny, Luke, that he's the boy who can see around corners and not to get big-headed about it. What subjects excite you? You'll find me embarrassingly remedial if it's outside my wheelhouse."

This wasn't true. He knew plenty about topics that interested me: the Soviet Union's invasion of Afghanistan, where Mr. Burr said Great Powers go to die; NASA's space shuttle project; and why LA still hadn't licked a smog problem that began well before I was born. As we chatted, Denny futzed around his office, picking up mementos and doodads, among them a vintage Geiger counter.

Dr. Feynman afterward asked if I minded if he and Denny stepped out in the hallway so he could hear in private "how his family was faring?" He told me to have at a bongo drum.

We left about ten minutes later, climbing down the same ladder we'd used to enter. I was sky-high that my new favorite Caltechian declared I could take myself "anywhere my curiosity and notepad lead me."

Denny, though, stood under a mounted light, looking anything but pumped. Buoyant at the chalkboard, he now plucked dust from his eyes, staring off into the forever-night down here.

"You ready to split?" he asked. "It's getting a little claustrophobic for me."

"What's wrong? You look bummed. Did he say something that got to you?"

He triple-clicked the flashlight to stall a reply. "*Nah*. It's not what he said. It's that he had to say anything at all."

I knew further questions would mean talking to a turtle retreated into its shell. We started walking back, Denny done shining his flashlight on curious things. The crash of footfalls and pitched voices behind us stopped me in my Pumas. I thought it was a Caltech security guard coming after us, or possibly something scarier; if it was the latter, I hoped Denny wasn't so morose he couldn't conk it with his flashlight.

Yet all that clamors isn't always sinister, and when he shone his flashlight on it from a distance, it reminded me of a floating genie surrounded by minions speaking to a turban. Closer to us, in the light cast from the bulb above a ladder past Dr. Feynman's office, Denny and I saw it wasn't someone on a magic carpet but a person in a backward Mount Waterman hat.

Then the clamor stopped, and with it, a grisly reality. Carl and RG were cradling Kyle, with their hands underneath his legs and his arms hooked around their necks. I could hear him groaning and babbling.

Denny put his flashlight on Kyle's face, and his pupils were dilated and black.

"He fell off the scaffolding by the wind tunnel," Carl explained, straining and winded. "They're doing repairs on it or something. He said he wanted to touch it because it was alive, and I grabbed him by the back of his shirt, but he still fell off the edge. It was a humongous drop, like two stories. His ankle: It's gnarly. Look."

Denny shifted his flashlight downward to Kyle's rolled-up pant leg, and I got a peek. That ankle wasn't for the squeamish: it was pink and bulging and the size of a baseball.

"The catwalk, while shrooming?" Denny said, irritated. "Why didn't you guys try to walk around a column on Suicide Bridge while you're at it?

"Pot meet kettle, space cadet," Carl yipped back. "You're not one to talk. None of us are tripping anymore, either. Not after we heard him land with a crack."

"What are you going to do?" I asked.

"Take him to Huntington," said RG, who was panting like Carl. "He needs a doctor."

"No, I don't," Kyle mumbled. "Just some ice, and I'll be mondo cool. But when did you guys grow antennas? *Uhhhhh.*"

CHAPTER SEVENTEEN
FREAK CLUB

Starving, I suddenly jonesed for a Bob's combo plate, both to satisfy my hunger as well as wind down from a tunnel adventure that expanded my horizons, even if it seemed to shrink my passenger's. He drooped in the car, unamused anymore that it sat illegally in our archrival's parking lot, not only dejected but, I don't know, decarbonated.

"Yeah, whatever," Denny said, absent his spark from an hour earlier. "Let's go."

We would, just not yet with us in such diverging headspaces, so I yanked the Celica key out of the ignition and dropped it in my lap. What better time than now, I realized, to do what I'd been wrestling with for a few months, and that was to trust him with the secret that I'd maintained for nine long years? "Random question," I said. "Did you ever see *The Day the Earth Stood Still?*"

Denny's heavy eyelids, aimed somewhere out the windshield, fluttered surprise. "That old flick? Yeah, like a million years ago. What does that have to do with a damn thing?"

"Because you're going to hear the day my Earth stopped."

He flicked the air vent with a prickly expression. "Spit out whatever you want to say," he gruffed. "I want this night to be over."

"Fine. You were right on Halloween when you said I was lying about how my mom died."

"No, duh," he replied, flicking my innocent air vent again. "It didn't take a polygraph to know that. You're a pretty terrible liar."

"Thanks, I think. Anyway, it wasn't a car accident on a foggy highway up in Ventura like I told everybody. She slipped in a bathroom at Bullock's picking up a pack of cigarettes and cracked her skull open on the floor. No one found her until it was too late. That's the long and short of it." I took a deep breath. "Would you want that advertised around school?"

Slowly, Denny turned toward me. "Not particularly."

For the following ten minutes, I fleshed in the details of my lowest of lows, details I'd entrusted to only one other person. Denny was dating her.

Six years before I arrived at Stone Canyon, my mom's Virginia-Slims addiction had threatened to leave her a divorcee in a house of smoke and cinder. Of all my father's beefs with her—the flash-fire temper, the disinterest in science, the oversleeping, those crosses and Bibles—cigarettes burning from morning coffee to bedtime reading was the most unbearable. The secondhand smoke scalded his throat, contaminated his clothes. When he did kiss her, he complained she had "sewer breath." When he didn't, the red-lipstick-stained butts littering ashtrays in multiple rooms reminded her why.

The morning of the day "it" happened began with her still asleep and him going through the house to round up every pack of Virginia Slims he could find, including her hiding spots for emergency packs in the backs of drawers. I watched while he ran all of them under the kitchen faucet and jammed them into the trash under the banana peels. Afterward, he set a pamphlet for a cold-turkey, smoking-cessation program down by the coffeepot.

Noticing the brochure when she shuffled into the kitchen in her bathrobe, my mom reacted predictably: she went apeshit without a single cigarette to calm herself.

"Dude, the way they screamed at each other, I thought our roof would cave in."

Fallen beams would've been preferable to what did collapse. My dad left for work to escape her meltdown, hoping she'd reconsider the pamphlet after she cooled off. But she didn't, and before the house stopped shaking, the doorbell rang; it was the older, neighbor-girl who babysat me. Mom, a moment later, hurried into my room, kissing the top of my fretting, little head. "All couples have arguments," she said in a voice hoarse from yelling. "Be a good boy until I'm back from errands. You never know what I might have for you."

A Bullock's customer found her dead in a pool of her own blood at noon.

She was sprawled inside the department store's Tea Room, upstairs from the main shopping area. Best that everyone could tell, she'd walked up the stairs there, since the ground-floor ladies' room had briefly flooded. After using a stall, she must've accidentally dropped her purse off the counter, and in bending down to retrieve it, whacked her head on the hard edge. Dizzy, she fell backward onto the unforgiving floor, conking her head with a bone-crushing force.

Inside her purse and Bullock's shopping bags, I told Denny, were reflections of her last-day-alive state of mind: a fresh pack of Virginia Slims she'd torn open, plus scarves, shoes, and blouses, price-tags still attached, probably to drive up her Mastercard bill that my dad was always on her about. They discovered five cartons of smokes, all purchased from Kloke's liquor store, in her car, and a pink box of deliciousness—buttercream vanilla cupcakes from Federico Bakery—to cheer me up by appealing to my sweet tooth.

"That's basically it," I said. "Now do you get why I bum out when you light up your Marlboros?"

Denny went from slouching to sitting up as my story Earth-skidding progressed. "Unfortunately."

If he appeared stunned, he was behind me. I'd unloaded all this without blubbering as I had to Eddy. Perhaps, after all this time, I'd cried the trolls of grief out of me.

"What happened?" he asked as I started the Celica, bound for a Bob's cheeseburger and cherry Coke.

"I just remember my dad taking me to a child psychologist because I guess I wasn't doing too hot. He had me draw pictures and play with sock puppets to force me to open up."

"Sock puppets? I'd want to punch them. But anything he say stick?"

"Not really. His message was that what happened to my mom would never happen to me. That's what he thought was my boogeyman, not walking around unsure where I was or feeling like I'd lost a body part."

Denny bunched his face. "To quote Carl, 'fucking-a.' That's a ton to hold in."

I got us moving north on Lake Avenue, driving past the department store I made a lifetime vow to never step foot in. "But I did start making a list afterward to remind myself of something. I used to carry it around in my wallet until the ink got all blurry."

"Of why you missed her?"

"No. I already knew that. My list was about the freaky ways that other people died. I was eight, nine."

"Freaky?" Denny's voice was coming out of its funk. "Too hard to say?"

"Nah, the opposite—it gave me comfort. Yeah, I turned into a bookworm, I guess to plug the emptiness. But I also became a fanatic about Ripley's Believe-It-or-Not, stuff like that. It was my way of saying, 'See, Bullock's Tea Room: You ain't so special.' Want to hear some examples?"

"Definitely."

In a few-minutes time, Denny learned about the ancient Athenian smothered by a pile of gifts from his grateful subjects, and the Byzantine emperor dragged sixteen miles through woodlands in the antlers of the deer he was hunting; about the public intellectual who laughed himself to death over a royal succession, and the defense attorney who accidentally shot himself demonstrating how guns unintentionally discharge. We both giggled about the French president who died during a mistress' blowjob, and the health fanatic who OD'd on vitamins and carrot juice. Sherwood Anderson, one of Mrs. Whitcomb's favorite writers, choked on a toothpick.

"All right," Denny said when I was done baring my soul. "See that payphone over there at the Mobil station. Stop and call your dad. Tell him you're spending the night at my house."

"Why?"

"You're not the only one with a freak story. And we can eat later."

—

We were westbound on the Foothill Freeway, heading for La Cañada, when Denny began confessing how his father's stood-up lunch date resulted in his house "going Hiroshima." Out the Toyota's windows, a soupy marine layer exiled the stars, pressing a spooky ceiling over cliffside Altadena and the lights sprinkling JPL.

Most times I'd been around his dad, he was in khakis and short-sleeve shirts, easygoing in his wire-rim glasses, always willing to let his opinionated kids dominate the conversation. He was taller than his sons, though just as lean, with reddish-brown hair thinning on top and an ever-present wry smile. I knew from Denny that the outdoors was his relief valve from family and work pressures. He'd take Saturday spins up Angeles Crest Highway on his Harley-Davidson and near-nightly jogs around fragrant Descanso Gardens. Aware I was a reader, Dr. Drummond talked books with me, joking he devoured Stephen

King for guilty pleasure and J.R.R. Tolkien, whose *Lord of the Rings* gave Bilbo his name, for imagination.

"Want to know the real reason I didn't go to the KISS concert with you guys last summer?" Denny asked. "It wasn't just because I hate those posers in makeup. I bailed because my family didn't know if we had to take dad to an asylum after the doozy he told us." He stared out of the window again, as if he were vacillating himself about opening up this box.

"And that doozy was?"

"I'm trying to figure out how to simplify it. One thing. Just hold off the ten-thousand questions until I do."

Denny's dad had received his Bachelor of Science in physics from Caltech, counting himself among Richard Feynman's most prized undergrads, and his doctorate there in geology, a more hands-on discipline. For years, Archie Drummond was a promising associate professor on tenure track. Yet when a better-paying, less-stressful administration job came open, he took it, leaving science, if only temporarily. A buck didn't buy what it used to when you had three kids in private school.

After July 2, 1979, nothing could buy what he'd lost.

Dr. D that day had his taste buds fired up for a lamb-kebab lunch plate from Burger Continental a short walk from Caltech's sleepy campus of nerdy, brilliant people. He ate there weekly if not more, and, for a trim person, could gorge himself like a sumo wrestler, easily putting away double skewers, heaps of buttery, Mediterranean rice, as well as hummus and grape leaves. (His fast-burning metabolism sounded similar to mine.) Of course, the exotic belly dancer shaking her hips for tips at the male clientele—the free side dish more than a few wives, supposedly, wanted off the menu—was another reason he dug Burger Continental.

"Things weren't perfect then," Denny explained. "Me and Daniel were fighting all the time, and mom was away more with her Republican Party cronies. But dad, he was our Rock of Gibraltar. When he got a fix for BC, though, it was watch out."

Dr. D knew someone else at Caltech infatuated with that spot and showed up to that man's classroom-lab to rendezvous for their planned lunch. Bizarrely, his ex-colleague, Dr. Petrus Visser, a geology professor never late for anything, wasn't there, and at first it was no sweat. While he waited, his dad basked in the room where he'd once taught grad-school classes alongside his affable, lambchop side-burned friend. It was nostalgia-time for him, inhaling the moldy scents of dug-up rocks. Sweeping his hands over Plexiglass boxes holding, Denny said, "every variety of stone you could think of, man, anthracite to verdite. I used to be play with them when visiting as a kid."

Once it got to 12:20, with a can't-miss meeting at 1:45, Dr. D decided he'd give his buddy another ten minutes until he'd walk over to BC by himself. It was then, bored and possibly stood-up, that he noticed that the machine that made him still pine for geology was all cued-up for an experiment.

"You know what a spectrometer is?" Denny asked.

"Not really."

"Didn't think so. It's like a magic-oven. Superheats objects to make them emit wavelengths so you know what's inside of them, chemically that is."

"I'll take your word for it."

"Caltech's famous for them. Used them on moon rocks, comets, bird fossils. When dad looked inside, there was a slab of rock in it. But just not any rock. It was this mysto one from Mexico that Eddy would love. Called the Esperanza Stone. Look it up. The superstitious Mayans claimed there was an inscription on it from God. Total bullshit; probably a meteorite. But some early-Pasadena guy, Charles Holder, brought a sample back and donated it to Caltech before it was the Caltech we know. Point is, whatever you believe about the stone, it was a major no-no for Petrus or anyone to be testing it, cuz it's supposed to be under strict lock and key as an antiquity."

No sooner had Dr. D realized that something was up (or afoul) than he recognized he wasn't alone in that vacant classroom. In a large mason jar, blocked before by three-ring binders on a metal table by the spectrometer, was a rat. A stupendously dead rat, to be exact. Denny said his dad hoisted the jar into the light, and its contents were as unappetizing as could be. Bloated torso, black patches on a decomposing stomach, stiff mouth ajar: your classic rigor mortis.

"It made zero sense," Denny said. "A rat corpse in a room devoted to rocks. But you know what also made no sense? My dad doing something on impulse, not by the book where you had to fill out forms in triplicate to even fart around the specimens. So, he ran the spectrometer just like normal. The rat coming back to life wasn't."

I almost choked on my saliva. "Back to life? *What?*"

"Yup. Crazy, huh? Something dad said was 'dead as a doornail' was running around inside the jar, or going up on its tiptoes like it wanted out. Nothing was rotting on it, either. In fact, it was more than healthy. Shiny, white fur, sharp eyes, springy feet. All impossible."

"Sounds so." I exited at Angeles Crest Highway, uncertain if I wanted to hear any more.

"Imagine being a man of science, a PhD confronting that?"

Denny said his father tumbled into speculation mode, suspecting it could've been the classroom fluorescents that made the rat appear dead before, and that it'd been positioned in the geology room as a gag. Still, when he checked the mason jar's lid, it was sealed airtight, so he questioned if the spectrometer's vibration shook the rat out of a low-oxygen coma or, alternatively, if he was in the middle of a vivid dream. Dr. D's last theory was the most fatalistic: an undiagnosed brain tumor was causing him to see things that weren't real.

"Were any of those it?"

"I wish, just not the brain-tumor part. After twenty minutes of running through every possibility, cursing to himself and getting emotional, which wasn't like him, dad said only one hypothesis held water. Ready?"

"How could I be?"

"Exactly. He'd resurrected a lab animal, either by himself or because of the stone and the spectrometer, and that the God he'd stopped believing in was giving him a golden opportunity."

—

We were now in my car at the curb outside his house, but Denny wasn't finished narrating how his earnest, high-IQ father became an unwitting Dr. Frankenstein.

"Mom got a call from a bartender at the 35er on Colorado; that's how we learned all this. It was three in the afternoon that day, and he told her to come pick him up because he was hammered and making a fool out of himself. Like going up to customers holding up a cage with the rat in it, asking them if they 'believed in miracles?' The bartender said the only miracle he needed was staying in business in a dogshit economy. The day after, dad convened a family meeting to give us the blow-by-blow. None of us believed a flippin' word of it."

"And that's how you lived all these months, in limbo?"

"I'll skip the crazier details, because we'd be here until sunup, but yeah, basically. During the day, dad was at Caltech. At night, it was all rat, all the time. Like wall-to-wall rat obsession in his study. At dinner, he'd say it was an incredible find that he had a responsibility to study. He thought it could be *the* next law of nature. And I shit you not, win him a Nobel. Nucking futs."

I swallow. "Jesus."

Dr. D, once a social drinker, afterward began drinking Tanqueray gin at alcoholic levels. At restaurants, it'd be multiple gin and tonics, then belligerence about handing over the car keys. Mortifying episodes at two Pasadena fixtures—the Greene Turtle by Parsons and Monty's Steakhouse on Fair Oaks—hardened the reality that Archie Drummond was going mad.

"Dad tried to pretend everything was normal, because that was mom's style. It wasn't. His work production went down the toilet. He stopped riding the Harley. But the fail-safe line? At a cocktail party for new faculty, he had one too many and cornered the school president. Said he needed to schedule a one-on-one with him about a 'phenomenal discovery.' He was slurring and begging. On Monday, *slit*. They fired him."

"They did?"

"Not a total disaster. He rents himself a one-room office below Bergee's doing business and insurance consulting. That part's OK because he's so damn good at it. After dark, that's when it gets whack, and he holes himself up with that thing. Some nights, he invites over biologist friends to examine it and performs experiments after they go. He said he's shot it up with chemicals that'd kill a hundred rats. On the bright side, he's not getting shitfaced in public anymore."

"Chemicals? Sorry, I'm know I supposed to wait to ask more questions."

"It's cool. Arsenic, cyanide, dioxin, actual rat poison. Dad's convinced himself the rat's unkillable. Claimed he cut the tip off its tail to measure coagulation and it grew back."

"I'm so confused. On numerous levels, honestly. But what did your dad's friend say? And what kind of name is Petrus?"

"Dutch. Specializes in crystals. Likes disgusting red herring. He told my mom he forgot about meeting Dad for lunch because he was down the hallway interrogating people about who left the dead rat in his room. He can't make a fuss, either. He knows dad busted him fiddling with the Esperanza Stone."

"Question on that."

"Don't bother asking—I can read your mind. Nobody thinks that rock or spectrometer had *anything* to do with this. Pure fantasy. Dad's been trying to replicate everything that happened, but that takes cooperation from Caltech, and that ain't happening anytime soon....You're the first one outside the family and his friends to know. Who'd believe it?"

I turned on the Celica's fan to get air blowing. "You're getting it in stereo," I said. "Eddy's past life, this. All the Big Man you don't want."

"Nice try for a laugh, but face the facts, Luke. They're two good people with mental problems. Eddy's a girl who had leukemia telling herself stories; dad's gone off the deep end. A psychologist we badgered him to see diagnosed midlife crisis. He never went back. A week at Betty Ford rehab? No change with the Tanqueray."

"And your mom?"

"What about her? They're not sleeping in the same room. Half the time I don't even know where she is. They'll probably wind up divorced, lonely, popping pills. Maybe joining a cult."

"Don't say that. It can't be that bad."

"Oh, it can't?"

—

Much as I worried my system couldn't absorb anymore, I knew I couldn't be another of Denny's missing persons. Under a dark, foggy sky flirting with mist, I schlepped behind him for the second time tonight, bundled in my corduroy jacket. Side gate into the backyard, past his mother's color-coordinated patio set, around the corner outside his father's study: Denny had brought me here to meet his dad's alter ego.

Twenty-feet shy, he stopped to finish the briefing. "Every Friday night, if mom isn't here, it's his Sunday."

"His Sunday. I don't..."

"Keep it down," he said, lowering his voice. "He prays to the rat in case it's holy. Let that sink in."

"But you said he was experimenting on it?"

"He's hedging his bets. Science or God. I'm telling you, he's not all there."

We duck-walked, all quiet, up to the sliding-glass door casting a dull, yellow light into the spooky backyard. Denny kneeled down along the window's edge with a sort of practiced despair in his eyes, while I folded myself along the other side for the carnival sideshow I never asked to see. When my knee touched the cold concrete, I quaked, hoping I was never the object of someone else's morbid curiosity.

"Three minutes, k?" Denny murmured.

Can't it be two? Our only ally here were fishbowl optics letting us peer in while the interior glare kept Dr. D blind to our voyeurism. Whatever we'd glimpse, I knew it'd be tricky to unsee.

My initial view was lowest to the ground: a brass-plated, liquor-cart-turned-rat-care station. The lowest shelf was dedicated to food, packed with labeled Ziplock bags containing sesame seeds, grains, and alfalfa. The shelf above it grew more ominous, arrayed with syringes, cotton balls, lidocaine, and marked vials of poisons. On the cart's top were pads of tea-green graph paper, which my own dad bought in bulk at Fedco.

Nervously, I looked up toward the figure Denny predicted would "weird me out," while boils of Cool-Whip-like fog trickled around us. What I'd give to be back in those tunnels.

Then *he* came into view, angled forty-five-degrees from us, which was forty-five too many.

It's not every day, after all, you have courtside seats to a grown man with a doctorate staging a warped crucifixion of himself. The Dr. D I viewed through the window was a spinoff Jesus not martyred for our sins, nails pounded into limbs by Roman thugs, but spellbound by what he suspected could be a sacred critter. In his reverence for that possibility, he'd strapped himself to a greasy black cross propped against the wall, hands and feet harnessed in coarse, hiking ropes fastened into the wood. His sacramental vestments—green, crown of thorns trimmed from a small Christmas wreath, and nothing else on except for a pair of Ocean Pacific swim trunks—were equally cuckoo. He was moonstruck, too, attention glued forward, chanting something inaudible.

"He prays to the rat in case it's holy. Let that sink in."

My eyes floated up that direction, anticipating a lab rat similar to those with life sentences in Stone Canyon's bio lab. Forget that. This rat had the dimensions of a grown possum and Bruce Jenner's athleticism, galloping nonstop on a wheel in his wire-metal cage.

"Told you," Denny said low-voiced. "Is that fucked up or what?"

We could hear the wheel screech and see it blurring RPMs. Run, run, run, run: That's all the enormous rodent did, besides occasionally gazing over at the human apostle in thrall to him.

The Jesus my mom had taught me about promised the faithful an afterlife in his Father's kingdom. My friend's father had given the animal he'd yet to determine was supernatural or scientifically explainable a three-story palace perched midway up a floor-to-ceiling bookshelf. The cage with the wheel was the lobby, connected to a smoked-ocher, double-decker Habittrail-cage enclosure adapted for the rat's girth. In the penthouse was a straw bed, bowl of seeds, extra water dish, and fake miniature log. The Habittrail setup I once had for "Ouchie," my skin-puncturing hamster, was a gardener's shack in comparison.

For piety, there was a Virgin Mary candle with flickering blue flame by the cage.

"What's he saying?" I whispered. "I can't make it out."

Denny pointed to words written out on spectrometer-wavelength paper taped behind his father's head. I ratcheted my neck back to read it.

"And they came, not for Jesus' sake only, but that they might also see Lazarus, whom He raised from the dead." —John, 12:9.

———

"The cross, before you ask, is an old telephone pole he found at a dump," Denny said after we departed the shrine for a seat on the diving board over his azure-lit pool. "He paid a carpenter to haul it over in his truck, cut it down to size, sand it, everything. Even sanitize the bird shit."

Then I was alone on the diving board while Denny retrieved us "memory-cleansers." I hoped they were kick-ass because nothing, including the seared image of the smoking electrocuted kitty at football practice, rivaled Dr. D's demented portrait. He returned with a film canister of his homegrown, purple-haired bud, two apricot fruit roll-ups, and his dalmatian, Oscar, who understood his boy needed him. Denny toked hard, then handed me his ceramic, Yoda-face pipe.

"You weren't kidding when you said nucking futs." I took a puff, careful to blow the smoke upward to avoid crop-dusting Oscar. "But something you said before, that inside your house was Hiroshima. Is that too nosy to ask about?"

"You're always nosy, but I sucked you into this. My folks were never lovey-dovey. The way they battled over this, what they accused the other with, that was the mushroom cloud. I wasn't going to tell you this, but mom's more than emotionally checked out. There's this scumbag trying to get Reagan elected that I think she's having a…you know."

I dove in to spare him. "And your sister and brother. How are they handling this?"

Denny plucked himself off a strip of apricot roll, his comfort snack. "Worse than me," he said, chewing. "Denise was only home from Vassar for two weeks last summer before the war zone made backpacking across Europe sound tempting. But Daniel, everything was so much better between us. He'd stopped terrorizing me. No more playing chicken with burning cigarettes over our arms. Or black eyes."

"Freshman year, I remember. Your hoodie year."

"He used to harbor this grudge that dad favored me because we both loved science, and he had his heart set on being a moneygrubbing lawyer. Our junior year, though, after he left for UCLA, that's when he started acting like a big brother. It was rad. The rat broke the peace."

"Just what you needed."

"You're telling me. My dad didn't only get falling-down drunk at the Greene Turtle. He did it *the* night that Daniel's girlfriend's family happened to be eating there. Total in-your-face humiliation for him. He just dropped his fork and left. Literally. He walked home—all six miles worth."

Around 2:00 a.m. a few weeks after that, Denny said he was jarred awake by a noise outside his dad's recently deadbolted study. When he went to investigate, he caught Daniel trying to break in with a screwdriver. "He was going to free that furball outside and get dad back into rehab. I got him to stop by telling him dad might try to kill himself if his higher purpose was gone."

"That didn't end it, did it?"

"You be the judge. A couple days later, mom's in Sacramento, probably not alone. I'm asleep when Daniel bursts in around midnight. 'Get up,' he says. 'Meet your new friend.' I'm still yawning when he throws a fucking live snake on my blanket. I scream, but Dad's too blackout drunk to hear. Daniel flips on my lamp. It's a rattlesnake, a three-footer. That's it, I think: I'm dying because my big brother needs to lash out at someone. Seriously, I'm about to jump out the window when he says not to spaz—the snake's decapitated! Gosh, how sensitive of him. He makes me hold the headless thing while it writhed and wrapped itself tight around my arm until it died. Answer your question?"

Dots converge. "Wait, the rattles you got pissed at me finding, the same snake?"

"You mean snooped? Yeah, I retraced where Daniel buried it, shoveled it up, and cut off the rattles as a keepsake. Reminds me what I can survive. In his defense, he did apologize at Christmas. A Christmas where mom and dad bought us all separate presents."

"You say Hiroshima? I say Dark Side General Hospital. The professor knows all about this, doesn't he?"

"Yup. He's dropped by twice and called weekly. If he can't talk sense to him, it's all hopeless. That's what he wanted to talk to me about when we visited."

Off in the distance, in the rolling Verdugo Hills behind his house, a pack of coyotes howled and bayed chasing its dinner or merely frenzying itself. Oscar's half-deaf ears twitched at the jackals, and I packed a second bowl. Denny kicked at the pool's tranquil surface with a Converse.

"Oh my God," I said. "We forgot all about Kyle. You think he's OK?"

Denny exhaled. "I hope. But I'd trade him that ankle for this. I'm scared, dude. Somebody doesn't go downhill like this unless something's very wrong."

He twisted away choking up, sniffling in a way unheard of from Stone Canyon's space cadet, and knowing he wasn't touchy-feely, I kept hands off. When he swiveled around, any tears were replaced by a smile at the absurdity of all this, followed by a gallows laugh. Being on the freak wavelength, I got it, chuckling with him on the diving board, just not so loudly to, in Cheap Trick-ian philosophy, give ourselves away. Authority figures assuring us the world was our oyster sure had a convoluted way of leading by example.

We hit the sack around 1:00 a.m. after watching some Johnny Carson and Wally George, reiterating that tonight's mutual admissions were our state secrets. Before we switched off the set, we agreed on something we'd been batting around before tonight's drama—starting a rock band to play a few summer parties, both of us eager to remove ourselves from parents who were lost themselves.

It took me a while to fall asleep on his trundle bed, not because I could hear the rat-wheel spinning down the hall, but because Denny told me his dad had named the animal. Stupidly, I asked him what?

"Can you say Lazarat?"

CHAPTER EIGHTEEN
SEMI-GODS

A month from diplomas, we already had one foot out the door, or so it felt sitting across from Felix Rodrigo for an early-bird dinner at Super Antojitos, the hole-in-the-wall specializing in foot-long, red-sauce burritos. Carl and I were making good on our promise to treat him on this his sixty-third birthday; he'd made good to look the other way when we ordered ourselves Dos Equis, if we limited it to a single brew each.

Our longtime Spanish teacher, a dead ringer in his forties for the womanizing casino owner in *The Flying Nun*, toasted us over scorching white plates and cold cervezas. To Carl, an NYU-bound cinema major, he said break a leg "en la Gran Manzana." For *this* future UC Berkeley freshman, major undeclared, he said: "Show those bomb-throwing liberals how to conjugate the subjunctive like a scholar. They could use it."

In his camel-hair leisure jacket and pressed brown slacks, Mr. Rodrigo had clung to his sixties' fashion sensibility into the precipice of the eighties. For years, he'd been Stone Canyon's language workhorse, teaching Spanish, French, and Latin, overseeing the department, even coaching tennis on the side. But Father Time was catching up, slowing his walk, silvering his hair. Most strikingly, it'd flattened his once-playful nature, where he'd only tease thumping us if we misbehaved, and, sometimes, given us a hothead, old man we didn't recognize.

For me at least, our *profesora de espanol* still had his tidy, pencil-parted mustache and golden voice—clues the suave Spaniard I met as a freshman was in there someplace. Carl and I, on this Monday in early May, had a plan counting on that. We'd pose Mr. Rodrigo million-dollar questions he could freely answer, now that we were short-timers.

Life as a Stone Canyon teacher?: "generally rewarding"; whether the class of '80 was as exceptional as the legend in our minds?: "Yes, until the class of

'81 rolls around"; whether he worried US troops, including possibly us as new draftees, would be shipped off to fight in Nicaragua, where a communist was just elected president?: "Well, it's not a zero percent chance because Carter's such a weakling, but we still have our Vietnam hangover, so I don't expect you'll be learning to fire an M-16."

Carl and I clinked Dos Equis to that.

"But let me ask you two something. Any reaction to the new teachers your headmaster continues to recruit? They as good as us dinosaurs with fountain pens?"

Our headmaster? Surprised, we answered that we preferred veterans like him and Mr. Burr.

"That's refreshing to hear because I'm not ready to be put out to pasture; I can't afford to with my wife being like she is. I'm not ready to say *buenas dias* to all you stupid burros, either.

I bumped Carl's shoe under the table. Since Mr. Rodrigo rarely spoke about his wife, the grapevine did, rumormongering she was either an invalid slowly dying from a degenerative brain disease or was his fictional spouse concocted for sympathy. Now, us two burros knew what few else did.

———

We were tandem again Tuesday for our next rite of sub-god status. This time, it was on top of desks, wearing paper crowns in the preposterous tradition for yearbook editors presiding over their final meeting. Spread below us were eight of our nine fellow club members, plus faculty adviser Harvey Burr, springy in his Colonel Sanders suit. Ten seconds of lively clapping for us was touching. The ten additional seconds was toady overkill.

Carl and I bowed quickly and hopped down quicker, crumpling our headwear.

"Don't forget, people, this was our inaugural year having co-editors," Mr. Burr said while we stood there, all awkward. "A successful experiment in a year of change, I say, and one of our best yearbooks ever. Of course, it's no co-hinky-dink that I was supervising."

Laughter, authentic and courtesy, did a lap around the drab, lower-school room where our JV football coach had taught us ancient history with gruff joy. In appreciation, I passed around, in this bunker under the bio lab, a box of Winchell's doughnuts. While I did, Carl quick-hugged Mr. Burr, a reputed germaphobe.

You could get wistful in these waning days, wondering if any college professor would be as influential as someone like Mr. Burr. Not every teacher tacked up revolving "Great Minds" posters or packed their pipe with Old-World care, nor termed the Founding Fathers "imperfect geniuses" and democracy "more fragile than we appreciate."

Nor was everyone as impassioned about decorum, as a memorable digression last week highlighted. Eddy, class bleeding heart, had said the Turner Thesis "whitewashed settler mass-murder against Indians," spinning plunder into something heroic. More than even her Pasadena-past-life story, she'd kicked the hornet's nest, upending a class where half the kids came from conservative families that idolized John Wayne.

Mr. Burr flailed his short arms, trying to halt everyone from squawking over one another. *"Order, order,"* he said. "Has Walter Lippmann, my lodestar, taught you nothing? 'When all men think alike, no one thinks very much.' Disagree civilly."

Nobody heeded his Walter-Lippmann-admonition on account of the proceeding thing to come out of his mouth. Mr. Burr's top dentures had not only broken loose from the roof of his Polident-caulked gumline. The force with which he'd yelled had caused them to shoot past his lips and onto the desk of a dumbfounded Cindy, who scurried out of her chair at the sight of his fake teeth. Campus laugh-track when it happened, mainly forgotten now, just not by sentimental me.

Today's lessons were of the more practical sort. Yearbook production was good for the landfill business, and wrap parties like this also functioned as unpaid cleanup jobs. I tore open a box of Hefty garbage bags; Mr. Burr prepared to make himself scarce.

"I'll leave you two feudal lords with your serfs," he said. "I have your finals to plot."

We put our backs into the tidying-up for twenty minutes, hacking on dust and hurling things with sweaty hands. We dragged over the larger-ticket items—the bent "guillotine" paper-trimmer and battered IBM Selectric typewriter with torqued space bar and Wite-Out stains. We rounded up the rejected photos, shredded, spaghetti edges, spent markers, and empty Elmer's Glue and Scotch Tape. A one-hundred-seventy-page, ad-supported yearbook doesn't paginate itself. Ten plump Hefty bags attested to that.

Everyone here was laboring for the cause, including my freshman "buddy" Nick Chance, everyone except for one absent member. It's not like Denny was tied up with sports because he didn't play any, or was at the final Stanley Kubrick Appreciation Club meeting slated for next week. Exasperating. Alarming. Since that revelatory March night that began in the Caltech tunnels, this had been his pattern. He'd become flakier about showing up when required while his moods remained a roll of the dice. Eddy confided she frequently had little idea where he went after school, "but it probably wasn't good."

More than his opposites-attract girlfriend, he was consistent in one facet. He'd voice the quiet part out loud. Like a social-studies discussion last week over America's most precious metal. Gold and silver were the class consensus. "Au contraire," he replied from his back-row redoubt. "It's plutonium, you know, for our warheads."

When the hydraulic door now groaned, Carl and I expected a contrite him to materialize. Nope, it was Mr. Pike, and he acted hesitant about entering. A sharp curl of the hand drew me to the transom, and I quickly knew why he wouldn't come in. From five feet away, his breath was a jet fuel of Wrigley's Spearmint and whiskey.

"Luke, when did the printer say it'll deliver the finished products?" he asked, a little marble-mouthed. "I need a carton for the board before a presentation. And I mean *need!*"

"It's a six-week turnaround, so by finals week they should be in." I tried not whiffing that mint-cut Jack Daniels tailing his words.

Before responding, he did something I'd never seen. He turned his head sideways and spat his Wrigley's into the hedges like it was a perfectly normal thing for a prep-school headmaster to do. "You come tell me, post haste, if anything changes. I'll straighten them out." No goodbye when he spun and left.

For the better part of a year and a half, Mr. Pike's daytime drinking was the subject that never grew old, both for the spectacle and sheer obviousness of it. A carload of gutsy seniors in the class of '79 had actually photographed him staggering out of Remy's Bar-and-Grill up Foothill—thirty-five-millimeter evidence that the man who patrolled the hallways and parking lots for rule-breaking mischief was a ruddy-cheeked moralizer who preached sobriety while liquored up.

None of those smoking-gun photos were shared with us, nor did they need to be. If Mr. Pike believed he could fake sobriety by relying on gum and a capacity to "maintain," he was stealing from our playbook. Still, no adult should be garbling his words or tripping on smooth concrete before 10:00 a.m.

But there was the Big Why, as in why someone who'd rescued a school from bankruptcy, raised a bundle to get us air conditioning, and introduced a gender revolution required a flask? The conjecture was tabloid-y, juicy, and somehow believable. Mr. Pike, the grapevine said, was trapped in an unhappy marriage to a jealous wife. A wife who'd apparently insisted he accept a West Coast job, after catching him at a trashy Bangor, Maine motel with a secretary at his previous school, or she'd divorce him for all he was worth. Three years ago, after reportedly spotting him talking with the gorgeous Mrs. John, she threw such a hissy fit in the clapboard home provided to the headmaster's family, that people outside could hear it.

Mr. Pike's purgatory beverage of choice: Jack Daniels or some facsimile.

As freshman, we caricatured authority-figures. As sophomores—roll Easter ski trip to Mammoth chaperoned by Darren Rucks, Mrs. John's twenty-eight-year-old replacement, who only got mad at our partying when we broke something—we capitalized on them. As juniors, aware our married art teacher ran off with a lesbian lover, we were titillated by them. Now as seniors, deluding ourselves we'd seen everything, we were jaundiced by it.

The firing of varsity football coach Bucky Mullins, the redneck who'd only been here since September, was a comeuppance that was personally gratifying. Because nothing stayed secret in this fenced-in acreage, we'd heard the Baton Rouge DA's office had issued warrants on him for gambling debts *and* assaulting an ex-player. Imagine that? At other schools, this would've qualified as long-lasting infamy. For us, a "Pearls Before Swine" yearbook entry.

When Denny slinked in five minutes before the bell, Carl flashed him a *where-were-you?* shrug while I slapped an empty Hefty bag in his arms. "Not a fantastic time," I said, "for your vanishing act. We've been busting our humps. Where were you?"

Denny's crooked grin was worrying. "Doing my patriotic duty," he said. "But I should've watched the time better."

"Patriotic duty? Do I want to know?"

"Probably not."

"I thought you backed away from that stuff. College ahead and all."

"I'll answer like a scumbag politician. No comment."

—

That same day, post soccer practice, I was back where I'd been so often, soaking in Carl's popular jacuzzi on La Cañada's not-so-storybook Beulah Drive. The company with us was once a regular here until a girl drove him off. I'd asked Carl if we could invite Rupert, assuming it'd be a sales job, and he stunned me by saying yes. Rupert did it again by agreeing.

Hot-tub jets blasting, I fancied myself as peacemaker and hoped to soften up the two combatants with my own running battles. "We've had some big fights at dinner, but this was Ali-Frazier," I said. "Charlotte was so scared she ate in her room. My dad said he'd withhold my tuition if I didn't enroll as an econ major. But I told him it's my life. *Mine.* He said, I quote, 'our negotiations aren't over by a long shot.'"

"Negotiations?" asked Rupert, beside me in a borrowed pair of Carl's Bahama trunks. "Your dad giving you a calculator for graduation?"

"The joke's on him. I'm making my living with a keyboard."

Crapshoot on what Rupert would receive at graduation. His cash-strapped parents were relocating to the Houston area, where his dad was lucky NASA hired him for its space shuttle program before JPL layoffs hit. The constant shuffling and money anxieties, I knew, left Rupert feeling the nomad. And because of Carl's hormones, he didn't even have a blonde, blue-eye-shade girlfriend to take his mind off his rootless base camp.

What Rupert did have was a toehold as a programmer, someone quick to understand the brute logic of computers eluding many of us. Only Denny, who'd puckishly unplug the computer-lab monitors if a lippy freshmen or junior-higher was bogarting them, blew through assignments faster. Here's the rub, though. Even excelling in the class I reviled—trigonometry by BASIC-computer language, which had to be a Geneva Convention violation—Rupert had no sanctuary.

Weeks earlier, our first-year teacher Eli Adler, who'd ignored the faculty's "senioritis" policy of reducing workloads in our final semester, had tried burning him at the stake in front of all of us. Rupert's perennially red eyes?: Proof, Mr. Adler said, he was a "pothead disrespecting everyone by toking before class." His daily sandals?: "what degenerates wear."

"Do us a favor," he said in his smear-job. "Drop out and enlist. The Army could use fresh meat as cannon fodder."

Nobody had told Arnold Horshack's thirty-year-old version—pocket-protector, dorkified glasses—that smog allergies enflamed Rupert's eyes, and that flip-flops were permissible. Or that the student he ridiculed had been accepted into elite Carnegie Mellon University but would be attending the cheaper University of Texas. How Rupert lasted that day without erupting was inspiring. How Mr. Adler drove home on tires that weren't slashed by us was miraculous.

But everything was calm now, if miles from warm and fuzzy, as Carl and Rupert chatted directly for the first time in months. *Protect the brotherhood. Mend it on "remember-when" lane.* This dreamer was proud of himself. When someone rapped on the swing gate into Carl's yard, I figured it was erratic Denny crashing my bid at jacuzzi detente. No glitch there.

"Oh, I didn't realize you three were together." It was Cindy, flummoxed by the scene after she'd stuck her head over the posts. "Carl, uh, I…I'm dropping off your copy of *Ordinary People* for English. I bought my own. I'll see you… uh…whenever. Bye."

Leery smile erased, Rupert didn't wait for Cindy's VW to chug off to fume at Carl. "You did that to rub it in, didn't you? The only thing I asked was not to flaunt your relationship when I'm around, but you had to score points." Even Rupert's mustache, a bad-hombre growth on the gentlest of people, bristled.

Carl's square, recently goateed face, which I joked had taken him from Brian Wilson to Bob Seger, was unsympathetic. "Quit acting so butt-hurt—I didn't know she was coming over," he said. "Let's not rewrite history, either. I didn't poach her from you. She came on to *me*."

Possible boy-on-boy violence from there. Rupert was no Moses, but his hands parted the hot tub's foamy waters to get close enough to give Carl a throttling. His counterpart put up his dukes like in an old-fashioned fisticuffs, neither of them natural fighters. I had to do something before someone was bleeding, so I grabbed Rupert under the armpits from behind to restrain him. His six-foot frame threw me off. I went for his arms again with much worse timing. Just as I thought I had him, he threw his right elbow back to cold cock Carl, but my jaw stopped that with a wicked shot that made my brain rattle around in its housing.

"*Damn*, Rupert," I said, testing if my jaw could still hinge. The hostilities paused while he and Carl processed the third-party damage. "This what a guy gets trying to get you two to make up?"

"Luke," he replied with an anguished face. "You all right? You know that was an accident."

"Yeah, yeah. Still."

Rupert hopped out of the jacuzzi before I could see straight, disappearing into the Drummond's house, presumably to change, and moments later, we heard his car burn rubber off Beulah Drive. History, Mr. Burr reminded us, doesn't always repeat, but usually rhymes, and for Rupert, his rhyme was being left out in the cold again.

—

Stakes high, villains close, it was so earsplitting inside our gym that you couldn't hear the perpetual white noise from the Foothill Freeway pulsing overhead. Five-hundred-or-so strong, our foot-stomping home crowd shook the retractable bleachers with every swish of the basket, every tenacious rebound. The electricity was unmistakable: This could be Stone Canyon's year.

Everyone was contributing. Neil Katz, campus's ultimate survivor, Occidental College in his future, broadcasted the game from the scorers' table with verve. Our cheerleaders, led by Cindy, were peppy Rockettes, scissor-kicking and pom-pom shimmying themselves breathless. The best team in years deserved no less for this first-round CIF playoff game against heinous Poly, a two-for-one opportunity that wasn't just another athletic brick in our wall.

Each time RG, our All-League point guard, drained another twenty-footer from the key, we erupted.

"Hey, hey, ho, ho, Poly's got to go," our cheerleaders yelled. *"The black-and-silver's on a roll."*

"Another moon shot," Neil would add, wedding RG's last name to his hot shooting hand.

Mr. Pike was seated mid-bleacher, below Denny, Eddy, and me up where the grandstands meet cinder block. Never has someone who had done so much for a place appeared to cherish it so little. His indecipherable expression, hands clasped behind back when not puffing Marlboros on campus strolls, made him the hardest book on campus to read, and we'd read like fiends. Sometimes I wondered what the disaffected Holden Caulfield would say about him that we didn't.

"Foul on Poly," Neil oozed into the mic. "Free throws for Stone Can-*yooon*."

A roar went up. The cheerleaders chanted. *"Hey, hey, ho, ho, Poly's defense moves slow-mo."*

Mr. Pike's reaction through eighteen minutes of action? Two claps and a sweep of the hair.

ZZZZZZ. Our piercing airhorn buzzer, also manned by Neil, was a sweet refrain. "The halftime score is…*your* Stone Can-yoon Mountaineers thirty-two, Poly seventeen. Refreshments outside."

Our boys trotted off the floor, arms raised to a standing ovation for a captivating performance. Then it was the wooden march of spectators' shoes streaming toward bathrooms and snack tables. The invasion of people's hyper little brothers and sisters onto the court for games of pickup and horse kept the zoo-like atmosphere going. Never much of a basketball fan, and even worse player, prone to clumsily dribbling off my high-tops, I still recognized the teams' differing intensities. We were radiating sheer want-to, hustling for loose balls, running the floor like we had afterburners in our sneakers. Poly's Nikes seemed fabricated from lead.

We hung back from the stampede, opting for scene-watching and plan-making. While Eddy and Denny talked postgame taco run, I couldn't help but watch Mr. Rodrigo by himself under the westerly basket, back from those boisterous kiddies hijacking the court. Worry lined his face, and he intermittently stared over at Mr. Pike as if he was the reason. I had a hunch, a hunch based on something he'd said near the end of his birthday dinner. It was about how he "might soon be an endangered species because of a few, isolated incidents."

A February "incident" might've already guaranteed that. We'd been reading passages of *Don Quixote* in Spanish when Kyle laughed. That's all. Mr. Rodrigo didn't warn him; didn't ask what was so humorous? He charged down the aisle like a Pamplona bull and slapped Kyle across the face with an open hand, saying, "I've had it with you, Hartsung." Kyle would've had every right to retaliate, but he packed up and left before his reactor core melted. Soon after, Kyle recounted, Mr. Pike walked by, inquiring what he was doing on the Senior Lawn when he should be in class. Kyle pointed to the red outlines of a hand mark across his cheek.

Perhaps, Carl and I should've thought twice about treating Mr. Rodrigo to burritos and beer after he cuffed our pal, instead of keeping the meal on the QT and telling ourselves we couldn't squander the precious chance to hear the inside dope from such a campus fixture. Yet that was weeks ago, so maybe something else embarrassing had motivated him to stand alone in apparent self-exile. It was the same way during the first half, him alone moping by the side of the bleachers, a multilingual outcast in pressed slacks and dull eyes.

Felix Rodrigo: donde esta tu viejo encantador? Unless that charming self was all an act.

"Hey, anyone, some help here? I need to drain the main vein." It was Kyle, fittingly, interrupting my armchair-detective work, calling out to friends in proximity.

Carl and I maneuvered over to where he sat, ankle casted after tumbling off that Caltech scaffolding, and helped him down the tricky steps. Carl then ambled over to Cindy, whispering something that made her giggle.

It was no "co-hinky-dink" moments later, when I stepped outside to size up the popcorn-Pepsi line, that Rupert cupped my shoulder. He was checking in on my achy jaw—for the tenth time—and about to split; too much Cindy-Carl for his Mountaineer spirit. "You up for a hike Sunday?" he asked. "Eaton Canyon waterfall?"

"Definitely," I said. "You sure you don't want to stick around for the second half?"

"I'm sure. I'll buzz you Sunday morning."

So much for my hot-tub truce. I returned to a grandstand scattered with wallflowers, misfits, creaky grandparents, and faculty. Up in the cheap seats where I'd been, Denny and Eddy hardly acknowledged me, preoccupied by their flirty spat. Denny was arguing he deserved a parking-lot cigarette, having cut back to three Marlboro's a day under Eddy's influence. She said, after goosing him in the ribs, that he could smoke to his heart's content; he just wouldn't be planting his "tobacco mouth" on her afterward. I wanted to barf.

Across the court at the scorer's table, tracking Neil was less nauseating entertainment. Reviewing stats and game notes on a clipboard, holding his head up without flinching about who had him in their crosshairs, he was Mini Mouse no more. He was still missing a verbal filter, but who wasn't missing something? I waved at him, and he waved back with an innocence the brutes couldn't beat out of him. He tooted a pair of airhorn blasts signaling five minutes before play resumed.

A dozen Poly players lopped out from the locker room, robotically lining up for a layup drill. Our team, I reasoned, hung back for the gamesmanship or an extended pep talk for the most consequential second half of hoops in forever.

Given that, I hadn't expected Joe Mendoza, our olive-skinned, feather-haired assistant basketball coach, to materialize first. Or that he'd fast-walk toward the bleachers with an anxious expression. At the first row, this young, Latino hire angled his hand as a visor, searching for somebody deeper in. How many else noticed I don't know, but he took the steps two at a time after he'd spotted Mr. Pike.

He greeted whatever rapid-fire news Mr. Mendoza delivered calmly, as if hearing about a paperwork snafu. Also listening in was Mr. Pike's semi-pervy associate dean of students, a demonstrable leer-er in a cardigan and tortoise-shell glasses. Message received, our headmaster departed the bleachers, walking at a normal clip alongside Mr. Mendoza into the bowels of the gym.

But Mr. Mendoza was soon back at grandstands' edge, hand-visoring for someone else. It took him longer this time to pick out the face he needed. Fifteen seconds of hearing him out was all Brian Tollner's father, a doctor at Huntington Hospital, needed. He hustled into the locker room in suit and tie, unconcerned about any subtlety.

With the crowd straggling in and Poly players circling their coach for adjustments, Mr. Pike reemerged maybe two minutes later, making a beeline not for the stands but for the scorer's table. He gestured at Neil, who handed him the microphone out of its silver cradle and walked out to center court for the announcement nobody saw coming.

"Everyone," he said, "may I please have your attention? And can folks near the doors ask those outside to step inside to listen? I'd appreciate it."

He stood there, mic in hand, as fifty or so spectators filed in, taking seats or standing by the double-door exits. I gazed at Eddy, who looked at Denny, whose eyes began to dart.

"I'm afraid I have some bad news," Mr. Pike said, subdued as an undertaker. "Apparently, half our team has contracted a severe stomach bug, probably from eating the same bad chow. It wouldn't be fair to them, or to the good people at Poly, to force them to compete when they're incapacitated. League rules, devastating as this is to say, require that Stone Canyon forfeit the game. We'll release more information when it becomes available. Drive home safely."

He gave the chrome mic back to a gape-mouthed Neil and returned, bearing upright, to the locker room.

Hot on his heels was a crescendo of booing, hissing, and mass grumbling. "I call bullshit," a Poly fan hollered. "I call Poly dirty trick," a Stone Canyon fan hollered back. Players' parents were less vocal, rushing across the floor toward the doors separating it from the dressing rooms and banging on them for entry. Cindy, meanwhile, huddled with the other dejected cheerleaders, having them drop their pompoms into a sparkly pile.

There went the season. There went aspirations for a championship payback.

And there went Denny, tugging his Stanford hoodie over his head, telling Eddy the lights gave him a bad headache, and head-flicking me a goodbye.

Soon, the wail of ambulances barreling into the lower-school parking lot drowned out everything. There'd be no more moon shots tonight.

CHAPTER NINETEEN
CAFFEINE GATE

I was seething red, with pals in the hospital, sirens in my ears, and the little culprit on the other end of the phone. "You're involved, aren't you?" I pressed him later that evening from my black-leather reading chair. "You always are. It's your MO."

"Those retards," Denny replied. "I gave them specific instructions. They were only supposed to swirl in a pinch....Hope those aren't famous last words."

Whatever those words were, they sounded more irked than panicked. Through them, I'd learn how good intentions became a misguided scheme, kept from me on a need-to-know basis.

The first takeaway: RG was the prime instigator, desperate to beat Poly for only the second time in eight tries, and with a UCI recruiter in the stands evaluating him. As good a season as we had, he wanted the team to have an edge, a secret weapon that'd bring home a banner over those Nancies in orange-and-white.

Consequently, at a school that emphasized chemistry, teaching kids well-acquainted with recreational chemicals themselves, RG consulted the brainiest boy in Oz.

Short of popping Black Beauties, Denny said he might have the perfect solution, speed that was both safe and attainable. "And you won't have to buy it from some sketchy, back-alley drug dealer, either," he told RG. Fritz Mueller, the thick-tongued German chemistry teacher who'd unretired from Lockheed Corporation to teach here, the one Denny fooled to write out the LSD formula, had taken care of that. Mr. Mueller, it seemed, preserved a large sample of the goods in a Tupperware container in his cabinet.

"Stoked," RG said. "How soon can you get it?"

This close to graduation, Denny said *he* wouldn't be getting anything. But, as long as he had no direct fingerprints, he'd help engineer the break-in.

And that he did, escorting RG by the chemistry room, telling how to jimmy the door open with a screwdriver at night, diagramming where the performance-boosters were. He'd research the proper dosage for caffeine-jolts later.

"I may not show it, but I'm tired of Poly eating our lunch," Denny said at conversation's end. "That's why I was late to the Yearbook Club cleanup. Once he's better, I'll call RG to get our stories straight. I can't take the fall because that dude blows at math."

Ironically enough, that same dude phoned me early Saturday evening, describing the team overdose in a frail voice. "I'm not drinking coffee until I'm thirty," was the first thing he said.

RG described a hyped-up locker room, with Zeppelin's "Achilles Last Stand," everyone's favorite pre-game song, belting out of a ghetto-blaster. While Coach Hoover sat in his tiny office, fine-tuning his game plan, RG was in a bathroom stall with three other starters. There, he dumped crystallized, caffeine powder kept in wax paper into Gatorade bottles purchased at Alcorn Liquor. Everyone afterward was hopping around, high-fiving, shouting slogans, champing for the opening whistle.

By halftime, though, it became a MASH unit in there. The caffeine-users had run off the court and proceeded, one after the other, to drop onto the cold floor. All their symptoms overlapped. They curled into fetal positions with intestine-twisting stomach cramps. They struggled to catch their breaths from accelerated heart rates. Two foamed at the mouth.

"Coach Hoover didn't know what to do, and he always knows what to do," RG said. "The absolute worst was that ambulance." He'd been on a gurney, speeding toward Huntington beside Brian, who had the longest neck in class and was the team's best power forward. Brian's dad rode along, guaranteeing them they'd be OK. But a son going into sudden cardiac arrest, requiring his father to shock his heart back into normal rhythm by electric paddles, wasn't OK. It was life-or-death borne by hoop dreams.

"Scariest moment of my life," RG confided. "I can't get the sound of those paddles out of my head."

"Sheesh. How much caffeine did you have in your system?"

"The doctor estimated twenty-five cups. Two grams worth or something."

"Two grams? What were you thinking?"

"I wasn't. Brian had like eighty cups in him. Denny said to measure out everything so we'd have enough to last through the whole playoffs. Seven games, if we kept winning. I guess we overdid it."

"Understatement of the century. What'd they put you through at Huntington?

I'm sorry I asked. RG said his breathing problems turned into an asthma attack in the ER, and he passed out. When he woke up groggy in a private room, he had a stomach tube down his throat and an IV in his arm, feeling "like a mummy." The tube delivered activated charcoal to sponge up the caffeine. The IV contained barbiturates (Benzos) to lower his racing heartbeat.

After the tube was removed, RG said he had to immediately fend off an avalanche of questions from parents both exhaling and furious. By the time he got home to his Linda Vista bedroom, surrounded by his drum set and phalanx of athletic trophies, Mr. Pike was bearing down.

Right off the bat, he knew it wasn't salmonella poisoning that sickened eighty percent of our starting lineup, as he suggested to a *Pasadena Star-News* reporter sniffing around about why the high-stakes game was forfeited. Mr. Pike sensed there was something fishy behind this, and in a hardball conversation with RG's dad, which RG listened in on from the other line, stated he'd "have no trouble collecting damning evidence meriting expulsion." He was already aware of missing caffeine and claimed someone had seen RG and Denny "casing" the chemistry room.

"Pike was on a rampage," RG continued. "He said if I didn't confess first thing Monday, I could forget about any scholarship offers and enroll in junior college because I wasn't smart enough for any Ivy League schools. Screw him. But my dad, he threw a nasty pick."

Yes, he did. Without a direct witness of his son pilfering the caffeine, RG's father told Mr. Pike, he had no case for expulsion. If he tried, he'd hire a shark of an attorney and sue Stone Canyon for failure to secure dangerous chemicals around minors. It'd happened before—with the lye. Something about a pattern of gross negligence.

"That shut Pike up," RG said. "So did my dad telling him he ought to go after the kid whose brainstorm this all was. I didn't know he'd try dumping it all on Denny to get me off the hook. It's gnarly. Never say anything, okay?"

"Fucking-a! Tangled web."

"And thing was, we probably didn't need any speed to beat Poly. Like that matters now."

———

His office, down a shabby hallway in a building slated for replacement, was a mishmash of used furniture that should've had a date with the county dump. The walnut desk had a white, replacement leg; the mismatched credenza begged for a lacquer job. Aside from a dated family photo and his mounted lacrosse stick, the room revealed little about its occupant, a man many regarded as a dour tyrant, others as our chain-smoking, school-turnaround artist.

The one incontrovertible fact: Mr. Pike was irate at the class of '80.

Crisscrossing weekend calls made plain he was taking "Caffeine Gate" personally. Like it'd robbed him of athletic bragging rights and fundraising ammo for this summer's $2 million pledge drive. The humiliation element he faced inside that full, energized gym went unstated.

I'd expected a tap on the shoulder from him, as others had been tapped for their grilling. Regardless, it was still a shock to the system when he did as classes let out on Monday.

He met me at the solid-core door, the one installed after Roland eavesdropped through his previous, paper-thin one, in a backup houndstooth coat. A fingers-crushing handshake later, I was on a cloth cushion, interrogation seat I'd largely managed to avoid for four years.

He's got nothing on you. So I reminded myself as he pulled up an adjoining guest chair by me and lit a Marlboro. He had the heat running on a seventy-eight-degree day. Why did I think he could've made a casting call for a funeral director?

"Luke, you probably know why I wanted to speak privately."

"I do. But before you…"

He cut me off. "I don't remember granting you permission to talk yet. Do you?"

"No, sir."

"Sir? Drop the choirboy act. This will go faster if you do."

"Yes, Mr. Pike."

"Let's get right to it. These are the things we know. Your good friend, Denny Drummond, assisted another close friend of yours, RG Moon, to bust into the chemistry lab and steal an enormous quantity of caffeine. We're quite fortunate it didn't kill any of our players. Now you may speak."

I did, too quickly. "If you know so much, why do you need me?" I crossed my legs to prevent my nervous foot from incriminating tapping.

"Fair question, fair question," he answered, that glower transforming into good-cop smile. "The guilty are pleading the fifth. Others are as well. I expect much more out of you."

Flattery as truth serum. "But I don't know everything that happened," I said, giving myself an out on that umbrella word, everything. "I won't make something up. Didn't Socrates say…"

Mr. Pike banged his armrest. "Stop trying to wriggle your way out of this, son, for both our sakes." He stabbed out his ciggy and dragged his chair closer for the next turning of his screw. "Socrates isn't in danger of not walking for graduation like you. Or having his transcripts flagged, Mr. Future Cal Bear."

"But you're asking the wrong person," I faux-protested. "I feel awful about what happened. Plus, forfeiting to Poly."

He used that adjective against me. "Then you must also feel awful that there are people who saw Denny sitting by *you* at the gym before the hubbub began, and people who saw him slither away when it did. You still want to maintain your Sergeant Schultz stance?"

Do something. "Denny had a headache or something. He said he didn't feel good."

"I'm sure he didn't. Knowing what he caused. Denny's got a brilliant mind, no one questions that, but he's not immune from consequences. Not this time. Boys were flopping around like fish on the locker-room floor because of him. Headache? Don't try my patience. Now, let's return to you."

He plucked a manila folder from his desk inbox, then held it up for my consumption. It was my official Stone Canyon transcript. I really was back at the Pit again, up against the lockers, waiting on an ultimatum. This bully-with-title traced a knobby finger down the summary page, flipping through the others, then rustling back.

"Overall, you've done well here. From a self-conscious, picked-on eighth-grader with braces to today, a fine student, Yearbook Club co-editor, Varsity soccer. Mrs. Whitcomb believes you have a real career in writing." *She does?* "But were you aware that several of your teachers consider you sneaky? Devious?"

That broke skin. "Um, no. They never told me that." *Way to take the bait, idiot.*

"I have my sources," Mr. Pike went on. "And a million better things to do than come down on an honors student, who probably thinks I'm being a hard-ass right now. Well, I know you're covering for buddies who played with fire. This wasn't a petty hallway scuffle over a girl."

"I realize that." Just like I realized that "Caffeine-Gate" was the buzz of campus and the focus of a quick-moving investigation. Mr. Pike and his pervy assistant dean had already searched Denny and RG's lockers and questioned every player. They'd quizzed Eddy and alerted Dr. Drummond (fortunately sober at that moment). They'd chided Fritz Mueller and chastised Coach Hoover for their inattentiveness.

"You know the cliché about how it's a small world, yes?

This isn't going to be about Disneyland. "Yes, Mr. Pike."

"I recognized a familiar name studying your file. Would you believe that a former lacrosse teammate of mine from UConn is on the Cal admissions panel? Good, old Connor Rhoades. We should catch up, I thought."

Don't. "Okay."

"You do understand, don't you, that I could interpret your silence as complicity? I admire your sense of loyalty. I do. It's noble, but the truth is paramount. I give you my solemn word no one will ever know that you identified Denny as the ringleader because we both know he was."

I uncrossed my legs, squirming, damp-backed, and succumbed to a quick pinkie gnaw. Mr. Pike was pressuring me with unveiled threats, more interested in Denny than RG when RG had started this, probably because Denny had outfoxed him on one too many occasions.

Mom, Bilbo: any help? Ray Davies, the poet in my ears, a salvation lyric? All crickets, backs turned. This choice fell to me.

At half a ton, too, the weight of it was a gravitational yoke confining me to this hot seat, making it perilous to spout off the obvious: Mr. Pike was browbeating me into betrayal by any other definition. Everyone keelhauled here—for disciplining, cowing, or other purposes—were familiar with the ditty Mr. Pike had laminated and hung above that lacrosse stick, if only because he recycled the line from poet Edwin Markham into his speeches with the frequency of someone garnering a royalty check.

"The cresting and crowning of all good, Life's final star is brotherhood."

"Come on," he said. "I don't have all day."

Then quit muscling me into outing my brother!

My options were as binary as a true-or-false quiz, a thumbs up or thumbs down in Caesar's Colosseum. I could save my own ass, justifying it as forced confession, and let Mr. Pike stomp Denny like Blur Öyster Cult's Godzilla stomped downtown Tokyo. Hell, it'd only cost him everything: Stanford, scholarship money, any slim hopes his splintered family stabilized. For sure it'd flame out my kinship with a friend whose dad lost his mind to a rat and his mom to Ronald Reagan—a friend who'd pushed me to stand up for myself, got me through math-y hells, introduced me to hidden worlds, while reminding me that living and existing are as different as the boob tube and a Griffith Park laser-light show.

But if I protected Denny, assuming Mr. Pike's threats were valid, there could go much of my everything: cap and gown at graduation, Berkeley, grudging respect from my father. He'd have his grand confirmation he'd need to puppeteer my life, noting how atrocious my judgment was.

Boiled down, I could sacrifice Denny to spare myself, or sacrifice myself to save Denny in a gamble that might sink all of us anyway. *What about your boozy truth, Mr. Pike?* My brother was right. It could be barber college here I come.

"With all respect, Mr. Pike, I think it's pretty unfair that you're roping me into this. Go ahead and wreck my life. I don't care." *Like hell you don't.* I rose out of my chair in sham umbrage, throwing my backpack over my supposedly principled shoulder.

The dark smile that creased his face was nothing like his blushing joy after inspiring the entire high school three years earlier with the feats of *our* school's founder, that friend of Lincoln's. He was a joyless soul now, not about to be outwitted again by the likes of us, outwardly as dogged for vengeance as he was accountability.

"You know, I think I will give Connor a…"

The small speaker attached to Mr. Pike's avocado-green phone crackled before he squeezed me further. It was the school secretary. "I know you said not to disturb you," she said, "but our friend from Caltech is phoning again. Third time today."

CHAPTER TWENTY
MOONLIGHT GRADS

The chartered Greyhound bus ferrying us toward the Pacific Ocean for Grad Nite was already bonkers, and we were still twenty miles from the beach—and only hours removed from the stiff orchestration minting us alums. Whirlwind or not, I never wanted this rolling elation to stop. Never wanted out of this red-eyed communion and mass goofiness, us together in a gray zone where we were still Stone Canyon's responsibility but no longer technically theirs.

"Don't make me be your mother," Darren Rucks, our lead chaperone, warned us before the bus left the lower-school parking lot stained by grease puddles and memories. "I was your age once. You'll hate yourself if you get so blotto you can't remember your last hurrah."

Kyle, eighteen and still punk, was impassioned for his final hurrah, though. "*Anarchy in the LC,*" he howled.

"*La CAN-A-DA,* our home and native land," Carl followed. "Suck it, hosers."

Mr. Rucks probably suspected what I knew: The two had pre-gamed behind an overpass column, torching bowls of Compact-O from a hollowed-out apple because they forgot the Zig-Zags. I stole a puff with them, then watched other classmates shotgun beers and gulp off flasks.

"Your funeral," tutted Mr. Rucks in his rumpled UC Davis sweatshirt. He gave us a derisive shake of his wispy-haired head and sat down by the driver with a crossword puzzle.

Rich as it was for the same teacher we'd occasionally swilled with to be promoting moderation, he already had two *I-told-you-so's* before we'd reached the Santa Monica Freeway. Russ and Benny, the artists in the class of '80, chain-smokers for whom Andy Warhol was messiah and Stone Canyon San Quentin, wouldn't be comatose long. Too much vodka, too soon had them in drunken slouches, slaughtering words. Only Russ managed to blow half of his cookies out the window; Benny spewed all of his on the Greyhound's beveled floor.

Notified that "something gross happened," Mr. Rucks was the least surprised and the first to pay for it. While everyone near the sour yak tried not hurling themselves, it was Mr. Rucks who had to enter the breach, tamp up the messes with a beach towel he ripped out of Benny's backpack, and squish the nauseating terrycloth into the bus's trashcan near the front. "Just what I needed," said the driver, a fiftyish black guy with rheumy eyes. "Teenage air freshener."

My money to vomit next? Ralph Billum, a light partier who prematurely drank himself asleep with his head between his knees and his Gonzaga U ballcap skewed sideways. People scooting by gave him a wide berth, fearing chunky eruption.

All in all, the cops would've needed a paddy wagon to haul in us minors for our adult companions: Coors, Mickey's Big Mouths, Boone's Farm, Southern Comfort, Smirnoff, whiskeys, plus a special trunk for the many strains of bud. In Stone Canyon tradition, Grad Night sobriety was practically a capital offense, so we couldn't disappoint our ancestors any more than we could forget the Turner Thesis or Pythagorean theorem. That'd be heresy. Besides, if we weren't sharp listeners, nobody would've heeded faculty goading us to bring "festive personal items" tonight. The result was a bumper crop of Wham-O and "As-Seen-on-TV" merchandise flinging around.

From my rear-seat panorama, my first pang of regret was not borrowing my dad's Betamax to videotape these last rollicking hours with familiar people the system designed to break apart. It was thirty-seven boys, two girls, and one alternate universe, albeit in slight retrograde. Fingers that'd gripped Blue Books and exhausting readings now monkeyed with Frisbees, Superballs, Silly String, Whoopee Cushions, and, yeah, a pair of flamenco castanets. Brian, recovered from his caffeine cardiac arrest, manned the ghetto-blaster, lip-synching to Devo's "Mongoloid." Mitch Wilkins, our BMOC quarterback—blond, chisel-jawed, a better socializer than student—demonstrated the skills he'd picked up from his love of old westerns. Five rows back, he tried lassoing a brown-skinned boy with a grown-up demeanor I had no idea knew how to be silly.

"Some aim, Mitch," Tarek Salah squealed, after Mitch whiffed again. "Back to the coral for you." Tarek was going to Harvard. Yale-admit Jodie Foster was his prom date.

We'd probably exchanged all of five hundred words over the years. But just because Tarek wasn't gabby, or taller than Mr. Burr, or anyone's definition of "cool," none of that could muddy the obvious: Barring calamity, Tarek, with his ferocious smarts and drive, would someday be the neurosurgeon of Saudi-Arabian-American descent he dreamed of being.

Kamran, the other Muslim in our class, had deserted us tonight, and though a shame, it was understandable. Tarek had emigrated with his parents from Tehran, and while he tried convincing people he was from "Persia, not Iran," he could never fully escape hateful taunts on campus after the hostage crisis. People humming the *"La Bomba Iran"* song on the field; the "towel-head" snickers in the hallway. You don't just brush that off for Grad Nite.

"Adorable, aren't they?" said Eddy of Mitch and Tarek. She leaned into me, fanning a pack of tarot cards. "You want a reading now or later? You can't avoid me forever. I'm less accurate after I've had a few."

"Later then. I like my psychics with double vision." I'd made her sit with me, having lost time with her to Denny and her new, after-school sewing business. "First things first. You glad you transferred?"

She put her cards away. "Academically, it was Mount Everest compared to Blair. And three times as weird. But it was the best year of my life. Short as this one will be."

I shut my eyes. "Not tonight with the past-life stuff. Some of that past isn't pleasant."

She pecked me on the cheek, big-sis apology-like. "I get that. One of these days…Until then, look who needs a cold shower."

Neil might need two. Aware that Cindy was a free agent after she broke up with Carl post-prom, he'd moved into the seat behind her, presenting her his "festive" item: a set of silver clacker balls, which most of us jettisoned in our Garanimals phase. What a pickup move, trying to charm his ways into her erogenous zones with kinetic action, one ball knocking into the other, transferring its energy, like a hypnotist's watch. Pathetic, sure, in a time of Pac-

Man and Missile Command, yet also reassuring. In our transitional moment, Neil's guilelessness remained intact.

"He really thinks he can get some with that, doesn't he?" I asked.

"She'd join the nunnery first.…By the way, a body snatcher grabbed Denny."

I spotted him mid-bus, deep in conversation with Glenn Wicks, tonight not in his usual khakis but Levi's and a Bobby Fischer chess-master shirt.

"He's been on good behavior all day," Eddy said. "It's scaring the hell out of me."

"Maybe he got religion after almost not graduating. There's no predicting him."

Only Eddy and I knew the reason that Denny was even on this party bus, and that was because his father had summoned the professor for intercession. I was in Mr. Pike's office when Dr. Feynman, Caltech's sensei of quantum-physics, rang, though I wasn't there for what he relayed. Denny was, and he said Dr. Feynman described him as "only guilty of a youthful indiscretion," alluding to a rocky home life as a variable. Should Mr. Pike expel him, Dr. Feynman said, he'd disassociate himself from Stone Canyon "and walk across the street to Poly. Denny, believe you me, is going to change the world, one line of computer code at a time."

As such, Mr. Pike had to swallow another bitter pill, needing the professor more than the professor needed him, and emceed graduation with barely masked spite. He hadn't forgiven anyone (despite the prayer service inviting grace), clapping through gnashed teeth as Denny raked in the awards— winner of the "Thaddeus Lowe Memorial Prize for Mathematics," the first ever "Alan Turing Computer-Science Prize," and recipient of a $5,000 scholarship to apply against his pricy Stanford tuition. Denny said Mr. Pike stared him directly in the forehead handing him his diploma. Was he ever grateful, too, that his kin, behaving today more Brady Bunch than Addams Family, had given him a finger-whistling ovation in our bunting-draped gym to soften Mr. Pike's rebuke.

Tarek, with his soaring GPA, was valedictorian. Carl, annoyingly good at whatever he tried, was runner-up. My trinket load wasn't theirs, though I did win the English award, made cum laude, and got into the National Honor Society. Mr. Pike had a pit bull snarl when my name was called.

"You must be so proud of your son," an effervescent Mrs. Whitcomb told my father on the field afterward. Behind us, a thousand Nikons clicked to families saying "cheese."

"I am, I am," he said. "This guy." *Then say it, Dad. Say you're proud.*

"He's been a treasure, though we still disagree about Hamlet," she said. "Luke knows this retiring, old woman will be watching anxiously for his byline."

"Byline?" my dad clucked in his checked coat. "We'll see where he goes in the real world."

Mr. Whitcomb, sampling my home world, arched an eyebrow and told me to keep in touch.

"Luke," Eddy now said, pinching my arm. "Come back, wherever you went." She pulled out of her bag a $9 bottle of Trader Joe Cabernet. "Only the best for tonight. Just us."

I smiled. "Can't wait. Especially after Oak Grove Park."

Never there again for me. Five days ago, after a group of us completed our last finals, mine a bloodbath trig/BASIC computer exam, which Mr. Adler devised to show us who's boss, we'd straggled down there with two six-packs of tallboys. None of us ecstatic, brain-zapped graduates were slam-dancing on picnic tables. We were slumped on parking-lot logs at noon sipping beers on empty stomachs. I was vegging out, staring at my Pumas, when a black boot entered my field of vision. *That's odd.* I followed that boot upward to beige pants with blue piping, a black ammo belt, then a CHP helmet—a helmet inside of which was an old acquaintance, the same Omar who'd chased Denny and me as freshman on his chopper. I always knew he'd get us.

"Now, what do we have here?" Officer Stroud asked.

Busted drinking underage, and in public, our gooses again should've been cooked. But Cindy, who'd never meant to divide us and seemed made of glass after she did, had some hero in her. It wasn't Odysseus, just effective. "Officer," she said, approaching him, eyes moist. "Can't you give us a break? We just got done with like fifty tests in a row. *You* must've gone through that. How about my friends dump the beer, and I drive them home? I haven't touched a drop."

The studly cop fell for Cindy's female wiles, leaving us bailed out again and her to contend with Neil's clacker-ball pickup attempt. "You should come over,"

Eddy and I overheard him say. "We'll steal my parents' schnapps and go see *The Empire Strikes Back*? We got a date, Princess Cindy?"

"Drats," she said. "My dad's taking us to the Caribbean. Maybe when we're back."

"That not what I heard," Eddy whispered. "She said her dad was taking her to the Burlington Coat Factory to get clothes for the fall semester."

Cindy, off to all-girls Smith College, would need something warm in Massachusetts. Eddy, quietly a top-five student, could stick with her eclectic sun outfits. Have I mentioned she snubbed Brown—*Brown*—to attend the very, non-Ivy League Fashion Institute of Design and Merchandising in downtown LA? It was affordable, close, and, best of all for her, an ideal place to help her launch clothing lines for cancer victims.

I, too, was ready for my future chapters, yet seeing the backs of these heads in tonight's feel-good pandemonium, I got this bittersweet aftertaste that self-absorption had cost me, that I wasn't as inquisitive as I thought. Four years into this, I'd hardly held a real conversation with the "others," with the isolated, the misunderstood, the lonely. It wasn't only Tarek. Ritchie Egleton was a language whiz who never hid being gay or his dislike of attention as the best hitter on our baseball team. Jonathon Kendrick was a ninth-grade chum who'd later stationed himself on our periphery, me never inquiring later what Stone Canyon was like in *his* shoes as an African-American.

Even there, on the freeway besides us, were other stories to be told: the immigrant family cramming six people into an economy car, the windburned painter changing lanes as if his life depended on it. The first bubble that needed piercing was my own because Pasadena wasn't the world. It wasn't even Pacoima. The *others*: that's where life's blood-and-glory resided in tantalizing diorama.

In separate news, our brotherhood still had blemishes. Carl and Rupert, even detached from Cindy, coexisted only by ignoring the other. RG and Kyle had a side dispute themselves—over unpaid gas money. Carl and I even squabbled over the military's compulsory Selective Service form in case of a draft (most likely for combat in Central America). I'd reluctantly signed. Carl stoutly refused. Whoever extolled senior-life as a smooth coronation sold us a bill of goods.

Now no more Debbie Downer. In row three, Adam Hosarian was a reminder that none of us were who we'd been before. Hairy-armed Adam had once stuffed Roland into a gym locker. Tonight, as Roland annihilated him in Rock'em Sock'em Robots, Adam's barrel-roll laugh echoed off the bus's welded ceiling.

"Yo. We need to start thinking about summer concerts. Like pronto, before Ticketmaster gets jammed up." It was Denny, squishing in beside us, and not as wasted as I'd assumed he'd be.

"Zep. Blur Öyster Cult. And yes, Luke, your patron saint Ray Davies and the kinkies."

"And what, no Eagles, only headbangers?" Eddy asked.

"Not true. I'll just need to sell a bale of weed to afford the duckets. What I do for you."

Normally, I would've followed up, asking him if he was still selling his fire-hills-grown ganja to those rough-and-tumble LC townies, but why harsh anyone's mellows? "Speaking of music, band practice in the tool shed Thursday? Carl and RG are game. Our first gig's two weeks out, and people are going to be ticked if Sparkly Eyes only plays the three songs we know."

"Don't get your knickers in a bunch," Denny said; he was our bass player, Carl the singer, with me on guitar, and RG on drums. "I'll be there. Maybe your neighbor's llama will jump your fence and chase you around again. I'd kill myself if I missed that."

"Lord," Eddy said. "Does Stanford really know what it's getting?"

—

Whoever picked Santa Monica's starched-linen Jonathon Club for our farewell dinner really should've researched us more. A ritzy meal for a class where a third of us parodied the stuffy Establishment? A sophisticated menu—baked Alaskan salmon, chicken Cordon Bleu—for Taco Bell tastes? A Disneyland all-nighter would've made more sense.

I was cloudy-headed, heart full, with pockets of dismay, when the Greyhound motored into the misty parking lot. The interior lights switched on, revealing eight dozing classmates on this day that seemed to start last year. "Go enjoy yourselves," Mr. Rucks said as people roused themselves. "Just do it responsibly. Nobody in the water. Nobody needing to be rushed to the ER.

The hundred bucks I'm getting doesn't include triage. You guys have an hour before dinner."

We filed off, some springing from the bus steps, some stumbling, others drowsy. While I waited to deboard, I watched Mrs. Rucks check if the prematurely sauced Russ and Benny were in any shape to rally. I'd wager no, neither of them reacting much to his shoulder-shakes or soft appeals. While they'd slept it off, he left the Greyhound, going toward the Jonathon Club, probably for Lysol and bucket to mop up the vomitorium.

On the beach, the unconsumed liquor and weed was downed and smoked on our sandy playground of unsyncopated bliss. Us Saturnalians got our share, as did the Dungeons & Dragons bunch hitting lightly off our doobies and showering everyone in cheap champagne. Blazing, we filled the night sky with Frisbees and other flying objects. We gamboled barefoot and played a spontaneous game of capture the flag with someone's spare shirt. This morning, outside after graduation, I'd flung my cap sideways, accidentally nailing Carl in the shoulder. After he half-tackled me on the shoreline, it was his chucklehead payback. "My clavicle," he said, "sends its regards. *Bwaaaaa.*"

Sitting down for dinner, I was wet, flying, and hardly the only famished grad. Once knives and forks got busy, sawing through petite surf & turf and celebratory cake, the plunge in crosstalk underscored to how us stars of the day were the last to eat. The most ironic thing the Jonathon Club served was coffee. I tried it, heavy on cream and sugar, and smacked my lips at the start of a lifelong addiction. Not for RG and Brian. They ordered Seven-Ups.

By eleven p.m., our less-chatter-boxy bus was long gone from Santa Monica, depositing us on Colorado Boulevard in east Pasadena for our nightcap. They'd kept the locale a surprise, and some of us booed, prejudging it a more tone-deaf choice than the Jonathan Club. Here we'd just graduated from one of California's hardest prep schools, and it'd culminate in a juvenile magnet under a mirrored disco ball? To me, all the earmarks of Mr. Pike's revenge tour.

Rental skates on, however, most of us regained second winds, even the hurlers and the hungover, and it was a boogie-licious kick in the pants. My dad used to drop me off here at Moonlight Roller Rink after my mom died to give me something to do for the afternoon, so the coordination was muscle memory. It was the goodbyes getting closer with every loop that I needed to out-skate.

On scuffed, polyurethane wheels, we lapped and swooped, crashed on bony hips, gently hockey-checked each other in the boards, no one telling us to stop. After a deejay took requests, we made it a shootout in our running, classic-rock-punk-new-wave war. I had him play "Another One Bites the Dust" to needle Carl over how far Freddie Mercury had fallen. He retaliated with "Silly Love Songs" to show me where the Beatles' legacy went. Kyle chose "I'm the Man" about a flimflam artist because RG owed him those forty bucks. RG's salvo was "Psycho Killer."

The People's choice highlight had to be Neil skating up to dream-girl Cindy, wooing her again with his clacker balls. She laughed him off. He skated backward around her. She veered away. He followed her, until his preordained, back-asswards-trip over a loose bootlace, which snapped the clacker balls strings, scattering eight shiny orbs across Moonlight's floor. In all his Neil-esque spectacles, this was the most Neil, thermos incident notwithstanding. We applauded. He bowed from a sitting position.

After twenty more minutes inside ankle-cutting skates with toe-jam insoles, I dropped into a plastic chair by the vending machines. Carl collapsed alongside seconds later, with dread gaining on him. His parents, who'd trusted their sons to throw gonzo parties and caretake their pet-menagerie when they traveled, parents who'd always appeared to us as the steadiest of couples, were mapping out a divorce.

"I got to make the most of this summer while the getting is good," Carl said. "They're putting the house on the market in September."

I gave him a side, bro-hug. "I still can't believe it."

"More proof," he said, eyes on Moonlight's beamed roof, "life's a shit sandwich. No matter how much bread you have, you still have to pick shit out of your teeth."

Rupert soon wobbled over on skates, and not to chat me up. "Carl, you wanna split a Snickers?"

Carl's expression turned from sulky to appreciative. "You're a God among men."

Rupert propelled himself toward the vending machine, and I needed answers. "Nobody told me that you two buried the hatchet?"

Carl stretched. "The hatchet kinda fell apart, tonight. After capture the flag, he walked up with a bota bag and said we should make it our peace pipe.

We remembered out there we were friends before Cindy. And it wasn't like either of us were getting laid."

I left for the head, and when I returned, Kyle and Rupert were mid-rink, trying to bounce my Nerf football off the disco ball; Mr. Ruck's arm-waving from the side wasn't deterring them.

I removed my skates, and Eddy glided over and copied me.

"I still feel like Dorothy leaving the Emerald City," she said, leaning down. "In twenty years, I wonder what they'll say about us girls. I should really write a book."

———

Kyle's dad, Wes Hartsung, was a successful insurance executive and former World War II bomber pilot who, Kyle once explained, would rather shop for his daughter's Kotex supplies than say boo about the carnage he saw and created in Hitler's Germany. At a school fizzy with "Great Men" fathers, he'd pulled off one mean feat, being both good *and* lower-g great. That's why we were here. The Hartsungs, having raised two older kids in the experimental seventies, preferred that Kyle and his cohorts commit their half-baked acts on their premises in case of trouble.

But trouble wasn't our business tonight so much as going extra innings together before getting lumps in our throats. It was 2:00 a.m., six of us lingering outside a two-story, Spanish Revival on Altadena's empty Midlothian Drive, haggard from the day and bruised from roller-skating crashes. A thick marine-layer fog that socked in Santa Monica had followed us to the inland foothills. June Gloom they called it.

"What's the story?" Carl asked, rubbing a sore elbow. "Just twiddling our thumbs?"

Denny's crooked grin had a notion. "How 'bout we twiddle this twister?" he said, pulling a pinkie-sized joint out of his hoodie pocket. He gave it a sniff. "Skunkier than real skunk. I wanted us to torch it in the Caltech tunnels, but that was the old Denny."

Rupert swiped sand off his neck. "The new Denny sure seems a lot like the old Denny."

"That he does," added Carl, a beautiful sight of reconciled brothers. "But never look a gift doobie in the mouth. You put it in yours."

RG flipped the collar on his letterman jacket in the chill. "That sounds a little gay. No hard feelings."

Denny shook out a Marlboro. "*Do-di-dooh*. It's always a debate with us."

This was going nowhere. "I don't know about you," I said. "I'm still hungry."

"You always are, but they did serve us kiddy portions," RG said. "Hey, Kyle, can we raid your pantry, one last time? *Pretty please*."

Four nodding heads made it a plurality, so Kyle, our pathologically likable outdoorsman, led us up the brick pathway toward his red-paneled front door. On the stoop, voice hushed, he issued us marching orders. "Shoes off and total radio silence. I mean it, nitwits. We have relatives in town for graduation."

Soon, we were tiptoeing down a pitch-black hallway, toward the Hartsung's cedar pantry, in filthy socks. I flashed back to our sophomore raid here after seeing *The Rocky Horror Picture Show* at midnight at the Rialto. We'd improved our skullduggery since then, hands placed on the shoulders of the person in front, steps timed to the tick of the grandfather clock. Kyle's parents, asleep in the upstairs master bedroom, could keep dreaming, undisturbed.

Or maybe not after Kyle stopped in his tracks, causing us to rear-end one another, accordion-like, on a carpet runner.

"*Fuck*," he whispered. "I think someone's up."

We knew what to do: We became mannequins.

"It's grandma," he said after more footstep analysis. "And she won't be cool with this. Bible Thumper. Coat closet now!"

We U-turned, trailing our host back the direction we entered. Then, with the faint snap of a door, we found ourselves hemmed into an enclosure never designed to accommodate six grown teenagers. Denny flicked his Bic for bearings; Kyle grabbed it with imperial intentions and re-flicked it. "Hang on," he whispered. "She's probably going to the kitchen for a glass of milk."

We'd all been, except for Denny, in football huddles together. But this huddle didn't require us getting out of a third-and-seven. It required aligning ourselves, among friends with dodgy breaths and in need of hot showers, away from potential noisemakers. Around us were plastic-wrapped dry cleaning and spare wire hangers, ski coats and rain jackets, multiple umbrellas, too. The thick scent of mothballs injected a hint of camphor forest.

My stillness poked at me in here. Carl was just bored. *"Attica, Attica,"* he murmured. Kyle clamped a hand over RG's mouth when he snorted at it. "Dude—shut up."

Unfortunately, grandma wasn't after milk. She was after the bathroom adjacent to the coat closet where we were isolated. Kyle unflicked Denny's Bic, plunging us into darkness, once she entered. We had one task, and that was not making a peep while an old woman did her business.

Simple? You try hearing the lacy scrape of bloomers wiggled to ankles, or the *"oof"* of butt-cheeks hitting a toilet seat. You go mute at the dainty stream of tinkle and *"ahhhhh."* Somebody let slip a *"hee-hee,"* and I bite the side of my hand not to duplicate it.

Grandma's pre-deuce farts, with the brassy toot of a jazz bugle, made me bite harder. Her grunting–*"Errrrr, errrr"*—had me wincing. When we heard, clear as a bell, the actual plops, it overcame Denny's defenses, and he let out a single, husky cackle that went through the wall.

"Is someone there?" Kyle's grandma inquired in a quavering voice. "Hello."

This time we kept quiet, and she returned to the matters at hand with two more rounds of grunt-and-plop. "No more fondue for me," she said to herself.

Only a cyborg would've been capable of squelching themselves for long after that. As soon as we heard the powder-room door open and the guest-room door close, we beat a sock-padding retreat to the door. From the porch, we scooped up our shoes and went to the street. Re-lacing them on the curb, we cried peals of laughter.

"If she'd had the runs," Rupert observed, "even the ayatollah would've lost it."

"Yeah, bad call by me," Kyle said. "I forgot that guest-room toilet is messed up."

"Now you tell us," Carl said.

It was 2:17 a.m. when Kyle crept back into the house and 2:21 when he shut the door bearing a box of gingersnaps.

"That's all you got?" Denny asked. "See you at 7-Eleven."

"Oh, yee of little faith." From inside the box, Kyle extracted everyone's snack of choice: Flaky Flix for me and Rupert, apricot fruit rolls for Denny, string cheese for RG, dry salami for Carl. "It's not a Bob's combo," he said, "but what is?"

We scarfed it all under the cottony mist and fifty-degree temps. Soon as we were done, Denny had his family-size doobie ablaze and being passed around. In a few minutes, with fatigued arms and grateful lungs, we'd reduced it to a flat roach.

"Fellas, shall we call it?" asked Rupert, raccoon-eyed. "I'm about to fall asleep on my feet."

Not yet. "What about the Thad, you know for old time's sake?" I suggested (read implored).

Everyone gaped at the other. The hallowed Thad? Un-broached until now.

"Luke Pukewalker has a point," Carl said, winking at me.

"Damn right, Zitty Stardust," I said winking back. Not bad for this wee hour.

"Wait," RG asked. "Kyle, your ankle shipshape for this?"

Kyle flexed it. "Bah, the doctor said not to, so let's go for it. Don't expect much air."

We'd conceived the Thad at a post-JV-football-game party in the Dieters backyard and limited it to special occasions ever since. Visualize Dan Aykroyd's Bass-O-Matic pureeing the Hokey-Pokey, athletic isometrics, and Ministry of Silly Walk outtakes into one ludicrous ritual.

I mouthed the magic words unlikely to be mouthed gain. "Okay, time to Thad."

Everyone assumed the designated stances, dead center in foggy Midlothian Drive. Knees bent. Palms slapped femurs. Necks bobbleheaded. Shoulders rolled worm-like precisely eight times. Why did we call it the Thad? Because, through it all, the tale of Stone Canyon's creator, with his aerial derring-do and gutsy ambition, was still the best story we'd ever heard, and we'd heard plenty.

"Now spin," I said. And we did, one-eighty-ing, landing in the same bent knee, femur-palming position. Our grand finale was a standing jump; Kyle phoned that one in.

"*The Thad is always rad,*" we said in union, muted so grandma wouldn't hear inside.

By now, we'd been up for close to twenty hours, everyone woozier than wired. Nobody wanted to say the lacerating words, but we pushed through, forging our goodbyes, hugging with extra force, pledging more get-togethers before college returned us to freshman, maggot-status. The jarring echo of car doors opening and closing in their vacuum seals symbolized the last metallic notes of adolescence, and it wasn't my fresh horizons that gave me goosebumps but the expiration of my posse.

I whipped my Celica around, slicing through the fog for my five-minute drive to the house where my voids remained, one in a shoebox.

CHAPTER TWENTY-ONE
CURSE OF THE WILD COYOTE

I'll miss this lumpy chair when I split for a cinderblock dorm room, even though I'm still murky about its origins. Inside its paint-scraped armrests, I'd lived a life. From the leathery con, I'd clipped articles on freak deaths after my mom's, and gobbled adventure-fiction as grief narcotic. Held my Wonder Beagle and tapped an angsty foot in brotherly tiffs. Coordinated 1:00 a.m. sneak-outs, dozed off to *King Lear*, and ribbed Carl for pronouncing sandwich "sangwitch."

Ever versatile, the chair tonight was my protective tower in another romantic flameout. Four days after Grad Nite, I was about to be single, and unlike with Beth, I was the breaker-upper this time. Stacie Hester was mounting little resistance, but that didn't mean scorched-earth was beyond her. Ours was a May-September romance that began in April when this older woman, a nineteen-year-old with button nose, full lips, and curvy bod, passed me a mouth-watering, chocolate-cream sandwich during one of her shifts at Wistaria Bakery in Hastings Ranch. I handed her back a dollar and the world's corniest come-on note, phone number below.

"If I said I liked your buns, would you hit me with an éclair?"

I was stunned she responded, and even more what an "other" like her could accomplish: paying her own freight behind that bakery counter, renting a Rosemead Boulevard apartment, attending Pasadena City College's nursing program at night, all unsupported by parents who'd she hinted were cruel.

Physical attraction aside, our relationship came with a timestamp on it. She was my date to our senior prom at downtown LA's Biltmore Hotel, me in a salmon-colored tux hamming it up with my well-glazed pals in the photo booth, around Jodie Foster, on the dance floor. Messed-up home lives or not, we must've presented as suburban boys clueless to how fortunate we were while she just hoped to make rent.

"Let's rip the Band-Aid off," I told her now. "I'm leaving for Berkeley in seven weeks."

"And I have to be up at six."

The click on the line signaled a call waiting, and I told Stacie I'd phone her back. "Please don't," she said. "Bye, Luke."

I hit the button. "Hey, you." It was Eddy, a panting Eddy. "How fast can you get over to Denny's? He's in deep shit."

"Again?" I said. "Put him on."

"I can't. There's a manhunt for him."

Why, Denny, why? Shaken, I told my dad a friend had a "minor crisis," skipping the manhunt part, and went Speed Racer on the freeway there, Eaton Canyon to La Cañada in twelve minutes. Parking was the hassle, because a county fire engine and four Sheriff's Department patrol cars, currently in front of the Drummond's house and its neighbors, ate up chunks of curb.

Eddy darted up to me on her stick legs, swathed in a pullover once I was out of my car. No marine layer tonight, only bone-white stars and a thwapping police helicopter overhead. "The professor," she said, nuzzling teary cheeks into my neck, "can't rescue him this time. He pushed his luck too far."

"Steady Eddy," as I called her, a roll-with-it chick who'd lilt, "Wherever you go, there you are," and "Never forget to shine inward," pulled back with a sheet-rock complexion. She'd gotten it with me only once before. Last summer, a random bloody nose briefly alarmed her that the leukemia was returning faster than her premonitions foresaw. It wasn't.

I walked her over to the Celica and sat her down in the driver's seat, away from the flashing lights and street clamor. She blew her nose in an old KFC napkin she rustled out of my glovebox, trying to settle herself. While she did, I eyed the two-dozen-plus neighbors, most in PJs and bathrobes, rubbernecking from lawns or sidewalk. There'd be no peace inside their homes with the racket outside. If wasn't the fire engine idling like a giant, red centipede and staticky walkie-talkies chirping away, it was the noisy copter with spotlight partially turning day into night.

"Where is he?" I asked. "And what'd he do this time?"

"The deputies, they're looking for him. But, Luke, he might have a gun."

I didn't think I heard her correctly over the mincing thud of the copter circling to the north.

"A gun," she mouthed.

I came around and sat in the passenger seat, and we both shut the car doors. *A gun?* It was too surreal for the willies but just enough for a pit in my stomach. This was bound to happen.

Eddy told the story fast, and if there was an instant theme for me, it was Denny joining Oedipus, Gatsby, and Garp, heroes whose worst enemy always lurked in the mirror. Except Denny wasn't a literary invention. Daniel, she said, got her involved after a breathless call short on details, pleading with her to drive over to help him, "find Denny before things turned gory."

On his doorstep, Daniel explained that he and Denny had a major fight this afternoon, and that he'd flown off in his muffler-rattling car. Home hours later, Denny was "out of his mind on angel dust. I couldn't get him to calm down. Maybe he'll listen to you."

I felt ill. "Angel dust? Shit, that's hard-core. I can't believe I'm asking this, either: Why the gun?"

"I can't believe I'm answering it," Eddy said. "You know how he's been obsessed about that big, mangy coyote that's been going after neighbors' cats? The one he calls Cujo?"

"Yeah. Isn't there an active pack in the hills or something?"

"Beats me. But he grabbed his dad's rifle and ran out of the house trying to shoot it. I was cruising around with Daniel searching for him when we heard the gun. It sounded like a cannon going off."

I pictured a muzzle flash. "He didn't kill it, did he? Cops don't swarm a dead coyote."

She sighed, and it was then I noticed the sweat matting that brown fro of hers. "Nope. The bullet went through the window of the house kitty-corner to his—the Katz's house, Luke. His parents are out there talking to the cops. How much darker can this get?"

No telling with him. I asked her where Denny's parents were, and Eddy said his mom was in DC, on Republican National Committee business, and his dad was back at Betty Ford, self-checked in on this stint. "I know about

Dr. Drummond. Denny told me a month ago; it kept me from letting him know I just wanted to be friends. He didn't want me saying a peep to you."

The stillness inside the car was torture enough, but everything unspooling outside was worse—the squad cars' light bars strobing patriotic colors into the night, the lookie-loos, the gut-wrenching intrigue of whether another gunshot was in the offing. "Should I go look for him?"

"Don't you dare!" Eddie yelped. "The sheriffs have their guns out. You want to die, too?"

Who said anything about dying? We exited my Celica to learn what we could, quickly appreciating two opposing camps pleading their cases to the police. Daniel, in a Dodgers sweatshirt and cargo shorts, talked to them with his hands behind his head like it'd fall off without them. On the other side of a Sheriff's cruiser was Neil's father, an eye surgeon, and his agitated wife.

Eddy and I moseyed over to them, just a couple of teenage eavesdroppers. Neil wasn't around. I could picture him in the basement, cowering behind some old ironing board, squeaking like he used to when preyed upon.

"For the third time, officer," Mrs. Katz said in her pink sweats, "that bullet came inches from striking our daughter in the back of the head while she was watching TV." She held up fingers mimicking how close. "Do something. And what's my son supposed to think? He took endless abuse at school and graduates, and now he might believe someone's shooting at him."

"Honey," Dr. Katz said, arm around her, "the police don't need to know about that tonight."

Another Omar who spotted us creeping up made himself into a cross to separate us from them and drove us back. A second later, it was clear the real plotline wasn't here. It was behind us, up near the top of the block in the direction of Descanso Gardens where some of the neighbors were pointing.

Two deputies jogged the way of their gesturing fingers, and that eardrum-blasting helicopter hovered over us again. Every one of us at ground zero stood frozen while three silhouetted figures bathed in the copter's million-watt spotlight emerged from the darkness.

It was ghostly at first, then brutally real. Denny, shirtless and bristling against his handcuffs, had two officers clamping him by the elbows, fugitive-like. Another pair of deputies trailed, one gripping a slim rifle, barrel pointed out. We hurried up toward them without any inkling of what to do, near enough to register the leaves and twigs tangled in his matted hair.

"Get your hands off me, you Nazi's," he ranted. "I told you I was doing a public service. That killer thing slaughtered Tinkerbell, the Harrison's cat, last week. Ask my brother. He knows I'd never shoot at a person."

"Sure, sure, kid," a neckless cop with sergeant stripes said. "Tell it to the judge after you come down from whatever psychotropic you're on. The innocent don't hide under bushes. So, you're under arrest. You have the right to remain silent. Anything you say…"

"Denny," Eddy cried out, "You keep your chin up. I promise it'll be OK."

Even wild and PCP-eyed, he was capable of breaking your heart. "It's *never* going to be OK," he keened. "Don't you see? That's the point of my whole, goddamned life!"

They shoved him into the back of the cruiser, and nobody had any clarity by the time it rolled off. It was followed by the other Sheriff's cars and fire engine, leaving only a smattering of neighbors outside. The Katz's were gone by then, curtains drawn over their spider-web-cracked front window. Not a single coyote bayed.

I escorted Eddy back to her Pinto, both of us hollowed out and grim, agreeing to speak in the morning. I was about to bounce myself until I noticed the Drummond we forgot—the Drummond sitting on the curb, rocking at the waist.

"This is all my fault," Daniel said, as if we were continuing an earlier conversation once I sat down by him. "I had to do something before that rat polished off what's left of the family. I know you know. This morning, I picked the lock on our dad's study, grabbed the cage, and released that fucker into the hills. Denny went ballistic, to put it mildly."

I didn't understand what "ballistic" meant, and regretted asking, because it was Denny storming around the house, predicting his father's suicide with his atheist path to God and/or ticket to a Nobel gone. It was him secretly talking to someone on the phone, then taking off for the afternoon, and returning "all loco." It was him admitting to his big brother that those ex-LC-High losers he'd been trafficking ganja to had sold him PCP, which can deceive people into believing they're Superman.

Daniel said all he could think to do was leave emergency messages for his absentee parents and make Denny a grilled cheese, like that'd detoxify him. And when the sandwich was ready, Denny was gone. So was their father's Winchester rifle, which he'd bought in response to the serial killers and murders in the news, storing it in his study with Lazarat and his shrine.

Hunched over himself on the curb, Daniel slowly began bringing his forehead down on his fist. "I should've relocked the door. I could've saved him from himself."

"No one could've," I said. "You tried. But he'll spring back." *Prince of trite: That's me.*

"You know what I hope?"

I winced. "What?"

"I hope a rattlesnake gets that overgrown rat."

—

It was Fourth of July at Bob's, and I'd rather not be here, but a deal's a deal. I'd promised Nick I'd treat him here to lunch, then show him around the teen Valhalla beneath Suicide Bridge, as thanks for his help on my Frank Flint essay. Rather than procrastinating, I should've gotten this Romper-Room chore over sooner. Now, I waited for Nick's mom to drop him off on a frenetic holiday. Waited when our band, Sparkly Eyes, should've been using this time for another rehearsal—in the parallel universe where we actually played our scheduled gig, instead of having to cancel it, and hadn't bickered so much over much over a set-list where the only tunes we finalized were originals that Ibanez-thumping Denny heralded as "wowzzerz's."

There'd be the thrill of the gunpowder air tonight, though, in the rockets get glare on the rim of the Arroyo, ogling the Rose Bowl fireworks spectacular with the first girl to whom I'd ever whispered, "I love you." Abby Lippincott got me, or the part of me willing to be got. Everything about this quiet knockout from Monrovia, from her honey-blonde hair and limpid, emerald eyes to poise and touch, made me jelly, made me dream-cast her as my Becky Thatcher. Kissing her was swallowing fireflies.

I was relying on Nick and my copy of *Fear and Loathing in Las Vegas* to distort the hours before I could clasp her hand. The curveball was seeing two ex-classmates in the booth adjacent to the one in which the hostess parked me. Warm hugs were exchanged.

"First Stone Canyon, now Bob's," I joked. "Where's girl-power headed next?"

Eddy, a Tomboy in hot pants today, smirked. "Anywhere north of the Mason-Dixon line. Where a gal of age can get an abortion and a good bowl of chili. No spying now."

"That'd be dullsville. I'm here paying my penance."

"I thought," Cindy said, "your penance was driving everyone to see the Pretenders at the Universal on Friday."

"That, too." I explained about waiting on Nick and cozied back up with Hunter Thompson. But you can't unplug your ears minus cotton, can you?

"Question, have you declared a major?" Eddy asked her tablemate.

"Business," Cindy said. "That's what my parents wanted. Said it gave me the most options."

"It does, and hot damn," Eddy said, accenting it with a clap. "I say we make a pact."

"A what?" asked Cindy, who viewed Eddy not the spunky unicorn like me but a superior being of her gender.

"A pact. After we're old, you know like thirty, and gained some real-world experience, we promise to get together. If my clothing company's doing well, I'll need a capable woman to take the reins before I go back to the good place. My best guess is that'll be around 1997."

Cindy hesitated before responding. "Geez, so specific with your omens. But yes, I could see that. Thirty's a long ways off, so I'm in, I think."

I'd just read the line "too weird to live, too rare to die" as Eddy pinned her CEO headhunting on the expectation of her premature death. I might've asked to relocate to another booth had she not then updated Cindy on another sensitive topic. While up to speed on it, I couldn't stop listening, Denny being the drug I couldn't wean off.

They'd arraigned him on a slew of charges: reckless discharge of a firearm, criminal mischief, consumption of a Class-C drug, evading police. The judge, however, wasn't ready to pigeonhole him as a criminal. He zoomed out, viewing a remorseful teen with no priors and genius potential, and ordered a psych evaluation at a Camarillo mental hospital.

Denny, in a call to me from a payphone there, said he wasn't surprised they'd diagnosed him a manic-depressive because it "obviously it runs in the family." It was how smoking angel dust while agitated made him fire at a cat-killing coyote that actually wasn't there; how it manufactured in his scrambled brain a " big, bad wolf with demon eyes someone had to mow down." He never would've done it, he added, if he'd been taking lithium, which the mental-hospital prescribed him as a mood-stabilizer. His luckiest break, hands down: The Katz's refusal to press charges.

And there were no dead bodies.

"That's killer," I said. "Whoops, great. Lesson learned, Houdini. Now we can still drive up to school together like we planned. Whoever said Cal and Stanford can't get along never rolled with us, right?"

"Stop," Denny said, flat-toned. "Stop. There isn't going to be any rolling. Stanford heard about the arrest and Caffeine Gate. They revoked my admission."

Silent scream. "That's not fair. No one got hurt. So what are you going to do?"

"I don't know. I vaporized everything when I pulled that trigger. I'll reach out when I'm out of here."

But there'd been no call, and none of mine returned. When I phoned his house's main line ten days later, his mom thanked me for being her son's loyal friend, before announcing that Denny had moved out of LA—to a location he requested stay undisclosed. I held my tongue from telling her she should be prosecuted for impersonating a parent. Suddenly, though, I understood why Eddy wouldn't disclose what her tarot reading of Denny on Grad Nite forecasted, after I'd batted away her two, drunken attempts to foretell what lay ahead for me.

Back at Bob's, waiting on Nick, fetishizing about Abby, the ten-pound anvil about to be dropped was reserved for last. Eddy asked Cindy how Neil's sister, Vicky, was faring, after the gunshot. Evidently, the two had been chummy since kindergarten.

"Fairly shitty," Cindy said. "Her dad had a heart attack last week. Who do you think she blames?"

One thing you could count on from the Stone Canyon class of 1980. We leave a mark.

—

Yearbook 1980 – Predictions by Luke Burnett & Carl Dieter

Most likely to purchase Wrigley's Spearmint on factory discounts: Mr. Pike.

Most likely to live an empty life with marvelous hair: Bitchen Mitch Wilkens.

Most likely to invest in waterfront real estate in Soviet Afghanistan: Neil Katz.

Most likely to make Swim Fins and Empty Kleenex boxes the New Adidas: Kyle Hartsung.

Most likely to attend 1,000 Grateful Dead concerts but recall only five: Carl Dieter.

Most likely to suffer lockjaw from posing nonstop questions: Luke Burnett.

Most likely to die and tell about it, regardless of whether you want to hear: Eddy Hollister.

Most likely to program an ICBM to shoot the moon for laughs: Denny Drummond.

PART III

CHAPTER TWENTY-TWO
THE RETURN

April 2000 Harvey Burr, bless his *Westward-Ho!* heart, today is a tottering widower in a Monterey assisted-living facility, with stinging neuropathy in his feet and the eternal fire of an educator. Every week, he's told me in our email exchanges, he invites residents into the drab community room for a brisk talk on forgotten US history. Like how US President James A. Garfield could've survived the 1881 assassination attempt on him—"if his doctors hadn't been such haughty nincompoops unwilling to listen to a woman physician." How the Pentagon's first nukes relied on German rocket engineers it "persuaded" to come stateside before the Nuremberg trials. "Wernher von Braun ring a bell?"

Typically, his lectures are greeted with applause, but a few cranks gripe his quaking voice is too soft for their hearing aids or that "he's a windbag with nothing better to do." He brushes it off, having heard worse, and concludes his emails to me with tasty quotes. His latest was from Ecclesiastes, after I referenced an article I wrote on a petro-oligarch of post-Soviet Russia.

"There's no new thing under the sun."

No slight, Mr. Burr, but there was plenty new under the La Cañada-Flintridge sky—millions of dollars in new. I was last here in '88, arm-twisted to man a fundraising phone bank, during a nail-biting Dodger playoff game when no one wanted to give. Earthmovers, concrete layers, and fat-cat-donor checks returned before I did. Now, twin smoked-glass buildings, one a science complex, the other a performing arts center, burst from the soil in Stone Canyon's southwestern corner, an upgrade from the bleached grass and wispy eucalyptus trees of my era. Everything's so freshly unwrapped: the expanded, Ethernet-wired classrooms and two-window snack bar selling salads and BLTs; the space-age gym with digital scoreboard. The twenty-screen computer center. Supposedly, there was a "relaxation couch" in the girls' room.

A stranger might confuse the place for a small liberal arts college whose teams played on *ESPN2*. In this whirl of change, the rattle-trap freeway overpass by the gym was Stonehenge.

Strolling around, I cringed at one sentimental casualty of our tribal kingdom. During the overhaul, they shrank our hallowed Senior Lawn, reducing to the width of a couple, miniature-golf holes. Whether sacrilege or sacrifice, seeing that ages you. Changes to the lower school broadcast there'd be no reverting to the days of pool tosses or the Piggy treatment. The locker-banks that'd been D-Rex's and Raggedy Angry's game reserve are history, ripped out for a custom music studio. It's shady as ever there, sitting under that overhang walkway, but a watchful camera enforces the sign. *"Our Honor Code Has ZERO Tolerance for Bullies."*

"Well, well, well—the famous writer in the flesh."

It's Cindy Lummis seeing me from the top of the recast stairs. We do little dances and embrace on this reunion day, different yet still the same. I've packed thirty pounds onto my string-bean frame, gray flecking the temples. Cindy, despite the crow lines and straightened hair, still resembled Barbie, just in peach eyeshade instead of indigo. A reverse, time machine has turned the past-us present.

"I prefer infamous," I said. "And look at you, future board member. Congrats."

"You heard, huh? So weird."

"Not to me."

"Well, we both know who they should've picked to break the glass ceiling."

"You'll rise to the occasion. You survived us."

It's freeform gab tramping over to the courtyard outside the Sherman Pike Administration Building. Then, once noticed, we're encircled by old schoolmates not far from the tapas and drinks on silver-and-gray tablecloths. Hearty handshakes morph into even heartier hugs and watery eyes. My delight tripled as the ex-Saturnalians joined the reacquaintances.

Carl's in from Portland, RG from time-frozen Sierra Madre. Kyle, professional-ski-bum-turned-G-man, X-rayed me with the same, old smize and Prince Valiant hair. "You steal a Dorian Gray on a reporting assignment or something?"

Though we only get together sporadically, our love language of insults has wondrously endured. It's a target-rich environment, too, with us approaching the interval between the last vestiges of youth and the commencement of the old people we might become. Male-pattern balding where there'd been walls of hair; love handles; corporate casual-wear; double chins.

"You betcha," I answer Kyle. "Don't you remember Mr. Pike pegged me as sneaky?"

"Aww, the good headmaster," Carl said, sashaying up. "If I wiggle my nose, I can smell the JD on his breath."

"He might've been a boozer, but walk around," I said. "Pretty impressive what he started."

"Don't you dare go conformist on me."

Carl, better goateed and more rough-hewn than in 1980, sported a new tattoo on his left arm: a spiky-haired Cheshire Cat. He wasn't inked six months ago when I flew up to Portland to attend a Pearl Jam concert together. That's Carl for you, always evolving, never shivering in the eclipse of anyone else's sun (including a brother making six figures at Enron Corporation). A successful theater director today, he'd been everything before: bookkeeper, beekeeper, carpenter, sous chef. Previous to that, he'd been an African tour guide drinking away his demons on safaris and riverboat rides trolled by hippos. Able to do it all, his ultimate mastery was attainment of the sober life. Proud of him as I am, Rupert won our air-miles contest. He'd jetted in from San Salvador, arriving with baggy eyes and in signature flip-flops.

Our class is one of four being honored today, with robust turnouts from the classes of '75, '85, and '90. Headmaster Darryl Schenker, who'd begun here as a hippie-ish, freshman English teacher my senior year, emceed the program like a pro. After the midafternoon reacquaintances, he formally welcomed us back, touting our contributions with the standard flattery, heralding us as the foundation, the "standard-setters ever part of Thaddeus Lowe's continuum."

Sappy, yeah, jingoistic, possibly, a naked bid for donations, no doubt. But I had this chest-full of pride, a conceit that maybe we *were* part of something monumental as guinea pigs.

And then I had to wreck it, wreck it by overthinking things just like I always did, letting myself do a head count. There went some of that buzzy glow. *Eleven*. Only eleven folks from our class of thirty-nine were present, less than any other class. Considering the twenty-year milestone for the first coed group, we should've taken over the joint, relishing our status.

But eleven: That's the tale of this tape. Where was Glenn Wicks, always more than his asthmatic-goober label: Evidently, rejecting us from Sherman Oaks, just across the Hollywood Freeway. Russ and Benny, our avant-garde artsy-fartsies: Apparently too preoccupied schmoozing San Francisco gallery patrons, or holding banners in a protest, to fork out a hundred bucks for a Southwest Airlines round-tripper. Scowling Kamran: He probably wouldn't have attended if he lived next door rather than Qatar. Other no-shows were either kids from famous families (your Rick Landau, your Adam Hosarian) or the likes of Tarek Salah and Jonathan Kendrick, people who'd had generally miserable experiences here getting educated to the max.

My takeaway was life at its rawest. Outer wounds bind. Internal gashes never scab.

Of all the legit reasons for blowing this off, there was no arguing with somebody being dead. Nobody went the same either. A depressed Brian Tollner cloistered himself in his garage with a running car. Roland Peters, born for the military, was killed on a Navy cruiser attacked by bomb-laden motorboats in the Persian Gulf. Mitch Wilkins, who'd dreamt of retiring to a Wyoming cattle ranch, drunkenly wrapped his SUV truck around a Las Vegas telephone pole one night at 3:00 a.m. Ritchie Egleton, dying of AIDs, bet the farm in Mexico on a miracle cure that proved to be fifty-thousand-dollar snake oil. Leukemia took Eddy down, more or less the month she predicted.

Among the living in our *will-he-or-won't-he-come* sweepstakes, the smart money was on Neil Katz as no-show. The last anyone heard, in a mid-nineties alumni update, he owned a boutique firm collecting debt from small businesses. In his photo, Neil had thinning, squirrel-colored hair, muscled biceps, and a McMansion in Bradbury, a gated, hillside community for high rollers east of Pasadena. When I read he donated his time as a youth Taekwondo instructor, it all added up. Neil's existence seemed dedicated to preventing a repeat of his prior one.

After Roland's plaque was dedicated, we crowded under a shaded picnic table to share tiny memories of the wiry, toe-headed boy who always obeyed the rules. After charting who else wasn't attending our missing-man formation, we picked up where we left off with crosstalk and catching up, joshing along memory lane, practically needing breadcrumbs to lead us back to where the day's nostalgic conversations began.

Eventually, Carl, Rupert, Kyle, and RG peeled off to tour the gentrified campus themselves. Again, it was just me and Cindy, a single mom who Eddy, true to her word, named as successor to take over her clothing line for cancer victims. On the one-year anniversary of her death, we met at Forest Lawn to lay roses on her grave. We even discussed redoing her tombstone to read what she'd desire: *"Here lies a woman who wants you to know mortality is nothing but a myth perpetuated by the Death Industrial Complex."*

"So, when's your first board meeting?" I asked under an eave by Mrs. Whitcomb's old room. "That should be…"

Before I could finish, my world goes dark as a pair of hands blind me from behind. I knocked them away and pirouette, hopeful it's who I want it to be.

"You have the twenty bucks you still owe me? That's before the compound interest."

"Naturally—but it was only five, you stinking liar."

I yanked him into a clench and thrust him back for a peek, my first since June 1980, seven-thousand-plus days ago. I wouldn't have recognized him without hearing that baritone husk. It's not that his features aged faster than ours, or that he ponytailed his shorter, blond hair. It was the fact he'd attended his reunion like it were a costume party, and he came as the boss.

The square black glasses, the beige cardigan, the obligatory khakis. This was Bill Gates, well, a shorter Bill Gates plastered with a crooked grin. I poked Denny's arm. "Just checking to see if you're real or a hologram." My snark pancaked his smile, so I backpedaled. "Sorry. I wasn't sure you were coming."

"Yeah, I wanted to keep it a surprise." The grin resumed. "Now, tell me everything."

"*Oh my God,* is that who I think it is?" Watching Cindy snatch Denny into her arms warmed the cockles. "You down from Seattle? Somebody said that's where you were."

"Actually, I moved back for work." *You what?* "Dang, Cindy, you get the prize for best-preserved."

"Preserved? I'm not strawberry jam." She lifted up his fake glasses, revealing pale blue eyes clearer than our last encounter. "And you're definitely not Bill Gates."

"Whatever we are, we're back together where it all started," he brayed.

Instantly, the two were as bubbly as everyone, reaching for wallet photos of their kids, not that I had any. Headmaster Schenker, a fiftyish, academic-sort with upturned eyes and pronounced jaw, hovered behind Cindy a few minutes later, apologizing to say he needed her to glad-hand a big donor from the class of '75. That left me with Denny, so much unspoken between us.

"So," he asked, "where's the rest of the fellas?"

I led him to the wrought-iron railing overlooking the lower school, feeling eyes on our backs. I knew it wasn't me people were bemused about. It's whether I was with Microsoft's chief or his imposter.

"In some ways, it hasn't changed at all," he observed. "Like an old shoe."

"Except we're ancient history. Remember 'smear-the-queer' from eighth grade? Just saying that today would probably get you suspended."

"No more gonzo, eh?"

"Try holistic."

"That's cool. But this rigmarole feels a little staid for me. Tell me there's an after-party."

I nodded, and we talked more about the campus makeover, just not in any natural cadence. It took my gumshoeing three years ago to hunt down his email address and nagging to spur him to respond. My long-lost friend kept our communications vanilla, and when I'd knock out a paragraph to rekindle connection, he'd reply with complacent one-liners. *"Damn, devastated to hear about that,"* or *"That's gnarly,"* or *"Gotta scoot, work's bananas."*

Being with him now, after he'd disregarded my most urgent email, I realized how much resentment I've bottled up, telling myself before it didn't matter. It did, and he knew it.

"I'm still in your doghouse over her, aren't I?"

My expression's lead. "That obvious?"

He squinted at me through his phony, Bill Gates glasses. "Yeah, you still purse your lips when holding something back. Let's get into it in private. I'll fill you in."

For festivities' sake, I put my issues with him on ice. "You're right. If she were here, she'd be chirping at us to be kumbaya. But what's with the getup?"

Denny chuckled. "Fun, shock value, cover, I guess. I was nervous showing my face after how things ended. Bill's a pal, and when I emailed him my idea of coming as him, he thought it was hysterical. He Fed-Exed me one of his real sweaters. So, I'm not a totally fake him."

I gave the sweater a tug. "I'm more of a Steve-Jobs-turtleneck-fan myself." *Don't get too chummy.*

"Hey, I got to snag something to eat," he said. "My stomach's bugging me."

Over at the table with the drinks and food, where I over-gorged on deviled eggs, Denny managed two bites before other familiar faces swallowed him up. Returning to my side afterward, his bright spirit didn't flicker, until he asked what'd been weighing on him.

"Any sight of Neil?"

"Not so far. Nobody really expected him."

"Shit. I was hoping he'd show. I must've tried twenty times to apologize directly to him. Make it twenty-one. I almost think he gets his jollies depriving me of that."

"*A-ha*, the plot thickens. I had no idea he was playing mind games."

"Mind games? After Columbine, I was considering wearing a bulletproof vest. No BS."

There's no time to comment on that, or the bloody school shootings we were never worried about, because other history wanted to say hello to him. I pointed at our old posse rounding the corner, and when Denny removed his novelty glasses, Kyle, Rupert, Carl, and RG trotted up, group-hugging him as if he'd reanimated from another dimension.

—

As one of two current locals, after years of bicoastal ping-pong, I suggested meeting in the pub always flying a Union Jack. Simple choice. The John Bull bar, on Fair Oaks Avenue, remained a favored watering hole for expatriate Brits, Anglophiles like me, and other thirsty sentimentalists, be they in flannel, leather, or stone-wash. On weekends, roustabouts and pickup artists, tread-wear airbrushed in the bar's neon light, joined regulars to knock 'em back.

Like Colorado Boulevard's Old Town, whose seedy pool halls, tchotchke shops, and round-the-corner drug deals were wallpapers of our youth, the John Bull was reimagined for the hipster crowd. In its original manifestation at a different site, this establishment was its truest self: a glorified dive bar decorated with British coats of arms. Whether you were out for a slump-busting hookup, room-temperature beer, or pinball-tilting on the patio, it was cheek-to-jowl with good-timers. While I preferred the louche John Bull from my college years, the joie de vivre still wakes up the echoes in every hoot and cackle.

We made base camp in a corner booth upstairs, away from the big-screen TV downstairs airing a Manchester United soccer match. As bachelor and disinterested cook, I've sampled all the pub grub here. "You can't go wrong," I said above the din, "with the bangers and mash."

At that, Carl's fleshy face came alive. "Wait, you talking about the food, Luke, or a girl you brought home from here?"

Game on. "Um, if you're only married a year and already need the vicarious thrills, hope you have a prenup. Anyway, I don't banger and tell."

"See there," said Denny, Bill Gates sweater and glasses shucked, waiting for the laughter to peter out. "That's the primo roasting among friends I need back in my life."

It was Kyle's turn now to needle guilt: "That's what you get for being a stowaway on the International Space Station, or wherever you were the last twenty years."

Denny glanced down and sighed, further confirmation there'd be no plug-and-play reintegration with us. Our waitress, a middle-aged woman in a ruffled, beer-wench dress, appeared at our table, pen out. I rode solo on the bangers-and-mash train. Carl, the foodie of the bunch, ordered the Cornish pastry; Denny, channeling *Braveheart* from his ancestry, went Scottish egg. Kyle and Rupert played it fish-and-chips safe. We hissed at RG, a Warner Bros. video editor, going with the burger, plain.

Food was one thing, but the drinks better tell our paths. Rupert, RG, and I ordered Guinness, Denny a pricy Balmenach Galore scotch. When Carl asked for an Arnold Palmer and Kyle black coffee, respectively, it was a bracing reminder that Father Time was watching, on the hook for nothing.

Thank God, I think, these ex-party animals made it out alive. That they'd steered their ships off the shoals of addiction that doomed an eye-popping number of acquaintances, no matter their talents or parents or sweet yearbook photos. Whatever our *smoke-this, chug-that* gestalt, nobody expected youthful indulgences to metastasize into such wide carnage. A Sycamore-tree-lined rehab center near Caltech, co-run by a celebrity doctor, had yet to save a single Stone Canyoner. A *Variety* article hinted about a future reality-TV series there despite that.

Eddy's funeral two years ago was the last time most of us were together. As the closest to her, it walloped me the worst. I had trouble for days getting out of bed with my first migraine, trouble accepting that circumstance had stolen another goodbye. Graveside, where mourners saw a polished coffin, I saw a debilitatingly-still box whisking me to tire-squished Bilbo, motionless under that white sheet. The priest was eloquent, speaking about resurrection, about Eddy's big heart, and yet I could only dwell on the poignant night we'd sipped Irish Coffees at Monahan's not far from the John Ball. I'd been nattering on about a scientific article I'd read predicting that in thirty years, genetic engineering would cure every type of cancer, asking, "where's the vaccine for humanity's assholes?" Eddy laughed, before adding that based on her latest portent, which she claimed now came to her in scalding showers, "I'll be dead in six months and be reborn in Pasadena sometime around 2025 to benefit from all those new remedies." Knowing I still cringed at her eradication talk, she did it anyway, I later recognized, out of love so I could brace myself for her void.

But that was Eddy. And I was sitting with brothers who'd stayed above ground.

Carl needed to bottom out in a drunk tank with a DUI, after years of blackout nights and fractured relationships, to retire the Stoli for good; through AA and grit, today he sponsors Oregon's most celebrated body-piercing artist. Kyle's pocket poison was coke in a screw-top vial, a college habit he carried over into an entry-level job at Squaw Valley, a Northern California ski resort. After shredding his ACL on a helicopter jump, he replaced his weekend nose candy for a daily addiction to Vicodin. Going from speed devil to opium-dependent was no way to live, and it stole everything: his job, a woman, that carefree, Altadenan air.

Both Carl and Kyle, however, had a trusty crane to lift them out of their rings of hell. Its name was Jerry Hoover, our old football coach and a recovering addict there for them 24-7. Kyle's rebound was particularly fairytale. Within three years of asking himself what he had to live for, he discovered his answer in the shimmering High Sierra outside his window. His zeal for the great outdoors turned into a master's degree in ecology, and when a government recruiter heard about him, it turned into the job of a lifetime as top aide to the US secretary of the Interior.

Rupert was never chased by that addiction dragon, gallivanting around the planet in small teams installing modern telecommunications gear in dicey, third-world countries. Getting high wasn't in his DNA like wanderlust or, foreign adventure was. That on multiple occasions he'd antagonized local mobsters and henchmen unfriendly to the regime contracting his services was his cost of international business. In a call last Christmas, he nonchalantly mentioned eluding a kidnapping attempt on a trip through Peru. "I wish it weren't so cloak and dagger," he said, "but you can't beat the thrill, or the paella. Better than being a desk jockey." True.

As a senior, RG was our tri-sport star, a guy with a pizza-shop girlfriend in tight Jordache jeans and a black Camaro that made us all envious. Today, he walked with a slight limp, our most likely to require a knee replacement, and drove a budget-friendly Accord. We hang out regularly and would've started a band if he wasn't stretched so thin. Responsibilities swamp him—young family, mortgage, taxing studio job—in a boat he paddled alone. Like all of us sons of parents who had us late, he neared middle age while his folks creaked into senior-citizen-hood. Caring for them would be less burdensome if his two wealthy, much-older sisters lifted a finger. They don't, still bearing grudges from their own rocky childhoods, dumping their responsibilities on a little bro as guiltless as he was overwhelmed. RG internalized that hurt, that backstabbing by indifference, and it was aging him fast, from the bald spot he termed his "fleshamaca" to the Rolaids consumption no gastroenterologist could endorse.

Since nobody knew Denny's recent past, he received the guest-of-honor treatment, everyone thirsty for details. He supplied just enough to quench it, recapping his ascent at Microsoft and settling down with a wife and daughter. Only semi-braggy, he said he'd been on a White House task force combatting fraudsters preying on Y2K fears. Next get-together, he promised to "scare the crap out" of us about how the Internet will eventually "light the world on fire. Once corporate money figures out to monetize the web, nothing—politics, shopping, borders—will be same. All of Microsoft's futurologists are predicting that so remember you heard it here first. Until then, you'll be happy to know I haven't shot at another coyote."

Denny's words, whether revealing or deflecting, parachuted us back to 1980 on the wings of "Hey, remember when…?" Two decades downstream, our memories were still spoken in shorthand. The poisoned thermos; D-Rex's goodbye party; the bobbing Bacardi; the war wagon; Caltech's tunnels; Rupert's bio-lab flies; my "Natural Selection Gave Me an Erection"; our final "Thad" outside Kyle's house. There were so many we tuckered ourselves out, ending on our double-barreled senior-class prank. One bunch had filled the office of our pervy assistant dean in a waist-high sea of Styrofoam packing pellets; the other had rewired the bell so it instead of buzzing, it played "Disco Duck" through the speakers until a near-stroking-out Mr. Pike had the lines cut.

Speaking of him, no one was surprised he'd died five years ago of emphysema. Nor that Felipe Rodrigo, our Spanish teacher, had keeled over in 1984 at the Eaton Canyon country club, where he'd been a part-time tennis instructor. Mr. Pike had fired him two years earlier over his combustible temper and, it pained me to say, doling out inappropriate hugs to coeds in the months before his shut-in wife died.

With that in the mix, we took a straw vote on most reviled teacher. It was Eli Adler by a landslide.

"Rupert," RG said, "tell Denny about your revenge. A chef's kiss on that one."

"He'll appreciate it," I added. "Revenge used to be Denny's stock-in-trade."

He shot me a scowl, and I didn't flinch. This was Rupert's moment. And what a moment it was rehearing how he never forgot the trig/computer teacher who'd shamed him our senior year, falsely accusing him of being an irredeemable stoner who should go die in a war. Seven years ago, Rupert had mailed Mr. Adler a package. Inside, was a *Wall Street Journal* feature that hailed Rupert as an "Elite IT Man Will Travel," and a copy of his ten-grand-a-month paystub.

"Fucking A," Carl said, getting inspired. "Let's not be those phonies who only promise to get together. Every other year, we're throwing our own reunion. C'mon, Vancouver, 2002?"

We answered, "*done deal!*" and "*hell yeah!*" plus a throwback "*psyched*" and "*stoked.*"

I never wanted this to end, the innate belonging, the unspoken love, grad-night reprised. We'd constituted nearly half of our class today, and we didn't come for deviled eggs. I was about to suggest another round, when Kyle consulted his Casio watch. "Shit," he said. "We've been here two-and-a-half hours, and I got a redeye to DC to catch."

And then there was two, since Carl's was driving Kyle to his departure gate in a rental car while RG, who was putting up Rupert in a spare bedroom, needed to be up early for a kid's little league game. I asked Denny if he was "up" to visit one last landmark, and he said he was. On our way out of the John Bull, the downstairs crowd erupted at a corner-kick goal, and the Brits in the bar drunkenly cheered, "*We're Man United. We Do What We Want!*" I whispered into my old friend's ear, "Remember how we used to?"

—

We were back at "the Point" for the first time since the Carter administration and *Van Halen II*, and nothing much had changed. Same taupe bluff towering over east Pasadena's New York Drive and its Medieval-looking flood-control basin. Same dusty parcels off limits to hungry developers blocks from my childhood house. Sometimes, after taking excessive antiaircraft fire visiting my now eighty-one-year-old father, I clear my head out here. The journalism awards, the recognition, the appearance on *20/20* about my piece on Eddy: I've given up trying to make him proud, aiming only to keep us on speaking terms, in honor of my mom.

Back in the day, the Point was in rotation with Smoke Grove Park, the underside of Suicide Bridge, and the Dieter's backyard for unfettered cavorting. The Point's open access invited us to do as we pleased, and where we pleased no cops or parents stymied us from lugging beer, weed, tunes, and questionable judgment near the sheer drop-off. Sometimes, in rare look-ahead moments, we'd ruminate if our teenage selves would recognize what life spit out decades on?

Sitting on a disgusting old picnic blanket from my trunk, I hoped *that* Luke could live with this rendition. Except for some romantic doldrums and a cantankerous father, I was in a fairly sweet place. Denny, candidly, rated little more than reverb, a colorful echo, an outrageous kid from an analog past. Although tickled to see him, the main reason I brought him here was a curious itch to understand what he'd turned into out of chaos.

Trick-of-the-trade tip: If you want someone closed to open up, open up first. So, he heard about my lonely freshman year at Cal taking general-ed classes in impersonal lecture halls, always the outsider. Feeling I was checking off someone else's box. Transferring to USC as a journalism/poli-sci major as a sophomore, over my dad's objections, was a fierce declaration of who-I-shall-be, in the best decision of my life. Post-graduation, I cut my cub-reporter teeth at the *Pasadena Star-News*. I also ended an impulsive marriage, after eight tempestuous months, to a future human-rights activist in a quickie divorce. (I demurred telling Denny I later broke off an engagement with another woman, never feeling the fireflies as I had with Abby.) Journalism substituted as my true love anyway, and I enjoyed a charmed rise up the ranks with staff jobs at the *Oregonian*, the *LA Times*, *Rolling Stone* (a boyhood-dream come true), and today *Golden State* magazine.

"Twenty years of life in ten minutes," I said. "You're up."

"Cool. But let me guess, what you're dying to know is why I went MIA?"

"Wrong. I know that part. I want to know why you stayed one."

Leaning back on his elbows, Denny laid bare the cost of that errant bullet. After Stanford dropped him, only one school was enamored enough of his high SAT scores to offer him admission. And still, he said, he needed five years to graduate from Cal Poly San Luis Obispo with a BS in computer science, having minored in class-ditching, dorm-room-trashing, and part-time-job firings, while ingesting every drug not named PCP. His aimless drift only stopped with fortuitous timing at a campus job fair, where he dazzled a Microsoft recruiter with his bravado and mastery of JAVA, FORTRAN, COBOL, UNIX, and other coding languages. By summer of '85, armed with a degree, he was in Redmond, Washington as a junior software engineer smart enough to recommit to his lithium.

The scene he left behind in La Cañada was a more tangled coda. The morning after he discharged that rifle, Denny said his father sped back from Betty Ford, sober for good this time, and immediately tried to smooth the Katz's traumatized feathers. At home, he hugged Daniel for a good two minutes, tearily thanking him for disposing of his obsession-inducing lab rat. Together, the two dismantled the shrine and makeshift cross, heaving the parts into Sports Chalet's dumpster. In the succeeding weeks, Dr. Drummond forgave his wife for bedding another man during his mental tailspin, just not for prioritizing Reagan's victory over Denny's psychological cries for help, something that went back years. Their divorce divided the kids, Denny and Daniel siding with their humbled dad, and their sister aligned with the mom.

For twelve years afterwards, Denny said, his father redeemed himself. Caltech's business office rehired him, and just in time to stave off several financial catastrophes. One day, however, he became lost driving home, then he was puzzled running the dryer. It was aggressive, early-onset Alzheimer's, and he died in his sleep in 1992, one of the few things Denny had shared in sporadic emails. His mom, who'd relocated to DC for an unglamorous job in the budget office, living with a man who cheated on her whenever she traveled, was in La Jolla today. She still worked for the GOP without being much involved in Denny's life. He's closer to Daniel, who has a family and a fifty-hour-a-week job at a Boston law firm (plus a lifelong hatred of rodents).

"So, that's how the cookie crumbled a long time ago."

When he yawned in the moonlight, I glimpsed rings under his eyes and thought he could use a few steak dinners to fatten up, probably from bypassing meals during his long hours coding. Next, he told the story of meeting his wife, Naomi, a "Bohemian" he fell for at first sight, their rock-solid marriage, and the bunny-toothed, four-year-old daughter, Joy, they loved to pieces. As to why he'd returned to Southern California, he said he'd embarked on a "major gamble," leaving a $200,000-plus job as a senior engineer in Microsoft's future-technology division to get the jump on the next digital revolution—mobility. With a gaggle of other ex-Microsofters following his lead, he was perfecting the software for something tabbed "SkyFile." Dumbed down, it'd let anyone with an Ethernet connection, wherever they were, to access their computer hard drives from a remote server, and with password-protected confidence.

"You want to run your desktop from Lagos or London, it doesn't matter, you can," he said. "Totally confidential, Jimmy Olsen. Billion-dollar idea. We're going to take it public. Notice I didn't spell out as much around the guys? Who knows if Rupert has pals at Apple or Google?"

Dr. Feynman, who'd died two years ago, after linking 1986's deadly explosion of the space shuttle Challenger on faulty O rings, was sure looking prescient. The professor just didn't know which corner the boy who visited him from the tunnels would see around.

I took a deep breath. "Look, it's been a fantasic day. And I don't want to cap it on a sour note, so just one more thing. Why did you ignore her when she asked for you? What would that have cost you?"

Denny levered up into a cross-legged position. "Now we're getting to the crux, aren't we? You've been waiting all day for this, haven't you?"

Pick your spot. "I wouldn't say waiting. But yeah, it's been on my mind."

"What can I say? I was a slimeball. You have to remember, I didn't know Eddy died until my brother mailed me your story in *Rolling Stone* about her, and then the little clip about it winning the National Magazine Award. I cried reading it, and you know I'm not a mawkish sort. Naomi got a little jealous about it when she saw my reaction."

"C'mon, man. I emailed you telling you she was fading, and how much it'd mean for a five-minute call. She was down to like seventy pounds." Even last year's AP English Class here knew that fact, after Mr. Schenker, fulsome in praise for the article, invited me to speak to the seniors about how the story came together and read the opening passage.

"The day before she died of at thirty-six, a fragile Jacqueline 'Eddy' Hollister was rolled outside her Pasadena, California hospice in a wheelchair, told that loyal customers who'd purchased the inexpensive and customized durags, blouses, and other garments her company manufactured for cancer patients wanted to express their appreciation. Weak, bald from the chemo, hardly able to sit upright, she expected to greet a dozen people, if that. Her math proved way off, because two-hundred had taken over the street, spilling out from an adjoining parking lot, serenading her goodbye with her favorite song, Carly Simon's 'Haven't Got Time for the Pain.'"

"I already said I didn't know," Denny said. "I was working insane hours. And even if I did," he added, pinching the bridge of his nose to reshore himself, "I wanted to erase that part of my past."

"By ignoring someone on their deathbed? Is that SOP for atheists?"

Denny's skin looked gray as I bared my fangs. "For what it's worth, I didn't tell her goodbye, either. I was in New York covering a global warming conference when she died. I figured she had another week. After everything she did for us, we should've been at her side."

Nothing was said after that elephant was released on the Point, the only sounds the thrush of cars on New York Drive and a talkative owl from an unknown tree.

"Feel better now?" he said, getting up, knocking dirt off the Bill Gates sweater he'd put back on.

"A tad," I answered with an ambivalent smile.

"Bottom line: I can't make amends to her, but I can to you. Why don't you drive down to the South Bay on Saturday for a BBQ at our rental. I'll introduce you to my better half and my little girl, demo SkyFile for you. We can adjourn to the garage afterwards for a little toke and a lot more discussion. I can't have you loathing me forever."

"I wouldn't be here if I loathed you. Understanding you is the toughie."

"Fair."

At our cars, there was a bro-hug and swapping of cell numbers and email addresses. "My head's spinning," I said. "Time and space, playing those tricks. See ya."

"I'll see your 'see ya' with something better. Later days, remember?"

———

Two Unisom's sleeping tablets might as well have been sugar pills for all the good they did a brain cache runneth over. It wasn't only the reunion and Denny but my second article for *Golden State* magazine, which paid better and grinded less than daily journalism, powering the insomnia. My expose was about a potential cancer cluster spoked around the Burbank headquarters of defense contractor Holtz Aerospace. My father had worked there out of Caltech and was furious I'd targeted it; just another grievance in our long list of them.

Denny's "Later Days," meantime, translated itself into *much* later. The following week came with no word about the BBQ. My voicemails and emails, similarly, went unreturned. So much for the more mature him grappling with the past. My Motorola Razor, in fact, didn't vibrate from him until July, three months after his exultation of how "crazy-good" it was to reconnect.

Done with the flake, I let his call go to voicemail and didn't bother listening to his message for days. Once I did, it wasn't the blarney, excuse-making I expected. "You have every right to want to kill me," he said in a strangely hoarse voice. "Before you do, I need your help while I'm still around."

CHAPTER TWENTY-THREE
KARMIC RAZOR

When he mentioned swapping rainy Seattle for LA's "South Bay," I repeated the mistake that'd gotten me chewed out as a cocky, young reporter. "If somebody tells you where they live, Burnett," my then-city-editor hollered across the newsroom, "be damned well sure you confirm which state." My sin: Assuming someone I quoted was from Pasadena, my birthplace, rather than Pasadena, *Texas*, where he was from. *Oops.* I assumed again with Denny, picturing him in a relaxed beach town inhaling saltwater air, noshing happy-hour nachos, digging toes into pristine sands only sporadically marred by oil spills or washed-up whales.

Manhattan Beach, Hermosa Beach, Redondo Beach: Someone poised for technological superstardom could buy themselves half a subdivision in any of these fog-and-sun communities. Except he hadn't, because Denny's "South Bay" was more south than bay, fifty-minutes or so below those adjacent cities, across the Orange County line in *Huntington Beach*.

Whether he bungled the coordinates from geographic amnesia, having been gone so long, or was flaunting his prospects to the boys at the John Bull, who can say? But he should've consulted his old Thomas Guide before shooting his mouth off. This I say with nothing against Huntington Beach from my inch-deep knowledge of it. Founded by a railroad baron. Subsidized by an oil-industry still pumping black gold. Abounding today in porn-shoots, the way it had sixties' surfing lore immortalized in Beach Boys' lyrics.

The mystery was what Denny was doing in a place seemingly so un-him. He didn't strike me as someone eager to fraternize with laid-off aerospace workers or, as dyed-in-the-wool iconoclast, pound beers with Rush Limbaugh Dittoheads or talk Metallica with skate-park skinheads. And what about his fealty to Dodger blue in proud Angels' country? Merely asking this measured how far we'd drifted. In the three months since I'd last seen him, the bigger question was why I'd lift a finger to help an accomplished nihilist who'd wounded so many by going over the top or staying AWOL when most emotionally convenient. Not only had I tormented myself debating whether to see him again should he resurface, but, sad to say, entertained the conspiratorial: That he'd attended the reunion in his Bill Gates' costume to soften us up to invest in his SkyFile bonanza. Profit off our brotherhood.

Relistening to his voicemail about needing a hand, a four-letter epithet couldn't be discounted: *user*. Would he soon be hinting I bring my checkbook?

Other parts of his story were as flimsy as wet newsprint, and it wasn't only pleading ignorance about Eddy until it was too late. Just as implausibly, he purported knowing nothing about what befell Nick Chance, when the only people on Earth who hadn't were either in comas or on nuclear submarines in the Mariana Trench. In late 1993 and early 1994, you see, our ex-schoolmate *was* the news. Every media titan—Barbara Walters, Larry King, Geraldo— were in Pasadena to report on whether my cowlicked-hair, ex-Freshman Buddy constituted a verifiable miracle or master of illusion? Don't ask me: I was tracking the circus from the *LA Times* Sacramento bureau, hoping that spectacular, curvy bridge hadn't produced another dead body.

In recap, Nick, then a laid-off, Wham-O product engineer, had gotten himself embroiled in a showdown with police after interrupting the lavish ceremony marking the bridge's eightieth anniversary. Nick, in his desperate last moments, had beamed images of 1913 Pasadena using an ingenious solar projector. Before sharpshooters could kill him and his protective beige dog, the two vanished in a powdery flash that, to this day, no detective, professional skeptic, forensic scientist, or Vatican investigator had debunked. Once Nick's girlfriend penned her Oprah-endorsed bestseller about him, hypothesizing Nick had been alive here before, much like Eddy asserted she had, it gifted billions of reincarnation-believers with an *I-told-you-so* and City Hall millions of dollars from the tourism and merch associated with being a mecca of spiritual intrigue. Stone Canyon itself was overrun with press inquiries and *CNN* cameras. You couldn't last a news cycle—or walk ten feet—without hearing the name "Nick Chance."

And I'm expected to buy Denny was deaf, dumb to that? More like disaffected, in spite of my profile on Eddy (into which I'd peppered Nick's life for context). A narcissist probably would've scrutinized that article to ensure I'd kept Lazarat and the Drummond name out of it, and then gone back to typing his Microsoft 1s and 0s. In 1980, I'd come yea close to not graduating because of him. In 2000, here I am in stop-and-go, Saturday-morning traffic on Interstate 5, in his service again, on a cryptic mission he'd only divulge in person.

"A dying man's wish." That's what he asserted calling back. *Dying?* I heard user-speak. Hence, this wasn't just ambivalent loyalty sending me south. It was almost a cold fascination to size up whether behind his plea he was a software charlatan or authentic desperado.

—

His townhouse, a stucco box mired at the end of a cookie-cutter cul-de-sac, was a study of rot in motion, hinting at bleak surrender inside. Seeing it through my windshield, the detached unit could've been the "before" photo in a property-sprucing brochure. Either that or sugar-plum dream for squatters. The lawn, a grizzly patch of browning grass and gopher holes, shouted neglect. So did the cinderblocks holding up a mailbox drizzled in gooey bird shit. Under the bent rain gutter were mud splatters. Over the living room's cathedral window, a bedsheet served as the curtains. The cherry on this hovel was the rooster-crowned weathervane. Normally strapped to one's chimney, Denny's hung by a slim wire over the porch, swinging in the ocean breeze.

He answered the door in baggy gym shorts and Blur Öyster Cult shirt trumpeting "Buck Dharma for President." It was disturbing how different he looked, clothes draping off him, his emaciated ribcage showing when he stretched for a handshake. He'd grown a goatee, too, but unlike Carl's, Denny's came in stringy white.

"I know what you're thinking," he said, greeting me in a low, sandpapery rumble. "But I'm not Fabio. I'm just too sexy for my shirt. Step into the palace."

I did, aghast at how sick he appeared, and unclear what he wanted. He instructed me to make myself comfortable while he whipped us up refreshments in the kitchen. As he rooted around, banging cabinets, I continued standing, surveying Denny-land in all its grandeur-less detail. It didn't take an architect to realize the floorplan here—high ceiling, wall-length mirrors—was a gimmick to trick buyers into perceiving something bigger than it was, with the rest pre-fab. All that I got. Yet where, pray tell, was his wife and daughter—and why was there little visible furniture save for an Ikea living-room set and empty U-Haul boxes stacked by the front door? The haphazardness suggested limbo, as if his family was on the fence about whether to unpack in this bizarre dump or gear up for a fire sale to erase its memory.

The engrained stench, which jumped right into your nostrils upon entrance, was little inducement for anyone to stay. If my nose was right, it was one part clinging pot smoke, one part ocean spray, the rest a moldy, cloying stink that pumped decomposition out of the cheap air ducts.

I had my head titled, checking for outbreaks of black mold, as my barefooted host waddled in from the kitchen. Scraggly arms held a tray with two steaming mugs of chamomile tea in white Windows98 mugs and a sleeve of Saltines and spread. Denny set the tray down on his coffee table, told me to sit on the couch, then dropped into the love seat diagonal from me.

He grunted *"oof"* reaching for his tea and made a raw-broccoli-eating face slurping it.

"This shit's like drinking a flower bed. My doc tells me it's good for digestion."

I sampled mine, and his "flowerbed" comparison was right. He downed his cup and with effort slathered a few crackers with butter, forcing himself to get them down. As he chewed, I stole glances and was relieved he wasn't clairvoyant. Had he been, he would've heard me clubbing myself for questioning whether he was a user, a bloodsucking flake. *How could this be?* Eyes like black moons sunk into his head, eyes tinted a sickening shade of daffodil yellow. Complementing that, he must've lost twenty-five pounds, as if he were on a starvation diet on the road to wasting away.

Damn him. He had been telling the truth, confiding that he had incurable hepatitis. That he was "a dead man walking," while I thought, give me a break! Now, I saw, his condition was sad, tragically so, and my suspicions about his selfish intentions dissolved on his dust-bunny-strewn floor. Guilt-flavored remorse, black-licorice-bad, nibbled at my stomach lining when I blurted out my existential question, one thirty-plus years premature if average lifespans weren't bullshit. "How advanced is it?"

Denny flopped the back of his ponytail into the loveseat's wrinkled cushion, and the stoicism in his raspy monotone sounded as if he was talking about somebody else's doomsday. "Advanced. Not that there's a good hepatitis, but I have the ugly duckling kind, Hep C with cirrhosis."

I set my tea down and leaned forward, trying not to visibly disintegrate in front of him. "Holy Christ, Denny, I am so, so sorry. I'm afraid to ask the outlook."

He wasn't afraid to give it. "Binary. If I don't get a liver transplant within the year, I'm good as gone."

"As good as gone." It was like hearing he'd drank antifreeze on a nonrefundable trip into oblivion. "It can't be that grim, can it? No treatment? Nothing experimental?"

"You are an optimist, aren't you? They can't delay it, only address symptoms. So it's either transplant or hasta-la-bye-bye."

"Jesus, how can you be so mellow about it? I'd be howling at the moon."

He twisted his neck side to side as if to test whether it, at least, remained operational. "Dude, what do you think I've been doing the last three months, besides trying to stay alive?"

I fell backward into my cushion, almost cramping up in my powerlessness to reverse the tides of someone I'd lightly villainized. "I don't understand. How'd you contract this? You weren't sharing drug needles, were you?"

That elicited a feeble smirk. "Oh, Luke, never stop being you. Quick timeout."

He whimpered reaching for the coffee table, and this time, his grimace almost had me feeling pain by proxy. His fingers crawled around inside the jumbled drawer for what they came for: A baggy of pre-rolled doobies and a Bic. There were no formalities like high school: He just lit one, inhaled carefully, then hacked for twenty seconds like a rookie, as if he'd ever been a rookie at anything. He directed me to grab my own, and I complied; he didn't want me, I guess, jittery about getting infected. Although I only smoked on weekends now, I burned through half my joint like it was 1980. Anything to be anesthetized.

"I wasn't shooting up or going to bathhouses. Who do you think I am?"

My head floated. "What should I think? You haven't even told me why I'm here."

He took another drag, then flicked his roach with a sizzle into a Diet Coke can. "Allow me first to narrate the lowlights. It's a funny tragedy when you think about it."

Dateline: Cal Poly San Luis Obispo. It was Denny's junior year, during a relapse of his "fuck-up days" precipitated by bad news from home that he wouldn't specify. He said it was a time of attending class and taking his bipolar meds when he felt like it, which mostly he didn't. One day, after a bookish neighbor in their student-apartment building complained about his all-night ragers, it was Pearl Gringle again in escalation. Late the following evening, a high Denny snatched his roommate's jackhammer, which he swung for his part-time demolition job, and with a *"Cowabunga,"* bashed the complainer's door off its hinges. Action, reaction. Another trip handcuffed in a police car, headed this time for a small-town jail cell with a urine-drenched bunk.

Future crackling in flames again, Denny didn't alert his family and was too chagrined to tap others for a bailout. With everyone transfixed by the 1984 Summer Olympics in LA, and a corresponding drop in crime, it was just him and a beleaguered jailer named Allen in the basement holding pen. A small TV in there aired clips of Carl Lewis and Florence Griffith-Joiner, but Denny's focus was Allen. He doubled as the station IT guru and was grumbling aloud over his ineptitude debugging the computer system cops used for bookings, court schedules, and staffing shifts. When the gawky, bulbous-nosed Allen looked like he wanted to punch out the noncompliant screen, Denny cleared his throat.

"Hey, want me to take a gander, officer? MS-DOS's my thang. That's an IBM XT, isn't it?"

Denny's civilian fingers were soon clicking and clacking a police keyboard attached to a computer, which Allen rolled into the cell on a cart and connected with an extension cord. It took Denny under four minutes to fix the code and reset the network, though he pretended he required fifteen so Allen didn't feel so rotten about himself. System rebooted, thankful his inmate was a hundred times the MS-DOS-man he was, Allen unlatched the cell door afterward. Denny's reward: Ten minutes in the bathroom to make himself presentable before he faced the judge.

Inside, it was drive-by cleanup, pits doused with wet paper towel, unruly hair wetted down, wrinkled shirt smoothed with faucet steam. Still, four days of unshaven stubble made him the degenerate in the mirror, and Denny couldn't have that. In scouring for an answer, he found a seemingly magical one in a blue, disposable razor on top of the paper towels in the trash basket. Shaving off growth with a dull, re-harvested blade "hurt like a mother." It reddened his cheeks, nicked his chin. The results, however, were incontrovertible. The judge gave him a slap on the wrist, sentencing him to fifty hours of community service and replacement of the caved-in door.

"Here's the kicker. When I got home, I was supposed to cram for summer-school finals, but by that night, no flippin' way, I was sick as a dog. Ralphing. Brown pee. Down for the count. After I got better, I sloughed it off as a jail virus I picked up. Now I know it was the Hep-C saying hello. The City of Hope doc who heard my medical history put that together. I got the junk in my bloodstream…because I'd cut myself with an infected razor. And now the monster's out of dormancy. You tell me: Isn't that the most warped kettle of fish you've ever heard?"

"By a mile."

"I do the cops a favor with their IBM. It costs me the back half of my life."

I stood up to do something—wrap my arms around him, kick out his grimy, bay window because he lacked the strength to break something. Even so, he motioned me down with an expression that was in no mood for tears, outrage, or dialogue about where this fit in our joint compendium of freakish calamities.

"And I bet you thought I was a lowlife for not calling you about that BBQ. Let me tell ya, I'd walk across hot coals to be that lowlife."

So, it was just him in this mold-pocked house, wearing a wedding ring for a wife who wasn't around in his dire hour. It incensed me, as it'd incensed me Denny wasn't there for Eddy. "Where's your family?" I asked with heat behind it. "They should be here for you."

He boosted himself up in his chair for a question he must've known was inevitable. "Yeah, you'd think. But Naomi, she basically moved out after the doctor lowered the boom. Don't get me wrong. We'd hit rough waters before. I'd go on coding benders, lose sense of time. I considered it commitment. She considered it compulsive. Whatever it was, not super for a marriage."

"And that has exactly what to do with hepatitis?"

"She grew up in a family outside Denver that made mine look like the von Trapps. Domestic abuse, drug abuse, child abuse; just put a name in front of the abuse and she lived with it. Here I come along, rescue her from that, and overall, we have a peachy life. When she heard I needed a liver transplant, *boom*, she couldn't hack it. So much for 'in sickness and health,' right? I love her, know this is excruciating. I just wouldn't have done Naomi like that if the situation was reversed."

"And your daughter?"

"What about Joy? They're in the apartment in Redondo Beach we leased after we packed up from Seattle. It was supposed to be a stopgap until we could shop for a house. Then my money got tied up in SkyFile. Then the diagnosis. We still talk every night between *Rugrats* and bedtime."

"Please tell me she doesn't know what's going on."

"She's four, so no. She thinks daddy has a nasty cold we don't want her to catch. Not a lot of options. Naomi hems and haws about coming back, and I'm not begging. I shouldn't have to."

He reached his arms upward stretching, while I re-moored my eyes on him, questioning this abandonment story. A wife of what, ten years, bolts refugee-style with their kid when her husband learns he's dying, all because of childhood flashbacks? There's got to be more to it. I make myself drop those suspicions, though. I was here as his friend, not a cynical journalist.

"So when you separated, she stayed in Redondo Beach, and you retreated down here?"

"One of the ex-Microsoft coders I'm working with bought this as a side investment after cashing out stock options. He's letting me live here for two hundred a month. The lawn and upkeep are on me. Green thumb, huh? Now, before I go crash, let's cut to it."

"Let's."

He omitted any preamble. "You ever write an apology letter—for someone else?"

I'm choosy with my words, unaccustomed to being baked so early, and never in this pinch. "I can't say that I have. Shouldn't the person asking for forgiveness do that?"

"Ordinarily. But every time I start a letter to Neil, I can't get past the fact the little shit keeps holding this over me. I need a different approach. So, who better than a Man of Letters to get the proverbial ball rolling. I can't let that night eat into my brain anymore."

I leaned forward again, peering into his cloudy, sulfur eyes. "I got to be honest, Den. You need to let this go, especially now. He already knows you're sorry. Stop giving him any power."

Denny stared at me. "You're the one who doesn't get it. I'm doing this for myself."

———

That day, I agreed to a partnership on the "Neil Apology Project." The division of labor was organic. From a rented hospital bed he stationed in the living room for convenience, Denny popped his meds, pestered his hepatologist about his liver transplant ranking, and banged out root-programming required to land SkyFile on the Nasdaq. From the *Golden State* magazine's suite in downtown LA, I put the finishing touches on my explosive story of human suffering and corporate malfeasance, sure, in my quixotic head, to make national news. Home at night in my apartment on Bellevue Avenue, I took decompressing jogs and ate like a Stouffer's microwave king. Afterward, it was laptop-time, research time, delusion time: The better I did motivating Denny to craft the perfect mea culpa, the better the odds I wouldn't be dry-cleaning my black, pinstriped suit for the first time since Eddy's funeral.

Life darkens. We bargain.

Nothing in seventeen years of writing prepared me for this assignment. How, after all, do you pour out somebody else's heart when it's been unmapped territory after living two states away? Night after night, I littered my floor with crumpled-up rejects masquerading as Denny's regret. *"Dear, Neil, words fail to convey..."; Dear, Neil: I never intended..."*

It all sounded too homogenized, too canned, so for motivation, I explored the past. At lunch, I hoofed it with my PB&J from the magazine's Sixth Street offices to LA's Central Library. Into the humid stacks I meandered, thumbing through books deconstructing how history's VIPs got on bended knee. Afterwards, we traded emails, sifting for a winner and tossing out the garbage.

"If it's so divine to forgive," Denny asked, when I brought him nothing but rejects, "shouldn't it be high-octane divine to seek it?" Sometimes, he'd blast out an all-caps missive at 3:00 a.m., after ten straight hours of programming he admitted his doctor wanted him to kibosh.

As if any expert could calculate what that imaginary coyote cost him. No matter, we had a plan. We'd perfect an apology, surprise Neil with a knock on his door, and see who was sorriest.

To: d.drummond@skyfile.com
From: lukelovesraydavies@earthlink.net
Subject: Clinton & His Zipper Throw Themselves at the Altar
In his public apology, post-blue dress, POTUS covers his bases by saying public displays of regret matter less than becoming a new him. It's Old Testament in self-flagellation, vague on sins committed, but psychologically cunning. Edited for brevity. Anything to recycle?

"...to be forgiven, more than sorrow is required....First, genuine repentance... to repair breaches of my own making....Second, an understanding that I must have God's help to be the person I want to be."

To: lukelovesraydavies@earthlink.net
From: d.drummond@skyfile.com
Subject: Clinton & His Zipper Throw Themselves at the Alter
Luke: major negatory, and I admire Slick Willie for his pro-technology views. I can't promise to ask for redemption from a white-bearded man on a throne who doesn't exist. Let's move on.

To: d.drummond@skyfile.com
From: lukelovesraydavies@earthlink.net
Subject: Karl Marx's Wah-Wah Non-Apology to Frederick Engels
How's this from the Father of Communism? Marx apologizes for his tone-deaf condolence note about Engel's dead wife by bellyaching about his own domestic discord. If Neil knew how family havoc drove you to fire that gun, perhaps he'd hear you out.

"It was very wrong of me to write you that letter.... However, what happened was in no sense due to heartlessness.... The landlord had put a broker in my house, the butcher had protested a bill, coal and provisions were in short supply, and (a sick daughter) was confined to bed."

To: lukelovesraydavies@earthlink.net
From: d.drummond@skyfile.com
Subject: Karl Marx's Wah-Wah Non-Apology to Frederick Engels
Brutal day health-wise after a few ones almost feeling human. Wahoo Tacos for dinner, puke-fest later. Only ramen for me today. Aside from Marx being an invertebrate, no way I'm laying this on anyone but myself. Get me something I can build off of. Ticktock before you're writing my obituary. Our mission impossible: Getting through to somebody who doesn't want to listen.

To: dennydrummond@skyfile.com
From: lukelovesraydavies@earthlink.net
Subject: Charles Darwin isn't sorry for his beliefs. Maybe you shouldn't be either.
Message received. Here's a blunt apology, if you call it that, from a man of principle. In 1880, a strange woman writes to Darwin, asking about his beliefs as a condition for reading his books. It's like she needs to know Darwin appreciates the suffering of Jesus, just like Neil, it appears, wants you to suffer as precondition for apologizing. Let's shame him for the sadist he is.

"I am sorry to inform you that I do not believe in the Bible as a Divine revelation therefore not Jesus Christ as the son of God. Yours faithfully Ch. Darwin."

To: lukelovesraydavies@earthlink.net
From: dennydrummond@skyfile.com
Subject: Charles Darwin isn't sorry for his beliefs. Maybe you shouldn't be either.
Darwin's great. This isn't. You're reaching. I need a springboard, not tangents. Tick.

To: d.drummond@skyfile.com
From: lukelovesraydavies@earthlink.net
Subject: We Screwed Up. You Weren't Witches After All

Enough with the guilt sandwiches, ok? I'm cramming this in while working on a story that could get my ass sued by very powerful people. Speaking of powerful, recall *The Crucible* from our reading list? Salem Witch Trial? Massachusetts jury sentences twenty-five people to death out of Puritanical paranoia. Shown evidence of wrongful conviction, the jury later makes a bogus apology. Not the judge, Samuel Sewall, who's so crushed he needs someone to read his apology for him. He believes God has punished him killing three of his daughters. (As atonement, he spends his last years protesting colonial mistreatment of Indians and slaves.) Compacted form here. Isn't there, God excluded, some Sewall in you?

"(Sewall)…desires to take the blame and shame of it, asking pardon."

To: lukelovesraydavies@earthlink.net
From: d.drummond@skyfile.com
Subject: We Screwed Up. Turns Out You Weren't Witches After All

Yo. Update first. Drove to City of Hope yesterday. My future isn't looking much better than the Salem witches: I'm No. 107 on the national liver-transplant registry. Hep-C's this boa constrictor, squeezing my time. But cross your fingers: They're starting me on a new drug (Interferon) that's shown promise for others. Let's ride with the good reverend. I can do something around blame and shame. Guilt sandwiches off the menu. Thanks for everything, your humble Space Cadet.

CHAPTER TWENTY-FOUR
WHAT SORRY GETS YOU

I'd volunteered three times, if not more, to slog through traffic to pick him up from Huntington Beach for our incursion behind enemy lines. He'd hear nothing of it, proclaiming he missed driving and didn't need me "babying" him. You didn't win arguments with Denny anymore, you negotiated terms, so I was under the pepper trees in front of my apartment as he roared up in his shiny black Audi A8.

"Hop in, loser," he said, from his rolled-down, passenger-side window. It'd been three weeks since work commenced on the letter. "You got the address?"

And hello to you. "Yep. And somebody's feeling better," I said walking over. "I still think we should go in my car, though."

He gunned the engine. "Not today," he said in a voice with more ballast in it. "Got to take charge while the Interferon is working."

Besides him in a bucket seat, I was heartened noticing other signs of minor rebound in his less yellowy eyeballs and more animated arms. His irreverence was too engrained to ever flag. "If Neil won't come to the apology, we'll bring the apology to Neil."

Obtaining his address, which Stone Canyon didn't have and the web didn't know, was reporting-101. It took me flipping through old phone books in the basement of the Pasadena Museum of History for his previously listed number, then a reverse directory to pinpoint the street. The word was already out on Bradbury, a speckle of a village where a low-end mansion, sans fountains or pillared Griffins, would cost you a cool three million.

Tearing east on the Foothill Freeway, Denny drove as leadfooted in his German performance vehicle as I usually did in my dented Acura with the fickle A/C and "No Comment" bumper sticker. Fast-lane only, seventy-five-mph cruising speed. Mercifully, weekend traffic was light, and his reflexes went untested during the fifteen-minute trip. I played navigator with my dog-eared Thomas Guide in my lap, with only a single reservation: I hadn't had time for a recon trip to scope out access. My oversight quickly became the day's first hurdle in rolling up to security gates deciding who got in and out of here. Seeing those yellow-striped, wooden arms, Denny banged his palm on the steering wheel, reacting like they were concertina wire.

"Oh, fuck a duck," he snapped. "Of course Neil has an HOA protecting him."

A uniformed guard would've turned us away, sending us to defeat, and maybe Denny down the drain. But that was hypothetical because there wasn't any photo-booth-sized guard shack, making a keycard reader the only obstacle between us and our appointed mission. Denny's face re-brightened when I told him we'd triumph if he pulled over to the side for a sec. The gods of contrition surely heard me, because not twenty seconds later, a woman in a white S-class Mercedes-Benz zoomed up to gate in a seeming rush. By the time she'd whacked her card on the reader, oblivious to us, I had Denny get his Audi on her tail to draft on her bumper before that wooden arm fell.

Neil's house sat on a bluff with a picture-postcard view of the sprawling San Gabriel Valley. Up in elevation, just below the Angeles National Forest, this would've been Frank Flint's archetypal burb. In Bradbury (population one thousand), exclusivity was its secret sauce to wall off the rat race, with equestrians welcome and few big-city headaches (schools, the needy) to accommodate. Nobody at Stone Canyon, where Neil shattered the Guinness world record for self-buffooning comments, could've predicted such a moneyed landing spot for him. Among his neighbors in these, affluent blocks were lightning rods, among them the black activist/developer who'd weighed blockading the Rose Parade and a scandalized televangelist. The only story I ever reported here involved the ambush, double-murder of race-car legend Mickey Thompson and his wife. Everyone here treasured privacy. Neil, seemed to me, craved peace of mind.

And if curb appeal was his bid to prove he belonged, a shamrock-green lawn, sculpted hedges, and a candy-red Porsche 911 in the driveway vouched he did. Indeed, between the landscaping and the Tudor-style mini-mansion— stone façade, crisscross-lattice windows—he'd re-created a British estate tucked into an old, LA smog belt. Neil's debt-collection business must've been a virtual ATM if it could gild this type of residential lily.

"You ready?" I asked Denny, idling in his Audi across the street.

"Ready to stop punishing myself and get this over with, if that's what you mean."

"And you're really not going to let me read what you wrote first?"

"Exactly. I want you to be surprised. And impressed."

Bad idea. "Your call."

"That's right. And since it is, not a word, Okay, about my condition. Pity's the last thing I need."

Climbing out of the car, it was eighty-five on a roasting, July afternoon. With both of us, by agreement, in long pants and dress shirts to reinforce the seriousness of our visit, tack on a few extra degrees. Now tack on a few more, because Neil's property wasn't just secure, it blared its outright hostility to strangers even contemplating walking up the path toward the door. If it wasn't the motion-detector lights at the corners of the house, it was the pair of ADT security cameras by the shrubs, and if it wasn't those, it was the spiked, iron gates cordoning off the backyard, declaring *don't even think about it.*

Neil, we both appreciated, had fashioned himself a fortress, and at the base of the porch, Denny mopped the sweat off his brow with the back of his arm. In crunch-time, self-reassurance he could get this done, he patted the folded apology note in his back pocket, the one he wouldn't let me vet, and we proceeded on this flier. Up to a wide, lacquered-wood door with iron knocker befitting Henry VIII we went. Instead of a doorbell, a buzzer and intercom were carved into the side. A can't-miss metal sign drilled in above NRA love. *"This house is protected by Smith & Wesson. Have a nice day."*

"Checkpoint Charlie here," Denny said, curling his fingers around the lion-faced door knocker. He rocked his head, getting himself in a groove, then let that knocker drop. The familiar, if less mousy voice reverberating through the speaker a few seconds later sent us glancing at each other with *here-goes-nothing* smiles. "Can I help you?" the voice said.

I pressed the button to speak first, just as rehearsed, while Denny double exhaled. "Hey, Neil," I said. "This is Luke, Luke Burnett from high school. Long time, no speak. So sorry for showing up unannounced, but this is an unusual situation."

Neil, the great and powerful Neil, made us wait on his steamy stoop for the courtesy of his reply. "Yeah, so unusual you evaded security to get in. What gave you the right do that?"

So much for *let-bygones-be-bygones* or, less probably, *how's it hanging?* "The gate arm was up when we arrived," I fibbed with principle, looking over at a Denny swaying on his heels. "And we would've called first, but your number's unlisted." Technically, that was accurate.

"We? Look, this isn't a good time. I'm packing for a trip. I'd appreciate it if you left."

I opened my mouth to respond, expecting this might happen, but Denny was too quick, bumping past me to press the buzzer, none of which we'd rehearsed. "Yo, Neil. It's Denny. Yeah, that Denny. After all these years, it's essential we speak face to face. All I'm asking is for five minutes of your time. I'd appreciate it."

We stood there, sweating and dreading for another disembodied communique.

"Well, if it's about what I think it is, there's nothing more to say than you've already said with your incessant calls and stuff. Now, tata you two."

Tata? That word was foreign to Denny's vocabulary, and his index finger shaded white pressing the speaker button again while his other hand fished out his secret letter. "As our old classmate Eddy would've said, *Whoa Nellie.* If you won't come out, at least let me read you something, real-quick, and we'll be out of your hair."

Another pause from the man behind squawk box. "Out of my hair," Neil said. "That's a good one." Droning before, his words took on a knife edge. "You have any idea what your bullet did?"

Denny gulped, then refortified himself. "Yeah, I have a pretty good picture."

"Let me widen the lens." I squeezed Denny's shoulder before the coming barrage, him inches from the intercom. "I bet you didn't know that my sister, the one you almost killed that day—I know, *total accident*—had just gotten home from college after being mugged back east with some sorority sisters. She'd wanted to use the car that night, but I borrowed it first to play night golf at the Arroyo nine-hole course, so I have to live with the guilt. Your bullet should've flown over *my* head. After you, she needed tranquilizers. And then there was my dad. You know that he dropped dead at the hospital visiting a patient a few years later. It couldn't have been that gunshot, could it Mensa man? Face facts: you buried us."

What the hell? Denny never briefed me on Dr. Katz. Irrelevant now, I told myself. This was psychological warfare that Neil kept winning—by hoarding his power *not* to forgive a man he didn't know now had little runway to secure it.

"You're real a piece of work," Denny barked, ditching preplanned civility for hot-breathed invective. "I knew you'd try scapegoating everything on me. Your old man was in bad shape before any of this happened. Our fathers used to be friends, remember? He'd had bypass surgery, took pills. Lost his spleen when we were juniors after someone stabbed him at some medical conference? You're conveniently forgetting that, aren't you, to play your little head games?"

Neil snickered. "You keep telling yourself that. And I have better things to do than listening to you feeling sorry for yourself. You dicks get off *my* property before I call the police. And never come back. Stone Canyon can burn to the ground for all I care."

The squawk box fell silent, and so did we. Back in the Audi, both of us perspiring, Denny looked disappointed but not decimated, bent not bowed. "I'm not giving up on this," he said, keying the car and cranking the A/C. "He's going to hear my side of things if I have to hold him hostage in a dark room."

Much as I wanted to grill him over Neil's father, I decided to let the porch fireworks fizzle out first. "That's the spirit. I say we bag out of here and grab an early dinner. We can't have you wearing down after all this."

—

I picked Saladang, a Pasadena Thai-food fixture just up the block from the John Bull. Overhead, in this large, cool industrial space, were exposed, black airducts. On the menu was every possible permutation of noodles, curries, stir-fries, and spicy meats—a little taste of Bangkok fifty yards from the grassy park where the homeless ate their dinners out of the trash.

"So," he said in a voice rougher than before, "what's good here, besides the beer I'm not supposed to have? Or the salt I can't eat?" He chugged his ice water, then hailed a busboy for a refill.

I ordered the BBQ chicken and a Thai iced tea, though I'd give anything for a frosty Singha. Denny: "Boring yellow curry, no spice at all, and a stupid Sprite." Our tiny, black-clad Thai waitress left, having no idea why Sprite wasn't smart.

"Out of curiosity, were you going to tell me about his dad? That's not some trivial detail."

"Not you, too? You're the newshound. I assumed you knew. Why would I hide it?"

Assumed; there's that water hazard again. "You tell me. But you still should've broached it."

Denny's red-rimmed anger at Neil's had become a stiff upper lip in his Audi. At our table, on the brink of a mini-fight with me, that brave face began unraveling into slow despondency. Predictable. What wasn't was the green pallor creeping around his gills.

"Point made. If I'm being a hundred-percent honest, I was afraid you wouldn't help me if I brought it up. But I meant what I said to him, about him making me the black cloud over the family. You never blamed Bullock's or your dad for what happened to your mom, did you?"

That was valid, valid and a mite offensive, so I pivoted. "Can you at least cut the suspense and show me the apology letter you were going to read? I have skin invested in it."

Our waitress, exquisite in her lousy timing, set down our appetizer, chicken sate with peanut sauce, no sodium, and then was gone.

"We'll need a do-over for that?" Denny said.

"Uh-oh. Why's that?"

"Don't be pissed. I tossed it out the window when you weren't looking on the drive here. I'm just so fucking tired of him, tired of punishing myself, and before you tell me to get therapy, I've had it and it was useless. Neil must've blanked out on all those times *I* defended him when the meatheads at Stone Canyon were making him their pinata. Notice I didn't bring that up?"

Much as I wanted to parry, I couldn't, not that with his chartreuse pallor. "Don't worry. We made first contact. Next time, we'll reapproach with better timing. Just no more withholding the whole truth, and nothing but. Roger that?"

"Sure, roger," he said with a sigh as our entrees and sides arrived in Saladang's customary food mountain. For someone not eating much, it'd be leftovers for days for him.

"Mass quantities, huh? Start digging in while I run to the can."

I'd been peeing more than usual of late, a byproduct of too much coffee in the vicious insomnia-caffeine cycle. A problem for another day. Or ever. When I exited the bathroom in the back and peered across the room at our table, my urinary tract was the least of my concerns.

Denny was slouched over his curry, and customers were starting to point. I dashed over, crouching by his chair to speak into his ear. "*Hey, hey*, what's going on, man? You all right?"

His head didn't move, only his lips. "Luke, take me to the hospital," he whimpered. "I'm folding in on myself."

Big breath. "You got it. Can you walk?"

"I, I…don't know."

I threw forty dollars down on the table and, with the whole restaurant gawping at our medical drama, lifted him up by his armpits out of his wicker chair. Clumsily, I slung one of his floppy arms around my neck and almost dropped his limp body getting it turned around. People idly watching us must've thought he was schnockered, and I thought *if only*. With his feet dragging, I hauled him to the front glass door with no idea how I could possibly open it without letting him tumble. Our waitress saved us, though, scurrying over to pop it open.

"Hope your friend all right," she said. "He look terrible."

———

You learned a bunch about our comically dysfunctional healthcare system when you stagger into the ER with a pal in liver failure, and are treated like it's the DMV. No one took to the intercom to summon a wheelchair or staff nephrologist. No one ordered a blood-panel "stat." They merely told us to sit down to fill out paperwork in a waiting room chockfull of hurting people. People holding icepacks to heads, pressing hand towels to bloody knees, clutching swollen bellies that should've been soft. Doctors weren't running this medical subway car. Insurance company CEOs and their lobbyists with concierge care for themselves were.

As if to normalize this upside-down-ness, the Huntington Hospital's community TV had "SpongeBob SquarePants" on to entertain the kids pulled in here either as patients or captives to their grown-ups' maladies. Tonight's episode was irony-rich. "Arrgh: Rock Bottom."

Weirdly, Denny had rallied a little, head upright, complexion less seafoam than before. Though I was still afraid to graze somebody glass-like in the car, he wasn't hesitant to elbow me. "Someone's checking you out, four rows over," he said. "Unless she has a thing for the dying."

Gallows humor, I now knew, was his way of staying alive. And I recognized the woman. She was the daughter of Harold Artemis, a retired Holtz Aerospace engineer I'd interviewed in person, her there every time, for my forthcoming story. He'd blown the whistle on the exotic chemicals that workers, supposedly acting on orders from above, had furtively dumped into the LA River and surrounding soil, starting in the Cold War era and ending when the firm decamped to Alabama. Holtz executives had escaped unindicted, while dozens of residents who'd lived around the fenced-off plants were stricken with eerily similar cancers and other ailments, plus contaminated properties they couldn't unload. Other Holtz employees were sick, too, in a reckoning only beneficial for the attorneys duking it out in class-action lawsuits.

Now, Heather Artemis' eyes sparkled at me, and the hazel light tantalized, setting off pinwheels, even picket-fence thoughts, as I veered around the ER obstacle course to claim the only other empty chair around. She explained that her dad—applauded by many for denouncing a *Fortune*-500 corporation, discredited by others as a disgruntled turncoat—came here by ambulance. It was kidney cancer, his price for handling those long-worded polymers and solvents of stealth technology rendering secret, military aircraft undetectable. After filling her in about Denny, I got her cell and email, outwardly so she could keep me apprised of her father, inwardly because we both were aware our chemistry was generating a dopamine energy field worth exploring.

"No ring on your finger, but still the smooth operator," Denny smirked. "So, what's the story on her? She's hot."

Ninety-six minutes later, he lay in a tilt-up bed in a ground-floor exam room overlooking an asphalt walkway. A tall, redheaded nurse with a caring smile flitted in and out, saying the backlogged ER doctor would be in after he dealt with "some criticals." On her third time in, she opened a saline IV while inquiring whether Denny was taking his bipolar meds? Her hunch: He'd been skipping his mood-modulating pills since feeling better on Interferon.

Gently questioned by her, the maniac in him, which I'd last encountered in June 1980, burst out of hiding, steamrolling the teasing, courageous, waiting-room Denny. The room vibrated with pent-up rage. "I see what's going on," he said in a throaty snarl. "You've written me off as a dead man. A statistic waiting for the slab. Like, why tie doctors up on a losing cause?"

The veteran nurse was unfazed; raving patients must've been another day at the office. "Mr. Drummond, you might've noticed it's a full house tonight. Nobody's writing anybody off."

Showing her what he thought of that logic, he swept the flamingo-pink, plastic water jug off the tray over his bed with the back of an arm, as if that'd teach her. The lid stayed locked, so there was minimal splash. "Don't insult my intelligence, lady," he said, dripping contempt. "I worked for Microsoft. I can smell a company line a mile away."

The nurse picked up the jug and set it on the sink. "There's no conspiracy, I assure you, so let's try to control ourselves. Tell me what you would like us to do?"

"Finally, you're hearing me. Call my hepatologist at the City of Hope. Get him here ASAP."

Now, I hoped, he'd behave, exhibit decency. I really was a Boy Scout. "If I wanted smoke blown up my ass," he said acidly, "I'd wander into a forest fire."

"Cool it," I said from the visitor's chair. "You're being mean when she's trying to help."

He wasn't listening. Between his "forest fire" snipe and now, he'd closed his eyes and his ears must've followed. The day's histrionics would've tired out the healthiest of people. But in the seconds that elapsed, the nurse and I saw it wasn't so much exhaustion shutting him up as his circuit-breaker tripping. All at once, his chest heaved, his breathing turned shallow, and his cardiac monitor started beeping. The nurse Denny had accused of withholding care remained poised, unlike me. She rocked his shoulder to gauge his responsiveness, and when there was none, slapped a black button on the wall. There'd been a lot of that going around today.

"What's going on?" I asked leaping up, knowing the answer wasn't going to be "nothing."

"Respiratory arrest. He's not breathing."

"CODE BLUE, ROOM 103," a prerecorded voice sounded and repeated over the ER loudspeaker.

Denny's face soon was blue. Not quite Violet-Beauregarde-*Willy Wonka*-blue, but a scary-enough blue that the nurse shooed me out of the room just before a cart, two white-coated doctors, and a pair of nurses flocked in. *Happy Neil?*

I backpedaled toward the waiting room, tracking the action, hoping against hope this wasn't it; that Denny someday would deliver his apology, that someone too young to die wouldn't. That should all else fail, I'd get a proper goodbye to the person nobody appeared capable of saving.

—

I'd forgotten where I was, and almost who I was after dozing off into a funky, sub-REM sleep. All I remember beforehand is pestering a businesslike nurse at the admissions desk, after being evicted from Denny's room as it degenerated from abuse to mayhem, about an update, then being scolded to "stop asking for information we're only allowed to impart to the patient's family."

"If you happen to see any of them here, let me know because they must be wearing their invisibility cloaks," I yapped. "The guy's pretty much alone. Doesn't that make me family?"

"No, it makes you a compassionate friend on the verge of being aggressive."

"For giving a shit?"

In the gray twilight of reanimating consciousness, I now twitched at the shadow lurking over me. My mind was neural slurry, so I kept it basic. *You're in the Huntington ER waiting room. There was a CODE BLUE. Denny's probably dead. And you have no right to know.* The rest were shards of memory, shapeless and fuzzy.

"Sorry to wake you," the shadow said. "You're Luke, aren't you? Denny's friend?"

My dusty eyes looked past her for reference markers. The hive of sick and injured was down to stragglers. The TV playing *SpongeBob* before now played *Touched by an Angel*. The wall clock read 2:47 p.m. I'd been zonked for hours.

"I think so," I said, pushing my memory to retrieve this face from its file. Got it. This was Naomi Drummond; at the reunion, Denny had shown me the wallet photo. Tonight, she appeared as wiped as I felt, her large, expressive eyes saggy, her cantaloupe-colored, V-neck sweater rumpled.

"The nurse said you were still out here. Sweet of you to hang around."

I could feel my stomach juices gurgling. The fiasco at Saladang, where neither Denny nor I touched our entrees, crystallized, and I scooched up in my chair. "And you must be the Naomi."

"Nice to meet you," she said, sticking out her hand and sitting in the chair opposite mine. "I wish it wasn't like this. I've been here since about eleven."

"I'm nervous to ask how's he doing? Is he…?"

Naomi massaged her neck. "Alive, yes. It was touch-and-go. They had to perform CPR on him."

"Jesus." More fragments from his room: his bluish face, that inert chest. "He was OK this morning."

"He's stable. They had to put a tube down his throat to get him breathing again. But that's out. He's getting oxygen through his nose."

"Wow, I'm happy to hear that….And you? How are you faring?"

Naomi's lips trembled, then stopped. "Shaky, petrified. Every other emotion. I hadn't seen him for a week. You probably know we're separated."

This was awkward. "Yeah, Denny shared a little. Brutal situation for everyone."

Her brunette hair was a deconstructing bird's nest, yet there was a composure to her. "If there's any silver lining, my mom gets to babysit and spoil our daughter. She and I didn't exactly have the best relationship, so it's something watching her down on the floor with Joy playing Pokémon."

"I'll bet." *Pillow, where are you?*

"How did this all happen, though? He sounded so much stronger on the phone?"

Best I could, I gave her the *HLN*-deep version: Denny recruiting me for the Neil Apology Project, the crash-and-burn in Bradbury, him drooping over his no-salt-or-spice curry.

"That coyote again," Naomi said like somebody else done with that pesky mirage. "He can't let it go, and Neil knows it. They're doing this juvenile dance. I truly wished they'd stop."

Denny had told me he'd met the "splendiferous" Naomi while accompanying his dad to a La Cañada AA meeting, in that church by Winchell's, in 1990. He was home to spend Christmas with the family, mother excluded, all-in on sobriety. She was a soft-spoken eccentric who owned a North Hollywood collectibles-shop selling and renting vintage set pieces. Once, Denny said, Naomi had managed the stress of making ends meet in hot-aerobics classes, but gradually she reached for the sherry bottle. One nightly glass became three, and three became her minimum.

Behind the dependency, I knew, their origin story was writing itself. As with so many from our generation, Denny would beat one addiction, only to have to crawl away from a subsequent one. He'd developed his latest similarly to Kyle as a weekend warrior, just not from skiing but from dirt-biking in Seattle's bumpy forests. When the weed and Advil no longer tamped down a throbbing lumbar, he was prescribed hydrocodone. Getting hooked with his genes was unavoidable, yet two fitful years of dependency later, he'd weaned himself off, vowing to never touch another opioid again. It'd been his third spin with chemical bondage.

He was back at that La Cañada AA the following day, not for lost sobriety but for Naomi. "Hello, I'm Denny and I'm a drug addict." Friends noticing their spontaneous attraction goaded the two to go out. They did—on an improvised first date culminating on a lookout over Angeles Crest during a meteor shower. "Love at first sights," Denny had exuded, "differences aside," Naomi being a Hindu-influenced Christian living with "a third-eye" activated by other people's pain chief among them. Yet, the couple paved over her spiritual callings (and goth crucifixes) and did separate activities on Sundays. The rest of the week, he'd told me, Naomi modulated his extremes and gave him reasons with her love not to self-destruct. She was his Eddy 2.0.

"On another note," I said, trying to reorient my sleepy head back in the present, "I know how grateful Denny was you took him to the hospital all those times before they diagnosed him. It was all news to me. We'd hardly communicated since high school. I don't how much he's told you about us savages."

She glanced toward the ER-bay door. "Quite a bit, after I dredged it out of him. He missed you guys. Were you all really trapped in a closet listening to an old woman go number two?"

"Yep. Tonight's a long ways from that."

I shouldn't have said that, because tears spilled down her alabaster cheeks, collecting under the shapely jaw of an obviously burned-out spouse. I hobbled over with one foot asleep to the nurses' counter and snatched a fistful of tissues.

"Thanks," she said, daubing her mouth. "I thought I was cried out." *I could relate.* After she blew her nose, she continued. "This might sound totally random, but did you ever catch the movie *Good Will Hunting*? You know, Matt Damon, Robin Williams?"

I wondered if this was her *The Day the Earth Stood Still?* "That is random, but yeah. Poignant."

"For the last ten years, I've lived with my own Will. Brilliant on the inside, reactive on the bad days. Over the past months, it's been too much of the latter."

I was tempted to add I knew *that* Denny from our past life. I couldn't. "Will, yeah, I get that comparison. Question, though, what's the prognosis? He getting out of here anytime soon?"

Naomi stared down at the wadded tissues in her palm, then back at me. "You know hospitals nowadays. Always trying to discharge people fast to save a buck. The doctor said he could be released in a few days. I'm hoping he'll let me stay with him in Huntington Beach until he's mobile. I'm expecting another battle. No offense, Matt Damon."

"I'll speak for him. None taken."

"Luke, you've gone above and beyond. Go home before you need an IV."

I yawned not for show but necessity. "I'll take you up on that." I pushed up on the chair to rise when she patted my hand to keep me there for a bit longer.

"Before you leave, tell me one thing. Why did Denny say I moved out?"

CHAPTER TWENTY-FIVE
REAL DEATH EXPERIENCE

I sensed it trailing behind, not so much a hooded creature measuring me with his scythe but a black dorsal fin lazily hanging back in case my lifeboat sprang a premature leak. That fin said nothing in this life was as seaworthy as it appeared, and nervy habits that I'd mostly packed away—the foot-tapping, the nail-chomping—rolled freely out of drydock.

Two weeks after Denny's resuscitation, a stabbing pain in my left side sent me down a hypochondriac's rabbit hole. Gallbladder disease (or the Big C) is what this liberal-arts major self-diagnosed, and I dialed my doctor for an MRI. If there was such a thing as a compassionate scoff, he gave me one, suggesting it was psychological and that I lay off the dairy and WebMD. Still, mortality was in the hopper again after my father underwent an emergency procedure to insert a coronary stent, something the surgeon said was a must to prevent a fatal heart attack they called a "widow-maker." I was grateful he was okay, not ready to let him go without some reconciliation, because without it, I knew he'd perpetuate our future battles from his grave. The expected passing of whistleblower Harold Artemis, protagonist of my article, was more of the same and worse. Another type of death then silhouetted itself on the horizon—the death of *my* career over a careless mistake in my story about him that could prove to be professional hemlock.

Except for my dad's stent, I'd concealed everything from Denny, who'd been sleeping on my couch the past few nights to be closer to the City of Hope for treatments. Someone like him—an emotional sphinx coding away on his laptop, head slumped in catnaps, only happy when his precocious daughter lobbied him for a Furby on their nightly calls—had too many woes to be anybody's trusted adviser. Hell, he'd refused to even confirm whether his little girl and separated wife were living in Huntington Beach or Redondo Beach (in the real South Bay).

My Catch-22 wasn't geography, though. It was what to do with him after Heather invited me to attend the meeting of a New Age club that flamed up my curiosity, among other things. Should I maroon him in my apartment with a bowl of microwave popcorn and TV, knowing disturbing new facts about him from Naomi, or trust his promise to "be a good boy in strictly observing mode" at this support group—a group, I should clarify, for people who'd escaped *their* bodies and lived to tell about it. Had Denny not been so screwed, I would've left him, but the sands of his hourglass were piling up at the bottom fast, and I couldn't live with myself letting more spill out because the old him had periodically escaped in these dying days.

—

The address Heather gave me, 78 North Marengo Avenue, was just a street and a number, devoid of any sentimental oomph. Until that is the old girl came into view, and the cityscape around it fell away. Those rounded windows, the terra-cotta roof, the stolid, almond-colored façade: Pasadena's historic YWCA building was a friendly ghost meriting my full-body goosebumps. Either I'd forgotten it was there or my subconscious auto-deleted it to shield me from backsliding into the blackest of pits. Nothing's lost forever, is it?

I threw the Acura into neutral in front of the Mediterranean gem synonymous with my mom. Every Sunday, she'd drive me here to learn Christ's teachings, and when the Bible-speak grew tiresome, there was post-sermon sugar (cookies, cake-pops, bottomless fruit punch) waiting to further indoctrinate us young souls. Suddenly, I was relieved the YWCA wasn't another casualty of gentrification, that the wrecking ball had gone elsewhere, and I was tempted to ditch my running car to go leap off the perimeter wall like I did for kicks at seven.

Stella Burnett, "Miss Southland 1940," was once a luminary at this offshoot Protestant congregation in the shadows of Pasadena's cupola City Hall. Nobody read the Gospel of Paul as theatrically, nobody organized holiday parties or charity raffles as meticulously. There she was the movie-star a swirl stuffy parishioners. You ought've to have seen her, huddling with the minister, confident and coiffed, free of a house with that low ceiling over who she could be.

"You're vegging out," said Denny, caressing a sore abdomen. "What gives?"

"I didn't realize the meeting was in here," I said, quickly summarizing my history. Another factoid soon shook loose, too: the same pathbreaking female architect responsible for the Hearst Castle (and that Xanadu, *Citizen Kane* mythos) designed this.

"That must be a trip," Denny said. "Hope somebody will be flashing back on me."

"There'll be plenty. And that's a ways off. But no fatalism tonight. We're guests, right?"

"C'mon, man. I don't have dementia."

So fitting for us: little ironed out, trap doors galore.

—

I assisted Denny, who now walked with a cane, up the stairs and into a marble corridor ambered in time. The ornate fixtures and wall casings were identical from before, and the lemony polish was breathing the past. Recognizing now that the Near-Death-Experience Support Group/San Gabriel Valley branch held its monthly gatherings in a room two doors down from where I learned water could be turned into wine, I yearned some to drink to celebrate my reattachment to this sacred building.

At the archway, I toggled my reset, repeating to myself I was here for Heather and, to a smaller extent, educating myself about the "other side" I sometimes fretted had lost my number. The unexpected spurt of nostalgia was a freebie, a lucky bonus for me to relive at 2:00 a.m. in bed.

I pulled one of the bulky, wooden doors, and Denny limped in behind, both of us surprised by the size of the crowd for such a niche subject. Any chance we'd slip inside undetected was dashed as soon as the roughly forty attendees swiveled our direction, probably thinking we'd entered the wrong room, us the youngest people in a maze of white- and gray-hairs milling around holding Styrofoam cups of coffee and brownies. After a minute, the majority nodded welcome to us, though some frowned eyebrows with mild suspicion.

Heather's "Luke, over here" by the window was the voice of social reprieve.

Until her, I'd never heard the acronym NDE, only anecdotal stories of people "crossing over" during violent accidents and medical crises. Interest, obviously, was zipping past cheesy TV mediums and into more intimate, story-sharing settings. Navigating around senior citizens toward her, Denny still limping behind, I peeked at a table with mainstream-looking books that someone must've toted from home. *The Journey of Souls; Many Lives, Many Masters.*

Nearing her, I reached out for a two-handed, condolence shake. She swatted that away, tugging me into a body-heat hug. "At least he died knowing he was a hero," she cooed into my ear. "And that's *all* because of your story." A peck on the cheek later, I was so daffy-brained that Denny had to introduce himself to Heather as my "plus one."

Afterward, when she went off to greet an acquaintance, some air leaked out of my Heather balloon. How gallant would she think of me if she knew she'd just flattered a disgrace-in-the-making?

Holtz Aerospace was livid at my article depicting it as an environmental rapist expecting taxpayers to foot the cleanup bill, and even more livid the EPA had launched an investigation. The company wanted my head on a platter and had threatened a multimillion-dollar libel suit against *Golden State*, singling out the only blunder in the piece. Among other evidence of skullduggery I'd cited was a grainy, backlit video, where an "insider" detailed a cabal of unscrupulous executives, corrupt lawyers, and *see-no-evil* regulators that did the company's bidding. But it wasn't evidence. It was a fake, an elaborate ruse by a Holtz operative to discredit the entire story, which the company knew was otherwise accurate, while smearing my reputation in payback. Had that apocryphal tape not compromised me, I would've blown open the slimy charade in a follow-up. Yeah, some Bob-Woodward junior I was. If nothing else, I'd probably get shitcanned.

Heather walked back with eyes still grieving for her dad and melt-in-your-mouth smile lines for me. *Don't make this about you.* "I'm so happy you're here," she said after we sat down. "I'm sure you have better things to do on a Friday night with your girlfriend."

"Actually, I'm single. And I was eager to come. You've gotten me curious about this stuff. There's a Vroman's trip somewhere in my future, Am Ex bill be damned."

Her dulcet laugh, the way she tucked her hair behind her ear, I could swoon for this woman.

"It's my third meeting here," she said. "I got interested a year ago, after my father woke up from his first coma. He had this giant smile on his face, and when he was well enough to explain, told an incredible story about traveling through a portal of lights and meeting a spirit guide for a life review."

"A spirit guide? What's that?"

"You got me, but whoever it was told him he was getting more time to mend fences with his siblings. It's one of those things you can't un-hear, you know?"

"I do know…from covering things on Earth. 'Un-hearable,' I'm trademarking that."

"Slow down," she said with a coquettish grin. "We'll need to negotiate first. I propose hammering out the fine print over El Cholo margaritas."

"You drive a mean bargain. Then again, margaritas are nature's perfect food, if blended, with salt."

"Purist. Let's make it a pitcher. And nachos. A week from tonight? I could use a hard…margarita."

"Me, too."

Our flirty chatter, paradoxical in this room of the macabre, paused while she reviewed an index card bulleting what she'd tell the group about her dead father, Harold. As for Denny, I couldn't ignore him after he collapsed his last time out in public.

Nor could I keep my stomach from bulging up into my diaphragm when he was no longer in the chair to my right. For everyone's wellbeing here, I prayed, let him be going for brownies.

It'd been atheist to the left of me (with my Godless-Big-Bang dad), and atheist to the right of me with him, who now looked better than he had at Saladang but worse than before Neil's *shove-that-apology*. I stood up, trying not to alarm Heather, sweeping the room. I wish I hadn't.

He was just where he'd promised *not* to be. Instead of the brownies, he was by the narrow podium up front, speaking with a seventy-something man who appeared to be club president. I gnawed a pinkie, hoping this wouldn't be an exploding cigar; perhaps Denny was networking, fudging in case of a Road-to-Damascus epiphany that'd bring him back here. The guy he was speaking to could've reminded him of a staple from our TV-generation: an older Fess Parker, who'd portrayed frontiersman Daniel Boone on the Disney series. Rather than

Boone's coon-skin hat, this gent wore a thin canula piping oxygen into his nose from a portable oxygen tank.

I acted blasé as Denny shambled back on his cane. "That was Louis, the head honcho," he said. "I was expecting a holy roller. He wasn't. He's rational. Wants to quantify everything."

"He says in his *strictly* observational mode. Don't forget our deal."

Then Louis flicked on the mic and reintroduced himself, saying he was a retired architect and "onetime, mouthy nonbeliever" who had to see the light to believe it during a botched lung-cancer surgery. "Now forget me. What a marvelous turnout for only our fifth meeting. We'll have to rent out the Pasadena Convention Center if we keep growing." He caught his breath before addressing housekeeping matters (meeting dates, dues, a possible holiday potluck), then said: "Without further ado, let's hear from anyone who hasn't spoken before. Come one, come all."

The NDE voyagers conveyed fantastic tales in five-minute increments. An Altadena dentist, who'd plunged from a steep hiking trail, recalled levitating out of his body, swept up in unconditional love equivalent to "a million shaking orgasms"; a "Light Being" soon sat him down on a bench overlooking a golden river. A West Covina CPA that paramedics discovered with no pulse after her car was T-boned shared a different itinerary. She said she'd been shepherded around the afterlife by a grandmother she intuitively recognized, even though that grandmother had died at the Dachau concentration camp years before the CPA was conceived.

At the sixth, supernatural recollection, getting the hang of things, my interest drifted from the afterlife to tonight's audience. Having covered the gamut, from Podunk council meetings to UN Security Council gatherings, studying group dynamics was a favorite hobby. Typically, my standard questions were who had the power and who wanted it, but that didn't translate here. It was the factions Louis hadn't acknowledged, manifested in what club members wore, who they applauded, where they sat. Even the cosmically transformed, I reckoned, had their homies.

And color me engrossed. The bloc sanguine about their encounters dressed like that with outer-worn crucifixes, crystal-encrusted necklaces, and other spiritual baubles. In my mind, they were "The Gratefuls," NDE-ers with no misgivings about choosing to return to Earth with damaged physical bodies and reinvigorated purpose. Their opposite numbers were what I deemed "The Regretters," who also claimed visiting kaleidoscopic dimensions outside of time-and-space constructs. For them, repatriation to the material world, either on their own volition or a nudge from above, saddled them with obvious returners' remorse over the double-edged sword of second chances. An ex-Occidental professor, who spoke from the side of his mouth after a stroke, got one's attention. The agonizing physical therapy, colleagues who mocked his paranormal travelogue, home recovery listening to Subway "Five-Dollar Footlong" ads on the quarter hour. "The passage back wasn't worth it," he lamented. "Not by a long shot. To quote Vonnegut, 'It is a mixed blessing to be brought back from the dead.'"

"Don't be so bitter," came a Grateful's voice from the corner. "You're living on house money. And can you put a cork in the Vonnegut?"

"Like hell I will," slurred the Occidental man.

Louis seized the mic, trying to quell the partisans split over the hereafter's picky admissions to its dreamy carnival. "Everyone, please, please stop with the sides. It's bad enough the scientific community, including Caltech, refuses to take us seriously. We can't afford to frag each other with the opportunities at hand....Anyone else care to speak?"

Heather did, detailing her father's NDE, phrasing it as the gift that'd buoyed him, a gift that gave *her* optimism she'd see him again. Not only was it touching; it stalled the grumbling and rivalries, and the old people hugged her like a long-lost granddaughter on her return to her chair. I stood to embrace her, as well. "Beautiful," I whispered. "I'm sure he heard that."

Before we sat down, I wanted Denny's impression, cynically frosted and all. Still, you can't converse with someone not present, and after a shiver arced through me spotting him back at the most dangerous place here—re-shaking Louis's hand, taking the mic from him—it was too late to slap duct tape around his mouth or fearmonger the crowd about sniffing a natural-gas leak.

"Hi, everybody," Denny said, trying to clear the croak out of his voice. "I'm Denny Drummond, and I wasn't intending to speak. You've inspired me to rethink that."

"Inspire away," said a member of the Gratefuls, an old guy with a colostomy bag bulging under his Tammy Bahama shirt. "Good to have a fresh face here."

"So my friend, Luke, over there by Heather, was nice enough to bring me tonight." *Nice or suicidal?* "And Louis, he encouraged me to open up. So I will. I have terminal liver failure. Highly overrated." He waited for the chuckles to ebb. "Thinking about my end, I came across a Woody Allen quote where he said, 'I'm not afraid to die. I just don't want to be there when it happens.'" More chuckles. "But I was at Huntington when they brought me back from dead."

"There's your mistake," editorialized a fifty-ish Regretter, a tubby man with a prosthetic leg in a pope-on-a-rope T-shirt. "When God ordered you to go back, you should've staged a sit-in."

Denny laughed like everyone, not a bomb-thrower about to come out of retirement, and I relaxed. When his crooked grin proceeded it, all I could think was: *He wouldn't. He couldn't.*

"And I wish God had spoken to me. Because you know what I glimpsed between worlds?"

"A star system," the pope-on-the-rope Regretter said, now playing the straight man.

"Absolutely nothing. A void. Abject blackness."

"That can happen," said a sclerotic woman in a wheelchair, sweatered-up on this summer evening. "Don't read too much into it. The Lord knows what he's doing."

"*Shhh,*" Louis said from a chair by the podium. "Let him finish. This isn't a revival."

From my right, flank seat, I leaned back, out of Heather's sightline, to mouth a series of *"Don'ts"* at Denny. He ignored me and what must've been my purple-faced horror.

"No disrespect," he said, "but some of you have convinced yourselves of things that didn't happen. What if there's *nothing* after this, and your out-of-body trips were perfectly explainable hallucinations caused by hospital narcotics? Or the evolutionary brain soothing itself in shutdown mode, like when somebody's drowning. Go read Christopher Hitchens or Richard Dawkins. To be born is to be extinguished."

By the instant groundswell of disgust, Denny might as well have dumped a bucket of honey over his head and invited a Grizzly for lunch. Booing and hissing poured from every direction, Gratefuls and Regretters united at last, with an intensity that shocked me. The able-bodied jolted to their feet, shaking fists, pointing arthritic fingers at my blasphemous plus one. These wrinkled NDE-ers wanted to skin him alive.

"You've got a sick-o sense of humor," bellowed the retired Occidental prof. "You a ringer?"

"Don't attack me," Denny said, doubling down in his godlessness. "Make peace with the abyss. It's not like you'll feel a thing."

"You're a tiny person" a woman I couldn't see said, before letting out a welp.

This was all my doing, all my gamble, and we had no escape plan. I didn't know whether to race up to read him the riot act for public embarrassment or be his Secret Service, wresting him to safety before his cane was used against him. But there'd be none of that because instead of tottering down the aisle at his own peril, he cut a sharp right toward the heavy door.

Louis, mic in hand again, worked damage control in the wake of Denny's two-minute stunner. "I think our friend mistook us for the Skeptic's Club that meets here every other Monday," he said panting. No one giggled. "Don't let somebody so detached rile you up. It takes bravery to live, and even more bravery doing it knowing what lies above."

His plea for calm had no visible effect on Heather, whose scrumptious face was bunched up like a gardening glove. "Tell me you didn't know your sociopath friend was planning to say those horrible things?" she said to me. "Look how upset he made everybody?"

"Believe me, if he weren't already dying, I'd be arranging his funeral. He's been pretty depressed. I guess he thought making waves would cheer him up." I reached for her hand. She retracted it like I had leprosy. "I never should've brought him."

"And I never should've asked *you* here. I was feeling empty. You made it worse."

"Please accept my..."

"I don't. And I'd hoped you and I...oh, forget it. And the margaritas."

She wheeled off toward a waxen Louis, who'd had to sit down and dial up his oxygen tank.

He wasn't in the corridor, the corridor pungent with memories of my gussied-up mom holding my little, cookie-crumbed hand, when I crashed through the door, searching for the human grenade launcher. He was outside, leaning against my car, bathed in streetlight, and standing on legs that probably shouldn't have descended those stairs alone.

"Go ahead and behead me," he muttered. "Just make it quick."

I stomped around to unlock and open the Acura's passenger-side door. My hand latched around his elbow to thrust him inside, and not tenderly either.

"Ouch, bro," he said. "That hurts. Careful."

"I'm not your bro."

This is what it had come down to: me manhandling someone who'd been so precious to me—someone I'd bled for, someone I believed had changed—into a car I never should've let him in, not with the cost-benefit analysis of friendship aways skewing destructively in his advantage. It was a short drive to my apartment, windows rolled down with my A/C leaking freon and neither of us in the mood for classic rock and old, frothy debates about best bands.

Denny didn't speak until the car idled at the mouth of my subterranean parking garage.

"You want me to leave Heather a voicemail castigating myself as a heathen?" he asked. "I'll tell her impulse control's never been my strong suit."

I hit the garage remote without replying to his fake offer. At my parking spot, I rolled the windows up, cut the engine, and contorted toward him for maximum impact. He twisted to face toward the window to reduce his exposure.

"You're terrified, I get that," I said through gritted teeth. "Even if you're not vocalizing it. Anybody would be flipping out in your situation. But that doesn't excuse tonight, Den. Not one shred. You always took things too far. This, though…blatant sadism. Hey, look me in the eye! I'm not talking to your goddamned ponytail."

He didn't flinch. "Those delusional geezers were lying to themselves with their mumbo-jumbo," he said in a scratchy husk. "Light tunnels? Guides? Somebody had to level with them."

"And you're that somebody, knower of all, I suppose. Screw you."

"You don't have the foggiest idea of who I am, or how preposterously I'm going out."

Another comment over the line, and I felt my blood pressure about to geyser through the sunroof. *"The fuck you say?"* I hollered. "My mom died picking up a pack of cigarettes. Oh wait, only your pain matters. That's why you freely spread it."

"How 'bout I do the world a favor and jump off Suicide Bridge. Unlike your pal Nick, I'll leave a body."

"Nope. Your guilt's no good here anymore. 'Preposterous?' Explain that or we're done."

That got him angled toward me, and trying to clear the mucous from his throat. Like everything about his biology, it was hopeless. "The bad news that triggered my bender from hell in college…"

"Yeah?"

"I suppose it's time to tell you. It was Stewey. Stewey phoning to tell me Neil's dad was dead. His croaky voice was now something you'd hear in an oxygen tent. "The upshot—me getting myself arrested and giving myself Hep-C from that razor. Happy now? Come to think of it, why the hell do I need you? My obituary's already written."

"Nice try. Another thing you withheld. You've turned willful amnesia into an art form. You must be proud."

"Man, I've never heard you yell before. And like you're so perfect."

Dumbest thing I ever did was waving the grenade-launcher back into my life. The smartest thing I *never* did: confiding to him that Holtz Corporation was breathing down my neck so he could manipulate that too. "Just admit it. Life bores you to tears. So, you amble by the carnage you've created and justify yourself as a martyr with a righteous cause. In twenty years, it's same ol', same ol'."

"Really? Was I a martyr when I saved your butt from D-Rex?" he said, trying to reach my volume with tender vocal cords just not having it.

"No, you were a troubled kid with a demented way of trying to make right. I'm not talking bipolar. I talking your need for stoking chaos when things get dark, like with your dad. Did you even care that I was the sacrificial lamb who almost lost his spot at Cal covering for you over the caffeine fiasco? A classmate almost died because of your bright idea."

He scrunched his nose, girding to roar back without the physical firepower to do so. "You're such a hypocrite," he said, straining. "I've Googled your articles. A house fern would know you're projecting your own issues about your dad on your subjects."

Gloves off. "If we're getting real, I think your atheism is total bluster. All of creation, possible multiverses, started out of nothing? But you love ruffling feathers, playing the cynic."

"Says you."

"How can your favorite group be Blur Öyster Cult when its biggest hit was 'Don't Fear the Reaper'? You know, 'the whole forty-thousand men and women every day'?"

Whoever knocked on the driver's side window nearly owed me a new pair of boxers. It was old Mr. Lainey, my landlord, a walrus-shaped fossil with a greasy combover and farmer's wardrobe; he complained incessantly about the noises feeding back on the hearing aids tucked inside his disgustingly hairy ears. I rolled down my window to smile him away.

"That was quite a ruckus you were making inside your car," he said. "I could hear it by the elevator bank, and you know I don't appreciate ruckuses. You already play your electric guitar too loud."

At amp volume one? "We'll watch it, Mr. Lainey. We were having a vigorous political debate. I'm for Gore. He's a Bush fan."

"Al Gore?" he pooh-poohed, the derision dancing on his suspenders. "Give me a break. Him and his global warming. And the Interweb. Like that's going anywhere. Keep it down, children."

Window back up, my voice dropped down. "Like I was saying, I doubt you believe the garbage you spew. Eddy, who you *wouldn't* call on her deathbed, and her past life; Lazarat; the Nick-mania you suspiciously claimed to have missed. Something's been trying to get through to you for twenty years and you've been flipping it the bird."

Denny started going green again, a flashing light to end this before he needed a reservation at the Huntington ER. In his greenness, however, he still remained a bombmaker. "Since we're being honest, maybe *you* needed all that garbage.

You know, to trick yourself you're not clutching pearls about dying someday. That cross under your shirt must be feeling hollow. Truth's a bitch, huh?"

My internal snarl was ready. "How rich...from someone allergic to the truth."

"Then extra-rich for you. You flayed me for turning my back on Eddy, but come clean. The real person you can't forgive for not being at her side is sitting behind your steering wheel."

Offloading his shame onto me. Ridiculing my belief (and everyone's) while he caws at the brutish hand of a cold, fickle universe. "Here's what's going down," I said in my calmest furious voice. "You can stay here another night. Tomorrow, I want you gone. Go stay with Stewey."

We sat there, in the spotty light of the oily garage, until Denny ended our confrontation with what mattered most to him, more certainly than life beyond death. "Guess this means you're done helping me with Neil."

CHAPTER TWENTY-SIX
ALL SAINTS, ONE SUCKER

Once upon a time, they'd called me "Lukenado." For them, an epithet, for me a reputation to uphold. While my mom wouldn't wait in line here at Vroman's Bookstore to pay, clasping her Michener, or Doctorow, or Christie, dreaming of parking-lot nicotine soon, I'd become a retail Category-4 for the blue-aproned wait staff employed as literature-lovers, not storm chasers. I'd rip books by their spines off their tidy shelves, jubilant hearing them clunk behind me domino-style. I'd swipe laminated bookmarks emblazoned with deep thoughts—Snoopy to Orwell—amd hide them in the kiddy-fiction section for a scavenger hunt management never requested.

"Mrs. Drummond," a miffed staff member would eventually ask my mom. "Can you *please* control your boy?"

Much as I'd merited it, they never outlawed me, and facial-recognition technology wasn't sophisticated enough to connect the adult-me with the rascally, radar-dish-eared child I'd been. No small break there. A Vroman's ban, in my season of dismay, would've been a kill shot to the spirit. I knew the layout of this two-story, Colorado-Boulevard institution like my way home because it was home. Hot new titles: Beckoning by the cash register; older fiction: winking from the eastern wall; biography: the money spot in the middle; self-help: rescuing those adrift by the stairs. When life bared its teeth, one store—the store businessman/naturalist Adam Vroman launched when Charles Holder was Pasadena's BMOC—was my bulwark, my portal out.

Lukenado days, where have you gone?

In the month since Denny made a fool out of us at the NDE support club, things that could've gone either way all broke the wrong way, and anxiety over them had me twisting in my bedsheets, bracing for the next day's humbling. That I was at Vroman's, book-browsing midweek itself was reality-buffering, me denying the fact that on the outside, the career interchangeable with who I was neared being dragged into a field for its public execution.

Golden State had really done it. It'd suspended me for a month without pay over the sham whistleblower video as upper management and the lawyers, the ultimate judge and jury, probed how this screwup could've unfolded. They'd already determined that my "failure to independently confirm the authenticity of the tape fell below standards of journalistic excellence." An Editor's Note in the subsequent edition acknowledged the mistake but said the magazine "otherwise stood behind the story." My stumper: how they could stand by the article, yet not the writer? Had it not been for my street-cred breaking stories and my prize-winning profile of Eddy, I would've been booted and stamped as damaged goods weeks ago.

Harvey Burr, naturally, kicked the bucket days later. The assisted-living center found our seventy-nine-year-old history teacher cold in his bed following a devastating stroke. Learning about it in an email blast, I visualized him above, in platform shoes and Colonel Sanders suit, at an Algonquin Round Table with idols Frederick Turner and Douglas MacArthur, and tried keeping that hypothetical afterlife front of mind over the mentor I'd lost. It spooked my dad when I informed him, not out of jealousy of what Mr. Burr represented but his reflex minimizing any talk of mortality as his own approached. Skittish, he did his usual deflection, reiterating his belief that I should quit journalism—and he had no idea how close that was to happening—to pen a hagiography of, what else, Caltech. I nodded, saying I'd mull it over when it was an automatic no, broiling inside about him refusing *my* requests, like giving me my baptism certificate, which he maintained he'd lost in his helter-skelter files. I didn't believe it.

RIP, Harvey Friggin' Burr.

The bad-news ricochet kept bouncing, as its wont, taking aim below the belt after I'd peed fire for days and self-catastrophized on WebMD for a few more. My New Delhi-born urologist, who'd stuck probes in holes where they were never belonged, guaranteed me I wasn't dying, "Just ordinary prostatitis" extinguishable with antibiotics. So far they hadn't worked, and instead of sexual euphoria, the gland responsible for it contorted me into a ball in the worst agony of my life. The New Delhi man preached patience, easy for him without a hot poker wrapped around his urethra.

Vroman's, needless to say, was as good an analgesic as existed, and today, I needed doubling up on the literary painkillers. I canvassed options like *Tuesday's with Morrie*, before scrubbing it as too close to an imaginary *Emails with Mr. Burr. Me Talk Pretty One Day* and *The Last Precinct* sounded like more innocuous palate-cleansers, and there I stood in line, braising myself in self-pity.

That's why I wrote off the feathery sensation, or whatever it was ruffling my outside shoulder, as a blast of Vroman's AC or, more likely, a jitter migrating up from a tapping foot. Whatever that airy nudge was, it pushed me to quit brooding and rotate my head to the left. In heeding the call, a fleeting glimpse of a promotional table was a tractor beam, and I ditched the line, ducking under the rope for a closer examination in one of those ironic-life junctures where you're uncertain whether to laugh or cry, grin or grimace.

Vroman's had devoted an entire table to a subject customers couldn't help but notice walking in, stacking books in a pyramid shape. The hereafter now came with bar codes in stories about earthbound angels and NDE, reincarnation and spirit contact, the mysterious Akashic Records, too. Suddenly, strangely, something burst out of me, and it was paramount I know if they overlapped with the yarns from the event my spiritual merchant of doubt had sabotaged that fateful evening. They did, and by the sheer variety, you'd suspect death was 2000's Hula-Hoop, a craze sweeping the nation. To gin up sales, a crafty marketer had scrawled, in upper-case letters on a posterboard, a celestial quote from the twentieth century's Greatest Man of science.

"COINCIDENCE IS GOD'S WAY OF REMAINING ANONYMOUS"
—ALBERT EINSTEIN.

I retreated a step, accidentally bumping into a customer, puzzled why I never knew the Father of Relativity (and onetime Caltech visiting professor) had said this, equally gobsmacked over its meaning. Being a free-will-er, I'd never considered God as a master choreographer in a cloaking device. Instead of feeling spiritually becalmed, though, it hit me like a blinding light, and I flung my Sedaris and Cornwall on the death-book table and hurried outside for blue sky.

It wasn't two minutes later on the sidewalk by Vroman's newsstand, asking myself if a second migraine was knocking, that my Motorola rang from an undisclosed number. Probably my *Golden State* editor ordering me to hand over my press credentials, as that's how things were trending. But it was Denny's oldest friend, phoning from the Mountain Time Zone, in what only a noodle-brain would interpret as something more than a haphazard occurrence.

—

From his love-rationed childhood, later outsourced to a New Mexico boarding-school, Stewey, I learned during our brief catch-up, had leveraged perseverance into a higher self. Once a double PhD earning big coin as a therapist for LA's neurotic rich people, today he traveled the state as a pro-bono shrink for California's obscenely crowded prisons. Off the road, he had his own family, as well as aging parents in a La Cañada palace whose tiniest needs trumped their son's biggest obligations. Even as a teenager around the Drummond household, he'd had an adult-ish face with a wavy "five-head" prone to wrinkle. That, I realized, was just the way it'd be for Stewey. Always.

"You know, if I wasn't bald before, I'd be pulling the last tufts out now," he said. "Naomi gave me your number. You're my last option."

"How bad?"

"Bad. We're talking like an animal crawling under the bushes to die."

Denny had returned to Huntington Beach after Stewey dropped everything to fly to Boulder, Colorado; his kid sister's condo had burned down in an electrical fire, a condo half-a mile from JonBenet Ramsey's hexed place, and she was a certifiable wreck. "Sis' needs me for a couple more days. You think," he asked, "you could get down there for a welfare check? I know you two had a barnburner of fight, but there's no one else. I've tried everyone in my contacts."

I bridled, with all the free time in the world, communicating that Denny was too radioactive for my stamina. "Bless you, dude, but I can't. What about his brother? His mom?"

"You know his family. They've already come and gone."

"Of course they have."

"How about this compromise? I'll call Daniel to nag him to fly back out from Boston when possible and you make one last trip. It's you or no one. Naomi said she and her Joy tried being around him again, and he's just too volatile. He's back to living on Red Bull and all-nighters' programming. When I asked him why he was burning the candle, being so sick and all, he blew a gasket and said this SkyFile thing was his only legacy worth leaving."

My head pounded. "Like I said, I can't, Stewey. I've seen how this movie ends."

"Even if he only has a month left? The City of Hope told him to get his affairs in order. Chances are you'll be last person from Stone Canyon he'll see."

"A private nurse?"

"We both know he'd roust her after one shift. Would it make any difference, any at all, if I told you that before he got huffy, I saw the book he'd been reading. It'll blow your mind."

—

Toggling stations on my drive south two day later, I landed on KABC, thinking how weird it was listening to talk radio when all that mattered to teen-me were catchy hooks and rebellious harmonies. What I'd give to go back to when rock, not hip-hop, was king and diseases were other people's problems.

The bottom-of-the-hour news was a buffet of good and bad: first functioning artificial heart, explosion of a Russian nuclear sub in the Barents Sea, high odds of thunderstorms tonight. They saved the local, event calendar for the end, probably because nobody was listening anymore, and nothing sounded riveting save for one happening. Tonight in Pasadena, near Vroman's, the city's most progressive church was bestowing a lifetime-achievement award on someone— of all the billions of people in the world—that Stewey had mentioned. Squatted on my cushion to keep my red-hot prostate from searing through my Levi's, I switched stations to KLOS.

Pinch me. Slap me. It was playing a song I'd never once heard on the airwaves, only record players. It was "Flaming Telepaths," as in Blur Öyster Cult's "Flaming Telepaths." *How was that for anonymity, Dr. Einstein?* Now, it wasn't only corrosive guilt propelling me south but a spur-of-the-moment brain stroke, likely as it was to backfire as grand delusion. Pumped, I called Stewey, and we agreed on a whopper to misled Denny into believing I was his taxi-service back to Stewey's guest room.

Besides, there was no way he could drive, greeting me as he did in a blotchy *"Don't Sweat Y2K"* T-shirt, drooping, plaid boxers, skin sagging off him at his door. "You," he said, scratching his butt-crack. "If you've come for the estate sale, try back in two weeks."

"Cool. But you were supposed to be ready so we can beat traffic."

No *"Got it, thanks for making that shit drive, need water?"* Only, "Wait outside. I'll be out in ten."

On the porch by his busted weathervane, in the humid, eighty-degree August sun, I wavered after seeing him, wavered about stringing coincidences together, debating whether to call Stewey in chagrin to say this was a mistake. The world I gleaned through Denny's screen door wasn't merely ramshackle. It was as unsalvageable as its inhabitant, trash everywhere, black mold leaching down a wall. A flipped-over U-Haul box in his living room was now a bedside table cluttered with pill bottles, a urine jug, paw grabber, and heating pad. His workstation was no longer that Ikea couch, either, but his living-room hospital bed blizzarded with laptops, Ethernet cords, CDs, and papers. If his life was an SAT question, the fill-in-the-blank choices would be: A) Tear-jerking; B) Unfair; C) Sepulchral; D) Tragicomic. It'd be better to hire a town car with an IV stand for him.

I had my cell out to phone Stewey when from deep within, I heard a shower nozzle squeak off, followed by the sounds of someone attempting to make themselves human. Coming into view, a skeletal, towel-wrapped Denny downed a handful of pills, chased them with Pepto Bismol, and coughed his way through two bowls of sativa. His last activity: Disappearing into the bathroom to ralph so intensely that his gagging shook the patio. In total, he was outside in twenty-five minutes in jeans gone baggy and a black, cotton Devo shirt. *"Got an urge, I wanna purge"* it read against a backdrop of band members in red "energy dome" hats.

I had to go through with my deception now. That skin-crawling vomiting, paired with Stewey's, *"Odds are you'll be last person from Stone Canyon he'll see,"* guaranteed that. Fraternal ties bound in eighth grade, compulsory heartbreak today for someone with almost no liver: name the emotional zip-ties as you will. If I couldn't save him per se, I'd try saving something else broken. Flip-flopping whether to "help" him was raw nerves, because this was *his* end.

Plus, I was about to be left behind by another departee victimized and bamboozled by stolen time.

Northbound on Pacific Coast Highway toward the freeway, my car's patched up air-conditioning directed jets of cool air at two people who'd rather not be together, nonetheless. He didn't speak for the first twenty minutes, until we were on the 605 Freeway passing Hawaiian Gardens (which I knew from reporting was neither Hawaiian nor garden). "I was going to take the bus, but Stewey, being all Nurse Nightingale, had to ask *you*, didn't he?"

"How do you know Naomi didn't? She still loves you."

This crossed a Maginot Line, earning me some bile. "Oh, so you know the lay of the land from what, a fifteen-minute conversation in the ER waiting room?"

"That's overstating things."

"Keep out of my marriage, Luke. Check that. Keep out of everything."

I tried. "OK."

He killed the rest of his portable Red Bull and let out a burp that smelled suspiciously (and grossly) of Del Taco. "How are you even here?" he asked with a gravel voice that wasn't going away. "Shouldn't you be at the magazine, tilting at windmills?"

"Day off," I said.

"Fine, but let's get something out of the way. If you think this is going to be an apology circle-jerk today, forget it. I'm not apologizing. Clear?"

"Windex clear." If he despised me now, wait until later.

It remained that way, tense and quiet, in the herky-jerky, northbound traffic. When we reached the Golden State Freeway, which was bookended by modern apartments and garish shopping centers pushed so close to the tailpipe-exhaust chute they should've built a giant iron-lung over it to cut the respiratory disease, I tried making benign conversation. The lackluster Dodgers; Mr. Burr memories. He grunted short responses that invited none back, so I gave up.

The least embittered passenger aboard kept its beak closed from the backseat, because Denny had drugged it asleep. The young cockatiel, a smoke-gray bird decorated with orange cheeks and a spiky, sunflower crest, had burrowed its head into its feathers, somehow gripping a perch inside a new cage while out. Not that he cared to elaborate, but Denny had to, saying he'd bought it from a pet store as a surprise for Joy, who now wanted a real animal, not an animatronic Furby. It's all he divulged, besides eye-dropping it Benadryl as "a road sedative."

I inserted a Kinks CD to transport me, and cringed inside, aware Ray Davies could've been singing about either of us.

> *"I'd really like to change the word*
> *Save it from the mess it's in*
> *I'm too weak, I'm too thin*
> *I'd like to fly but I can't even swim."*

Only one person knew how Denny had come undone, and for Naomi, it began after his birthday a year ago, when he'd lamented over not having racked up the mega-accomplishment folks had predicted. He deduced he needed a catalyst, and shaving hours "wasted" on sleep would be his tactical advantage. Soon, after exhausting workdays at Microsoft, he'd brew an after-dinner pot of Seattle French roast—later supplemented with Red Bulls and possibly amphetamines—and grind through the wee hours on his keyboard. While his wife and daughter snoozed, he was in the basement root coding for SkyFile, his post-corporate Golden Ticket. When bleary-eyed and in need of a break, he'd stop to review the online filings for a frivolous lawsuit accusing his semi-estranged mom and two partners of swindling investors in a complex, Laguna Beach real-estate transaction. For Naomi, this was wondrous proof Denny still loved someone who hadn't loved him very well back, proof he was the bigger person.

Still, that compulsive schedule—the eighty-ninety-hour workweeks, the zombie energy by the weekends—would've fried a superhero. For him, it did something worse: it torqued who he was, deforming him from family man to grouchy, capricious one, from bravura software designer to underperforming employee. When he announced he was quitting Microsoft, bosses who once would've thrown money at him to stay threw a standard goodbye party instead.

The change in latitude Naomi hoped would usher in changes didn't. Cooped up in their Redondo Beach two-bedroom, Denny remained a sleep-deprived workaholic now prone to dramatic mood swings. At South Bay markets and gas stations, someone always respectful to blue collars got snippy. Waitresses slow with their service heard earfuls. Naomi, soft-spoken but never meek, eventually staked her ground. No more dining out or nookie, she warned him, until "you address whatever demons you're carrying around. And get back on your meds."

Her ultimatum reduced the vulgar behavior, but it had minimal effect blunting his all-nighters or codswallop excuses about finding a local psychologist. Far worse, the Mayday call for wholesale change arrived too late.

Soon after our reunion, Naomi said, Denny's urine squirted out the color of iced-tea. His appetite then nosedived, followed by violet, nebula-looking bruises from barely touching the furniture. He pooh-poohed it all as iron deficiency, yapping at Naomi to stop being a Cassandra.

"Everything's going to be better after SkyFile goes public," he'd say. "I'll take six months off. Besides, I had grandparents who lived into their eighties. You married into superior genes."

A May fireworks show on a Huntington Beach pier also confirmed a breeder reactor of unresolved issues still resided within. They were driving home in the Audi when from nowhere, a tinted-window Corvette swerved into his lane. In a kneejerk pursuit, Denny didn't just forget lessons from the late seventies about giving maniacs on the road a safe cushion. He metamorphosed into a road-rager himself. For three, white-knuckle minutes, he wove in and out of traffic tailing the Corvette, flashing high beams, running yellow lights, while Naomi begged for him to pull over. He wouldn't, so drenched in sweat, risking her own safety, she unbuckled her seatbelt and scrabbled into the rear seat to stretch her body around their car-seat-strapped daughter. It was only then, after Naomi made herself a human shield, that he suspended the chase.

"After I stopped shaking, and he quit apologizing, I got it," she told me at the Huntington. "His childhood—it was still terrorizing him."

After more questionable decisions, including being diagnosed with Hep-C and yet continuing to code until 3:00 a.m., he announced she'd be better off without him. Nothing she tried—getting hysterical, showing him honeymoon scrapbooks, asking who'd windmill Joy around, lighting sage to chase off negative energy—dissuaded him. The next morning, he wrote her a check for living expenses and packed up for Huntington Beach. I kept my lip buttoned about being briefed on his doom-loop, knowing my asinine notion would've gone *kablooey* on the launchpad.

Now, eighty-five minutes and three freeways after setting out, we reached Valley Boulevard, the dead-end drag where the unfinished Long Beach Freeway unceremoniously fire-hosed an endless stream of cars into the gristle of machine-shop, mom-and-pop Alhambra. If Denny knew a scintilla of what I had in store, he'd stomp the floor for me to let him out.

Appreciating that, I went east where I'd normally go north, trekking to California Boulevard on the fantasy he might soften up glimpsing monuments from our colorful youth. We passed Burger Continental and all its ghosts, with Caltech and its own not far off. We passed markets where we'd bought eggs for Halloween night and underage Mickey Big Mouths for ourselves. Down the block from the restaurant we'd be patronizing was Cheesewright Studios, the possible, Manhattan-Project site that'd once so fascinated him we planned to sneak in there the summer after graduation, until his coyote blast through Neil's window removed it from the calendar.

Denny handled these fading glories much like the drugged cockatiel in my Acura's rear seat. By the time we'd arrived in the parking lot, he was sound asleep, head against the car window, drool zigzagging down his chin as if he was in his own Benadryl stupor.

———

The red, vinyl world of Bob's Big Boy, where waitresses once flew around and Clip-on tolerated us in the *cha-ching* of active cash registers, was in the throes of its own death spiral. Seated mid-restaurant, we could've sprayed pesticide and not tainted the plates of the other dozen or so scattered customers. The peeling laminate heralded where this was going: Rebirth or burial. Bob's only path out of culinary extinction was the Coco's chain rumored to be interested in a greasy-spoon takeover.

Before anyone came over, a yawning Denny grilled me about why we were at an unannounced stop? I told one truth (that I'd only had coffee all day) and one lie: Bob's was ten minutes from Vroman's, where Stewey would be picking him up at 7:30. OK, he said, why *there* and not Stewey's La Cañada Mid-Century? My follow-up fabrication was shaky, if quickly concocted: Stewey needed to ship a box of self-help books, including some Tony Robbins, to the insecure sister whose condo was no more. Even in his dire state, he would've seen through my

Tony-Robbins flourish had our waitress not materialized exactly when she did. It was old reliable for me, a cheeseburger-combo plate and cherry Coke. Denny copied my order, meaning his mutilated liver would be on its own against Bob's saturated fats.

A busboy set down waters, and his sulfury eyes tracked my fingers fishing into my shirt pocket for two Tylenol Extra Strength, my fifth and sixth pills today. He didn't know, because I figured he wouldn't care, that my pelvis was clocking in at pain-level four. Or that just sitting here, on upholstered seats that only appeared cushy, was a grin-and-bear-it proposition. I certainly wasn't about to wander out to the car where we'd left the cockatiel, windows down, for my embarrassing butt cushion popular with hemorrhoid sufferers. He'd witnessed me sitting on it before without even a baseline "bummer."

My right foot, as customary these days, began tapping the base of the rusty table with a metronome beat. I'd stopped trying to tame it, and Denny noticed the crushed ice in our waters vibrate in rhythm. Consequently, he surprised me when he asked, with a smidgeon of humanity, "You're hurting, aren't you?"

Let me count the ways. "Nothing compared to you."

"That wasn't what I was asking. Man, you love asking questions. Answering them not so much."

"Silence or character assassination; that's how this is going to be?"

"Why are we here?" he asked. "Really here? A walk down memory lane isn't going to solve a thing. Me. Us."

At that instant, I was positive he'd foil my plot, recognize he'd been kidnapped, and make a scene. All I could think to do was sidetrack him with a narrative nearly as pathetic as his own. And why not? Here, I'd been condemning him for bear-hugging his own darkness when I had trouble pinpointing much light in myself. Going on sheer hunch—in other words, classic, Luke-ian decision-making of late—I recapped the job suspension, my enflamed nether-regions, the self-doubt, my wobbly compass. Denny needed somebody else's misery to soften his own, and I had a summer clearance sale of personal schadenfreude to offer.

"Gnarly," he said, emotionless as before. "And the stress? Looks like it's eating you alive."

A jab of pain in the groin preceded me asking, "That transparent?"

"Transparent? It practically took out a billboard above the Commerce Casino. The pad in your car was a dead giveaway."

"Yeah, such a giveaway you ignored it until now, you mean?"

"Martyrs only dwell on themselves, remember? And your nails, *yuck*, let me see what you've done to them."

"Yes sir, Omar." Palms facing me, I lifted them off the sticky table.

"Crap, you absolutely slaughtered 'em, didn't you? I think Joy's are longer. You must bite them bloody."

"They haven't been like this for years. And that was during some fierce deadlines."

At seventeen, Denny reserved his caustic judgments for two-faced adults. Now I was one. "Don't kid yourself. Going *way* back, you always could get yourself wound tight."

"You're thinking of someone else."

"No, I'm not. It wasn't there when you were scamming on the babes or getting 'attaboys' for your writing, but it was always there. Accept it. You're hard-wired for anxiety. This isn't some bug."

"Not some bug?" Those words, his blistering assessment at odds with a generally, happy-go-lucky view of myself: My armpits tingled, and making it worse wasn't the pain in my groin. It was Denny shredding my sense-of-self with the detachment of one of my dad's industrial, air-conditioning foreman analyzing a defective evaporator.

"Just for the hell of it," he continued, "I boned up on more of your old stories after our fight. The greedy subway contractor. The assemblyman bribed by a slumlord, the guy who fled the country after you got done with him. Glad you weren't on Microsoft's case."

"Afflict the comfortable, comfort the afflicted. Yada, yada." Maybe he should've taken the bus.

"It all goes back to your dad trying to wrap you around his finger. Who'd a thunk he'd still be in your head?"

Denny, my comrade from Mr. Pike's bullshit bag of brotherhood propaganda, had slashed me with this before. "As you said."

Be they truth-telling or vindictive digs, I triaged myself, repeating inside that he really didn't know me or what I'd achieved. It was venom from someone struggling to gash more than three bites off his burger or get down half a dozen fries, someone whose hair was no longer dirty blond but completely white. Ten minutes later, Denny pushed his plate aside, popped an Interferon, and consulted his watch. "It's 7:15," he said. "Let's get my corpse in the car so we don't keep Stewey waiting."

After we split the check and I ordered my cherry Coke to go, Denny lifted up on his metal cane, glowering at me not to even suggest helping. In our last seconds in Bob's, I took a last gander at a place that, much like us, was a shell of its old self. And in gazing around to bid it adieu, the sun shined on me for the first time in months, providing just with what I needed: The rush that maybe *this* wasn't all in vain.

Sitting alone in a booth, where the future host of *Late Night with David Letterman* once laughed at our stupid teenage tricks, was none other than Lance Drexx. Always quick with a face, I'd recognize that Magic-Eightball lazy eye anywhere. To think he'd been the one who'd connected Denny and I together at the Pit—in 1976.

"Get a load of the guy in the corner." I pointed with my elbow.

Denny squinted for a second. "D-Rex?" he said. "What are the fucking odds?"

"You're the math savant. You tell me?"

He quickly lost interest because, it seemed to me, his only interest was getting to my car without face-planting on those feeble legs of his. As he shuffled away, I lingered, watching the ex-King of the Dead Arms stuff his maw with a club sandwich while constantly checking his cell for a call or text that wouldn't arrive. *Chew and check, check and chew.* No longer monstrous, Lance Drexx was now a flabby, balding nobody spilling out of a bleached-Polo-shirt without any corrective glasses.

Time tight, I caught up with Denny, not hard with him moving at one mph, in the lot Bob's shared with a strip mall peddling Brazilian waxes and vintage trading cards. Peculiar day today, with otherworldly thunderheads, white and pewter, over the San Gabriels. Three minutes in the oven and my shirt was slick. At the car, Denny glimpsed in the back, where the cockatiel remained passed out, and dropped into my passenger seat.

On the driver's side, I tapped my pocket. "Shit," I said, "I left my wallet inside." Denny had his head flopped, cheeks lime-ish, when I returned. Engine on, I made a right out of the lot, going toward Colorado Boulevard.

"You get him good?" he asked, seeing right through me again.

"Oh yeah," I said, chronicling how I'd stomped down the sidewalk, the sidewalk blocks from where Bullock's, she of Streamline Moderne architecture and unforgiving ladies' room floors, had morphed into Macy's. Told him how I'd rapped on the window outside where lonely D-Rex sat, stepped back, then hurtled my Styrofoam cup of cherry Coke against the glass with a violent *whap*. "I had to take my shot."

What I didn't confide to Denny after his personality vivisection of me: D-Rex had no idea who I was, what kind of demented individual would do such a thing, and neither did I.

CHAPTER TWENTY-SEVEN
THE STAGES OF DENNY

I saw the crowd jostling in through the church's open doors, he saw the black letters on the white marquis fronting the gothic tower, and with our visions colliding, whatever we were before—irate brothers, shaky-semi-friends—lay in tatters now.

"Stewey," Denny barked. "He narced I had her book and put you up to this, didn't he?"

Fatal illness hadn't reduced his processing speed, only that once-booming tone. "Just about the book. The rest is on me. Surprised?"

From Colorado Boulevard, I swung a right on Euclid Avenue—a right instantly bogging us down in traffic crawling into a teeming parking lot. Denny sucked his teeth before huffing, "This is bullshit. No way, no how I'm going in."

I gave him silence, steering the Acura around the congestion, focusing on how to get a defiant nonbeliever into a house of worship. I sped up the street and whipped an illegal U-ey, then slowed along the curb outside All Saints Church, banking on kismet that often freed parking for me. When a dark SUV in a primo space pulled out, I throttled into the slot it left warm.

"FYI," I said, engine off, "there's no one in science like the woman you're throwing a hissy fit about hearing. There's a movement promoting her for a Nobel. She's no joke."

His scowl said I was the joke. "How could you, man, knowing what you know?"

"Exactly."

Denny clawed his cell phone out of his pants pocket, flipped it open, and slapped it closed. "Dead battery, doesn't that take the cake? Let me borrow yours so I can call someone."

I shook my head. "Nope. Mine's out of service for you."

He stuffed his cell back into his loose jeans. "For your FYI, I got her book because I wanted to know what stage of grief I was in. That's all."

"I could've saved you the money. You're in the forever insufferable stage."

"*Ooh*, got me good. Where's the closest ATM? I'm calling a taxi."

"At the mall, half a mile away. And you have it wrong. She's here to receive an award and discuss her latest book. It's all about NDE—her own. You're not interested?"

"Obsessed…Stewey never was going to pick me up, was he?"

"No. Again, this was all my idea. Just lock up when you leave."

"You really are such a douche…"

I was out of the Acura, walking toward the august church that would've fit in the English countryside, before my saturnine whatever-he-was could spit the word "bag" out. He waited until I'd taken ten steps before he banged his cane against the window.

—

Sixteen years out of college, after covering ghoulish murder trials and other depravity, after global-conferences where it was pick-your-mass-horror—babies with AIDs, bad actors with nukes—I nurtured a hypothesis: Planet Earth was a self-devouring organism too complex to survive, an ouroboros doomed by voracious appetite. And that Mr. Burr was wrong, even on his deathbed, when he reminded this ex-pupil the *real* Golden Rule was "that those with the gold made the rules." I wrote back begging to differ, saying the Golden Rule is half-artifice, insisting you live it with a cynical awareness it'll be unlikely reciprocated.

Yet, nothing dehumanizing was being consumed here, if the visceral goodwill of the near-standing-room-only crowd was much barometer. Maybe it was this brittle day, but the air in here struck me as its own type of fragrance system, so instead of the church's musty, incense-infused scent, the positivity transported you to a jasmine meadow unsoiled by anyone's blood. The only unclaimed seats, two aisle ones in the second-to-last pew, were the far bleachers, and I reasoned in grabbing them that they were preferable than leaning against the back wall with someone openly hostile to being here, fantasy pasture or not.

On a bunting-wrapped riser in front of the altar, a seventy-something Dr. Elizabeth Kubler-Ross and All Saint's house reverend, a bearded, forty-ish man named Terrance McKay, sat on overstuffed chairs in an interview format. Under the lowered lights, from our position at the rear of the nave, they were stick figures, giving us no choice but to watch from a screen above the stage televising them to a crowd I ballparked around three hundred.

Between my feet was the brass-tined cage with the slumbering cockatiel; bringing it indoors was my only concession. Between Denny's knees was the cane I'm sure he wanted to use on me.

"Reverend McKay, know how much I'll treasure this recognition from a church with such a distinguished history of social activism on behalf of the marginalized." She lofted up the quartz, heart-shaped award and bowed her head. *"All Saints, you humble me."*

Award? How late were we? I tapped the shoulder of an old woman in black-cat glasses in the pew in front, inquiring what time this began? She said seven, "now shush." This all made sense. The radio had bungled tonight's start-time, and what we missed only heaped more pressure on me.

"What was life serving the dying?" the honoree began. *"Strange, but not why you'd think."*

In the tabloid-celebrity era, it was refreshing seeing someone who'd earned her fame behave so indifferently to its trappings. For this grand occasion, the internationally-known doctor dressed androgynously: pink button-down shirt, white slacks, wispy, gray hair in au-natural curl. Hers was a face, with its sharp nose and aquiline features, you'd see in Renaissance-Era paintings, except for large glasses that '70s Swedish tennis champion Bjorn Borg might've donned.

And Denny's reaction to this feted public figure? Closing his eyes and, presumably, muting his ears, as if her speech was a nuisance he'd need to grit through. I'd put so much effort into tricking him in here, I'd given little consideration to whether his contemptuous veneer was even crack-able at this point. It could make someone question if he'd subconsciously arranged this for himself, if this wasn't so much for the terminal as much the living's death of self-belief?

Dr. Kubler-Ross, thankfully, wasn't chintzy with her storytelling, describing aspiring to be a physician by grade school and a father who believed she'd top out as secretary or maid. During World War II, she aided refugees escaping Nazi, Germany, and later, hitchhiking across Europe between med school and residency, discovered her purpose at Poland's Majdanek concentration camp, where POWs had drawn white butterflies symbolizing their post-gas-chamber selves.

"I knew then psychiatry was for me, but not a psychiatrist like Freud."

From our back pew, it was impossible knowing who occupied the better seats, though a lateral view revealed cadres of blue-hairs, middle-agers, nuns in habits, and others, some clutching her books to their chests. Under the edge of the spotlight, they'd rolled up a phalanx of sick and wheelchair-bound people like this was Pasadena's Lourdes, France. Somewhere out there, in the darkened rows, were probably the NDE-ers and maybe dreamy Heather, who I hadn't completely written off. Knowing that and what else I had riding, I buzz-sawed any nail not already chomped down toward their cuticles.

Dr. Kubler-Ross, in her clip-tongued English, said she realized hospitals mistreated or ignored the dying at her first job. When she substitute-lectured to medical students at her next posting, she took an extraordinary career gamble: She invited a teenager dying of leukemia up to answer questions. It disconcerted her that those future-MDs were too jittery to capitalize on her bravery, so they hid behind the clinical, asking anodyne things. White cell count, chemo effects. They were cowards throwing away a chance.

"This girl became so frustrated she interviewed herself. 'Why won't anybody be honest? Why don't they ask me what it's like knowing I'll never go to a prom?'"

Denny, eyes shut, fidgeted at that tearjerking passage, while I flashed to Eddy. Up front, on the table between the honoree and the emceeing minister, light shimmered off her "Distinguished Service Award."

"Even before 'On Death and Dying,' my first book, was published, I was an outcast. The medical Establishment hated me for speaking out on the ultimate, taboo subject. I had to, because the terminally ill, especially children, were being systemically deceived. Doctors and nurses promised patients they'd recover if only they took their medicine and battled their diseases, when they knew full well their patients weren't going to be better. I learned if you were truthful, it lifted an immense weight off of them and, almost majestically, brought then solace."

While she paused for a sip of water, the awestruck crowd barely rustled. "Some heavy stuff," I whispered to Denny. "But that's not why you're here."

My olive branch proved a twig. He sucked his teeth again and pretended I wasn't there.

"…So, what was the catalyst to expand my focus from comforting the dying—and I've treated more than twenty thousand over the years—to studying death as a concept? It began with an apparition and cascaded into my own experiences, which I steeled myself to write about in my new book. It's titled 'The Wheel of Life' for a reason."

The first to spin that wheel, she said in her unflamboyant style, was a punctual ghost. Decades earlier, in a Chicago office building, she'd been dreading admitting something to the hulking, pastor-friend who for years ran their popular "End of Life" seminars with her. Convinced she was too worn down to continue them, she lingered by the elevator bank with the man, readying her bombshell, when someone appeared. Someone only she detected.

"I know this woman, and she is staring at me, I told him. My partner stepped into the elevator like a getaway car, as if I was hallucinating. Initially, I feared the same. Why? This woman, Mrs. Schwartz, had died years ago." The audience buzzed and murmured. 'Do you mind if I walk you to the office?' Mrs. Schwartz asked. 'It will only take two minutes.' I thought this can't be real, or that I needed a vacation, but I touched her, and her flesh was warm so I agreed. At my desk, the ghost said, 'I came back to tell you not to give up your seminars.' I had to feel my coffee cup to assure myself I was OK. Then I got a better idea: I asked her to write something on a pad of paper to prove this happened."

More buzzing, more crowd stirring, more Denny tuning out.

"In closing, I'd presumed she would be my only visitor from the other side. She wasn't. I'd have an out-of-body experience that resolved a serious bowel obstruction. I photographed a fairy. God, I believe, was challenging me. Witnessing the supernatural can be difficult on relationships, and I went through a divorce. Despite that, I'd meet spirit guides, witness ectoplasm transform at a séance, and spent a harrowing night feeling the suffering and grief of many of my patients, before a swell of enlightenment in a giant sphere of light. Yes, this little psychiatrist whose father didn't understand her."

The standing ovation that followed bounced off All Saints' stained glass and high rafters, shaking the pews with a seismic rumble more rock-concert than crusader's gospel. Everyone was glassy-eyed, staggered by her accounts, including me. Everyone except one audience member.

"Now have I paid enough?" Denny asked, at last deigning to look at me, his betrayer.

I transferred the birdcage, which had attracted a few stares and snide judgments walking in, from my feet to my arms, relieved that the cockatiel was awake, proof it wasn't some Monty-Python-esque gag at a solemn event. After reverend McKay announced there was time for a Q&A, I told Denny I'd cave to his wishes, suggesting we depart to beat the mob out the door.

—

Outside, a light rain fell in the tropical-like air and claps of thunder detonating off Mount Wilson foretold a Pasadena sky about to open up. Deluge, drizzle: what did it matter? At this rate, lightning strikes could've spelled out Denny's name in an ancient font and he would've called it humdrum meteorology. My plot, whatever its vague goals, was about as effective as the apology blooper on Neil's porch. Yeah, some winners we were—one fading, the other's career toast; one so furious at his ending he resented everybody, the other swinging a cage with a groggy bird.

The Acura was fifty feet away. Probably best I cut my losses, drop him off early at Stewey's, and accept this as the flop it was. Ironically, too, I'd written my last story for the *LA Times* here, reporting on a Nelson Mandela peace speech at All Saints about how he'd forgiven his apartheid masters in that sublime voice of his. Until now, I'd forgotten some of us were permitted afterward to interview him in a new reception room behind the stone-slabbed church.

As rain slapped down on us, the Mandela-rush slipping away, I time-traveled back to informing Stewey that I couldn't take Denny anymore; that, in fact, no human could. By that conversation's second replay, I felt almost nauseated, repulsed not so much with the Ratso-Rizzo sourpuss limping beside me but myself. Repulsed I'd reverted to quitter-mode again, to *Puke Skywalker* again, folding my tent in nothing-flat just because a longshot bid hadn't panned out.

In that liquid air, I soon heard something else: Mr. Burr in my ear, telling me to suck it up, to dig deeper, and Dr. Einstein's Austrian tongue saying nothing was random besides perceptions. You never know where a spidey sense originates, you just know to heed it. So, in my second, dumb impulse of the day, I handed a damp, impatient Denny the birdcage, trotted to my car with that lucky parking spot, and was back at his side in two shakes.

"I don't know what you're up to with that," he grouched. "Whatever it is, forget it."

The "that" was my laminated, *Golden State*, magazine press pass dangling from my neck on a lanyard. "On it," I said, without specifying what the "it" was.

From the sidewalk, we heard a sonic wall of applause signaling the formal end of the SRO event. In a few minutes time, my window for what I'd hastily devised would close, meaning we needed to hurry. I couldn't have anyone watch me frog-marching a plainly infirm man toward that reception room. I couldn't have anyone pushing off a left hand vised around Denny's forearm to accelerate his turtle pace. If anyone heard the f-bombs he unleashed at me as I steered him into another trap, they'd have every right to detain me in a citizen's arrest.

With no one around, nor much strength in his legs to resist, my Luke-ian impulse lived, so hail that. My hunch—that the reception door would be unlocked for All Saint's VIP—kept it going. I put the birdcage down on the rainy pavement and notched the door open.

"This is cruel and unusual punishment," Denny said. "Mind telling me what you're doing?"

I buffaloed him inside without replying and let the self-closing door do the rest. On a beige credenza was a rose-carnation bouquet from Jacob Maarse, Pasadena's priciest florist, a gift bag of swag, and four bottled waters. I tucked the birdcage behind the flowers for safekeeping.

"I wish I weren't dying," Denny said, tamping at a messy ponytail gone beaded with rain.

"Me, too."

"Because if I weren't, I'd kick the ever-loving shit out of you. Colossal waste of time."

Even dying, he talked like a longshoreman. "Waste?" I said. "I'm getting you a one-on-one with the expert on what you tried dozing through."

He hitched over to a cloth couch with an Afghan throw blanket and dropped backward. "This is your gimmick? Having the Kubler-Elf dame save my soul? Shoot me now."

"I've considered it."

When I peeked through the lace curtains of the window to gauge her whereabouts, something about that, or the intensity of the moment, released what I wasn't positive was even releasable. At last, my old classmate buried his face in his hands and broke down. This wasn't hysterical wailing from an Italian funeral, more weeping behind fingers, uncorking sighs suppressed for months, stamping of feet. The last time I'd seen Denny in tears: the night I thought *poor dude* twenty years ago, after he'd shown me his cross-strapped father worshipping a lab specimen.

"I'm just so…pissed off," he said, sponging up tears with the collar of his Devo shirt. "This can't be my life, and you're rubbing my face in it." More weeping, more sighing, more stamping, then the question that froze me. "Besides some nostalgic sense of loyalty, what's in it for you?"

A piece of me hoped he knew. I'd shillyshallied outside his moldering townhouse earlier today, ultimately moved by baseline pity as a suitable camouflage for the strands inside me wondering where the magic in the world redolent in our youth—the hot flame of excitement, of discovery, of possibility— had buried itself. Denny stared at me hard with sick, daisy-yellow eyes I tried averting by snatching him a complimentary Arrowhead water off the table.

"As your puppet, I deserve to know."

"Jesus, fine," I said, taking the water bottle from him and twisting off the cap because his fingers were too weak to do it. "I'm not letting you snip your mortal coil without last contact, because I tired of getting gyped that way."

"So, you're driving me into the ground, when I'm already halfway there, so you can make peace with loss? The bargain's not worth it. How 'bout I say goodbye…"

Voices outside the door stymied Denny from completing an expedient farewell, aimed at my psychic Achillies Heel, as his shortcut back to my Acura. Plus, we were in too deep, with no way to sneak out (or hide in a closet), things always so accessible as teenagers.

"Yes, yes," Dr. Kubler-Ross said. "Thank you, reverend, for a spectacular evening. Give this old woman fifteen minutes to rest her bones. My assistant scheduled a town car outside for me at nine." She popped the door cradling her award and halted, registering us intruders. There was Denny on the couch, shrunken and fragile, and me in the corner, the cockroach in the lights.

"Oh," she said in a startled tone. "I didn't realize anybody would be in here." I walked over while her eyes floated up to my press pass. "Are you with the media?"

"Yes…but not tonight. And apologies for our intrusion. It must've been a long day for you."

"Longer than I hoped," she said, not hiding that was directed at us.

"I snuck my friend in here hoping you could speak with him. I'm Luke, that's Denny." I shook her tentative hand; Denny flicked a wrist. "I know it's rash, but he's quite ill—and an atheist. If you need to call security, have them throw me out. He's in a bad way."

"Actually," Denny said in his hoarse register, "I don't know what I am except, excuse my French, royally fu…royally f'ed. Late-stage hepatitis C. Way down on the liver transplant list. Way up on the hopelessness meter."

I had no idea how'd she'd react: Shriek for help, declare she had nothing left to give, flee into the thunderstorm?

"I hadn't expected a counseling session," she said. "Only some time for myself."

That's it, I supposed. A Hail Mary that never should've been thrown. Why did I even try?

"Still," she said with a teensy smile, "whose schedule is their own?" After she set her award down on the credenza, trundled over to the couch, and sat down beside Denny, I told myself to breathe again. "Being so late, however, I'd appreciate candor. It's Denny, correct?"

"Yep."

She was a thin, rawboned woman with inquisitive eyes magnified by those oversize, square glasses. She massaged her neck, scratched an arm, then gave her unexpected patient a sweep—his black-checked Vans, the withered torso, eyes more yellow than blue. The doctor was in. *Hallelujah*.

"Let's get right to it. What's your deepest fear, besides anyone you'll leave behind?"

Denny replied, eyes re-shut. "Gosh, I don't know, extinction? Being squashed like a bug on a windshield?"

"I see, I see," she said. "Maybe it'd help for starters if you told me what you do for a living?"

Denny hesitated, wriggling up on the sofa. "Computer programmer. Fifteen years at Microsoft. Quit recently to strike out on my own."

"Interesting. Strike out on what? A new computer?"

He looked up at the ceiling of this comfy greeting room, willing himself not to blubber. "No, to roll out a new technology I developed. Lets anyone access their hard drive anyplace with Ethernet. Called SkyFile. Not that I'll be around to see it sink or swim."

Her gears, her psychiatric-gears, turned, and if this wasn't for Denny, I would've whipped out my proverbial notepad. "Let me ask you this. In your field, algorithms are vital, yes?"

"Uh, yeah. Pretty much our bread and butter. Why does that matter?"

Before their choppy dialogue sputtered on, a noise behind the gift bouquet, the bouquet we'd given her no chance to sniff, got our attention. From the wall where I leaned, I saw it was the forsaken cockatiel struggling to fly after Denny's antihistamine sedation. Twice, it'd flapped itself up to the lid of the cage only to spiral to the bottom on wings unable to sustain much lift. Now, it squawked a garbled bird-hiss.

"What was that?" she asked.

"A bird Denny bought for his daughter," I answered out of turn. "It's waking up."

"I see," she said. "Now, Denny, I want you to think radically, so radically you view this life differently than you ever have. Consider it one itty-bitty set of numbers in an infinite algorithm. The day is fast approaching, I believe, when the most obstinate Western scientists, be they astrophysicists or biologists, will appreciate God as master mathematician. That track?"

He sniffled, gloomy as he'd been in Huntington Beach, rasping badly as ever. "No, it doesn't. Not at all. Where's the evidence the universe is anything more than chaos, huh? Things crashing into each other at ferocious speeds because nothing's in control. I don't believe in ghosts or heaven, either. That's for suckers. No insult to you."

Another teensy smile. "Insult? My good boy, I adore skeptics. People espousing big things must face difficult questions. But I'll let you in on a secret I don't state publicly, because those religious groups, your Evangelicals, would have me deported back to Zurich. My dealings with that fraudster in San Diego, who entangled me in his healing center, was bruising enough."

"Can you get to your point before I vomit on your nice shoes?"

"Vomit? We wouldn't want that, would we? How to phrase this?…After thirty-five years of study, I suspect we have everything backward. Please hear me out against your doubt. This, where we are now on Earth, isn't our ultimate destination. It's *the* before, the pre-life. The afterlife you claim doesn't exist is where our true selves reside. Everything we've ever learned, over innumerable lifetimes, crystallizes there. You won't read that in traditional scripture."

Denny stared down at his cane and up. "You won't find a lot of things in the Bible. Like reality."

The doctor re-kneaded the back of her neck, as if strategizing how to ditch us. Also enthused to go was the cockatiel bouncing off the cage in repetitive flapping and falling.

Unexpectedly, the doctor boosted up off the couch and walked toward the racket, moving the cage in front of the red-white bouquet, and hovered her face over the top. "Now, now, you," she said maternally. "You must rest. There's a little girl who's going to need you." She soft-clucked her tongue at it, and the bird about to inflict brain damage on itself transformed before us. The thing hopped on the perch, wrapped talons around it, and began pecking at its cuttlefish bone.

While she'd worked her magic, Denny coughed, slurped water, and tried without success to clear the frogs from his larynx. He'd always bristled at authority figures, and his latest one was a cockatiel whisperer. "For argument's sake, let's say there's a .1 percent chance you're right. People used to think the Earth was round when it's an oval distorted by gravity."

"True," she said.

"But causing pain for others, that was my stock-in-trade. Ask Luke. If there's an afterlife, which I still highly doubt, Satan will be peeling my skin off for eternity."

That didn't throw her off. "I'll take a leap. You're a lapsed Christian who's watched *The Exorcist* more than you've attended church services in the last ten years? Am I close?"

"It is a horror classic."

"A dark sense of humor, that's beneficial. And I'm a psychiatrist, a unique one at that, but no all-knowing expert of what cannot be measured. That said, I've never counseled a single patient who had an NDE report they'd spent any length of time in fiery damnation."

"You're just saying that because you're the death lady."

The death lady? To her? He's never changing. Not in a hundred lives.

"You are *eigensinnig*, headstrong, aren't you? Hurting others, you might've noticed, is the fundamental human condition. As is love, sacrifice, confronting adversity…ingenuity."

Denny fell back into the sofa. "Understood," he croaked. "Box checked."

"*No*, it's not," I said, though she hadn't asked me. "He's faking it. Look at him." The Swiss shrink did.

"For an obviously intelligent person, you're too dug into your dogma. You refuse to believe a mysterious, impossibly complicated system is pulling for you. I use Windows. Every few years there's an update for improved versions, no? That's how I envision souls. Unlike Windows, there's no sales tax on them."

I covered my mouth to giggle while Denny-the-doubter pushed himself up again on the couch. "So God's a software designer?" he said. "If that's your message, forget it. You either believe in God or science. Black and white. No straddling."

"Can't you see, they're cojoined?" she said annoyed. "And understanding the system is no prerequisite whatsoever to benefiting from it? No genius has solved that paradox yet."

I shot my mouth off again. "Speaking of geniuses, Richard Feynman, you know the Caltech physicist, was Denny's high school mentor. I was in his office when Denny nailed a math problem very few could. He said Denny was so smart he could see the future."

"That's some high praise. Everyone knows about the legendary Dr. Feynman and quantum mechanics. A mischievous character, too, based on what I've heard."

The shadows around Denny's face remained. "And if he were alive, he'd know I was a ginormous failure who drove his potential into the side of a building."

"Stop punishing yourself," she snapped, Denny wearing thin on her. "Being a martyr gets you nowhere." He and I traded glances. "You subscribe too much to linear time. Why not dream of being the first spirit to write the algorithm for a soul. It might require, I don't know, a trillion lines of code and ten-thousand lives to get there. You'll have time."

"A trillion? This is ridiculous."

"Well, how can you believe in thermodynamics, that energy can change but neither be created nor destroyed, and reject that applies to humans as carbon and energy? Now that's illogical."

She let that hang, and, much to my shock, some blood returned to Denny's wan face, a fissure in his atheist ice-sheet. "Let's say we are energy. How," he asked with a swallow, "is that fair to a four-year-old girl who'll grow up without a dad?" Another exhale later: "Or the wife who tried keeping me from imploding?"

"Are you well enough to stand?" she asked. "This needs to be said on your feet."

"Not really."

"I'll interpret that as a yes. Get up."

I helped lift him up on his shaky legs, and Dr. Kubler-Ross grunted getting vertical herself. She then took his hands in hers, something she'd probably done a million times. Outside, rain lashed the windowsills. Inside, an electrical charge prickled my skin.

"Let's go back to God as a software designer. Picture him attaching invisible wires that carry vibrations between him and all of creation. Learning this lesson nearly killed me, all right? Those you're connected to will forever populate your existence. These aren't just words to trick you."

"But I fell into a coma and didn't enter any tunnel," he said pleadingly. "Where's my cosmic trip?"

"Waiting. There's an adage from Eastern religions, which I'll paraphrase. It goes 'Not for me.' Not everything we believe we're entitled to is given in a single life. Because where would the future adventure be? Or the accumulated knowledge? Or for you, the breakthroughs?"

Her closing argument wedding God and numbers was a stimulus that didn't produce any chemical hocus-pocus. Only an unfettered smile on Denny's face for the first time since our reunion. "I do know one thing," he said, his hands still clasped in hers.

"Tell me," she said eagerly. "I want to know. It's late."

"You're not the quack I believed."

She grinned broadly, as she had on stage, and took a step back after I handed Denny his cane. "I'm relieved to hear that. Just let what I suggested marinate... Now, before you go, you must tell me who those peculiar individuals are on your shirt? I've been wondering what 'got an urge, I wanna purge' means? Is it a joke about eating disorders?"

Denny and I smirked at each other, and everything tight before was loosened. Still, how could we explain a New Wave phrase about devolving civilization to someone whose musical tastes probably ran to Abba? The knock on the door spared us from answering.

"Dr. Kubler-Ross, it's Joe, the security guard. Everything all right in there? Somebody said there's people in there with you."

She nodded at us before replying. "Yes, perfect. I'm just speaking with two old friends. And their bird. We're wrapping up."

Quickly, we bade our farewells, expressed our appreciation. We'd had a moment, the three of us. I shook the doctor's hand. Denny double-gripped her fingers like a secular angel.

—

In the car, with the thunderstorm howling off toward San Bernardino, he winced in his seat, twisting toward me. "That was one ballsy play, d-bag," he said. "How can I ever thank you?"

I keyed the Acura. "Know a miracle urologist? Or *The New York Times* hiring editor?"

"No, but I wish we could blaze a bowl and see if Caltech has a secret cryogenics chamber to freeze me until there's a cure. I've heard rumors about something under Beckman Auditorium."

"A cryogenics chamber? You never said anything about that?"

"We've had a few other things going on."

I inserted the Kinks back into my CD player for the drive to La Cañada, and "Waterloo Sunset," with its wistful tale of paradise through a windowpane, caressed us. I was hamming up the *"Sha-la-la"* chorus part when a coughing spasm racked Denny, a spasm unlike any I'd ever heard. I turned the stereo off, regretting not having water. When his coughing jag wouldn't abate, Denny tugged a handkerchief out of his pocket and hacked into it. In the dashboard light, once the convulsion was done, he peeked at it and so did I. The hankie was speckled in blood.

"Don't wig," he said. "This is like ninety percent better than yesterday. The doc said the blood was from straining my throat, that's all."

"Me wig? Never." Yet I was scared. Scared to ask him if he'd changed back from an "ist" to an "ian"? Scared there wasn't enough time. Back into my CD player went "Waterloo Sunset" and Ray Davies' flowing "dirty old river."

At Stewey's curb, Denny stretched to hug me in another novelty. While he did, I remembered the red dots on the hanky of someone with a blood-transmitted disease. *Stop it.* There was that connected-wire theory to plumb, and I chided myself: no more WebMD.

"Can you believe what she said at the end?" he asked, before he allowed me to help him out.

"My head's still woozy. Which line?"

"About how I could thank her by having a terrific death and a wondrous afterlife?"

"Are you going to take her up on that?"

"How could I possibly know. Before she started making sense, something else she said gave me an idea—a mega idea. I'm getting it down on paper to give to my SkyFile team."

"And that is?"

"If the math of our lives is all around us, why can't data be, you know, kept in the air? The best hard drive could be…no hard drive. Store everything digital outside in like, um, in a cloud server. Cloud computing. Sound nutso?"

"To the guy who barely passed BASIC? Definitely nutso. I'd pounce on it."

"Plan to. And I have a confession, dude. Before we met her, I was planning to get even by hacking into your magazine's server so I could read their emails and tell you what they really thought of you. Most network security is child's play. But you redeemed yourself, so no hacky for you."

CHAPTER TWENTY-EIGHT
HIDDEN STILLNESS

On the Monday after Denny's *Come-to-Kubler-Ross* moment, his email dinged at 3:07 a.m.

To: lukelovesraydavies@earthlink.net
From: d.drummond@skyfile.com
Subject: Homecoming for a jackass
Yo. Guess who's moving back into the townhouse? Naomi and Joy should be in Huntington Beach anytime, and I'm Chlorox-ing everything. Trying not to huff the fumes. Joy named the cockatiel, which she's already gaga for, Harvey Bird. Wonder where she got that? I'm still feeling like shit but a million-bucks better, if that doesn't sound nucking futs. Talk to your face tomorrow.

On Tuesday, this rolled at 1:56 a.m.

To: lukelovesraydavies@earthlink.net
From: d.drummond@skyfile.com
Subject: On the mend
The worm's starting to turn. City of Hope upped my Interferon and enrolled me in an anti-viral drug trial that keeps the virus from spreading. First infusion, two weeks out. But having the fam back = best pharmaceutical. Told Naomi no-more coding all-nighters. My SkyFile team, FWIW, doesn't know what to make of the cloud-server idea. Any-who, you up to get the band back together for the Neil Apology Project? Who knows where I'll be in a month?

Thursday brought another sprig of optimism.

To: lukelovesraydavies@earthlink.net
From: d.drummond@skyfile.com
Subject: More upswing

Stop the presses, Jimmy Olsen. Feeling the best I have since Spring. Played Math Blaster with Joy. She's demanding something harder now. Took a walk around the block, cane-free. Even logged some well-earned conjugal time with Naomi (who hid my laptop for our afternoon delight). I'm pretending no dusk after this dopamine dawn.

Re. Neil. Remember how he used to say *The Beverly Hillbillies* was his favorite show and all the shit he caught for it? Saw a rerun and my muse went off. Worth finishing out?

"Wanna hear the story 'bout a boy named Neil? A squeaky, little runt bullies turned into meals. And then one class, at our Lord of the Flies, he destroys a toxic thermos, right under our eyes. Soap lye that is, gnarly sodium hydroxide. Time goes by and we're freshman turds no more. From peach-fuzz chins to seniors packing condoms. But when a coyote prowls, just after graduation, I'm baked on angel dust and shoot a hallucination. For the next twenty years, all I offer are 'I'm sorry', but Neil and his fam do nothing but rebuff me. No matter what I do, no matter who I help, the pain from that window is the curse without end."

PS. I'm betting Naomi compared me to Matt Damon in Good Will Hunting. She always does that. But I'm much better looking than him, and Ben Affleck, honestly, smokes you.

I emailed him back that while funny, rewritten lyrics about rednecks in LA was too slick for its intended audience. And that while I might not be Ben Affleck, Heather, before she nixed our Margarita-night, said I could've been Chachi's brother. Denny replied Saturday.

To: lukelovesraydavies@earthlink.net
From: d.drummond@skyfile.com
Subject: Blip

Good call on the Hillbillies schtick. In other news, been sick as a mofo. Yakking. No energy. Fever. Possible drug reaction. Naomi's been my Wonder

Woman, though. I wasn't a jackass pushing her away. I was an ogre. Gotta stop. My side's killing…

A follow-up email, after that gut-wrenching ellipsis, was delusion. I emailed him back four times and compulsively rang his cell. Hearing nothing, I jumped to Naomi's number in more futility. When I called Stewey, he said his luck reaching either of them was no better than mine, and we agreed that Denny's worm had probably gone the wrong direction.

Eventually, the obvious told me where Denny was, and journalism taught me that passivity was for chumps. On Monday evening, after more one-way communication blitzkriegs, I decided to plow eastward, through rush-hour traffic on the Foothill Freeway, toward the City of Hope in Duarte, a small, concrete-riddled town below Neil's Bradbury.

My Motorola shook just after I crawled past Sierra Madre.

"Luke, it's Naomi. We're at City of Hope."

"What I figured. Believe it or not, I'm actually on my way."

"You better step on it. He needed an ambulance last night after collapsing in the kitchen. They've given him morphine for the pain and he's losing it. Him and opioids don't mix well."

"Understood."

"And he's asking for you. Head to the pediatric unit. That's the only space they had."

—

Denny's dwindling hours were in a cheery hospital room, tucked in a kiddy bed where his feet stuck way over the edge. Across from him, a wall-length mural depicted the Arroyo Seco at century's turn, with splashy impressions of Cawston Ostrich Farm, the Raymond Hotel, Busch Gardens, Suicide Bridge, and the Mount Lowe Railway. Sick children needed wonderlands to voyage to; question was whether their doctors were honest with them about their odds.

There was no time, though, for a scattered mind, and not a second for irony, wisecracks, even Nick Chance allusions. How could there be as Naomi, looking frazzled and emotionally bludgeoned, conferred by the window with a stocky nurse? She hugged me when I came over, saying, "All his organs are failing." She'd begun scrolling through his phone's contact list to alert everyone. "I don't know what else to do for him," she whimpered.

"You're doing it," I said, empty encouragement to someone past bromides.

Already here, sitting bedside, was an older, silver-haired lady with elegant features and a grounded aura. It was Jill Livingston, Naomi said, a longtime friend of Denny's from AA. When I padded over, she was trying to sweet-talk him to stop ranting or they'd have to medicate him further. Leather restraints around his arms and legs suggested that'd been a losing battle.

Denny flopped his head to my side once I entered his field of vision; it gutted me seeing his face reverted to the walleyed desperation I'd first seen in June 1980. "*Luke*, oh man, oh man!" he said, ignoring Jill. "Not a moment too soon. You've got to bust me out of here. The babies! They're falling out of the painting."

"Painting?" I asked.

"The one with Jesus down the hall. He wants us to put them back. I don't get why no one is doing anything. Animals could attack them. Where's my clothes?"

Jill got up, quick-introduced herself, and walked over to wrap her arm around Naomi. I took her seat and held Denny's restrained hand. For all the uplifting frescoes I'd walked by, all those sunny paintings on a sterile floor outfitted with needles, I hadn't seen one of Christ or any man-eating predators.

"Denny, please," I said. "Calm down. Nobody's in any danger."

He squeezed my hand. "Yes, they are. Are you blind? There's a creature out there with black eyes and big teeth. It wants to eat them. Do something."

Like what? The morphine-IV in his arm had addled a brain long free of this type of chemical so he wouldn't get addicted again. The byproduct? A mind resurrecting the phantom coyote into an active, child serial-killer. "OK," I humored him. "I'll take care of it later. Take a nap."

His gravelly voice jumped. "*Stop pandering me!* I don't need a nap. I need to save those kids. But no guns. We might hit Neil."

There it was: Besides the Afghanistan poppy, Neil remained very much in his frenetic, neural hemispheres. Despite my continuing, "it's OK, it's OK," his babble grew into bellow, and a head nurse, a fifty-ish black woman with lidded eyes and a wristguard, entered to overhear a burst about "big teeth."

She spoke with her colleague and Naomi after that, then walked over. She had a pre-loaded syringe in her Velcroed hand, and my ancient dread resurfaced.

"Wait," I said. "What is that?"

"Dexmedetomidine. It's a tranquilizer. Listen to him. He's talking like a wild man."

"Can't you hold off for a sec? I have stuff to say to him, if this is it."

"Like what?"

"Things I haven't said before. How much he's meant. What we've been through. Goodbye."

"Luke," Denny raved, oblivious to the approaching needle. "What's happening? Where's that light in the corner coming from? It is going to hurt those kids' eyes."

"See," the nurse said. "He's in no position to hear anything heartfelt."

"Yes, he is," I objected, restraining tears. "Denny, reset yourself. Don't go yet."

The nurse pointed at a green monitor showing his elevated heart rate. "He needs this." I kept holding his hand while she injected fluid into his IV. In five seconds, he stopped talking.

Ten minutes later, leaving the ward slump-shouldered, Naomi hustled up to me. "I almost forgot," she said, handing me a Scotch-taped closed envelope. "He put this together a few days ago. He said you'd know what to do with it but didn't want you opening it until, you know."

—

When she phoned later, numbness in her voice, I knew. Knew he was dead. Knew there'd soon be shockwaves liquefying the soil under our feet. Tender as her story was, it still ended in his apocalypse, and there'd be no structural haven for us.

Last night, she said, after the Dexmedetomidine wore off and the pediatric ward's lights were dimmed, Denny was no longer agitated. He was in only minor discomfort, and of astonishingly sound mind. In his absurd, kiddy hospital room, they'd stroked hands. Shed nostalgic tears. Effused over the whip-smart daughter they hope would attend Stanford in his stead.

"But it got late, and he started going downhill. We said, 'I love you' again for the hundredth time, and I told him not to go anywhere while I went to pee.

Eight cups of coffee, ya know? I came back, pecked him on the lips. Sat back down. He took two more breaths."

I tensed. She sighed. "He died at one-oh-one a.m."

1:01? The witching hour for programmers?

I blanked out on anything she said afterward, hanging up with a brick in my belly. The news, however predictable, shrunk my apartment into a claustrophobic box. I couldn't focus my eyes, couldn't think straight. I chugged a bottle of Gatorade. Took a hot shower. I needed out, so I rounded up my weed and two Budweisers, pep-talking myself to hunt for him, even in hologram memory. Those antibiotics had doused the fire in my prostate. They'd never heal this. One man's cosmic journey is another's gaudy fabrication.

Being in no shape to drive, I did, of course, crisscrossing Pasadena in the fugue of grief's hearty fog machine. I slow-motored across the bridge, underneath which Denny and I enjoyed so many giggles, straining for him but just seeing rounded concrete. I whipped the Acura around on Linda Vista Avenue, hoping perchance for remnant fumes of him at Caltech, the Point, Bob's Big Boy. Stone Canyon's old, pot-dealing, wedgie-pulling lower parking lot: why not?

Why anything. I reversed course again, wheeling up Foothill Boulevard. A dissociative blur later, I was sitting on the bench at Descanso Gardens we'd often hung out on, smoggy sunrays bouncing off his Tommy-Shaw-ette locks. I torched a bowl in his honor, nursed a beer, praying I'd glimpse a certain superhuman rat amid the sweet-smelling flora and fauna. Nothing filled this empty vessel that'd gone 0-for-4 on goodbyes: mom, Bilbo, Eddy, now him. You lose that much, some of you goes missing. If it keeps happening, and you get no genuine closure, no raw-eyed declaration of what they meant, let alone a fanciful *see-ya-later*, it's like that part of you never even existed.

By late evening, I'd crashed through the first three stages of grief, mucking between the bogs of depression and worse depression. My only palliative was shallow formality: Informing the ex-Saturnalians, who, bless them, were as concerned about my shaken well-being as Denny's morbid particulars. Nobody was skipping his funeral.

I switched off my computer and girded myself for Denny's farewell communique. My fingers had never trembled like they did slicing open the sealed envelope Naomi passed to me, because I'd be reading from the dead.

I'd anticipated one document, the final draft of the Neil-apology letter he asked I read at his service, yet there were two.

The other was, and I don't bandy the term lightly, a jaw dropper: a copy of a long email on something uber-personal, along with his handwritten note.

"In appreciation for everything, I snooped through your father's computer and think I solved one of your mysteries. Hey, I only promised not to hack your magazine's server."

—

Two days after Denny discovered whether Dr. Evelyn Kubler-Ross knew her hereafter, my father and I locked horns over the secret borne from Denny's adept hacking. If I'd been a neutral observer, rather than the long-lost victim of what he discovered, this is the essay I *would've* composed about the avoidable damage of primordial lesions exposed to sunlight.

The bushy-haired man skips any knocking or pleasantries, storming into the room to wave papers at an older gentleman in a leather recliner as if they were incinerating his fingers.

"What are you doing here? You only come over on Sundays," says Leonard Burnett, a longtime widower and recently retired industrial air-conditioning magnate. "You should've called ahead." Vexed at the interruption, he plops the Caltech alumni magazine he'd been reading on a side table.

Luke Burnett, Leonard's youngest son, drags over a rounded chair for an impromptu showdown. "I could care less about etiquette," he says. "Or your opinions of me. Today, you're coming clean about something from the past. Our past."

While an August swelters outside, there's a decided frostiness between them in the jumbled, burnished-wood den with cottage-cheese ceiling.

Octogenarian Leonard has a Roman-emperor quality to him, with a full head of short, white hair; a flat, tri-level nose; and an unflinching frown. He's in khaki slacks, a floral short-sleeve shirt, and nerdy sandals with black socks. His boy, with his larger eyes and smaller mouth, is dressed casually in green cargo shorts and black Nikes.

There's little resemblance between them and an excess of tension around them.

"I don't have to do anything," Leonard says, snapping his neck up. "And I don't appreciate you bursting in with an attitude." He narrows his dorsum, suggesting he'd be giving no quarter.

Luke's golden-brown eyes laser in. "I came here with one question: Were you ever going to admit that you lost me on the day mom died?"

Leonard's impassive mask remains. "That's what's got your goat? Something from 1970? I can't remember what I had for lunch last week."

Luke scoots his chair up even closer; another few feet and they'd be touching noses. "Let me dust off the cobwebs. I wandered away when you were at Huntington Hospital to deal with her body."

Leonard twitches. "I don't have to take this. Come back after you've cooled down."

Luke, right foot tapping the cream-colored shag, doesn't move. "Wrong. You do have to take it. And you might not have loved her anymore, but you had all that history together. Three sons. Your Horatio Alger story. Some good years. A freakish, trip-and-fall later, kaboom, you're a single parent."

Leonard hesitates before replying, as if a thick fog around a lost memory is burning off. "You were eight," he says. "Quit generalizing."

"I knew it. You do remember. Thing is, dad, I'm beginning to myself."

"Enlighten me," Leonard says, crossing liver-spotted arms.

"I plan to. First image: I'm by myself in a freezing, white room. There's large silver drawers along one wall and empty, steel tables in the middle, except for one. I did what any flipped-out kid would. I tiptoed up to it and lifted up the sheet. It was mom under there, my dead mom, the worst sight a boy could see." Luke's eyes glisten, his voice cracks. "I touched her cheek, and it was ice cold. I saw the dried blood around the gash in her skull. I tried shaking her awake, calling her name. She was sickeningly still."

Leonard rubs his face, his body language shifting from raw offence to defensiveness.

"I'm fairly certain I got hysterical and banged on the morgue's doors for somebody to let me out," Luke says. "Let me out before I was still, too. It felt like I was pounding for hours, but it was probably only minutes. You must not have realized I'd left your side until you finished signing all the paperwork in the little office they had you in. I'm not upset about that. Mistakes happen. I'm appalled you squelched ever telling me."

Leonard dodges his son's eyes, peering around the study appointed with a wide, teakwood desk, a Formica counter supporting an old PC, and a mirrored stand supporting a miniature Apollo Eleven rocket.

"Do you also recall not speaking for a week afterward?" Leonard asks. "Or not eating anything but peanut-butter-and-banana sandwiches? Or bashing your old chair with mom's ashtray? We had to buy you a new one. I was so worried about you. And we all know about hindsight."

"I don't remember any of that, not yet, but I'm asking you what your plan was? Make sure I survived and hope I'd forget being trapped in a morgue? With my mother's corpse, that is."

Leonard slams his hand on the armrest. "Damn it, I wasn't thinking that far ahead! Who could? I was doing everything in my power to keep you from being committed. I had to drag you to a child psychologist, that Dr. Webster. He gave me two options: dope you up on tranquilizers or try hypnosis to erase your memory of that black day."

Luke blows air out of his cheeks. "Unbelievable."

"I didn't want you taking pills. And after a few sessions, the hypnosis worked. You were sad about losing your mom but weren't behaving like a mental patient. And they were using hypnosis back then on everything—weight loss, gambling, smoking."

Luke's hands, the ones with the papers clenched in them, go behind his head as the tension ratchets. The small, physical distance between father-son is wide as an ocean. "All these years, you watched me biting my nails, anxiously drumming my foot like now and you still sat on this? And for what? Because the Great Man knows better?"

Leonard sneers. "You're in no position to judge. And this was confidential. Who told you?"

"A brilliant friend who cared about me hacked into your computer. And before you accuse me of egging him on, I had no idea. He discovered a 1995 email from Dr. Webster. He was about to retire and pitch a book about his most intriguing cases. Like mine. He needed your permission. Want to see my evidence?"

Leonard recrosses his arms. "No. And you'll be relieved to know I denied him. Bet your snoop never mentioned that. It's always the parents' fault nowadays. I was trying the best I could."

"You quote you, 'Trying doesn't cut it.' And I still can't believe you withheld this."

"All right. When would you have had me tell you?"

"Hmmm, I don't know. How about when I fainted after seeing Bilbo at the veterinarian's? That was obviously me flashing back to mom."

Leonard's puckered face is of someone realizing he can't win this dispute. "I was an engineer running myself ragged for the company and keeping you upright. I'm not a shrink. How could I have put your nervous habits and that incident in the morgue together?"

"How about by paying more attention to your son's emotions than his math grades."

Luke rises up from the chair. His father gestures for him to sit. His son disregards it.

"I love you, Dad. You've done a lot of great things for me. But having my memory jogged by that email, it's a major deal."

"To you it is. I wish you'd get over it. I was looking out for your best interest."

"For a while yes, and then you stayed silent about me getting lost in the morgue as some sick instrument of control. It could be you didn't even realize it. You're accustomed to controlling everything."

"And?"

"And if I don't visit for a bunch of Sundays, you'll know why. I'll be trying to figure out how to forgive someone incapable of apology."

EPILOGUE
STARRY

The funeral nobody could brace for was held at Altadena's Mountain View Cemetery five days after Denny's departing kiss with Naomi. Seventy people, I'd estimate, turned out, among them his big brother, Daniel, whose face remained Denny's spitting image, and their stooped mother in a black veil and Christian Dior purse. Stone Canyon headmaster Schenker and a pair of subordinates attended to pay their respects, as did a barely-keeping-it-together Stewey and a downcast Cindy Lummis on an uncharacteristic, bad hair day. For her and our circle at Eddy's service, this was surreal repetition, a reminder the class of '80 only had so many bodies left to offer up.

The most famous mourner spaced out gazing at Denny's slate headstone, as if struggling to comprehend his ex-star programmer was history at thirty-eight. Join the crowd. "This way, Bill," somebody eventually said, veering him and some of his Microsoft associates toward the grave for a grave dirt-throw that was nobody's idea of a fond farewell.

All in all, I recognized about fifteen people, testimony to the lives Denny touched or tousled outside our group. His cremated remains were certainly in rarefied company with the other long-term tenants here. TV "Superman" George Reeves. Black Panther Eldridge Cleaver. Ex-California Governor Henry Markham. Science-fiction-writing prophet Octavia Butler. Naomi told me she'd tried having him interred near the two achievers he'd particularly relish, but the plots around Richard Feynman and Thaddeus Lowe were all spoken for.

Correction: there were sixteen folks in attendance I knew, and Denny would've been rubbing his palms together in glee, realizing everything was lined up.

During the speeches, Neil stood in the far back in a navy blazer with a solid baseball cap tugged down low over his eyes. Mr. Incognito must've read the alumni email about the memorial, and curiosity and/or spite lured him out of his gated McMansion for funky Altadena, which I always regarded as a Venice Beach with hiking trails and eccentric shopkeepers.

I'd Googled him after he'd squawk-boxed us off his property in July, and while he didn't carve out a large, online footprint, there was enough about him in trade publications and message-board threads to assess who he truly was. His debt-collection-firm's strongarm tactics had gobbled debtors' homes, bank accounts, college funds. The owner of a family-run, El Monte aluminum company now in bankruptcy wrote that Neil was "an iron-pumping, pinstriped weasel probably feasted on during high school."

After the Presbyterian rent-a-pastor did his thing, Naomi, Daniel, and a semi-catatonic Stewey gave their eulogies. Denny, the organic genius who nailed an A on his honors chemistry final while coming down from an acid trip; Denny, the incandescent scamp who lived to needle up-tight adults; Denny, the romantic who wrapped himself in valor no matter the cost, and was there— okay, usually—in a pinch.

Heavy-limbed, I was last up, presenting a highlight reel of a friendship that started with a haymaking JanSport and culminated with his unforgettable, atheism-believer encounter with the "death lady." I just had one more topic to broach, in the hardest speech of my life, and the Stone Canyon brotherhood took up position.

"Denny," I said, "was an incomparable cat; I think everyone here would concur. In that vein, he requested that I read an apology about an incident from decades ago that troubled him to the end." I gave a bowdlerized account of that night—excluding, for decorum, the PCP, insane father, and possibly immortal rat—and unfolded the note from my suit pocket.

Out of the corner of an eye, I saw Neil's Adam's apple spasm, then him backpedaling away from the horseshoe mourners had formed around the hole in the ground where Denny's copper urn lied. There was nowhere for him to go, though, for he'd been surrounded on the sly.

Carl, goateed and tatted, bracketed one side with a theatrically puffed-up chest. Kyle, who'd demurred a run for Congress after his Polynesian-American wife was diagnosed with breast cancer, flanked the other. Behind, ensuring Neil didn't twirl and run, was Rupert, still jetlagged after flying in from a big IT job in Crimea near the Russian border. RG, who'd begun seeing a therapist to unpack a childhood around boozy, warring parents, was in front, posting Neil up like the All-CIF guard, in white-boy 'fro and 'stauche, he'd been.

At some point, they had to grab his squirmy shoulders when he attempted boogieing out of there. You think many "Great Men" fathers would've delivered for a fallen brother like this?

"Dear, Neil: I tried. Tried everything to atone for the terror my bullet sicced on you and your family. Nothing made a dent. When I learned I didn't have much time left, I engaged a friend I didn't deserve to assist me with a note of contrition, and to motivate me, Luke dug up notorious ones from Bill Clinton, Karl Marx, and the Salem Witch Trial's judge. But they weren't good enough because I wasn't good enough. While this will be excruciating for my family to hear, I have to be honest. I didn't originally steal my father's shotgun to kill a vicious coyote. I stole it to put the barrel in my mouth to stop the heartache I caused others. A voice inside said don't. Live. I still fear the reaper, not as much as before, and am sorry about something else. It's you, Neil, the-once-persecuted-now-persecutor-Neil. Perhaps it's time for you to heed the words of Lawrence Sterne, an author at Fuller Seminary down the road. 'To forgive,' he wrote, 'is to set a prisoner free and discover the prisoner is you.' You do as you please. I'm liberated."

—

I could only handle an hour at the wake Stewey hosted, preferring the comfort of a dark, dreary cave. Home, I shed my funeral suit and dialed up the A/C. Poured myself a stiff drink and kept my apartment lightless save for the green desk lamp by my Mac in the bedroom. Everything I wanted gone still lurked behind. That black fin. The weight-belt of sorrow. The disenchantment with a cosmos that sometimes gets it yayas out depriving you of what you crave most. This wasn't the giddy future Stone Canyon promised us at seventeen. This was the scheming magic show where you no longer sat awestruck in the audience. You merely waited your turn to be the sequined victim sawed in half by a smug illusionist.

I'd hardly used my computer the last week, so with nothing to lose that I hadn't already obliterated, I reckoned why not see what other dire things were about to roll at me downhill. I scanned the emails, ninety-seven total, bottom up for a change. There was one tabbed "Urgent" from *Golden State's* libel lawyer that smelled distinctly of a pink slip. There was a benevolent Nigerian prince offering me a two-hundred-percent return if I advanced him $50,000. There was one from Heather that self-survival screeched at me to bypass for now.

I clicked exactly none of them.

I toggled my cursor up listlessly to the top of the screen for the last unread, bolded email. It'd crashed my in-box at 1:01 a.m. August 10, 2000. Baffingly, it bore neither sender nor subject line, and it took six months off my life and two cuticles off my left hand before my mouse engaged it, because that exact date was emblazoned in memory. The type was so light on the page it bordered on being invisible. Accident? I think not.

To: lukelovesraydavies@earthlink.net

From

Subject:

"Yo—Starry, starry, this real life. Doubt it's mois? Tomorrow's results. Lame Dodgers 2, Braves 7. Microsoft-stock closing price: $24.86. KLOS song of the day: 'Come As You Are.'"

The adrenaline, the possibility/impossibility, the humongous-ness of it: five seconds later, I was drenched in sweat, toes hot, cheeks flushed, hands moving hyper-speed across the keyboard researching what I could on websites crawling molasses-slow to plant obstacles in my path. But *Jesus*, once they'd stopped buffering! Retinal pyrotechnics. The email that couldn't have correctly predicted the Dodgers' score and *KLOS'* song-of-the day had predicted what couldn't be known to us mortal peons. Just like Mrs. Schwartz's benevolent ghost.

The only fact I couldn't verify online was Microsoft's closing stock price on August 11, so I flew to my recycling bin, rooting through my stack of *LA Times*, throwing unneeded pages in the air behind me until I traced the stock agate for the right day. Sure as my name is Luke Millikan Burnett, my eyes glommed onto the unbelievable: *$24.86,* down-to-the-penny-right.

I reminded myself, heart sledgehammering, what a gifted editor once advised: "Better right than rushed. Mistakes can kill." And on something this mysterious, this reality-shattering, I had to be sure I wasn't trapped in some wishful-thinking psychosis, and worked the problem for all I was worth. I double-checked each prediction, and after certifying them, pivoted to the other telltale data. I typed the email's ISP—101.01.01.01—into a search engine that pinpointed exactly where the servers were based, down to the city. It came back "Unrecognized."

"Unrecognized." How? Was I now the woozy survivor seeing things? Was this grief in reverse, throwing me into shock-y delusion to exert its staying power? Had Neil tasked someone to hack me after Denny ripped him a new one from beyond? Or, was this a Holtz Aerospace covert-op, attempting to gaslight me by Vulcan mind fuck, betting that'd polish me off?

As much as I hated doing it at midnight, I phoned Naomi, who couldn't sleep, either. Was she "absolutely positive," I asked, trying not act as fiercely jacked-up as I was, that Denny died at 1:01 a.m. and "precisely then? You didn't misread the clock through your tears?"

"It was 1:01. You don't forget that. It's on his death certificate, too. Why does that matter?"

I told her I'd get back to her, then immediately called and woke up my Mac computer answer man, Scott. After he whined me to let him do it tomorrow and I fought him, insisting this was life or death, he stumbled to his computer, and I forwarded him the email, stressing I needed to hunt down the origins "in a massive way."

I waited on the line, both feet tapping, while he performed multiple layers of digital sleuthing.

"Weirdest anomaly I've ever seen," he said five minutes later. "I don't have a logical explanation. The Bulgarians don't even use an ISP like that. It's whack— like it came from outside the Solar System. Now I won't be getting back to sleep."

There'd be no shuteye for me tonight, maybe not for days until I knew the truth of this anomaly, so I rubbed my eyes, pressing my face toward the screen to return to the email to flyspeck every letter, every number. In scrolling down, those same eyes almost rolled out of my head, because there was another line written in the faintest of type at the very bottom of the page.

To: lukelovesraydavies@earthlink.net

From:

Subject:

Lukey, even in stillness, everything's moving. Later Days.

"Even in stillness?" I could've nabbed two Pulitzers, forged peace with my father, even slipped a ring on Heather's finger in a happy-ever-after and that couldn't hold a Roman candle to what was jitterbugging through me at this electrifying moment.

"Later Days." I'd been rescued from a dungeon by a *see ya.* Catapulted out of darkness by an untraceable ISP. It'd be my golden secret.

Old ghosts instructed me what to do, so I flung myself back to 1979, hopping from couch to coffee table to love seat just like we would at free-for-alls at unchaperoned parties. Instinct then whispered the perfect encore, and I bounded with a thump on the floor toward my stereo, rummaging through my CD collection for the only song in the universe that mattered. Seconds later, Blue Öyster Cult's "Godzilla" exploded out of my speakers with power chords and lyrics that'd defined our era. Said who we were.

"Unrecognized," my ass. If Mr. Lainey, my walrus of a landlord, evicted me tonight, I'd go with a half-gainer, for this I knew through my cell-level jubilation.

Denny lives.

THE END

ACKNOWLEDGEMENTS
& DEDICATION

A heartfelt thanks to the following people, without whom this book would've never gotten off the starting blocks: David Ferris, Dr. Mark Fishbein, Brad Hall, Dr. C. Jane Hayes, Phil Johnson, Dr. Michael Marzec, Rob McLinn, John Plum, Chip Ritter, Annie Taylor Garner, Beverly Tookey, Kim Foster-Tookey, Lilly Tookey, G.R. Walper, and Joe Weller.

To the people at Rare Bird Books, who've always supported my writing: know I remain in awe of your talents, dedication to the literary craft, and devotion to getting important books out into a chaotic world. You make the impossible possible on a daily basis. I'm talking to you Guy Intoci, Hailie Johnson, Alexandra Watts, and, of course, Tyson Cornell, my muse, forever friend, and fellow Cheap-Trick fanboy. Deep appreciation also to my agent, Jeff Berg, developmental editor, Seth Fischer, and copy-editor (and old reporting pal), Steve Eames, for your dogged efforts shaping this manuscript through its numerous iterations and author freakouts. God Bless you all.

This book is dedicated in loving memory to Thomas Tookey (1962–2018), genius, troublemaker, innovator, husband, father, brother, son, friend, and incomparable spirit. Later Days.